THE RETURN OF HER BILLIONAIRE HUSBAND

MELANIE MILBURNE

REVELATIONS OF A SECRET PRINCESS

ANNIE WEST

MILLS & BOON

First Published in Great Britain 2020
by Mills & Boon, an imprint of HarperCollins*Publishers*
1 London Bridge Street, London, SE1 9GF

The Return of Her Billionaire Husband © 2020 by Melanie Milburne

Revelations of a Secret Princess © 2020 by Annie West

ISBN: 978-0-263-27806-4

MIX
Paper from
responsible sources
FSC® C007454

This book is produced from independently certified FSC™ paper
to ensure responsible forest management.
For more information visit www.harpercollins.co.uk/green.

Printed and bound in Spain
by CPI, Barcelona

THE RETURN OF HER BILLIONAIRE HUSBAND

MELANIE MILBURNE

To all the parents who have lost a baby at birth.
Your journey through grief is unimaginably painful
and long-lasting. My thoughts are with you. xx

CHAPTER ONE

THERE WAS A weird kind of irony in arriving as maid of honour for your best friend's destination wedding with divorce papers in your hand luggage. But the one thing Juliette was determined *not* to do was spoil Lucy and Damon's wedding day. Well, not just a wedding day but a wedding weekend. On Corfu.

And her estranged husband was the best man.

Juliette sucked in a prickly breath and tried not to think of the last time she'd stood at an altar next to Joe Allegranza. Tried not to think of the blink-and-you'd-miss-it ceremony in the English village church in front of a handful of witnesses with her pregnancy not quite hidden by her mother's vintage wedding dress. The dress that scratched and itched the whole time she was wearing it. She tried not to think of the expression of disappointment on her parents' faces that their only daughter was marrying a virtual stranger after she got pregnant on a one-night stand.

Tried not to think of her baby—the baby girl who didn't even get to take a single breath...

Juliette stepped down out of the shuttle bus and walked into the foyer of the luxury private villa at Barbati Beach. The scarily efficient wedding planner, Celeste Petrakis, had organised for the wedding party to stay at the villa so the rehearsal and other activities planned would run as smoothly and seamlessly as possible. Juliette had thought about asking to stay at another hotel close by, as she didn't fancy running into Joe more than was strictly necessary. Socialising politely with her soon-to-be ex-husband over breakfast, lunch and dinner wasn't exactly in her skill set. But the thought of upsetting the drill sergeant wedding planner's meticulous arrangements was as intimidating as a cadet saying they weren't going to march in line on parade. Juliette had even at one point thought of declining the honour of being Lucy's maid of honour, but that would have made everyone think she wasn't over Joe.

She most definitely was over him—hence the divorce papers.

'Welcome.' The smartly dressed female attendant greeted her with a smile bright enough for an orthodontist's website homepage. 'May I have your name, please?'

'Bancroft…erm… I mean Allegranza.' Juliette wished now she had got around to officially changing back to her maiden name. Why hadn't she? She still didn't understand why she'd taken Joe's name in the first place. Their marriage hadn't come about the normal way. No dating, no courtship, no professions of love. No romantic proposal. Just one night of bed-wrecking sex and then goodbye and thanks for the memories. They hadn't even exchanged phone numbers. By the time she'd worked up the courage to track Joe down and tell him she was pregnant, he had insisted—not proposed, *insisted*—on marrying her soon after. They'd only lived together as man and wife for a total of three months. Three months of marriage and then it was over—just like her pregnancy.

But once Joe signed the papers and the divorce was finalised she would be free of his name. Free to move on with her life, because being stuck in limbo sucked. How would she ever be able to get through the grieving process without drawing a thick black line through her time with Joe?

She. Had. To. Move. On.

The receptionist click-clacked on the computer keyboard. 'Here it is. J Allegranza. And the J is for…?'

'Juliette.' She wondered if it would be pedantic to insist on being addressed by her maiden name while she was here but decided against saying anything. But why hadn't Lucy told the wedding planner she and Joe were separated? Or were Lucy and Damon still hoping she and Joe would somehow miraculously get back together?

Not flipping likely. They shouldn't have been together in the first place.

If her childhood sweetheart, Harvey, hadn't taken it upon himself to dump her instead of proposing to her, like she'd been expecting, none of this would have happened. Rebound sex with a hand-some stranger. Who would have thought she had it in her? She wasn't the type of girl to talk to stag-geringly gorgeous men in swanky London bars. She wasn't a one-night stand girl. But that night she had turned into someone else. Joe's touch had turned her into someone else.

Note to self. Do not think about Joe's touch. Do. Not. Go. There.

There was not going to be a fairy tale ending to their short-lived relationship. How could there be when the only reason for their marriage was now gone?

Dead. Buried. Lying, sleeping for ever, in a tiny white coffin in a graveyard in England.

'Your suite is ready for you now,' the reception-ist said. 'Spiros will bring your luggage in from the shuttle.'

'Thank you.'

The receptionist handed her a swipe key and di-rected her to the lifts across the hectare of marble floor. 'Your suite is on the third floor. Celeste, the wedding planner, will meet with the bridal party for drinks on the terrace, to go through the rehearsal and wedding timetable, promptly at six this evening.'

'Got it.' Juliette gave a polite movement of her lips, which was about as close to a smile as she got to these days. She took the key, hitched her tote bag over her shoulder and made her way over to the lifts. The divorce papers were poking out of the top of her bag, a reminder of her two-birds-one-stone mission.

In seven days, this chapter of her life would finally be over.

And she would never have to think about Joe Allegranza again.

There was only one thing Joe Allegranza hated more than weddings and that was funerals. Oh, and birthdays—his, in particular. But he could hardly turn down being his mate's best man, even if it meant coming face to face with his estranged wife, Juliette.

His wife…

Hard to believe how those two words still had the power to gouge a hole in his chest—a raw gaping hole that nothing could fill. He couldn't think of her without feeling he had failed in every way possible. How had he let his life spin out of control so badly? He, who had written the handbook on control.

Mostly, he could block her from his mind. Mostly. He binged on work like some people did on alcohol or food. He had built his global engineering career on his ability to fix structural failures. To forensically analyse broken bridges and buildings, and yet he was unable to do anything to repair his broken marriage. Fifteen months of separation and he hadn't moved forward with his life. *Couldn't* move on with his life. It was as if an invisible wall had sprung up in front of him, keeping him cordoned off, blocked, imprisoned.

He glanced at the wedding ring still on his finger. He could easily have taken it off and locked it in the safe, along with Juliette's rings that she had left behind.

But he hadn't.

He wasn't entirely sure why. Divorce was something he rigorously avoided thinking about. Reconciliation was equally as daunting. He was stuck in no man's land.

Joe walked into the reception area of the luxury villa where the wedding party were staying and was greeted by a smiling attendant. 'Welcome. May I have your name, please?'

'Joe Allegranza.' He removed his sunglasses and slipped them into his breast pocket. 'The wedding planner made the booking.'

The reception attendant peered a little closer at the screen, scrolling through the bookings with her computer mouse. 'Ah, yes, I see it now. I missed it because I thought the booking was only for one person.' She flashed him a smile so bright he wished he hadn't taken his sunglasses off. 'Your wife has already checked in. She arrived an hour ago.'

His wife. A weight pressed down on Joe's chest and his next breath was razor-edged. *His failure* could just as easily be substituted for those words. Hadn't the wedding planner got the memo about his and Juliette's separation?

The thought slipped through a crack in his mind like a fissure in bedrock, threatening to destabilise his determination to keep his distance.

A weekend sharing a suite with his estranged wife.

For a second or two he considered pointing out the booking error but he let his mind wander first... He could see Juliette again. In private. In person. He would be able to talk to her face to face instead of having her refuse to answer his calls or delete or block his texts or emails. She hadn't responded to a single missive. Not one. The last time he'd called her to tell her about the fundraising he'd organised for a still-birth foundation on their behalf, the service provider informed him the number was no longer connected. Meaning Juliette was no longer connected *to him*.

His conscience woke up and prodded him with a jabbing finger.

What the hell are you thinking? Haven't you done enough damage?

It was crazy enough coming here for the wedding, much less spend time with Juliette—especially alone. He had ruined her life, just like he had done to his mother. Was there a curse on him when it came to his relationships? A curse that had been placed on him the day he was born. The same day his mother had died. His birthday: his mother's death day.

If that wasn't a curse, then what the freaking hell was?

Joe cleared his throat. 'There must be some mistake. My...er...wife and I are no longer together. We're...separated.' He hated saying the ugly word. Hated admitting his failure. Hated knowing it was largely his fault his wife had walked out on their marriage.

The receptionist's eyebrows drew together in a frown. 'Oh, no—I mean, that's terrible about your separation. Also, about the booking, because we don't have any other rooms and—'

'It's fine,' Joe said, pulling out his phone. 'I'll book in somewhere else.' He began to scroll through the options on his server. There had to be plenty of hotels available. He would sleep on a park bench or on the beach if he had to. No way was he sharing a room with his estranged wife. Too dangerous. Too tempting. Too everything.

'I don't think you'll find too much available,' the receptionist said. 'There's several weddings on this part of Corfu this weekend and, besides, Celeste really wanted everyone to stay close by to give the wedding a family feel. She'll be gutted to find out she's made a mistake with your booking. She's worked so hard to make her cousin's wedding truly special.'

Joe's memory snagged on something Damon had told him about his young cousin, Celeste. How this wedding planning gig for her older cousin was her first foray into the workforce after a long battle with some type of blood cancer. Leukaemia? Non-Hodgkin's? He couldn't remember which, but he didn't want to be the one to rain on Celeste's first parade.

'Okay, so don't tell Celeste until I make sure I can't find accommodation. I'll do a ring around and see what I find.'

He fixed problems, right? That was his speciality—fixing things that no one else could fix.

And he would fix this or die trying.

Joe stepped back out into the sunshine and spent close to an hour getting more and more frustrated when there was no vacancy anywhere. Beads of sweat poured down the back of his neck and between his shoulder blades. He even for a moment considered making an offer to *buy* a property rather than face the alternative of sharing a room with his estranged wife. He certainly had enough money to buy whatever he wanted.

Except happiness.

Except peace of mind.

Except life for his baby girl...

His phone was almost out of charge when he finally conceded defeat. There was nothing available close by or within a reasonable radius. Fate or destiny or a seriously manipulative deity had decided Joe was sharing a room with Juliette.

But maybe it was time to do something about his marriage. Keeping his distance hadn't solved anything. Maybe this was a chance to see if there was anything he could say or do to bring a resolution to their situation. Closure.

Joe walked back into Reception and the young receptionist gave him an I-told-you-so smile. 'No luck?' she said.

'Nope.' Luck and Joe were not close friends. Never had been. Enemies, more like.

'Here's your key.' The receptionist handed it over the counter. 'I hope you enjoy your stay.'

'Thank you.' Joe took the key and made his way to the lift. *Enjoy his stay?* Like that was going to happen. He'd been dreading seeing Juliette again, knowing he was largely responsible for her pain, her sorrow, her devastation. But at least this way, in the privacy of 'their' suite, he would be able to speak to her without an audience. He would say what needed to be said, work out the way forward—if there was a way forward—and then they could both move on with their lives.

CHAPTER TWO

JULIETTE HAD A refreshing shower and was dressed in a luxurious bathrobe with her hair in a towel turban. The bespoke bathrobe—apparently all the wedding party had them—had her initials embroidered over her right breast—JA. Which was a pity because the bathrobe was absolutely divine and she hated the thought of tossing it in a charity bin. But maybe, once she got home, she could unpick the embroidery and embroider JB instead.

The wedding planner had certainly pulled all the stops out. There were handmade chocolates with the bride and groom's names on them by the bedside, plus spring water bottles labelled with a photo of the happy couple. It was hard to look at her friend's blissfully happy smile in that photo and not feel insanely jealous.

Why couldn't she have found a man to love her like Damon loved Lucy?

Juliette had thought her ex, Harvey, had loved her. How could she have been so blind for so long? Harvey had said the three little words so often and yet they had meant nothing.

She had meant nothing.

And Joe hadn't loved her either, but at least he hadn't lied to her about it. Their relationship hadn't been a love match but a convenient solution to the problem of her accidental pregnancy. A duty marriage. A loveless arrangement to provide a secure home and future for their child. She had known it from the start and still married him because she couldn't bear to face the disappointment on her parents' faces. The disappointment she had seen throughout her life—every school report, every exam result, every time she failed to gain their approval. Every time she failed to live up to the standards set by her exceptionally talented, high achieving older brothers. And her parents, with their multiple university degrees. Even her very existence had been a mistake. She was a mid-life baby born to older parents who thought their childrearing days were over. And they *were* over, so they'd outsourced the rearing of Juliette to a variety of nannies.

Juliette placed her hand on the flat plane of her abdomen, her heart squeezing as she thought of the precious life she had nurtured there for seven months. Her baby might have been an accident but no way would she ever think of Emilia as a mistake. Oh, God, she shouldn't say her name, even in her head. It brought her so much pain, so much anguish to think of Emilia's tiny little crinkled face, her tiny wrinkled legs and arms. Little arms that would never reach up to her to hold...

Juliette turned to the task at hand, determined to

keep control of her emotions. She was moving on, processing the grief the best way she could. Part of that process was getting through this weekend and handing over the divorce papers to Joe.

She was still deciding which dress to wear to the drinks and rehearsal and had her choices laid out on the bed. The very *big* bed with cloud-soft pillows and gazillion thread-count Egyptian cotton sheets. It was similar to the bed she and Joe had spent that one-night stand in, having off-the-Richter-scale sex.

A night she couldn't erase from her brain or her body.

She swung away from the bed and snatched up her make-up bag from her open suitcase. She needed armour and not just the cosmetic sort. She needed anger armour. Anger was her friend now. Her constant companion. It simmered and smouldered deep in her chest like lava inside a grumbling volcano. Anger was her way of punching through the blanket of despair that had almost smothered her after losing the baby seven months into the pregnancy. A despair so deep and thick it had taken every particle of light out of her life. Happiness was something other people experienced. Not her. Not now. Not ever. A part of her was missing.

Broken. Shattered.

And all the King's horses and all the King's men were not going to be able to put her back together again.

Juliette was on her way to the bathroom off the bedroom to do her make-up when she heard a brisk knock on the door of the suite. Thinking it was a waiter bringing the pot of tea she had ordered a short time ago, she called out, 'Come in. Just leave it on the table, thanks.' And went into the bathroom and closed the door.

She heard the suite door open and the rattle of a tea cup and saucer as presumably the tea trolley was wheeled in. Then the door closed again with a firm click.

Should she have given the waiter a tip? Probably not while she was dressed in a bathrobe, even if it was the most deliciously soft fabric she had ever worn against her skin. Not that she had too much spare cash lying around for tips. She refused on principle to touch the obscenely excessive amount of money Joe put in her bank account every month. Guilt money? No. Those were relief funds. *His* relief. He hadn't got there in time for the birth, but when he came in half an hour later she hadn't seen a father grieving for his stillborn baby girl. She had seen relief washing over his features. She had seen a man who was relieved his sham of a marriage now had an excuse to end.

Their baby had died and so had any hope of them remaining together.

They were a mismatch from the start. Hadn't she always known that on some level? He was suave and sophisticated and super intelligent. A self-made man who answered to no one but himself. His cool aloof-ness had drawn her like a moth to a dangerously hot flame.

And it had burned her in the end. Even after three

months living together as man and wife, he had always kept an emotional distance, which had reinforced every fear she harboured about herself. It mirrored the emotional distance she'd experienced from her parents while she was growing up. The sense she wasn't enough for them—not clever enough, not pretty enough. She always felt they were holding back, keeping her to one side, *compartmentalising* her.

Juliette picked up her foundation bottle, took off the lid and released a sigh. Joe had done the same. He had travelled abroad for most of the time they were married, leaving her stranded at his villa in Positano. As far as she could see, he hadn't made any adjustments to his life by marrying her. He had expected her to do all the adjusting. She had moved countries, left friends and family behind and lived in a large villa with no one for company other than a rotating agency-recruited team of household staff. None of whom stayed long enough for her to learn their names, much less their language.

Juliette picked up her foundation brush and ran her fingers over the soft bristles. Of course, she was always there waiting for Joe when he returned, and she couldn't fault their physical relationship. It was as exciting and pleasurable as ever but it niggled at her that he seemed to spend more time away than he did at home. What did that say about her? Hadn't her parents done the same? So many trips abroad, lecture tours, sabbaticals, leaving her languishing and lonely in boarding school.

Juliette applied some foundation to cover the dark shadows that seemed to be permanently under her eyes. There was nothing she could do about the shadows in her eyes—they were also permanent. She put on some eye shadow and then a coat of mascara but she left the lip-gloss for after she had her cup of tea. She unwound the towel from around her head and shook her shoulder-length hair loose. Looking at herself in the mirror, there was no sign she had ever carried a baby to seven months' gestation. Her weight was back to normal...well, the new normal, because her appetite was hardly what anyone could call enthusiastic these days. Her hair had grown and thickened up again after a lot of it falling out due to hormones and deep emotional stress.

She looked like the same person...but she was not.

Juliette came out of the bathroom and walked into the lounge area and immediately saw the tea trolley next to the table by the window. She heaved a sigh of relief. A proper pot of tea with a silver tea strainer. No musty little tea bags and lukewarm water for this wedding party guest.

Big tick for you, Celeste.

Juliette could smell the bergamot notes of the high-quality Earl Grey in the air...and something else. Something that struck a chord in her memory and made a faint prickling sensation tiptoe across her scalp.

She swung around from the tea tray to see her estranged husband, Joe Allegranza, seated on the sofa behind her. A gasp rose but died in her blocked throat, her hand coming up to her chest to hold her leaping heart in place.

'What the hell are you doing in my room?' Her voice was a fishwife screech, her pulse a thud-stop-thud-stop hammering in her temples.

Joe rose from the sofa, his expression as unreadable as one of her father's astrophysicist research papers. 'It's apparently our room.' His deep baritone with its rich Italian accent made something in her stomach swoop.

Juliette frowned so hard a year's supply of Botox would have given up in defeat. Two years' supply. '*Our* room? What do you mean "our" room?'

'There's been a mistake with the booking.'

She narrowed her eyes to hairpin slits. 'A mistake?' She knew all about mistakes. Wasn't he her biggest one? She wrapped her arms around her middle, wishing she wasn't naked under the bathrobe. Wishing she had more armour against the tall, unknowable man in front of her. She needed heels the size of stilts to get anywhere near his six-foot-four height. She needed her head read for even noticing how gorgeous he looked, dressed in dark denim and a sky-blue open-necked shirt that highlighted his olive complexion.

She drank in his features, hating herself for being so weak. The determined jaw, the slash of aristocratic cheekbones, the ink-black eyebrows over hooded eyes the colour of centuries-old coal. The sensual mouth that had wreaked such havoc on her senses from the first time he had smiled at her, let alone kissed her.

But she was not going to think about his kisses. No. No. No.

Nor his earth-shattering, planet-dislodging lovemaking. No. No. No.

What she had to concentrate on was her anger. *Yes. Yes. Yes.*

'Juliette…' His voice had a note of authority that made her spine stiffen. 'The way I see it, we have two options here. We either go downstairs and make a fuss and thereby draw a lot of attention to ourselves, or we suck it up and leave things as they are.'

Juliette unwound her arms from around her middle and widened her eyes to the size of the saucer under her bone china teacup. 'Are you out of your mind? Why can't we go downstairs and tell Reception they've made a monumental error? But wait—isn't this the wedding planner's mistake? Celeste Petrakis was the one who organised the accommodation. She's being paid a ridiculous amount of money to make sure everything runs smoothly. This—' she pointed her finger between him and herself '—is not what I'd call running smoothly.'

A frown drew his eyebrows closer together and he looked down at one of his rolled-up sleeves and flicked off an imaginary piece of lint. The gold glint of his wedding ring on his finger stopped her heart for a moment. *He was still wearing his wedding ring?* Why? She had left hers at his villa in Positano, but hardly a day went past when her thumb didn't go in search of them on her finger like a child's tongue checking the vacant space left by a missing tooth.

His gaze came back to hers—dark, deep, mysterious. 'Celeste is Damon's cousin. This is her first job after being sick with blood cancer. It would upset God knows how many relatives of his if we make a big deal about this. Greeks are all about family. Besides, this is Lucy and Damon's wedding and I don't want to draw unnecessary attention to our situation.'

Juliette chewed at her lip, knowing there was a lot of truth in what he said. Wedding party guests were meant to be the supportive team, not the main event. And it made sense not to make a fuss, given Celeste's health issues. She admired the girl for getting back out there, and with such focus and dedication. Juliette hadn't been able to illustrate another children's book since she'd lost the baby. Her publisher and editors, and Lucy who co-wrote the books with her, had been incredibly patient but how long would that continue?

'But what if one of us stayed in another room? Another hotel? There are plenty of hotels further down the—'

'No.' There was an intractable tone in his voice. 'I've already spent the best part of an hour trying to find somewhere and drawn a blank. Lucy and Damon wanted the wedding party staying in one place. And there are no other rooms vacant here. So we will have to share.'

Juliette swung away and began pacing the floor, her arms wrapping around her body again. 'This is ridiculous. I can't believe this is happening. A weekend of sharing a suite with you? It's…it's unthinkable.'

'You've shared much more than a suite with me in the past. Our first night together was spent in a room very much like this one, was it not?' His coolly delivered statement triggered a firestorm in her body, sending waves of heat coursing through her flesh.

She didn't want to think about that night and how her body so wantonly, greedily responded to him. How her senses had reeled under the ministrations of his touch. How many women since their breakup had enjoyed the pressure of his mouth, the smooth, hard thrust of his body, the sensual glide of his hands? A hot spear of jealousy drove through her belly, sending pain so deep into her body she only just managed to suppress a gasp.

Juliette sent him a glare hot enough to blister the paint off the walls. 'How many women have you shared a hotel room with since we separated?'

Something moved across his features like a zephyr across a deep dark body of water. 'None. We are still technically married, *cara*.' His voice had a low and husky quality, his eyes holding hers in a lock that felt faintly disturbing. Disturbing because she found it almost impossible to look away.

She frowned, opening and closing her mouth in an effort to find something to say. *None?* No lovers since her? What did that mean?

She swallowed and finally found her voice. 'You've been celibate the whole time? For *fifteen* months?'

His crooked smile made something kick against her heart like a tiny invisible hoof. 'You find that surprising?'

'Well, yes, because you're...' Her words trailed off and her cheeks grew warm and she shifted her gaze.

'I'm what?'

Juliette rolled her lips together and glanced at him again. 'You're very good at sex and I thought you'd miss it and want to find someone else, many someone elses, after we broke up.'

'Have you found someone else?' A line of tension ran from the hinge of his jaw to his mouth.

Juliette gave a choked-off laugh. Her, sleep with someone else? The thought hadn't even crossed her mind. Which was kind of weird, come to think of it. Why hadn't it? She was supposed to be over him. Wouldn't being over him mean she would be interested in replacing him? But somehow the thought of it sickened her. 'No, of course not.'

Joe's eyes were unwavering on hers. 'But why not? You're very good at sex too. Don't you miss it?' His deep and husky tone was like dark rich treacle poured over gravel.

It wasn't just her cheeks that were hot—her whole body was on fire. Flickering flames of reawakened lust smouldering in each of her erogenous zones. Erogenous zones that reacted to his presence as if finely tuned to his body's radar. Her body recognised him in a thousand and one ways. Even his voice had the power to melt her bones. Her flesh remembered his touch as if it were imprinted in every pore of her skin. Hunger for his touch was a background beat in her blood but every time his gaze met hers it sent her pulse rate soaring.

And she had a feeling he damn well knew it.

Juliette smoothed her suddenly damp palms down the front of her bathrobe, turning away so her back was to him. 'This is exactly why I don't want to share a room with you this weekend.'

'Because you still want me.' He didn't say it as a question but as a statement written in stone.

Juliette turned and faced him, anger rising in her like a pressure cooker about to explode. Her body trembled, her blood threatening to burst out of her veins. Should she mention the divorce papers burning a hole in her tote bag? The thought crossed her mind but then she dismissed it. She planned to hand them to him once Lucy and Damon left on Sunday morning for their yachting honeymoon. It would spoil the happy couple's celebrations if the hideous D word was mentioned.

But Joe had mentioned the other dangerous D word. Desire.

'You think I can't resist you?' Her voice shook with the effort of containing her temper.

His eyes went to her mouth as if he were recalling how she had shamelessly, brazenly pleasured him in the past. His gaze came back to hers and something deep and low in her belly rolled over. 'I don't want to fight with you, *cara*.'

'What *do* you want to do then?' Juliette should never have asked such a loaded question, for she saw the answer in the dark gleam of his chocolate-brown eyes.

Joe closed the distance between them in a number

of slowly measured strides but she didn't move away. She couldn't seem to get her legs to work, couldn't get her willpower back on duty, couldn't think of a single reason why she shouldn't just stand there and enjoy the exquisite anticipation of him being close enough for her to touch.

He lifted his hand to her face and skated his index finger down the curve of her cheek from just below her ear to the bottom of her chin. It was the lightest touch, barely there, but every cell in her body jolted awake like a dead heart under defibrillator paddles. Every drop of blood in her veins put on their running shoes. Every atom of her willpower dissolved like an aspirin in water. She could smell the lime notes of his aftershave cologne. She could see the sexy shadow of his regrowth peppered along his chiselled jaw and she had to curl her hands into fists to stop from touching it. She could see the lines and contours of his sculptured mouth, could remember how it felt crushed to her own.

Oh, dear God, his mouth was her kryptonite.

'Take a wild guess what I want to do.' His voice was rough, his eyes hooded, the air suddenly charged with erotic possibilities.

Juliette could feel her body swaying towards him as if someone was gently but inexorably pushing her from behind. Her hands were no longer balled into fists by her sides but planted on the hard wall of his chest, her lower body pulsing with lust-heated blood.

His hands settled on her hips, the warmth of his broad fingers seeping into her flesh with the potency of a powerful drug. His black-as-night gaze went to her mouth and she couldn't stop from moistening her lips with the darting tip of her tongue.

He drew in a sharp breath as if her action had triggered something in him, something feral, something primal. He brought her even closer, flush against his pelvis, and her traitorously needy body met the hard jut of his.

His mouth came down to within millimetres of hers, his eyes sexily hooded. 'This was never the problem between us, was it, *cara*?' His warm hint of mint breath caressed her lips and her willpower threw its hands up in defeat and walked off the job.

Juliette's heart was beating so fast she thought she was having some sort of medical event. 'Don't do this, Joe...' Her voice didn't come out with anywhere near the stridency she'd intended.

He nudged her nose with his—a gentle bump of flesh meeting flesh that sent a wave of longing through her body. 'What am I doing, hmm?' His lips touched the side of her mouth, not a kiss but so close to it her lips tingled all over. He brushed her cheek with his mouth and the graze of his stubble made something hot and liquid spill deep and low in her core.

Juliette's lips parted, her lashes lowered, her mouth moved closer to his but then a stop sign came up in her head. What was she doing? Practically begging him to kiss her as if she was some love-struck teenager experiencing her first crush? She drew in a sharp breath and stepped back, glaring at him.

'What the hell do you think you're doing?' Nothing like a bit of projection to take the focus off her own weakness.

His cool composure was an added insult to the tumultuous emotions coursing through her body. 'I would only have kissed you if you'd wanted it. And you did, didn't you, *tesoro*?'

Juliette wanted to slap his face. She wanted to claw her fingernails down his cheeks. She wanted to kick him in the shins until his bones shattered. But instead her eyes filled with stinging tears, her chest feeling as if it were being squeezed in a studded vice. 'I h-hate you.' Her voice cracked over a lump clogging her throat. 'Do you have any idea how much?'

'Maybe that's a good thing.' His expression went back to his signature masklike state. Unreadable. Unreachable. Invincible.

Why wasn't she shrugging off his hold? Why wasn't she putting distance between their bodies? Why was she feeling as if this was where she belonged—in the warm protective shelter of his arms? Juliette slowly eased back to look up at his face, her emotions so ambushed she couldn't find her anger. Where was her anger? She *needed* her anger. She couldn't survive without it pounding through her blood. She blinked back the tears, determined not to cry in front of him.

'I don't know how to handle this...situation...' She swallowed and aimed her gaze at his shirt collar. 'I don't want to ruin Lucy and Damon's wedding but sharing this suite with you is...' She bit her lip, unable to put her fears into words. Unwilling to voice them out loud, even to herself.

Joe inched up her chin with his finger, meshing his gaze with hers. 'What if I promise not to kiss you. That will reassure you, *sì*?'

No! I want you to kiss me.

Juliette was shocked at herself. Shocked and shamed by her unruly desires. She stepped out of his hold and wrapped her arms around her body before she was tempted to betray herself any further.

'Okay. That's sounds like a sensible plan. Let's decide on some ground rules.' She was proud of the evenness of her tone. Proud she had got her willpower back into line. 'No kissing. No touching.'

Joe gave a slow nod. 'I'm fine with that.' He walked over to the sofa and sat down, hooking one ankle over his muscular thigh.

He was fine with that?

Everything that was female in Juliette was perversely offended by his easy acceptance of her rules. Surely he could have put up a little bit of resistance? But maybe he had someone else he wanted to kiss and touch and make love to now. Maybe he was tired of being celibate and was ready to move on with his life. It had been fifteen months after all. It was a long time for a man in his sexual prime to be without a lover. A tight pain gripped her in her chest and travelled down to tie tight knots in her stomach. Cruel twisting knots that made it hard for her to breathe. If she didn't pull herself into line, her grey-blue eyes would turn green. She had no right to be jealous. She had left their marriage. She had divorce papers in her bag, for pity's sake.

'Good.' Juliette's tone was so clipped it could have snipped through tin. 'But of course, that leaves the tricky problem of what to say to Lucy and Damon when they realise we're sharing a suite.' She walked over to the bar fridge and took out a bottle of water, unscrewing the cap and pouring it into a glass. She picked up the glass and turned to face him. 'Any brilliant suggestions?'

Joe's expression was still inscrutable but she could sense an inner guardedness. His posture was almost too casual, too relaxed, too calm and collected. 'We could say we're trying for a reconciliation.'

Juliette took a sip of water before she gave in to the temptation to throw it in his face. She put the glass down on the counter with a clunk. 'A reconciliation? For a marriage that shouldn't have come about in the first place?'

A knot of tension appeared beside his mouth, his eyes locked on hers in an unblinking hold. 'I wasn't the one who left our marriage.'

Juliette stalked over to the windows overlooking the white crescent of the sand and the turquoise water of the beach below. She took a shuddering breath. 'No, because you weren't fully in it in the first place.'

The silence was so long it was as if time had come to a standstill.

She heard the rustle of his clothes as he rose from the sofa. Counted his footsteps as he approached her but she didn't turn around. He came to stand beside her, his gaze focused like hers on the beach below.

After a long moment, he turned his head to look at her, the line of his mouth bitter. 'If you were to be truthful, Juliette, you weren't fully in it either. You were still getting over your ex. That's why we hooked up in the first place, because you couldn't bear to spend the night he got married to one of your so-called friends, on your own.'

Juliette wished she could deny it but every word he said was true. She had been shattered by Harvey's betrayal. They had been dating since their teens. His affair with Clara had been going on for months and Juliette hadn't had a clue. The night she'd thought Harvey was going to propose to her, he'd told her he was leaving her. Harvey Atkinson-Lloyd, her parents' choice of the perfect son-in-law for their only daughter. The daughter who, unlike their high-achieving sons Mark and Jonathon, had failed to do anything much else to win their approval.

Juliette ground down on her molars, torn between anger at Joe for pointing out her stupidity and anger at herself for making a bad situation worse by falling into bed with him that night.

She turned to face him, chin high, eyes blazing. 'So, what's your excuse for hooking up with me that night? Or do you regularly sleep with perfect strangers when you're working in London?'

An emotion flickered across his face like an interruption in a transmission. A pause. A regroup. A reset. 'It was the anniversary of my mother's death.'

His tone was flat, almost toneless, but there was a stray note of sadness under the surface.

Juliette looked at him blankly. 'But I don't understand... I thought you told me your mother had emigrated to Australia. Wasn't that the reason she wasn't able to come to our wedding?'

'She's my stepmother. Both of my parents are dead.'

Had she misheard him back when they were together? She tried to think back to the conversation but couldn't recall it in any detail. She knew his father had died a few years back but he had barely mentioned his mother. She'd got the sense it was a no-go area for him, so she hadn't delved any further.

They hadn't done much talking about each other's family backgrounds, mostly because he was away such a lot. Their brief passionate reunions when he came home between trips were physical catch-ups, not emotional ones. She had wanted more than physical intimacy but hadn't known how to reach him. Every attempt to get closer to him had failed, with him leaving for yet another work commitment. It was as if he sensed her need for emotional connection and found it deeply threatening. But, to be fair, she too had been pretty sketchy with her own issues to do with her background, not wanting him to know how out of place she felt in her academically brilliant family.

'I'm sorry...' she said, frowning. 'I mustn't have heard you correctly when you told me that when we were living together.'

His lips moved in a grimace-like smile that didn't involve his eyes. 'My father remarried when I was a child. But when he died ten years ago, my stepmother and two half-siblings emigrated to Melbourne, where she has relatives.'

'Do you have much contact with them? Phone? Email? Birthdays—that sort of thing?'

'I do what is required.'

Juliette was starting to realise she didn't know very much about the man she had married in such haste. Why hadn't she tried a little harder to get him to open up? Her shock pregnancy had thrown her into a tailspin. And when she'd finally worked up the courage to call him and tell him, he had flown straight to her flat in London with a wedding proposal. A proposal she had felt compelled to accept in order to mitigate some of the shame she had caused her parents in getting herself 'knocked up' after a one-night stand.

She looked at him again, wondering how she could have been so physically close to someone without knowing anything about him. 'How old were you when your mother died?'

Joe glanced at his watch and muttered a soft curse. 'Isn't there a drinks thing soon?'

'Shoot.' Juliette gave a much milder version of his curse. 'I'm not dressed and I haven't done my hair.'

He picked up a tendril of her mid-brown hair, trailing it gently through his fingers. 'It looks beautiful the way it is.' The pitch of his voice lowered and his eyes were a bottomless black.

Juliette swallowed and tried hard not to look at his mouth. 'Ahem. You're touching me. Remember the rules?'

He released her hair and stepped back from her with a mercurial smile. 'How could I forget?'

CHAPTER THREE

JOE DROVE A hand through his own hair once Juliette had retreated to the bathroom. No touching. No kissing. Sure, he could abide by the rules. But he hadn't realised it would be as difficult as this. It had been hard enough trying to erase the memory of her touch when he was living thousands of kilometres away. But sharing a suite with her this weekend was going to test his resolve in ways he wasn't prepared for.

He hadn't expected the chemistry to still be there. He hadn't expected the hot, tight ache of desire to grip him so brutally. He hadn't expected to feel anything other than guilt about how things had panned out between them. The guilt was still there, spreading cruel tentacles around his intestines like a poisonous strangling vine. Tentacles that crawled up into his chest and wrapped around his heart and squeezed, squeezed, squeezed like a savage fist.

Truth was, he'd been almost relieved when she hadn't answered his texts and emails. It meant he didn't have to face the train wreck he'd caused. The further along her pregnancy went, the longer he'd stayed away on business. Business others under his employ could have easily seen to. But no, he had wanted—*needed*—to throw himself into the distraction of work, because watching Juliette growing with his child had secretly terrified him. What if she died during childbirth? What if, like his mother, she had a complication and no one could save her?

Had he caused the loss of their baby by not being there? Had his absence caused Juliette unnecessary stress? Hindsight was all very well, but he had thought he was doing the right thing at the time. They weren't in a love relationship. They had married for the sake of the baby and Juliette had seemed okay with that arrangement. Providing stability and security had been his focus.

His focus since their separation had been channelling his efforts into fundraising for a stillbirth research foundation. It had been his way of dealing with his own grief. He considered it far more productive than falling into a heap like his father had done. Joe wanted the money raised to help others, to prevent others from experiencing the devastation of losing a child at birth. Research was expensive and counselling services were always seriously underfunded. But that was changing as a result of his efforts. His own regular large donations along with the fundraising programme he had orchestrated would hopefully reduce the number of stillbirths across the globe.

Joe changed into his fresh clothes and unpacked the rest from his small travel bag and hung them in the wardrobe next to hers. He touched the silk sleeve of one of her tops, lifting it to his nose to smell the lingering scent of her signature perfume. For months after she'd left, he couldn't go into the bedroom they had shared. He'd got his housekeeper to move his things into another room. A room without memories and triggers.

He slid the door closed on the wardrobe, wishing he could lock away his desire as easily. He'd wanted to kiss her. No doubt about that. His lips still burned with the need to feel the soft press of hers. Joe knew he was wrong for Juliette. He was relationship poison. He couldn't seem to help destroying those he cared about. But seeing her again made him realise there was unfinished business between them. Was that why he hadn't made more of a fuss about the booking mix-up? Yes, he'd been concerned about upsetting Damon's young cousin, Celeste, but he might have found some way to resolve the situation even if he had to stay on the other side of the island. And, truth be told, he could have refused the invitation to be Damon's best man in the first place and no one would have blamed him.

But he hadn't because on some level, be it conscious or subconscious, he wanted to be here for the weekend on Corfu with Juliette. On neutral ground. Somewhere where there were no triggers and tripwires to the heartbreak of their past. It suited him to be in close proximity to her, to reassure himself he hadn't totally destroyed her as well as their relationship.

A relationship that might have had a better chance if their baby had lived.

A tight ache spread through his chest when he thought of that lifeless little body. His baby girl with her little wizened pixie face, her tiny feet and hands, her permanently closed eyes.

Was there some sort of curse surrounding him and birth? His own birth had brought about his mother's death. His birthday—the day in the year he dreaded more than any other—was the anniversary of his mother's death. The very same day he had met Juliette in that London bar that had changed both their lives for ever.

The bathroom door opened and Juliette came out with her hair fashioned in a stylish knot on top of her head. 'Bathroom's all yours,' she said, avoiding his gaze.

Joe swept his gaze over her candy-pink calf-length dress with its waist cinched in with a patent leather belt and her matching high heels that showcased her slender ankles. He had never met anyone who could look so effortlessly elegant. Whether she was wearing track pants and a sweatshirt or designer wear, she always took his breath away. And when she was naked he forgot to breathe at all. 'You look stunning.'

Her creamy cheeks pooled with colour. 'Thank you.' Her gaze flicked away from his and she moved past him to get to the wardrobe. 'I'll just get my evening purse.'

Joe had to clench his hands into fists to stop himself touching her. The suite wasn't large enough to keep a safe distance. It needed to be the size of a small nation for that. The suite was mostly open-plan with a king-sized bed dominating the bedroom area, with no door between that and the lounge area. No more than a metre or two from the bed was a sofa and single armchair and coffee table and there were minibar facilities near the windows to maximise the view over Barbati Beach. The en suite bathroom was luxuriously appointed but was hardly what anyone would call spacious. For a honeymoon, it would be ideal.

But they weren't on a honeymoon.

Juliette opened the wardrobe and took her purse from one of the shelf compartments. He watched as her eyes went to his clothes hanging next to hers. Saw her teeth sink into her bottom lip and a small frown pull at her forehead.

'Is that against the rules?' Joe asked, leaning against the wall near her. 'To have our clothes touching?'

She stiffened and then shut the wardrobe with a little more force than was necessary. Her cheeks were a fiery red, her grey-blue eyes reminding him of a storm-tossed sea. 'We wouldn't need rules if you would stop looking at me like that.'

'How am I looking at you?'

She pursed her lips and put her chin up at a haughty height. 'Like you want to touch me.'

'I do want to touch you but the rules are the rules.' Joe wanted to touch her so badly it was all he could do to keep his hands under control.

She swallowed and her blush deepened. She dropped her evening purse on the bed and adjusted the belt around her dress. 'I should never have slept with you in the first place. It was totally out of character for me to do something like that.'

'I know it was,' Joe said, pushing himself away from the wall to approach her. 'That's why that night was so memorable.'

She frowned. 'Are you saying...*you* found it special?'

He gave a crooked smile and, before he could stop himself, he stroked a lazy finger down the curve of her cheek. 'I'd never met someone like you before.'

'Because I wasn't madly in love with you like most women are?' Her eyes glittered with sparks of cynicism.

He traced the outline of her lush mouth, knowing he was breaking the rules but unable to resist the temptation. 'You weren't interested in my money or my status. You just wanted to be distracted from a bad day, just like I wanted to be.'

Her tongue swept over her lips and she gave another audible swallow. 'Joe, we're going to be late for the drinks thing.'

Right now, Joe didn't care if they never made it to their friends' wedding. Being with Juliette— breathing in her scent, feeling the softness of her lips under his fingertip—made his blood pound with longing. A slow drag began pulling at his groin—a primal need he had shut down, ignored, blocked out with work, pulsed to vibrant and undeniable life. He slid his hand to the nape of her neck, meshing his gaze with hers. 'Why aren't you telling me to stop touching you?'

She gave a shuddery breath and her gaze dipped to his mouth. 'I—I don't know...' Her voice was whisper-soft.

He brought up her chin with his finger and locked her gaze with his. 'I'll tell you why, *cara*. Because deep down you want to be touched by me. You think a bunch of silly rules is going to damp down the explosive chemistry we still share?' It certainly wasn't damping down his. Not one little bit. He could feel the electric energy passing between them like a hot fizzing current. He could see it reflected in her eyes—the flicker of her eyelashes, the dart of her gaze to his mouth, the quick sweep of her tongue over her lips.

But then her gaze hardened and she placed her hand around his wrist and pulled it away from her face, shooting him a laser-like glare. 'There is no chemistry. I don't feel a thing where you're concerned. Not a damn thing.'

He captured her hand and tugged her close against his body. 'Want to put that to the test? One kiss. Let's see what happens.'

'Don't be ridiculous.' Her expression was scathing but her tone contained a trace of something else. Something that sounded very much like a dare.

Oh, he dared all right.

Joe breathed in the achingly familiar scent of her, brought his mouth as close to hers as he could without actually touching her lips. 'Just one little kiss.'

'You think I won't be able to help myself, like the night we met? But I can and I will.'

'Prove it.'

Her eyes went to his mouth. 'I don't need to prove anything to you.'

'Prove it to yourself then.'

She wavered for a moment, her eyes going to his mouth and back to his eyes. Then her eyes glazed over with chilly determination. 'Okay. I'll show you how immune I am to you.' She rose on tiptoe and planted a brief chaste kiss on his lips. She lowered her heels back to the floor and gave him an arch look. 'See? No fireworks.'

Joe gave a soft chuckle and released her. 'Probably just as well. I don't think anyone, least of all Damon and Lucy, are going to believe we've reconciled.'

A frown pulled at her brow. 'You're not going to...?' She clamped her mouth shut and turned away to reach for her purse on the bed. 'So, what are we going to tell them?' Her back was turned towards him, her hands fiddling with the clasp on her purse but he could see the tension in her slim back and shoulders as if she was bracing herself for his answer.

'We'll tell them the truth.'

She swung back round to face him, her expression wary. 'The truth?'

'That we're mature adults who are in the process of an amicable separation. Sharing a room for a couple of nights will not be a problem for us.'

Her brows rose. 'Amicable? Not a problem? Funny, but I don't see it quite that way.'

'Think about it, Juliette,' Joe said. 'We could go out there and pretend to be back together and then you'd have to allow me to touch you. Otherwise no one is going to buy it. I'd have to hold your hand, slip my arm around your waist, kiss you. You'd have to lie to your best friend. Is that what you want?'

Her small neat chin came up and her grey-blue eyes pulsated with anger. 'I want this weekend to be over. That's what I want.'

'Yeah, well, I want that too.'

Then maybe he could move on with his life.

CHAPTER FOUR

THE WELCOME DRINKS party was on the terrace in front of the infinity pool that overlooked the beach. The area was decorated with lanterns with golden flickering candles inside and honeysuckle and orange blossom scented the evening air. A champagne tower was on a table festooned with ribbons and posies of flowers on each corner. Two waiters dressed in white shirts, black trousers and black bowties were on standby to hand around a delicious-looking array of finger food. A string quartet was playing at one end of the terrace with a backdrop of cascading scarlet bougainvillea. There was a large sandwich board framed by pink and white flowers with a large love heart in the centre with Lucy and Damon's names written in beautiful calligraphy. Juliette had never seen such a romantic setting and tried not to compare it to her own wedding reception.

There certainly hadn't been any sandwich boards with love hearts on them.

Celeste Petrakis, the wedding planner, a slim young woman in her early twenties with short spiky black hair, was carrying a tablet in her hand and came dashing over to Juliette and Joe as soon as they came out to the terrace.

'Oh, my God, I'm so sorry but I think I've messed up your booking,' Celeste said. 'I only put down one J Allegranza on my list. I don't know how I got that wrong. I know Damon told me you guys were separated but I must have forgotten. Blame it on my chemo brain or something. I'm so embarrassed I want to die.' She clamped a hand over her mouth, her big brown eyes going wide as if she was worried she was going to get struck by lightning by a vengeful God. 'Oops. Didn't mean that. I've spent the last two years trying *not* to do that. But, seriously, I'm awfully embarrassed all the same.'

Joe stood close to Juliette but didn't touch her. 'It's fine, Celeste. We have no problem sharing a room.'

Juliette forced her lips into the semblance of a smile. 'Yes, indeed. So please don't worry, Celeste. You've done a brilliant job of organising everything. I've never seen such a lovely setting for a wedding. It looks like it's going to be an amazing weekend for Lucy and Damon.'

Celeste clasped a hand to her heart, her eyes dewy with emotion. 'Does that mean…? Oh, how romantic! I'm so happy for you both. We'll have a special toast for you guys later toni—'

'No.' Joe's tone was as blunt as a sledgehammer on a slice of sponge cake. 'We're not back together.'

Celeste's face fell and she bit down on her lip. 'Oh…sorry, I misunderstood. Do you want me to organise a fold-out bed for you? I mean, you might not want to share—'

'That would be wonderful, if there's one available,' Juliette said, trying to ignore the magnetic heat of Joe's body within touching distance of hers. If she moved even a fraction of a millimetre her arm would brush against him. It was almost impossible to control the urge to do so.

Touch him. Touch him. Touch him.

The chant was trying to keep up with her racing pulse.

'I'll see what I can do,' Celeste said, glancing between Joe and Juliette as if she couldn't quite work them out. 'I can only apologise again for this stuff-up. I would hate for you to be inconvenienced by my mishandling of—'

'Don't stress,' Joe said, moving slightly, his arm brushing against the bare skin of Juliette's, sending a shivery sensation through her flesh. 'It's not a problem.'

Juliette moved half a step away and gave the wedding planner a rictus smile. 'We don't want to draw attention away from Lucy and Damon. It's their special weekend, not ours.'

'Thank you for being so amazingly good about it.' Celeste gave them a finger wave and dashed away to greet some other guests coming out to the terrace.

Juliette glanced up at Joe. 'I need to speak to Lucy. She'll stress if she thinks I'm not okay about this. It'll ruin her wedding day for her if she's worrying about me—'

'Then pretend to be okay. It's not that hard.'

She glowered at him. 'Easy for you to say, Mr Show No Emotion.'

Joe shrugged and turned to look at the guests coming out to the terrace. 'It doesn't mean I don't have them.' The bottom register of his voice throbbed with something she had never heard in it before.

Juliette frowned and chewed on the inside of her lip. He was always so aloof and distant. He was like a steep and rocky island she continually circled, looking for a place to anchor.

His eyes met hers in a lock that made the backs of her knees shiver. 'This weekend could be a blessing in disguise. It could be a chance to sort out some of our issues. Not in the presence of other people, but while we're alone.'

While we're alone.

Juliette had to do everything in her power *not* to be alone with him. The only time she wanted to be alone with him was to hand him those hot-off-the-press divorce papers. 'I don't think our issues are the type that can get sorted out over a weekend, Joe. Not even over a lifetime.'

'Maybe, but at least we should try. I have some regret over how I handled our relationship.'

He had regret? She didn't want to hear about his supposed regret. She had regrets in their multitudes. She had known he had only married her out of duty and she had married him anyway. He had been there for her on his terms, not hers. It had been a fly-in, fly-out marriage that was doomed from the start.

Being with him now reminded her of how stupid she had been.

She'd foolishly believed their baby would bond them—would help him fall in love with her as well as their child. She had *wanted* him to love her. Wasn't that every girl's dream? If he had loved her then it would have made her feel better about how they had come together in the first place. It would absolve some of her nagging guilt about her own feelings. She had fallen in lust with him. Simple and bald and blatant as that. Lust was what she still felt for him and it had to stop.

She had to stop fuelling the fire that blazed inside her.

Juliette sent him an icy look. 'There isn't anything you could say to me that would make me want to resume our relationship. Nothing. So don't get any funny ideas that this weekend is going to magically fix what wasn't right in the first place.'

A waiter approached with a tray of drinks and Juliette took a glass of champagne. She was acutely conscious of Joe standing beside her, his arm brushing hers as he reached for a drink sending another hot shiver coursing through her body. Nerves and other emotions she didn't want to think about had her halfway through her drink before Joe had even taken a sip.

'Did you hear me say I want us to get back together?' There was a bite in his tone that nipped at her feminine pride. His eyes were espresso coffee dark and glittering with barely suppressed anger. 'That's the last thing I want.'

Juliette took another sip of champagne and then looked down at the remaining bubbles in her glass. 'Good to know.' It was good, wasn't it? He wanted out. She wanted out. Why then was her chest feeling as if something heavy was pressing all the air out of her lungs? She rapid blinked to clear her suddenly blurry vision, her throat so tight it felt as if a champagne cork was stuck halfway down.

Joe released a long slow breath and moved closer again, resting his hand on the top of her shoulder. The anger had gone from his gaze, to be replaced by a brooding frown. 'I apologise for being blunt but what's done is done and can't be undone.'

Juliette summoned her pride back on duty and brushed off his hand as if it was soiling her dress. 'I thought we agreed not to touch?' Her tone was sharp, her glare cutting.

'Please welcome the bride and groom.' Celeste's cheery voice rang out and the string quartet accompanied Lucy and Damon as they came out onto the terrace to cheers and applause from the assembled guests.

The press of the other guests gathering for a better view brought Joe to stand shoulder to shoulder with Juliette to make more room. Juliette painted a smile on her lips while her elbow landed a surreptitious jab in his ribs. He gave a low grunt that sounded far sexier than she had bargained for and a wave of heat rose over her skin. The steel band of his arm came around her and his hand glided down to her hip in a hold that was blatantly possessive. She glanced at his left hand resting on her hip and saw the gold glint of his wedding ring. The ring that claimed her as his. She was conscious of every point of contact as if her body had been finely programmed to recognise his touch.

She could have been blindfolded and still known it was him.

Lucy and Damon approached arm in arm and with wide smiles. An aura of happiness surrounded them and Juliette wished some of it could brush off on her. Why couldn't she have found happy-ever-after love?

'Oh my gosh, I can't believe my eyes,' Lucy said, grabbing Juliette in a bone-crushing hug that almost spilt the rest of her champagne. 'What's going on? Don't tell me you two are—?'

'No.' Joe's strident tone served to underline the word and land another free kick to Juliette's self-esteem. His arm dropped from around her waist and he added, 'There was a mix-up with the accommodation and we're trying to make it easy on Celeste, who double booked the room.'

'Oh, well, then...' Lucy's eyes began to twinkle as brightly as the princess diamond ring on her finger. 'I hope it won't be *too* much of a problem for you sharing?' There was a wink-wink-say-no-more quality to her tone.

'No problem at all.' Juliette kept her features under tight control but she couldn't control the creep of warm colour she could feel pooling in her cheeks.

Or the lingering hot tingle on her hip where Joe's hand had rested just moments before.

Damon grinned and grasped Joe's hand. 'Who knows what a weekend on Corfu will do, eh? Great to have you both here to share our special day with us.'

'I wouldn't have missed it for the world,' Joe said with an enigmatic smile.

After a moment or two, Lucy and Damon moved on to greet other guests, and Juliette lifted her glass to her lips and drained it. 'No problem sharing a room. Who knew what a consummate liar I could be? Go me.'

Joe's expression was shadowed by a contemplative frown. 'As I said, we could use this weekend to help both of us move forward.'

She raised her brows, sending him a scathing look. 'And how do you propose we do that? Hmm? Kiss and make up? Thanks, but no thanks.'

He took her empty glass off her and placed it on the stone balustrade nearby. 'It would be a start, don't you think?' His darkened gaze dipped to her mouth as if he were recalling every kiss they had ever exchanged.

Juliette's lips tingled and she fought not to lick her lips to draw any more of his attention to them. She sent him an arch look. 'That's how we got into this mess, if you remember. You kissed me.'

One side of his mouth came up in a sardonic half-smile. 'I seem to recall you made the first move.'

She ground her teeth so hard she was worried they would turn to powder on the spot. Did he have to remind her how forward and brazen she had been that night? So reckless and out of character. She shot him a pointed glare. 'You didn't have to take me up on it.'

'You seriously overestimate my willpower, *cara*.'

Juliette's chin came up. 'You'd better make sure it's in better shape this time around.'

One of his ink-black brows lifted. 'For when you beg me to take you to bed, you mean?'

Her hands clenched into tight balls by her sides in case she was tempted to slap him. 'Not going to happen.' She injected as much confidence in her tone as she could.

His lazy smile made the base of her spine fizz and tingle. He picked up one of her fists and gently prised open her fingers, his thumb stroking the middle of her palm in a way that was unmistakably sexual. His gaze held hers in a mesmerising lock no amount of willpower to resist could ever have matched. 'You shouldn't be ashamed of our chemistry.' The pitch of his voice lowered to a knee-weakening burr.

Juliette pulled her hand out of his, rubbing at it as if he had burned her. 'I'm not ashamed. I'm disgusted. And for God's sake, stop touching me.'

His smile didn't fade but a line of tension appeared next to his mouth and his eyes hardened. 'Careful, *cara*. We're in public, remember? Sheath those pretty claws until we're alone. Then you can rake them down my back to your heart's desire.'

Juliette had to blink away the scorching-hot images his words evoked. Her body was on fire, swamped with memories of his masterful lovemaking. It had taken her almost two years to be able to reach an orgasm with her ex and even then it was hit and miss thereafter. She had practically orgasmed on the spot the moment Joe kissed her the first time. He never took his pleasure before he satisfied her. He knew her body better than she knew it herself. She had explored every inch of his and, by doing so, had found a passionate and adventurous streak in her personality she hadn't known existed. Standing within touching distance now made her body miss him all the more. She could feel a magnetic pull towards him as if an invisible current of energy was calling her back to base.

To distract herself, she took another glass of champagne off a passing waiter. She figured it was better to keep her hands and mouth otherwise occupied.

'Do you know any of the other wedding party guests?' Joe asked after a long moment.

Juliette crossed her arms and cupped one hand under her elbow, holding her champagne glass in the other hand. 'Only Lucy. And Damon, of course. I haven't met any of the four other bridesmaids before because they're friends Lucy made since moving to Greece. What about you?'

'I'd heard about his cousin Celeste but not met her before today. But I've met two of the bridesmaids once or twice before.' He took a measured sip of his drink, lowering his glass from his mouth to glance at the view over the terrace.

A dagger of jealousy jabbed her in the gut. 'Oh, really?' Juliette made sure her tone was just mildly interested when in fact she wanted to know dates, times, places and whether he had been to bed with either of them. How could any woman resist him? She certainly hadn't been able to.

Joe turned to look at her with an unreadable expression. 'It's kind of ironic how Damon and Lucy met through us, isn't it?'

'Ironic in what way?'

He gave a one-shoulder shrug and looked down at the contents of his glass, twirling it to set the bubbles spinning. 'They seem pretty happy together. Whether or not it lasts is another thing.'

'Do you have to be so cynical? They're in love. Anyone can see that. That's what we were lacking. We married for all the wrong reasons.'

He didn't respond and instead tipped his glass back and drained it. She couldn't take her eyes off the strong tanned column of his throat and the peppery regrowth on his jaw that, in spite of a recent shave, was already vigorously reappearing. How many times had she felt his stubble against her soft skin? On her face, on her belly, between her thighs...

Juliette suppressed a shudder and turned to look at the other guests milling about for the next part of the entertainment the wedding planner had organised. Which bridesmaids had Joe met before? The blonde one? The sleek raven-haired one? The one with the big boobs and legs that went on for ever?

Joe held out his hand for her empty glass. 'Would you like something soft this time? Orange juice? Mineral water?'

Juliette handed the glass to him, being extra careful not to touch his fingers. 'Are you hinting I might drink to excess and make a fool of myself?'

He drew in a breath and pressed his lips into a flat line before releasing it. 'Look, I know the situation this weekend is hard on you. It's the first time we've seen each other face to face since you left.' His hands were thrust in his trouser pockets, his broad shoulders rolled forward. 'I would have preferred meeting with you in London but you didn't respond to any of my attempts to contact you.'

Juliette had ignored his texts and emails for months. She had even blocked his number on her phone. It had been her way of punishing him for not being there when she'd needed him the most. But in a way she had punished herself because she had made herself completely isolated. Her friends and family had tried to support her but, a few months in, they were all suffering compassion fatigue. Even Lucy, with the distraction of her wedding preparations, hadn't been as available to her, especially since Juliette hadn't felt up to illustrating the books they wrote together since the loss of Emilia. She'd desperately needed to be with someone who knew and understood what she was going through—the grief, the pain, the loss. She looked down at the flagstones at her feet rather than meet his gaze. 'I wasn't ready. I found it too…triggering.'

He moved closer to her and lightly touched the back of her hand with one of his fingers. 'That's completely understandable.' His voice was gentle as a caress and her hand tingled as if it had been zapped by a live current.

Juliette brought her gaze up to meet his. 'Do you think about her?'

His eyes flickered as if he was suffering a deep internal pain and only just managing to control it. 'All the time. That's why I've regularly donated to and been fundraising for a stillbirth research foundation for the last few months. I wanted to do something positive to help others in our situation. If you'd happened to read any emails from me, you would have known about it. I donated money on behalf of both of us.'

A stillbirth research foundation? Juliette's heart contracted. *He had been fundraising for a stillbirth foundation?*

The anger she wore like armour dropped away like a sloughed skin, leaving her feeling stripped of her defences. Defences she needed to keep her from getting hurt all over again. She hadn't read any of his emails for the last fifteen months. She had marked them as spam and felt immensely satisfied doing it.

Knowing now he was doing something for others was all very well, but what about helping her through the worst time of her life? She had stood by their baby's grave alone. Time and time again, she had grieved in isolation. 'But I don't get it. You tell me you've donated money and, knowing you, it would be a significant amount, but you haven't once visited her grave since the funeral.'

His mouth went into a tight line. 'Graveyards aren't my thing. I prefer to pay my respects in other ways.'

Every week when Juliette visited her baby's grave, she hoped to see flowers or a card or toy left by Joe. But there was nothing. She couldn't understand it and nor could she forgive it, in spite of his generosity to others. He came to London for work regularly—how hard would it have been to drop by the cemetery and hand-deliver flowers or a soft toy? Or didn't he want to be reminded of their baby and their broken marriage?

'Were you keeping away in case you ran into me?' She couldn't tone down the accusing note in her voice.

He looked down at her with an unreadable expression. His features could have been carved in stone. 'How often do you go?'

'Every week.'

'Does it help your grieving process?'

Juliette blew out a frustrated breath. 'Nothing helps with that. But at least I feel I'm not ignoring her.'

'Is that what you think I'm doing?'

She raised her chin to a combative height. 'Aren't you?'

He drew in another sharp breath and turned again to look at the view. His posture was stiff and tight as if invisible steel cables were holding him upright. 'There's no right way to grieve, Juliette. What works for one might not work for someone else.' He spoke through gritted teeth, his hands thrust back in his trouser pockets.

'And is your grieving process working?'

He turned his head to look at her with a grim expression. 'What do you think?'

Juliette shifted her mouth from side to side and looked away. Trouble was, she didn't know what to think. He had never behaved the way she had expected him to behave. He hadn't expressed the words she had wanted to hear or done the things she had hoped he would do. Their relationship had been based on his sense of duty towards her and the baby, so when the baby was lost there was no reason to stay together. He hadn't given her a good enough reason to continue their relationship. He hadn't expressed any feelings for her. But then, neither had she for him. She had been incapable of expressing anything but profound grief, which had in time morphed into anger.

She schooled her features into coolly impersonal lines and turned to face him again. 'I think you're secretly relieved we no longer have a reason to stay together.'

His jaw worked for a moment and his mouth tightened into a flat line. 'Let's leave that discussion until later. We're at our friends' wedding, remember?' And, without another word, he turned and left her with nothing but the company of the ocean-scented breeze.

CHAPTER FIVE

AFTER THE BRIEF wedding rehearsal Joe made idle conversation with some of the other guests but his mind was stuck on Juliette. He kept searching for her in the knot of people, a tight fluttering sensation going through his chest every time he caught sight of her honey-brown head in the crowd.

He had thought often of going to the cemetery where their baby was buried in England but each time he baulked. His father had dragged him to his mother's graveside to pay his respects on each and every birthday until he was a teenager. It had been a form of torture to stand by that headstone knowing he was the reason his mother was beneath it. No amount of wishing and praying and hoping could bring his mother or his baby daughter back. No number of visits, flowers or cards could undo what was done. He had always found his father's way of grieving a destructive process. Joe had chosen a different outlet—a constructive way of processing his grief by raising money for the research that would hopefully save lives and, no doubt, relationships.

But now, touching Juliette, standing next to her, breathing in the scent of her stirred his blood and upped his pulse and made him wonder if there was a chance something positive could come out of their situation. The chemistry was still there, as hot and electric as ever. The explosive chemistry that had kick-started their relationship was the one thing he could rely on to get it going again. He felt the pull of it like an invisible force drawing him to her. He'd had to stuff his hands in his pockets to stop reaching for her. He couldn't be in the same room as her without wanting her. Damn it—he couldn't be in the same country without aching with the need to take her in his arms.

Juliette turned and looked at him across the now moonlit terrace and a small creature scuttled through the ventricles of his heart. Girl-next-door-pretty rather than classically beautiful, she still had the power to snatch his breath. Her grey-blue eyes reminded him of a deep stormy sea with shifting shadows. Her slim frame was ballerina-like with a natural elegance of movement. And her skin was pale but she had a dusting of freckles over the bridge of her upturned nose that reminded him of sprinkled nutmeg. Her mouth was a Cupid's bow of pink lushness that drew his gaze like a magnet and he realised with a sharp pang how much he missed her sunshine-bright smile. Not those fake ones she flashed when required but a genuine one that lit up her face and eyes.

Juliette's gaze shifted back to the older couple next to her who were the bride's parents, but Joe could see she wasn't really engaged in the conversation. She kept chewing at her lower lip and fiddling with the clasp of her evening purse as if she couldn't wait for the evening to be over.

And soon it would be over and they would be alone in their suite.

The string quartet was playing dance numbers and several couples were dancing further along the terrace. He remembered the first time he'd danced with Juliette, how she had moved with him with such natural rhythm as if they had been dancing together for years.

Making love had been the same.

After their one-night stand and they had gone their separate ways, he hadn't been able to get her out of his mind. He'd had commitments back in Italy and then another project in Germany but he hadn't stopped thinking about her. And then, out of the blue, she'd called him and told him she was carrying his child. The news had stunned him. They had used protection but fate had decided to step in and create a new life. A life that hadn't lasted long enough to take a single independent breath.

Joe let out a long sigh as the familiar pain seized his chest whenever he thought of his tiny baby daughter. He blamed himself for not being there when Juliette went into early labour. Perhaps if he had been there to take her to hospital earlier things might have panned out differently. There were so many things he wished he had done differently.

Joe wove through the small crowd to join her,

taking one of her hands in his. 'Would you like to dance?' He figured it was one way he could legitimately hold her in his arms. And, more importantly, stop her from dancing with anyone else.

She looked as if she were about to refuse, but then she shrugged, not quite meeting his gaze. 'Sure. Why not?'

Joe led her to the part of the terrace set up for dancing, overlooking the ocean below. The string quartet was now playing a romantic ballad and he gathered her close, moving with her to the slow rhythm of the music. 'You didn't look like you were enjoying the conversation you were having back there,' he said, breathing in the flowery scent of her hair.

Juliette glanced up at him with a frown. 'Was it so obvious?'

'Only to me.' He led her further away from the other guests who had joined them on the dance floor. 'Do you know Lucy's parents well?'

'Pretty well. I spent a fair bit of time at their house when Lucy and I were teenagers.' She gave a little sigh and added, 'I was really envious of her. Her parents were so different from mine.'

'In what way?'

She didn't respond for so long, he wondered if she hadn't heard him. But then she aimed her gaze at his shirt front and spoke in a low tone. 'They were so... so uncritical. I don't think I've ever heard them say anything negative about her or the choices she made.'

Joe eased back to look down at her. 'And your parents were critical and negative?'

She gave a little eye-roll and lowered her gaze back to his shirt front. 'Not so much when there's an audience. They're way too polite and subtle for that. But I know how much I've disappointed them by not being as academically gifted as them and my two older brothers.'

Joe couldn't say he was all that surprised by her confession. But it niggled him that he hadn't drawn her out a little more on her family while they were living together. What did that say about him? What sort of husband didn't show an interest in his wife's background?

A husband with a troubled background of his own who wanted no questions asked, that was who.

Joe had only met her parents and brothers twice—at the wedding and then Emilia's funeral. The funeral was a bit of a blur to him and they hadn't been particularly warm towards him at the wedding—but he hadn't been expecting them to welcome him with open arms. They'd been polite in a stiff upper lip kind of way, but then his courtship of their only daughter hadn't exactly been ideal. A one-night stand pregnancy was hardly the way to impress and win over in-laws but he hadn't wanted his child to grow up without knowing him. Marriage had been the best option in his opinion.

Their child had to come first—the baby had been his top priority.

Her parents hadn't come to the hospital when they'd lost the baby as they were on a long-haul international flight. Juliette had flown to England to visit her parents before they'd left for a three-month tour abroad. She had been booked on a flight back to Italy the next day when she'd gone into labour. He'd flown back as soon as he heard but he got there too late.

'But you're so talented, Juliette. Your illustrations are amazing. Aren't they proud of your work?'

Her gaze was downcast, her mouth downturned. 'I'm the only person in my family without a PhD. I barely scraped through my GCSEs. A children's book illustrator isn't what they consider a worthwhile career, especially as I don't even have an art degree. They're proud I've had stuff published, sure, but they still see it as a kind of hobby.' She gave another sigh that made her slim shoulders go down. 'I haven't done a sketch in months so maybe they're right. It's time to find something else. I don't know how Lucy has put up with me this long. It's not just my career on hold, but hers too.'

Joe placed one of his hands along the curve of her creamy cheek, meshing his gaze with her troubled one. 'You don't need to think about a career until you're ready, *cara*. I've been depositing funds in your bank account to more than cover any loss of income.'

A tinge of pink spread across her cheeks but a determined light came into her eyes. 'I don't want or need your money. I haven't touched a penny of it.'

Joe brushed his thumb pad across the small round circle of her chin. 'You hate me that much?'

Something flickered in her gaze until her lashes came down over her eyes to lock him out. 'I never wanted your money. That wasn't why I married you.'

She stepped out of his hold and crossed her arms over her body as if she were cold but the night air was balmy and warm.

'Yes, well, we both know why you married me.' Joe couldn't remove the cynicism from his tone in time. 'You wanted to show your cheating ex you'd moved on.'

She pressed her lips into a flat line, the colour in her cheeks darkening. 'That's not true. It had nothing to do with him. I can barely remember what he looks like now. I thought I was doing the best thing by the baby by marrying you. Anyway, you were the one who insisted on marriage. I would've been just as happy with a co-parenting arrangement.'

'Have you heard from your ex? Do you ever see him?' Joe wasn't sure why he was asking because he didn't want to know. He could do without the punishment, the torture, the despair of imagining her with someone else. He had never considered himself the jealous type. But the thought of her being intimate with someone else made his gut churn. The thought of her having another child with someone else sent a tight band of pain across his chest until he could hardly draw a breath.

Juliette flashed him an irritated look. 'I hardly see how it's any of your business who I see or don't see.'

Joe led her by the elbow away from the other dancers to a quieter part further along the terrace. 'It's my business because we're still legally married.'

He lowered his hand from her elbow but he had to summon up every bit of willpower he possessed to stop from pulling her back into his arms and crashing his mouth down on hers. To remind her of the passion that sparked between them. The passion that was charging the atmosphere even now.

Which brought him to a perplexing question—what the hell was he going to do about it? He had already made mistakes with Juliette. Big mistakes. Mistakes that couldn't be undone. Would it be asking for trouble to revisit their relationship? To see if it was worth salvaging?

Her gaze glittered with defiance. 'I find it highly amusing how you're suddenly so interested in my private life after all these months.' She glanced at his mouth as if she was expecting him to do what he was tempted to do. 'And why do you keep wearing your wedding ring? It seems rather pointless.'

Joe reached for her left hand, running his thumb over her empty ring finger. He was expecting her to pull away but, surprisingly, she didn't. Instead her gaze meshed with his and her tongue darted out to sweep across her lower lip, her throat rising and falling over a swallow.

'It's not entirely pointless. It keeps me free of unwanted female attention.' He waited a beat before continuing. 'I still have your wedding and engagement rings.' Joe wasn't sure why he was telling her that snippet of useless information. Did it make him sound like a sentimental fool who hadn't got over the walk-out of his wife? Should he tell her he hadn't removed one article of her clothing from his wardrobe? That he couldn't even use the same bedroom they had shared as it caused him too much gut-wrenching pain? And don't get him started on the nursery. He hadn't opened that door once. Not once. Opening that door would be tearing open a deep and devastating wound.

Juliette glanced down at their joined hands before returning her gaze to his. 'I'm surprised you haven't pawned them by now or found someone else to give them to.'

Joe stroked the soft flesh of her palm, watching as her pupils flared and her breath quickened. 'They belong to you.'

Her chin came up, an intransigent light sparking in her eyes. 'I don't want them.'

'Maybe, but still you want me.' Joe brought her hip to hip to his body, his gaze lowering to her mouth. 'Don't you, *mio piccolo*?'

Juliette licked her lips again, her eyes flicking to his mouth. 'No.' Her tone was firm but her body swayed towards him as if propelled by a force bigger than her will to resist.

He tipped up her chin, stroking her lower lip with his thumb. 'Pride is a funny thing, is it not? I would like to say I don't want you either but I would be lying to myself as well as you.'

She drew in a breath and released it in a shuddery rush. 'Joe...please...'

'Please, what?' Joe cupped one side of her face with his hand, the other hand going to the small of her back to bring her even closer to the throb and ache of his lower body. 'Are you going to deny what you're feeling right now? What you've felt from the moment I walked into the suite this afternoon? What you felt the first time we met? It's why you blocked my phone and emails, isn't it? You don't want to be reminded of what you feel for me.'

Juliette swallowed again, her hands creeping up to rest against his chest, her gaze homing in on his mouth. 'We're separated now and—'

'We're not separated this weekend. We're sharing a room. Sharing a bed.'

'No, we're not.' Her hands fell away from his chest, her gaze defiant. 'Celeste said she was going to get a fold-out for—'

'I spoke to her a few minutes ago,' Joe said. 'She wasn't able to get one in time for tonight but she'll try again tomorrow.'

Her gaze flicked back to his, the line of her mouth pulling tight. She stepped back, her posture stiff, guarded. 'We both need to move on with our lives. It would only complicate things to go backwards instead of forwards.'

She placed her left hand against her temple and closed her eyes as if in silent prayer. 'Please, Joe. Don't make this harder than it needs to be.' She lowered her hand from her face and looked up at him again with an expression that shone anew with determination. 'I'm going back to the room. To sleep. *Alone.*'

Juliette managed to slip away without any of the wedding party noticing and went back to the suite and closed the door with a heavy sigh. She'd been so tempted to dance with Joe all night, to find any excuse to be in his arms again. But that was the pathway to heartbreak because they didn't belong together. Not then. Not now.

If only her body didn't keep betraying her. It was so hard to keep her distance when he only had to look at her and her resistance melted. She had lowered her guard enough to tell him about her frustrating relationship with her parents and her doubts over her career going forward. It was a moment of weakness and yet she had drawn comfort from sharing so openly with him. He had been supportive and understanding in a way she hadn't expected.

And then there was the stillbirth foundation…

She couldn't get it out of her mind—how he had raised money for much-needed research. That all this time she had been judging him for not grieving the way she expected, but he'd been doing what he thought would help others. It made it harder for her to access her anger, to keep her emotional distance.

But it didn't mean they had a future together.

How could they when they weren't in love, had never been in love and would only be together for the sake of physical chemistry? That wasn't enough to build a marriage on, especially a marriage that had suffered such a tragedy as theirs. A marriage that would never have come about if it hadn't been for her accidental pregnancy. She wasn't the type of woman he normally dated. She wasn't sophisticated or super-smart and no one could ever call her supermodel beautiful. She would never have been his first choice of bride if she hadn't fallen pregnant.

Juliette pulled the clips out of her hair and tossed them on the dressing table on her way to the bathroom. Joe's shaving things were on the bathroom counter and his bottle of cologne right next to her cosmetics. A soft fluttering sensation passed over the floor of her belly. Sharing a bathroom was such an intimate thing to do. Would she be strong enough to resist the temptation he offered? She picked the cologne bottle up, took off the lid and held the neck of the bottle to her nose, closing her eyes to breathe in the citrus notes. She put the bottle back down and put the lid back on.

She had to be strong enough.

She *had* to.

Juliette came back out to the bedroom and glanced at her tote bag, where the divorce papers were stashed. On Sunday, after Lucy and Damon sailed off, she would whip them out and wave them under Joe's nose, not before. It gave her a sense of power to know she had them there, waiting for the right moment. He thought he could snap his fingers and she would come running back to him as if nothing had changed. Everything had changed.

She had changed.

And she wasn't changing back.

Joe came back to the suite later that night to find Juliette asleep in the bedroom with a bank of pillows dividing the king-sized bed in two sections. The bedside lamp was still on and the muted light cast her features into a golden glow. She had taken her hair down and it was spread out over the pillow. Her make-up was removed, leaving her skin as fresh and glowing as a child's. Her mouth was relaxed in sleep, her lips softly parted, her breathing slow and even. He reached up and loosened his tie, slipping it from around his collar and tossing it to the chair in the corner of the bedroom.

Juliette's eyes sprang open and she sat upright, blinking at him owlishly. 'Oh, it's you...'

'Thanks for the hearty welcome.' Joe began to unbutton his shirt.

Her gaze narrowed and she pulled the bedcovers further up her body. 'What are you doing?'

'What do you think I'm doing?' He shrugged off his shirt and tossed it in the same direction as his tie. 'I'm getting undressed.'

'Can you do it in the bathroom?' Her cheeks were a bright shade of pink and her eyes kept avoiding his. 'And please wear boxers or something. And stay on that side of the bed.'

'It's a bit late to be shy, *tesoro*. I'm familiar with every inch of your body, as indeed you are with mine.'

She threw back the covers and dived for the bathrobe that was hanging over the back of another chair. He caught a tantalising glimpse of café-latte-coloured satin shortie pyjamas, one of the shoestring straps on the camisole top slipping off her shoulder to reveal the upper curve of her breast. She thrust her arms in the bathrobe's sleeves and knotted the waist ties around her middle with unnecessary force, sending him a scalding glare. 'Fine. Have it your way. You have the bed and I'll sleep on the sofa.' She began to stalk past him but he caught her wrist on the way and stalled her passage.

'Don't be so dramatic.' He let her arm go, opening and closing his fingers to ease the tingling sensation touching her had produced. 'I'm not going to force myself on you. You have the bed. I'll take the sofa.'

She bit down on her lip and glanced towards the other section of the suite where the smallish sofa was situated. 'You're too tall for it. You won't sleep a wink.'

He wasn't going to sleep a wink anyway, not with her so temptingly close. Seeing her all sleep tousled with so much of her creamy skin on show was already stretching the limit of his self-control. 'I'm sure we can manage to share a bed for two nights without crossing any boundaries.'

She fiddled with the waist ties of her bathrobe, her teeth still worrying her lip. 'Okay. But you have to promise not to touch me.'

He placed his hand on his heart. 'You have my solemn word.'

Juliette pursed her lips, her gaze searching his for a moment. 'Why do I get the feeling you're laughing at me?'

He lowered his hand from his chest and dropped it back down by his side. 'Believe me, *cara*. It's been a long time since I laughed.'

Her eyes fell away from his and a shadow crossed her features. She turned back to the bed and climbed back under the covers, pulling them up to her chin and turning her back to him. 'Goodnight.'

Joe's gaze went to the box of sleep medication on her bedside table. He came over to her side of the bed and perched on the edge. 'How long have you been taking those?' He pointed to the medication sitting next to a glass of water.

Juliette turned over onto her back, her expression defensive. 'I only use them when I can't sleep.'

'And how often is that?'

Her eyes shifted out of reach of his and her fingers began plucking at the hem of the sheet. 'More often than not…' Her voice was hardly more than a whisper.

Joe stroked back a strand of hair from her forehead, his chest so tight he could barely inflate his lungs to breathe. Guilt rained down on him over how he had handled the last few months. She had suffered alone when he should have been by her side. He'd thought keeping his distance was what she wanted but it clearly hadn't helped her through the grieving process. It certainly hadn't helped him either. So many platitudes sprang to his lips—like the irritating comments other people had made to him.

Time is a great healer.

It will get easier.

You'll be stronger for it.

Instead, he stayed silent.

Her shimmering gaze met his and his chest tightened another painful notch. 'I can't help blaming myself. Maybe I shouldn't have flown home to England to visit my parents before they went on their trip. I didn't need to go. I could have asked them to visit me instead.'

And why had she flown home to England? Because he'd been away on yet another work commitment, leaving her to fend for herself. If anyone was to blame, it was him. Joe took one of her hands and anchored it to his aching chest. 'No. You mustn't blame yourself.' His voice was so rough it could have filed through metal. 'You had a dream pregnancy up until then.'

Her mouth twisted. 'You weren't there for the first three months. It wasn't such a dream pregnancy then. I was sick just about every day.'

Joe wished he had been there but she hadn't told him until she was twelve weeks along. He laid her hand on his thigh, moving his thumb over the back of her hand in slow soothing strokes. 'I was going to contact you so many times after we slept together that night.'

A frown creased her smooth brow. 'Were you? You never told me that before.'

Joe gave a wry half-smile. 'We hadn't exchanged numbers but I managed to find your details online because of your publishing career. I thought of emailing you numerous times, suggesting we meet up for a drink or something.'

'Why didn't you?'

'You were still getting over your ex. I didn't think you were ready to move on.'

She lowered her gaze and slipped her hand out of his hold and grasped the edge of the bedcovers. 'I think I was over Harvey as soon as he told me he was in love with Clara. But you would've only been offering a fling back then, not something lasting.' She issued it as a statement rather than a question.

Joe stood from the bed and looked down at her, unwilling to confirm or deny it. He had never felt the need to settle down with anyone long-term. He'd preferred to live in a world outside permanent attachment. A safe world. A world where he couldn't hurt or be hurt in return. 'Try and get some sleep, *cara*. Goodnight.'

Juliette listened while Joe had a shower in the bathroom. She tried to stop her mind filling with images of him under the hot spray of water, tried to stop thinking of the times she had shared a shower with him in the past. The blistering passion, the drumming need, the explosive orgasms.

She groaned under her breath and turned so her back was facing the bathroom, tucking her legs up close to her torso and squeezing her eyes shut. She waited for him to join her in the bed, waited for the familiar press of his weight down on the mattress, her senses so alert she knew it would be impossible to settle into sleep. She opened her eyes and saw the medication next to her glass of water. She sat up, pressed one out of the blister packet and swallowed it down with a gulp of water.

She lay back down and waited for the slow but inexorable drag down into mindless slumber...

CHAPTER SIX

JULIETTE DIDN'T KNOW how long she had been asleep
when she woke. It was still dark except for a beam
of silvery moonlight peeping through a gap in the
curtains, illuminating the bed...*the half empty bed*.
She sat up and pushed her hair away from her face
and frowned at the vacant space beside her. The pillows were undented, the sheets smooth, showing no
sign Joe had even momentarily lain down beside her.

A perverse sense of pique washed over her. Why
hadn't he slept beside her? Did he find her repulsive? Was she worried she might cross to his side of
the bed? She pushed off the bedcovers and, ignoring
the bathrobe laid over the chair, padded through to
the sitting room area.

Joe was sitting in a slumped position on the sofa,
his long legs stretched out in front of him, his head
on one side, his eyes closed in a deep sleep. He was
naked except for a bath towel anchored around his
lean hips.

Juliette knew she should tiptoe back to bed. Knew
she shouldn't feel a smidgeon of compassion for him

for having spent an uncomfortable night sleeping upright. Knew she had no right to stare at his tanned athletic body bathed in moonlight, making him look like a Greek god rather than human. But her feet seemed to be anchored to the floor, her eyes drawn to him with the force of an industrial-sized magnet.

She wasn't aware of making a sound but suddenly his eyes opened and he blinked and sat upright, scraping a hand through his already tousled hair.

'Was I snoring?' he asked with a grimace.

'No. Is that a new habit you've acquired since we...?' She left the sentence hanging but couldn't explain why. He'd told her there'd been no one else since she'd left but one day there would be. That was something she didn't want to think about too closely. Someone else in his life. In his bed. In his arms. Experiencing the mind-blowing passion she missed to this day.

Joe drew his legs to a right-angled position, leaned forward and rested his forearms on his thighs. 'Not that I know of.'

There was a moment of silence. A silence so loaded the air seemed to be weighted, making it hard for Juliette to breathe.

'Why didn't you sleep in the bed?'

Joe lifted his head to look at her, his eyes so dark they could have been black holes in space. 'I didn't want to disturb you. You looked like you needed your sleep.' His voice had a rough edge that made something in her belly lose its footing.

Juliette rolled her lips together and came a little

closer, drawn to him as if her body had a will of its own. 'Joe…it's okay if you want to share the bed. Really, we're both mature adults and—'

'It's fine. I got a couple of hours. It's all I need.' He rose from the sofa, securing the towel around his hips, and walked over to the windows, pushing the curtains further aside to look at the moonlit view.

She couldn't take her eyes off the sculpted perfection of his back and shoulder muscles, taut buttocks and his long strong thighs and calves below the hip-height towel. Just knowing he was naked under that towel was enough to send her female hormones into a cheerleading routine. Sensations stirred low in her body—sensual, erotic memories of his thick, hard presence moving within her.

Joe turned from the window and brushed his hair back from his forehead. 'Go back to bed, Juliette.' His tone was part stern authority and part growing impatience.

Juliette took a step towards him. 'Joe…'

He closed the distance between them and placed his hands on the tops of her shoulders. The warmth of his fingers seeped into her flesh, awakening needs and desires she wasn't sure she could control. His hooded eyes drifted to her mouth, his breath hitching, his body so close her breasts brushed against his chest. The smooth satin of her shortie pyjamas couldn't hide her body's reaction to him. She could feel the tensing of her nipples, the spreading tingles in her breasts, the smouldering heat in her core.

His hand cupped one side of her face, his thumb

moving across her cheek like the arm of a slow-beating metronome. 'Kissing you would be the easy part. Stopping at one kiss, however, would be something else.' His voice was so rough it sounded as if he'd been gargling with gravel.

Juliette's gaze lowered to his sensually shaped lips and something in her stomach fell off a high shelf. 'Who said I wanted you to kiss me?' Her voice was too breathy to relay the cool indifference she'd aimed for.

One side of his mouth tipped up in a crooked smile that did serious damage to her resolve to resist him. His thumb stroked across her lower lip, back and forth in a mesmerising, spine-tingling rhythm. 'When I arrived here this weekend I was so determined I wasn't going to do this.'

Juliette hadn't realised she'd moved until she found herself flush against him, the hard jut of his hips, the proud rise of his male flesh setting her body on fire. 'Do what?' Her voice was so soft it could barely be called a whisper.

'You know exactly what.' And his mouth came down and covered hers.

Juliette knew she should have pulled away right then. She should have stopped it from going any further. She shouldn't have allowed herself to be tempted, much less give into it. But as soon as his lips met hers, something hard and tight and bitter inside her collapsed like a house of cards. His lips moved against hers in an exploratory fashion, as if he was reminding himself of her contours, her taste, her texture. She groaned and opened to him and his tongue met hers in an erotic dance that made the hairs on the back of her neck tingle and the base of her spine fizz.

Her hands moved from his chest to link around his neck, her fingers playing with the thick black strands of his hair. He made a low growling sound deep in his throat and changed position, deepening the kiss until the bones in her legs threatened to melt like candle-wax in a cauldron.

Joe's hands framed her face, his breathing almost as hectic as hers. After long breathless moments he lifted his mouth off hers, gazing down at her for an infinitesimal pause before sealing her lips once more with a softly muttered curse, as if he too hated himself for his weakness where she was concerned.

One of his hands left her face and went to the small of her back, pressing her closer to the tantalising ridge of his male flesh. His other hand went to the nape of her neck, his long fingers splayed into the tingling roots of her hair. Shivers coursed up and down her back, her inner core hosting a welcome party, darts of pleasure shooting between her legs.

Joe lifted his mouth off hers and placed his hands on her hips, stepping back from her a fraction. 'I think it might be time to stop.' Something in his tone belied his words—the gruffness, the rueful note, the chord of longing so low she might have missed it if she hadn't been feeling it herself.

Stop? Now?

When her body was screaming for the release it craved? And why the hell hadn't *she* been the one to stop this madness? She felt hot shame flushing into her face and she shoved his hands off her hips and stepped further back, chest heaving as if she were an affronted heroine in a period drama. 'What the hell do you think you're playing at, kissing me like that?'

One of his ink-black eyebrows rose in a sardonic arc. 'I could ask you the same question.'

Juliette couldn't hold his gaze and swung away. 'I'm going to have a shower. It'll soon be time to get up and get ready for the wedding anyway.' She strode into the bathroom and locked the door, leaning back against it with a ragged sigh. Why had she allowed him to prove how weak she was? How vulnerable to his touch? How lacking in immunity?

How dangerously ambiguous her feelings...

The wedding was to be held in the morning on the beach. Somehow Juliette had managed to shower and dress without running into Joe. He had left the suite while she was in the shower, and because she was heading to Lucy's room for a hair and make-up session with the other bridesmaids she didn't expect to see him again until the ceremony.

Lucy handed Juliette a glass of champagne on arrival. 'Get that into you. Now, tell me how last night went. Did you guys kiss and make up?'

Juliette took the champagne but decided against taking anything but a token sip. 'Let's talk about you, not me. Are you nervous?'

Lucy beamed. 'Me? Nervous? I can't wait to marry Damon.' Her smile dimmed a little. 'I just wish things

were better between you and Joe. Are you sure there's
no hope of a reconciliation?'

'It's not what either of us wants.'

'Are you sure about that? I saw the way he was
watching you last night. He could barely take his eyes
off you. And when you two were dancing, well, anyone would have thought you were—'

'We're not.' Juliette's tone was emphatic. She
opened the long narrow box that contained Lucy's
hand-embroidered veil. 'He slept on the sofa.'

'Oh...'

Juliette turned to look at her friend. 'I don't want
your wedding to be spoilt by my dramas with Joe.'
She painted a bright smile on her face. 'Now, let's get
you ready to marry the man of your dreams. Your
dress looks amazing, by the way.'

Lucy twirled this way and that in her voluminous
tulle and satin dress. It made her mixed-race complexion look all the more stunning. 'You don't think
I look too much like a meringue?' There was a dancing light in her eyes. 'It was a toss-up between this
one and the figure-hugging one we looked at together
in Mayfair but I've always wanted to be a princess
for a day.'

'You look exactly like a princess,' Juliette said,
trying to ignore a tiny jab of envy. 'A princess in
love.'

Joe stood next to Damon under the canopy of tropi-
cal flowers that had been set up on the beach. He was
trying not to think of his own wedding, how differ-

ent it was from this one. If he and Juliette had married in a more relaxed and informal setting, would it have helped? His goal had been to get married to her as soon as possible for the sake of the baby. The cold and austere village church where generations of her family had been christened, wed or buried would not have been his first choice. But he had wanted Juliette to feel supported by her family, given he had none to speak of.

Damon nudged him. 'Here they come.'

Joe turned and saw Juliette leading the way up the flower-strewn red carpet that had been laid down on the sand. She was dressed in a deep blue satin dress the colour of the ocean that pulsed nearby. The dress clung to her body like a slinky glove, outlining the gentle swell of her hips, the narrow waist, the slight globes of her breasts. There was a garland of flowers in her hair, giving her an *A Midsummer Night's Dream*, almost ethereal look. His chest tightened, his breath stalled, his guilt throbbed. He had failed her in so many ways. He had made promises to love and protect her but he had failed on both counts. Romantic love was something he had never committed to. He doubted it even existed except perhaps in rare cases.

It had certainly never existed for him.

But seeing Juliette walking towards him now, something shifted in his chest. A slippage. A softening. A tightly locked space slowly opening…

He snapped it shut. *Bang.* Bolted the door.

He was comforted by the all too familiar jolt of his

emotions shutting down. It was safer not to feel too deeply. To leave stray feelings unexplored. To deny them access through the firewall of his control tower.

Juliette met his gaze and a tremulous smile formed on her lips. The soft lips he had kissed early that morning and only just managed to stop kissing before he lost control. Kissing her made him realise how dangerous it was to be around her. It made him want her. Need her. Crave her. But how could he hope for a rerun of their relationship? What right did he have to insist on a second chance? It would only cause more pain, more heartache. It was practically his brand—projecting pain, heartache and loss onto the people he cared about. It was better he didn't care. It was better he didn't want. It was better not to hope.

Her gaze moved away and a sense of disappointment sank in his stomach like a stone.

Her smile was for the crowd, for appearances' sake.

It wasn't for him.

Juliette couldn't look at Joe without blushing over their kiss that morning. She couldn't look at him and not think about their own wedding. Their cold and duty-bound wedding where the promises he made had meant nothing.

But had hers meant something? Anything? Juliette gave an inward frown, wondering why her conscience was bringing this up now. She hadn't been the one to insist on marriage. She had done the right thing in telling him he was to be a father, to give him the option of being involved or not. She could have refused his offer... *Why hadn't she?*

Juliette stood to one side of Lucy and Damon as they exchanged their vows. Both had tears shining in their eyes, their love for each other plain to see. She glanced at Joe to find his gaze trained on her, his expression grave. She bit her lip and looked away again, her heart feeling as if squeezed by an invisible hand.

Maybe she had judged Joe too quickly. Hadn't her parents always complained about her impulsive nature? Her tendency to act first, ask questions later had often caused her to regret her actions in hindsight. She had not only not asked Joe the questions, she hadn't even allowed him to contact her. She had blocked him at every turn.

It was excruciatingly painful to confront her role in the breakup of their relationship. Would she be making a huge mistake in pursuing a divorce? But how could their marriage continue if Joe didn't love her?

The newly married couple kissed and the guests clapped and cheered and again Juliette was reminded of the brief kiss Joe had given her at their wedding, and the less than enthusiastic applause from the handful of guests, her parents in particular.

After Lucy and Damon's official photos were taken further along on the beach, the mostly informal and relaxed reception was held in the villa's ballroom overlooking the beach.

Juliette got up to dance with three of the other groomsmen to avoid dancing with Joe. She was worried she would betray herself in his arms, reveal things about herself she knew she shouldn't be feeling while she had divorce papers to hand to him. Dance after dance, drink after drink, she worked the room as if she had graduated as star pupil at Social Butterfly school. But inside she was shrivelling up, struggling to cope with pretending to be happy. One of the guests—another cousin of Damon's—was heavily pregnant and every time Juliette looked at her she felt a hammer-blow of sadness crash over her.

Juliette took yet another glass of champagne off a passing waiter and turned to find Joe standing beside her.

'Is that a good idea?' He nodded towards her glass, his expression brooding.

She arched her brows. 'Since when did you join the Temperance Society?'

He took the glass out of her hand and placed it on a nearby table. 'I think you've had enough.'

'I think you need to back off,' Juliette said, glowering at him. 'Just because you're not having a good time doesn't mean I can't.'

'*Are* you having a good time?' His gaze was as pointed as his tone. But then he released a heavy breath and added with a frown, 'You're pretending, just like I am. But doing a much better job of it than me.'

Some of Juliette's anger faded. She couldn't explain why—it just slumped inside her like a windless sail. 'It's a form of torture, isn't it? Watching other people being happy.'

'*Sì.*'

Juliette tried to read his expression but it was like trying to read a cryptic code. Or maybe it was because her head was starting to pound from all the champagne she'd consumed. Or maybe it was because she knew she was getting closer to the moment when she would hand Joe the divorce papers. She couldn't allow her defences to let her down now. She had come on a mission to get those papers signed. One kiss did not a reconciliation make. She pinched the bridge of her nose and winced. 'I think I need to go to bed. Do you think Lucy and Damon would be offended if I slipped away now before they leave?'

Joe glanced to where the happy couple were dancing cheek to cheek. 'No. I don't think they'll mind. Come on—' he held out his hand '—I'll walk you back to our room.'

Joe led Juliette back to their room. *Their room.* One last night suffering the torture of having her close enough to touch. Close enough to remember the potent magic that brought them together in the first place. Close enough to regret how he had handled every step, every stage of their relationship. Close enough to wonder if there was a chance—a slim chance—she would consider trying again.

The idea crept into his head and looked around for a place to get comfortable, pushing his conscience, his fears, his doubts out of the way. He wasn't imagining the chemistry still between them, was he? It was as strong and pulsing as ever. Their kiss had proven how strong their connection still was.

How could he forgive himself for not at least exploring the possibility of reconciling?

Joe closed the door of their room but he realised immediately his timing was way off. Not only was there a fold-out bed set up in the sitting room area but Juliette looked tense and on edge. Her teeth chewed at her lip, her eyes not quite meeting his.

'Are you okay?'

She nodded and sat on the sofa and held a scatter cushion against her body like a shield. 'I will be. I just need a glass of water.'

Joe fetched her one and brought it back to where she was sitting. She took the glass from him, guzzled down the water and then handed the glass back. 'Thanks.'

'Another one?'

'Not right now…' She tossed the cushion aside and reached for her phone in her purse and switched it off silent. 'I forgot I promised I'd send my mother a picture of Lucy and Damon.' She clicked the necessary keys and the sound of the message pinging through cyberspace filled the silence. She continued to look at her phone, her forehead wrinkling in a frown. 'Joe?'

'Mmm?'

She lifted her head to look at him with a puzzled expression. 'This email here that just popped into my inbox. Is it spam? It says you and I have been nominated for some sort of fundraising award. It says we're Fundraising Couple of the Year.' She held the screen up for him to inspect.

Joe leaned down to read the email, and then

straightened to take out his phone and clicked on his own emails. He was copied into the same email she had received. What sort of twisted irony was that? *Couple of the Year?* They were no longer a couple. He slipped his phone back in his pocket. 'No, it's not spam. Remember I told you I'd donated on your behalf? And raised funds through various other means. I sent you emails about it but you chose not to read them. There's a fundraising dinner in Paris next month. We've been invited to go and—'

Juliette sprang off the sofa as if one of the springs had poked her. 'Are you out of your mind? I'm not going to Paris with you. It's completely out of the question. Everyone will think we're still together.'

'So, what if they do?'

'We're not together, Joe.' A stubborn edge came into her voice, her grey-blue eyes steely. 'Just because we've shared a room this weekend doesn't mean anything.'

Joe took a deep breath. No way was he going to that fundraiser without her. It was the perfect opportunity to spend more time with her. This weekend wasn't enough. How could it ever be enough when he wanted her this badly? 'Juliette. This is not about us. It's about helping others who experience what we went through. If we don't show up as a united couple, then how will it look?'

Her expression tightened. 'It will look exactly as it is. We. Are. Separated.' The emphasis on each word was like three punches to his gut. She went over to her tote bag in the corner of the room and pulled out some papers and came back to thrust them at him. 'Here. I've been saving these for now.'

Joe's gaze narrowed as he saw what it was. Legal papers. *Divorce papers*. A pain spread like fire through his chest, searing through flesh, pulverising bone, taking away his breath.

So, his time in limbo was over.

Juliette had already made up her mind. She had come to their friends' wedding with divorce papers for him to sign. It was over. No sequel. No reruns.

The End.

A streak of stubbornness steeled his spine and his gaze. Their marriage would end on his say-so, not hers. No way was he signing divorce papers at his best mate's wedding weekend. He took the papers off her and tossed them onto the seat of the sofa as if they were nothing more than yesterday's newspaper. 'I'll sign those when I'm good and ready. Come to Paris with me and then I'll give you a divorce.'

Her chin came up and her eyes flashed. 'You're blackmailing me?'

He gave a grating laugh. 'Damn right I am. What were you thinking, bringing those to your best friend's wedding? I thought you had more class.'

She picked up the legal papers and carefully fed them back inside the envelope. Her movements were calm and controlled but he could see the effort it cost her. Her jaw was tight, her mouth pressed flat, her anger a palpable presence in the room. She put the envelope back in her tote bag and faced him with fire and ice in her gaze. 'We'll discuss this again in the morning. I have a headache and don't want to argue with you right now.'

Joe locked his gaze on hers, his own anger stiffening his spine. Anger so thick and throbbing he could feel it pulsing in his veins like a thousand pummelling fists. 'You'll hear the same thing from me in the morning. I will not sign those papers until I'm good and ready. End of.' He turned and walked out of the suite and closed the door behind him as firmly as a punctuation mark.

Juliette winced as the door shut behind him. She let out a ragged breath. *That went well.* She tugged at the pins holding her hair up and shook her head to loosen the strands. It didn't help her headache, nor did the thought of confronting Joe again with the divorce papers. Why was he being so stubborn and obstructive? Hadn't he said being together again was the last thing he wanted? Or was he interested in a little affair with her until after Paris? She couldn't allow herself to be used in such a way. She wouldn't allow herself to be exposed to more hurt when he failed to support her in the way she wanted. *Needed.* He was all for helping others in their situation, but what about helping her? Supporting her?

When Juliette woke the next morning, after a fitful sleep, she found a note propped up on the bedside table, written in Joe's distinctive handwriting.

See you in Paris,
Joe.

She glanced around the room. His luggage was gone. There was no trace of him in the suite. It was as if he had never been there with her.

Isn't that the truth?

She gritted her teeth and scrunched the note up in a ball and threw it at the nearest wall. 'I'll see you in hell first.'

CHAPTER SEVEN

One month later...

JULIETTE WEIGHED UP the options of informing Joe she would be calling on him at his villa in Positano or showing up unannounced, to hand deliver the divorce papers. She would get those papers signed if it was the last thing she did. She'd had zero contact from him since Lucy and Damon's wedding—not that she had contacted him either. Still seething with anger at the way he had issued her with an ultimatum, and the way he'd left without saying goodbye, it had taken her this past month to feel ready to face him again.

She was *not* going to be controlled by his outrageous demands.

In the end, Juliette decided to just show up at his villa, suspecting if she gave him the heads-up he might find a convenient excuse for not being there. She had heard via Damon that Joe was currently at his luxury villa high in the hills overlooking the Mediterranean ocean, so she was confident it wouldn't be a wasted journey. Besides, she still had a key and, unless he had changed the locks, she would stay there until he returned even if it took a week or two. Those papers needed to be processed and they could only be processed if he signed them.

That was her goal.

Her mission.

Get a divorce. Get on with her life.

But, due to travel delays and her taxi taking several costly—and she thought deliberate—wrong turns, Juliette didn't arrive until late in the evening. Which was deeply annoying, as she hadn't planned on staying longer than the five or ten minutes it would take to get the papers signed. She dismissed the taxi, figuring she would call another one as soon as she was done and then go to the hotel she'd booked online before flying back to London tomorrow.

She was reassured that some lights were on in the villa and pressed the doorbell. No answer. She pressed it again. And again. Still no answer. There was a security camera at the front entrance, so she knew if Joe was inside he could see it was her. Why wasn't he answering the door? And if he wasn't home and one of the household staff was there, why weren't they responding?

It was way too early for Joe to be in bed…although if he had someone with him… Juliette tried to ignore the sharp jab of pain that suddenly assailed her. He had to move on some time. He would definitely do so once their divorce was finalised.

Why was she getting upset about it? It was petty and immature of her. She was over him. She *had* to be.

There was no going back.

Juliette reached in her bag for her key and placed it in the lock, praying he hadn't changed the alarm code, otherwise the security system would screech loud enough to hear in Naples. She opened the door and, wheeling in her overnight bag, stepped inside and closed the door softly behind her.

'Hello?' Her voice echoed through the marble foyer and somewhere further inside the villa she heard something fall over and then Joe's deep voice letting out a filthy curse.

Juliette left her overnight bag at the front door and walked further into the villa. 'Joe?' She went to the smaller of the two sitting rooms, where she could see a pool of soft light shining from the door that was ajar. She pushed the door further open and saw Joe standing near the drink's cabinet with a shot glass of spirits in his hand. The room was in disarray. The sofa scatter cushions were askew, one of them on the floor some distance away as if it had been thrown there. The air was stale as if the windows hadn't been opened in days. Newspapers littered the floor and there was an empty pizza box with traces of topping—olives, capers, mushroom—stuck to the cardboard.

If Joe looked shocked to see her suddenly appear announced at his villa, he didn't show it on his face. He simply raised the glass to his lips, tipped back his head and drained the contents, before wiping the back of his hand across his lips.

'To what do I owe this honour?' His tone was bitter, his eyes bloodshot, his hair tousled, his lean jaw shadowed with at least two days' stubble. His shirt was creased and untucked from his trousers, giving him an unkempt look that was at odds with the man she knew. It was one of the things she secretly admired about him. He took care with his appearance. He wasn't a junk food eater. He didn't drink to excess. He was careful about over-indulging. Unlike her ex, whose idea of a gourmet meal was a deluxe burger at a fast food chain. And who had embarrassed her on more than one occasion by drinking too much and acting inappropriately.

Like *she* could talk after all the champagne she'd drunk at Lucy and Damon's wedding, but still...

Juliette frowned, shocked to find Joe in such a state. 'Are you...drunk?'

He gave a twisted smile that didn't reach his eyes. 'No, but it sounds like fun. Want to join me?' He placed his glass down on the drinks cabinet and reached for the bottle of spirits.

She dropped her tote bag on a nearby chair and came further into the room, stepping over the pizza box and a collection of newspapers. 'I'm not here to party, Joe.' She injected her tone with as much gravity as she could even though it made her sound like the fun police.

He poured a measure of spirits into the glass and she was relieved to see it was only a few millimetres, not centimetres. 'Want one?' He held the glass out to her with a daredevil light in his dark eyes.

'No, thank you.'

'I can open some champagne for you.' His smile had a hint of cruelty about it. 'We could get drunk together and see what happens.'

Juliette pressed her lips together as if she were channelling a starchy schoolmistress. 'That won't be necessary. I don't have anything to celebrate.'

The glint in his gaze hardened to flint. 'Not even my birthday?'

Juliette stared at him for a stunned moment. How could she not have realised? She had never actually celebrated his birthday with him as they hadn't been married long enough. She'd seen it on his passport, though—April the fifth.

But wait... That date rang another bell...

What twist of fate had her coming to visit him on the *exact* date they'd first met? 'I didn't realise until now—we met for the first time on this day. But I thought you said it was the anniversary of your mother's death?'

'*Sì.*' His expression was masked. Stony, cold, emotionless—all except for a shadow lurking at the back of his gaze.

She frowned as she tried to join the dots. 'Your mother died on your *birthday?*'

He put the shot glass down with an audible thud. '*Sì.*'

Her throat was so clogged it felt as if she'd swallowed one of the scatter cushions. 'How old were you?' Her voice quavered with emotion, imagining him as a young child dealing with the loss of his mother. Why hadn't he told her when they were together? Why had he kept such important information about himself a secret? And why hadn't she delved a little more deeply—tried to get to know him better? They hadn't been married long and they hadn't married for the usual reasons, but that didn't absolve her. She hadn't taken the time to understand him, to uncover the enigmatic layers of his personality.

'Thirty-three minutes.' His tone was flat but his eyes were haunted. Black, brooding, bleak.

Juliette's mouth fell open and her heart slipped from its moorings. 'Thirty...? Oh, Joe, you mean she died *having* you?'

He turned away to put the lid back on the bottle of spirits, a frown pulling at his forehead. 'It's why I try to ignore my birthday. There's nothing to celebrate in knowing your birth was responsible for someone's death.'

Juliette came over to him and touched him on the arm to get him to face her. 'I can understand how you, or anyone, would feel like that. But you mustn't blame yourself. It could have been a medical error or—' Even as she said the words, she realised how unfairly she had blamed him for their baby's stillbirth. Guilt was a heavy stone in her belly—crushing, punishing guilt.

He removed her hand from his arm. 'Look, I know you mean well but I'd rather not talk about it right now.' He rubbed a hand down his face, the rasping sound against his stubble loud in the silence. He let out a long breath and added, 'Why are you here? Have you changed your mind about Paris? It's next weekend. Don't forget—no divorce without it.'

The divorce papers could wait. Handing them to him on his birthday seemed a bit crass, considering the circumstances. Besides, her feelings of remorse were so overwhelming she didn't want to do anything she would regret later. She had enough regrets. As for Paris… Would it hurt her to go with him? Maybe it would help both of them find some measure of peace going forward.

'I'm not just here about the divorce. I wanted to come anyway…for another reason.'

Joe took a bottle of water out of the bar fridge and unscrewed the cap, his gaze watchful. 'Which is?'

'Erm…research for my next book.' It was a lie but she could make it true by doing a few sketches while she was here. That was if he hadn't thrown out her art materials. She had taken virtually nothing with her when she'd left. And he hadn't sent any of her things on to her. She couldn't possibly leave him tonight, not on his birthday. At first, she'd thought he was properly drunk, but she realised now he was in a brooding mood and tired. As if he hadn't slept in weeks. And he looked like he'd lost weight—his cheeks were hollow and fine lines ran down either side of his mouth.

He moved past her and sat on one of the sofas, his long legs stretched out in front of him and crossed at the ankles. He took a couple of mouthfuls of water, his gaze tracking back to her as if he couldn't help himself. 'How long do you plan to stay in Italy?'

Juliette sat on the opposite sofa and placed her hands on her thighs. 'I haven't decided. I thought

I'd see how I go… It's been a while since I've drawn anything—I might not be able to do it any more…'

Joe took another mouthful of water and then his gaze locked back on hers. 'Where are you staying?' There was a guarded note in his tone.

'I booked a small hotel down near Fornillo Beach.'

His jaw worked for a moment. 'Are you with anyone?'

'No.'

Silence ticked past.

Juliette tucked a strand of hair back behind her ear for something to do with her hands. She felt restless and on edge, uncertain of how to behave around him. Way too tempted to behave in ways that would make a mockery of the legal document in her overnight bag, still on the floor in the foyer. She wished she had the courage to walk behind the sofa where he was seated and massage his tense neck and shoulders like she used to do.

Joe leaned his head back against the sofa cushions and closed his eyes. 'I'll let you see yourself out.'

She was being dismissed.

A wall had come up and she was on the wrong side of it. But something kept her seated on the sofa, something kept her gaze focused on the lines and planes of his face, something breathed life into a dead place deep inside her heart. Juliette felt the stirring in her chest, the slow unfurling of closed wings, the gentle flap of hope coming to life. Hope that their relationship might not be in its last throes but had the potential to rise again.

But better this time.

She hadn't taken the time to get to know him in the past. Her shock pregnancy had propelled them too fast into marriage without the appropriate getting-to-know-you lead-up. And the devastation of losing their baby had blinded her to the things that had worked well in their relationship. Could they possibly build on those things?

'Joe?'

He cracked open one eye. 'What?' His one word, somewhat sharp reply wasn't encouraging but Juliette was starting to realise he was probably feeling uncomfortable with her seeing him in less than ideal circumstances. He felt vulnerable and unguarded and for such a control captain that was anathema.

Juliette glanced in the direction of the kitchen. 'Do you mind if I make myself a cup of tea?'

'Go for it.'

'Do you want one?'

One side of his mouth tilted in a bad boy smile. 'I'm not ready to be a teetotaller.'

'I know you're not drunk. You're only pretending to be.'

He leaned forward to rest his elbows on his thighs and lowered his head into his hands. 'I didn't ask you to come here. I'd rather not have an audience right now.' The *keep away* quality in his tone didn't daunt her. Not now she knew how vulnerable and exposed he felt.

Juliette came over and perched on the arm of the sofa next to him. She raised her hand and began stroking her fingers through the thick strands of his black wavy hair. He gave a low deep groan but didn't push her hand away. Every now and again her fingers would catch on a knot in his hair and she gently untangled it.

After a while, he raised his head from his hands and looked at her with his pitch-black eyes and something slipped sideways in her stomach. 'You should have left five minutes ago.' His voice was so rough it made the hairs on the back of her neck tingle.

Juliette idly ran her finger down the slope of his nose. 'Why should I?'

He grasped her wrist with the steel bracelet of his fingers and her heart gave an excited leap. His fingers were warm, the tensile strength an erotic reminder of other parts of his body that were hot and strong and potent. 'Because I might not let you go.'

Was it the whisky talking? Or was he expressing feelings he had hidden from her in the past?

Juliette used her free hand to stroke his richly stubbled jaw. 'Joe…why didn't you tell me about your mother when we got married? You barely told me anything about yourself. And when I fished for information, you would shut me down or distract me with something else. Or disappear for days on end with work commitments.'

His gaze shifted from hers to stare at her wrist in his grasp on his lap. His other hand came over the top of her captured hand and his index finger traced each of the tendons on the back of her hand. 'There wasn't much to tell. My birth caused my mother's death and my father did his best to raise me but her death was a dark cloud over our relationship.'

'Do you mean he blamed you?'

He gave a lopsided twist of his mouth that wasn't anywhere near a smile. 'Not in so many words. But every year on my birthday since I was old enough to remember, he would take me to the cemetery and make me tidy her grave and put flowers there. I hated going. I found it creepy, to be honest. I put my foot down when I was fifteen and said I wasn't going again. And I haven't. Not once.'

Juliette's heart contracted. She could picture him as a small toddler, not quite understanding why he had to perform such a morbid duty. And then in the years while he was growing up, still being forced to confront the reality of his mother's death and his innocent part in it. So many pennies were dropping in her head she was surprised Joe couldn't hear the loud tinkling. Was that why he had been so distant and aloof at their baby's funeral? He had been almost robotic, hardly saying anything to anyone, not showing any emotion and not comforting Juliette in the way she had needed. Was that why he had never visited their baby's grave? And during Juliette's pregnancy, the further along it went, he had retreated into himself, closed off, distanced himself. Had he been terrified all along that the same thing could happen to her that happened to his mother?

'Oh, Joe…' Tears stung her eyes and she turned her hand over in his and gripped him tightly. 'I wish

I'd known. How terrible that must have been for you as a small child.'

Joe released her hand and rose from the sofa, moving to the other side of the room with his back towards her. 'Why are you really here, Juliette?' His tone had a cold razor-sharp edge. Accusing, cutting, callous.

Juliette swept her tongue over her carpet-dry lips. 'I told you—I'm doing some research for—'

He swung around to face her with a brooding expression. 'You're a terrible liar.' He moved across the room and rummaged amongst some things on the small table near a pile of books. He picked up a pen. 'Got the divorce papers with you?' He clicked the pen open and smiled a savage smile. 'Where do I sign?'

Juliette rose from the sofa and hugged her arms around her middle. 'It's a really dumb idea to sign legal documents when you've been drinking even a small amount of alcohol. I think we should talk about this some other time.'

He clicked the pen on and off several times and she got the feeling it was his way of counting to ten to control his simmering anger. After a moment, he tossed the pen aside and walked past her out of the room, throwing over his shoulder, 'I'll let you see yourself out. I'm sure you haven't forgotten the way.'

Juliette closed her eyes against the sting of his parting words. But there was one thing she was certain of—no way was she leaving tonight. Not until they had chance to talk about things they should have talked about months ago.

* * *

Joe had enough trouble resisting Juliette when he was stone cold sober and even though he had only had a couple of shot glasses of whisky he knew it was wise to keep his distance. He was disgusted with himself for indulging in a pity party on his birthday. He mostly tried to ignore the date but this year had brought it all back. The anniversary of the day he'd met Juliette. The amazing night of hot sex he hadn't been able to forget. The amazing night that for once had made him forget what day it was. The amazing night that had cumulated in a pregnancy. A doomed pregnancy, because that was the sort of stuff that happened to him, right? He had a poisonous touch and it was no good thinking it was going to change any time soon. If ever.

He knew why Juliette was here. Those wretched divorce papers. He couldn't put off signing them for ever. English law stated a couple married in England could be granted a no-fault divorce after two years of separation. They had now been separated for sixteen months.

In another eight months they would both be free. *No-fault?* Of course there was someone to blame. Him.

CHAPTER EIGHT

JULIETTE WAITED DOWNSTAIRS until she was sure Joe had taken himself to bed. She went back out to the foyer and carried her overnight bag rather than wheel it, so as not to disturb him. There were several spare bedrooms on the second floor to choose from. The master bedroom door was closed and in darkness, so she assumed Joe had settled down for the night. She toyed with the idea of checking on him but decided it was best to leave him to sleep off his devil-may-care mood. She didn't trust herself around him, especially when he was in such a reckless state of mind. Besides, re-entering the room they had shared during their short marriage would test her in ways she wasn't sure she could handle. Too many images came to mind of her being in that bed with him, her legs entangled with his, her body responding to his surging thrusts with wanton abandon.

She suppressed a delicate shudder and continued on her way to one of the rooms further along the wide carpeted corridor until she came to the closed door of the nursery. She stopped outside, unable to take another step. It was as if a thick glass wall had sprung up in front of her and she could go no further until she glimpsed her baby's room—to see if it was as she had left it.

She had decorated the nursery herself, spending hours in there painting a frieze for the walls, making a mobile for the cot, placing soft toys on the floating shelves she had designed and got made specially. She'd chosen the pink fabric for the curtains with fairies and unicorns on it and made them herself. Every stitch, every brushstroke, every item had been placed there with love. Love for her baby.

They had found out at the twenty weeks scan they were having a little girl. At first, Juliette had wanted to leave it as a surprise but Joe had wanted to know. She understood so much more about him in hindsight—his uneasiness at that and the other appointments she'd managed to drag him to. She'd put his lack of enthusiasm down to the fact the pregnancy wasn't planned, that they weren't in love with each other, that they were only together because of the baby. But now she could see how difficult those appointments must have been for him. How he would be thinking of his mother and how his mother's pregnancy with him had ended in his birth and her death. If only she had known, if only he had told her, maybe their relationship wouldn't have floundered so badly after losing their baby.

Juliette still couldn't say her name out loud. Emilia. Once she'd been out in London and a young mother had called out to a small child with the same name. Juliette had to leave the store—she didn't even stay long enough to buy the things she had come for. She couldn't hear that precious name without going to bits.

How would it feel to walk into her nursery?

Or had Joe redecorated the room since she'd left? Had he stripped his villa of any record of her and the baby? The need to know was unbearable, even though she knew by opening the door she would be tearing open an already raw and seeping wound.

She took a deep breath and turned the handle and pushed the door open, reaching for the light switch on the wall. It was like a time capsule. Nothing had changed. The toys with their soft little bodies and sightless eyes were keeping watch over the empty cot. The hand-embroidered quilt was smoothly tucked in, the sheets neatly folded. The cross-stitched sampler she had made was framed above. *Emilia.*

Juliette's throat closed, her heart gave a spasm, her eyes filled. Joe hadn't changed a thing. Everything was the same. Everything. She walked further into the room and touched the mobile over the cot, sending it on a gentle rotation. She didn't have the courage to turn on the nursery rhyme music. There was only so much heartache she could stand.

She brushed at her eyes with the back of her hand, stepping away from the cot to pick up one of the soft toys off the shelf. It was a floppy-eared white rabbit with a pink satin bow. She held it to her face, breathing in the still newish smell, wondering if there would ever be a time when she would be able to think of her baby and not have this aching weight pressing down on her chest.

Juliette put the rabbit back on the shelf and went to the chest of drawers next to the change table. She pulled the first one open and looked at the tiny vests and booties and onesies lying there. She picked up a pair of booties—booties she had knitted herself. She swallowed and put them back and closed the drawer, her eyes burning, chest aching, emotions smashing through her like brutal, punishing waves.

She walked back to the door and turned for one last look at the room. Could there be anything more heartbreaking than an empty nursery, never used?

And then, with a sigh, she switched off the light and softly closed the nursery door behind her.

Juliette went further along the wide corridor to the spare room furthest away from the master bedroom. She opened the door and switched on the light but stopped short when she saw Joe lying face down on the bed. Naked. *Gulp.* He was soundly asleep, his strongly muscled legs splayed across the mattress, his arms resting either side of his head.

She ran her hungry gaze over his toned back and shoulders, feasted on the taut shape of his buttocks, his hair-roughened legs. She came closer, reaching for the throw rug on the foot of the bed, gently easing it out from under his feet and laying it over him to keep him from being cold, even though it wasn't a particularly cool night.

Why was he sleeping in one of the spare rooms? Why not in the master bedroom?

Juliette began to step backwards away from the bed to leave the room when he opened his eyes. He turned over onto his back, the throw rug slipping to barely cover his pelvis. Dark masculine hair arrowed down from his muscle-ridged abdomen, disappearing under the throw rug, but her memory filled in the rest of the picture for her. Hot colour rushed to her cheeks and her pulse flew off the starting blocks and raced and raced and raced.

'I—I'm sorry...' She backed further away from the bed. 'I didn't know you were sleeping in here.'

He sat up and pushed his hand through his sleep-tousled hair. 'I sleep better in this room.' He yawned and threw off the throw rug, stood and stretched, and her female hormones jumped for joy.

Juliette turned her back so quickly she became lightheaded. Or maybe that was because the sight of him naked was enough to make her faint. With desire. 'Could you please cover yourself?' She sounded like a prim spinster from another century but she couldn't look at him without wanting him.

Joe came over to her and placed his hands on the tops of her shoulders. Juliette sucked in a ragged breath, her senses reeling at his closeness. She could feel his body heat—*his naked body heat*—behind her, tempting her to lean back to feel the deliciously hard ridge she was almost certain would be there.

He leaned down to place a kiss just below her left ear and she tilted her head sideways to allow him access, her will to resist evaporating. 'Haven't you heard that saying—*let sleeping dogs lie*?' The soft movement of his lips against her skin, the waft of his warm breath, the deep rough burr of his voice was enough to make her legs fold beneath her like severed marionette strings.

'I told you—I didn't know you were in here. I was looking for somewhere to sleep and—'

He turned her to face him, his eyes sexily hooded and focused on her mouth. His thumb came up and brushed her lower lip, and something deep and low in her belly rolled over. 'Sleep with me.'

It was a command rather than a request and for some reason she was fine with that. More than fine. She didn't want to overthink why she was standing in the circle of his arms with her body burning with lust. But somehow, being back in this house with all the memories it contained shifted something in her—especially now she understood more about him. Things about his personality that made her see him in a totally different light. A light that drew her closer and closer like a storm-tossed dinghy towards the strong, steady glow of a lighthouse. Right now, all she wanted was to be in his arms, to feel the potent power of his body within hers, to feel nothing but passion, lust, longing and have those primal needs satisfied. By him.

Juliette placed her hands around his neck, pressing closer to the hard heat of his body, her body responding with humid heat of its own. She could feel the slick preparation of her inner core, the dew of arousal signalling her readiness, her eagerness, her wantonness. 'Are you telling me or asking me?' Her voice was just shy of a whisper but still managed to contain a spirited note.

He gave a crooked smile and drew her flush against him. 'Right now, I'd get on my hands and knees and beg if that's what you wanted me to do.'

She stepped up on tiptoe and brought her mouth to just a breath away from his. 'This is what I want you to do.' And then she closed the distance between their lips.

He made a desperate sound at the back of his throat and his arms tightened around her. His lips moved against hers in a series of hot presses, massages, nudges, teases. She opened to the commanding thrust of his tongue, the blatantly erotic movement sending lightning strikes of electricity straight to her core. Flickers and flames of want leapt through her body and she wondered how she had managed to survive so long without this conflagration of the senses. Her body was alive and wanting, aching with the need to have him deep within her.

Joe lifted his mouth off hers and started working on her clothes. 'Let's get rid of these. I want to look at you. All of you.'

Juliette tried to help him but her hands weren't cooperating. Besides, they were already occupied exploring his muscled chest and toned abdomen on her journey down to his erection. She took him in her hand and stroked him the way she knew made him wild for her.

Joe groaned and pulled her hand away. 'Let's get you naked first.' He continued to remove her clothes and each time a slip of fabric fell away from her body she shivered as his glittering gaze ran over her. 'You're so beautiful. So hot. I'm going crazy here.' His fingers struggled with the fastening on her top. 'Damn it. Why do you wear such complicated clothes?'

Juliette laughed and helped him with the fastening, leaving her in nothing but her bra and knickers. His hands cupped her breasts and even through the delicate barrier of lace her flesh leapt at his touch. Her nipples tight, her breasts tingling and sensitive, her inner core aching with need.

Joe placed his hands on her hips, his expression now gravely serious. 'Are you sure about this, *cara*? We can't undo this once it's done.'

Juliette brushed her lips against his. 'Totally sure. I want you. Don't make me wait any longer.'

He brought his mouth down on hers in a firm kiss that spoke of his own escalating need. Their tongues met and tangled, heat flaring between their bodies like an out of control fire. Joe deftly unclipped her bra and it fell to the floor at her feet. His mouth lifted off hers as he slid her knickers down her thighs. She stepped out of them, kicking them aside with one foot, and then moving close to his body again.

He cradled one of her breasts in his hand, his thumb stroking her budded nipple, sending shivers shooting to the core of her being. He brought his mouth down to her breast, his tongue circling her nipple, his teeth gently grazing the sensitive nub and his lips caressing the dark circle of her areola. Tingles coursed through her body, hot tingles and fizzes that sent her senses into a frenzy. Need throbbed and ached between her legs in a pounding rhythm in time with her racing blood.

'You have no idea how long I've ached to do this...' His voice had a ragged quality as one of his hands cupped her mound.

Juliette gasped with delight when he inserted one thick finger into her wet heat. 'Oh, God, I've missed this. I've missed you.' She shuddered from head to foot as his finger caressed her, his expert strokes sending hot streaks of longing down through her pelvis.

He brought his mouth back to hers in a long drugging kiss that made her forget about everything but the sensations coursing through her body. He tasted of salt and a hint of whisky and danger but she was addicted to all of it. Addicted to all of him. The flickering caress of his fingers sent her catapulting into a dizzying flight, spinning her into an abyss where she was conscious of nothing but the exquisite sensations rippling through her.

Juliette gripped his shoulders with her hands. 'Don't let me go. I might not be able to stand upright.'

'I'm not letting you go. I haven't finished with you yet.' His rough tone and strong hands made her insides quiver like an unset jelly.

He walked her to the bed, laying her down and coming down beside her, his dark eyes unashamedly feasting on her body. He trailed a lazy finger from the upper curves of each breast, down her sternum to the tiny shallow cave of her belly button. He spread her thighs and brought his mouth down to the secret heart of her body. She sucked in a breath, heady anticipation for his touch sending another hot shiver down her spine. His tongue tasted her, teased her, tantalised her into another earth-shattering orgasm. It went on and on, sending shudders throughout her flesh until she was breathless and gasping.

Joe placed his hand on her abdomen, his gaze doing a slow appraisal of her body. 'I want you.'

Take me. Take me. Take me.

Juliette panted it under her breath, her heart still hammering in the aftermath of ecstasy. But her body still craved him, it craved his presence deep inside and she reached for him, cupping him in her hand. 'What are you waiting for?' she said.

He eased her hand off his erection. 'I need to get a condom. Don't go anywhere.'

'I won't.' Juliette lay back and watched him hunt for a condom but it was taking too long. Her need for him was throbbing like a tribal drum between her legs—deep, pulsing, insistent.

He opened his wallet and swore, tossing it back down again.

Juliette propped herself up on her elbows. 'What? Don't you have one? What about in the bathroom?'

Joe came back over and leaned down to press a hot hard kiss on her mouth. 'I'll be right back.'

Joe hoped he still had condoms that weren't past their use-by date. Using protection was an issue, irrespective of whether they were officially back together or not. The thought of exposing Juliette to another pregnancy, another terrible loss was out of the question. But what was this…this interlude for Juliette? What was it for him? Just a quick scratch-the-itch-and-regret-it-in-the-morning?

Either way, it was a risk he was prepared to take. He wanted her. He wanted her with an ache so hot and hard and tight it was making him crazy. Making him think beyond tonight. Making him hope they might salvage something from the train wreck of their relationship.

Joe rummaged in the bathroom cupboard off the spare bedroom and found a couple of condoms in his toiletries bag he used when travelling. They had been there for months without him even noticing. But why would he have noticed them? He hadn't been interested in sleeping with anyone since Juliette had left. Not just because he considered he was technically still married, but because he couldn't stomach touching another woman. Being with any woman other than Juliette was repugnant to him. In the past, he'd had his share of casual flings—more than his share. His wealth and status made it easy to pick up casual dates. He had not even thought about it before he'd met Juliette. It was like following a script: drink and/or dinner, dive into bed with an equally enthusiastic and willing partner.

It had worked until it hadn't worked.

He'd met Juliette, they had a one-night stand and whoomph. He hadn't been the same since. He hadn't slept with anyone else since the night he'd met her. Not even when he had no contact with her for three months until she tracked him down to tell him she was carrying his baby. He'd blamed it on his work schedule—he was too busy, travelled too much, was too tired for the chase. All those things might well have been true but he knew deep down it was because sleeping with Juliette had shifted something inside him and he couldn't shift it back. But he would have to find a way, because there were no guarantees she would stay if he offered her a reconciliation.

He had to remember: she'd come here to get the divorce papers signed. Her willingness to sleep with him was probably nothing more than a parting gift. A farewell... Insert coarse swear word. That was all it could be, right? Why was he thinking it could be anything else?

Joe went back to the bedroom to find Juliette lying on her stomach with her chin propped up on her hands. He drank in the smooth curves of her spine and bottom, his lower body twitching with impatience to glide between her legs and thrust home.

'Did you find any?'

He held them up in his fingers. 'Only two, so if you have any ideas of a marathon you'd better hold that thought.'

Something passed over her features and her eyes momentarily slipped out of reach of his. 'What are your plans for the rest of the weekend?' Her tone was casual. Too casual.

Joe came and sat beside her on the bed, placed his

hand on her hip and turned her so she was lying on her back. He leaned closer, placing his hands either side of her head, caging her in, his gaze feasting on the sweet globes of her breasts. His groin pounding with feverishly hot blood. 'Shouldn't I be asking *you* that question?'

Her eyes flicked to his mouth. 'I don't know what this is…' She touched her hand to his jaw, grazing her fingers along his stubble. 'I mean…what we're doing…'

'Seems pretty obvious to me, *cara*.' Joe leaned on one elbow and traced his finger around one of her nipples in a lazy circle. 'We're getting it on.'

She pulled her lower lip partway into her mouth, releasing it again, her eyes still troubled. 'Break-up sex? Or…something else?'

It was the million-dollar question Joe didn't have an answer for. He kept his expression casually indifferent when inside he was mentally holding his breath. 'What else could it be? You came here wanting a divorce.'

A small frown pulled at her forehead and her finger brushed over his lower lip. 'I came here determined to get you to sign those papers. It was my goal. My mission…but now…' She gave a tiny sigh and her hand moved to the back of his neck, bringing his head closer. 'I want you to make love to me. I know it's probably wrong or inconsistent of me when I've been waving divorce papers in your face, but it's what I want for now. Just while I'm in Italy.'

A break-up fling with his soon-to-be ex-wife.

But Joe wanted her any way he could have her. 'I want you to stay until after the Paris fundraiser.' He knew he was taking a risk using such a commanding tone but did it anyway.

Her eyes flicked to his mouth and her tongue darted out to lick her lower lip, tightening the ache in his groin another unbearable notch. 'Okay. I'll go with you to Paris.'

'Good. But as long as we're both clear on what this actually is.'

Was *he* clear? The only clarity he had was that this felt right. Having her here in his arms. The trouble was…how was he going to let her go when it was time for her to leave? Or could he dare to hope she would stay? But that would mean resuming their marriage and look at what a rubbish job he'd done of it the first time around.

'I want you, Joe.' Her voice was as soft as her touch.

'I want you so badly.' Joe covered her mouth and lost himself in the hot, sweet temptation of her lips. His tongue met hers and a lightning bolt of lust shot through his groin. He gathered her in his arms, their legs tangling in a way that was achingly familiar and yet no less thrilling. It was like discovering her body for the first time—the dips and slopes and contours, the honeyed secret of her centre, the taste of her mouth and the feel of her breath mingling intimately with his.

He left her mouth to kiss his way down the scented hollows of her neck, over the delicate scaffold of her collarbone, all the way to her breasts. He took each nipple in his mouth, rolling his tongue over the tightly budded flesh, his blood thrumming with excitement. Her soft breathless groans, the arching of her spine, the folding out of her knees to welcome him made his heartrate spike. No one could turn him on like her. No one got him so worked up and ready to explode. No one.

He slipped on a condom and, putting a hand under her left hip to tilt her towards him, entered her with a deep thrust that made the hairs on his scalp stand up and a shudder ripple through him. She welcomed him with a gasp and began moving with him, her smooth slim legs in a sexy tangle with his. It was too hard for him to slow down as he'd planned. Too hard to resist the magnetic pull of her silken body. He thrust and thrust, his blood racing like rocket fuel through his veins, his skin tingling from head to foot. He placed his hand between their rocking bodies to caress her.

She threw her head back, writhing and whimpering as her orgasm took her away and carried him with her. The tight rolling spasms of her body sent him flying into the stratosphere. He buried his face into the side of her neck and groaned and shuddered and shook as his release powered through him in pulses and waves and ripples, taking him to a place beyond thought. Beyond the ugly divorce word, beyond the lonely emptiness of a future without her in it.

Beyond anything but mindless, magical bliss.

CHAPTER NINE

JULIETTE WOKE TO find herself spooned in Joe's arms. One of his legs was flung over hers, his head buried against the back of her neck, where she could feel his deep and even breaths stirring her hair. One of his hands was resting on her ribcage and he murmured something unintelligible and glided it up to cup her breast. She shivered with longing, her inner core contracting with the muscle memory of their passionate lovemaking during the night.

He groaned and sighed like a satisfied lion and propped himself up, turning her so she was on her back, his dark gaze smouldering. He brushed her hair back from her forehead with a touch so gentle it made something in her chest spring open. 'So here we are. The morning after the night before.' His tone was playful but she sensed an undercurrent of gravity.

She pushed back his hair from his forehead with her splayed fingers. 'You probably need to find a better way of getting through your birthday without drinking on your own or having one-night stands with strangers.'

He circled her mouth with a lazy finger, his gaze suddenly inscrutable. 'Is that what last night was? A one-night stand with a stranger?'

Juliette lowered her hand to his jaw, stroking his lean cheek with a feather-light touch. 'You don't feel like a stranger to me now. Not after we talked about... stuff.'

A frown flickered on his forehead and his gaze became wary. 'Is that why you slept with me? Out of pity?'

She pulled her hand from his face and jerked her chin back in shock. 'How could you think that? I wanted to make love with you. I practically begged you to.'

He placed a firm hand on the flank of her thigh to keep her moving further away, the heat of his touch sending a fizzing current to her core. 'There's probably a lot of stuff I should have told you before. But I try to forget about how I came into the world. I don't like thinking about it, much less talking about it.'

Juliette slid her hand back to rest against his cheek, her thumb stroking back and forth over his prickly skin. 'It must be awful to not look forward to your birthday. It must have been so painful growing up without a mother, especially feeling so guilty about how you lost her. But it wasn't your fault. Your father should've made that absolutely clear.'

His gaze flickered with shadows, as if he was leafing through his childhood memories like fanning through the pages of a thick book. 'He was grieving for a long time. I didn't understand that until I was much older. He was like a zombie walking through life. He was only a young man. My mother was the love of his life—they met in primary school. They married at twenty-one.' His mouth twisted and his eyes briefly squeezed shut as if he was experiencing the most excruciating pain. 'And she was dead at twenty-two. She didn't get to live the life she'd planned. She didn't get to reach her potential, to do the things most people dream of doing.' He swallowed and continued in a strained tone, 'I hated going to visit her grave. I felt sick to my stomach, because I knew I was the one who put her there. Who robbed her of everything: the man she loved, the future she'd dreamed of, the family life she longed for. I took it all away from her.'

Juliette blinked back tears. 'Oh, Joe, I wish I'd known all that before. I feel so annoyed at myself for not pressing you to tell me more about yourself. Is that why you found my pregnancy so unsettling? I sensed you were staying away longer and longer, the further along the pregnancy went.'

He took one of her hands and brought it up to his chest, holding it against the steady thump of his heart. 'I wanted to support you—that's why I married you, to provide for you and the baby. But when I saw your belly growing bigger each week, a vague panic set in and I could only quell it by distracting myself with work. I don't think I was entirely conscious of it at the time—why I was feeling like that. I just felt compelled to work as hard as I could. But I see how you would've read that as something else.'

Juliette swallowed a knot of emotion in her throat. 'When you got to the delivery suite… I thought you looked relieved… I hated you at that moment. I couldn't believe you were being so brutally insensitive.'

A flash of pain went through his eyes and his fingers on her hand tightened. 'I was relieved. Relieved you hadn't died.' His voice sounded rough around the edges, raw and uneven. 'I didn't think about the baby at that point. All I could think on my way into that room was, *Has it happened again? Have I killed my mother and now my wife?*'

Juliette bit down on her lower lip until she was sure it would draw blood. She couldn't believe how blind she had been. How blinkered she'd been to think he hadn't cared about her and their child. She pulled her hand out of his so she could hug him around the neck. She rested her cheek on his chest, her throat so tight it was aching. 'I've made so many mistakes. I'm sorry for misjudging you.'

Joe rested his chin on the top of her head and stroked her hair with his hand. 'We've both made mistakes.' His voice was a low, deep rumble against her ear. 'I guess the thing to do now is not make any more.'

Was *this* a mistake? Lying in his arms, wanting him with a need so strong it throbbed deep in her core. A need that made a mockery of the divorce papers she had brought with her. Joe hadn't said anything about loving her. And nor had she to him. She still wasn't sure how to describe her feelings for him.

They had been under layers of bitterness and anger and grief and were only now rising to the surface. One thing she did know for sure—they didn't feel anything like the 'love' she'd thought she'd felt for her ex. They felt strong and lasting, healing and hopeful.

How long Juliette wanted to stay with Joe was not so easy for her to acknowledge—even to herself. She'd only booked her hotel for one night, as she'd planned to fly back to England once the divorce papers were signed. But spending the night with Joe and finding out so much more about his background made her reluctant to rush off home without spending a bit more time with him. To answer some important questions that were niggling at her conscience.

She felt foolish and immature for being so intransigent in Corfu about going to Paris with him, but was it too soon to jump back into their relationship? Was it too soon to hope he would grow to love her as she was growing to love him? Or maybe she had always loved him. From the moment they'd met she had felt something shift inside her. The connection they'd formed had rocked her to the core and not just because of the pregnancy and its tragic outcome. Her misplaced anger towards him had covered up her true feelings. Feelings that had sprouted at that first meeting but had been poisoned and almost destroyed by the tragedy of losing their little baby.

'I know you're busy with work but I can hang out here and sketch and relax by the pool until we go to Paris. I'll try not to get in your way.'

One side of his mouth lifted, his gaze gleaming

with unmistakable desire. 'You can get in my way all you like.' He traced her mouth with a lazy finger. 'The more the better.'

Juliette shivered at his tingling touch. 'You don't mind me being here?'

'Not at all.' And his mouth came down and confirmed it.

Juliette woke later that morning to find the bed empty beside her. She glanced at the clock beside the bed and was a little surprised she had slept in for so long. How could it be nine in the morning? She couldn't remember the last time she had slept so soundly. Her nights were usually disturbed by restlessness and sleeplessness, rumination and regret.

She threw off the bedcovers and slipped on a bathrobe. *Joe's bathrobe.* She breathed in the scent of him, her senses whirling, her belly fluttering, her heart swelling as she recalled his exquisite lovemaking during the night.

How could she regret last night? It was impossible. She felt close to Joe in a way she had never expected to feel. Knowing more about his heartbreaking background had softened her anger towards him and directed it more at herself. Her own grief had blinded her to the reality of his. Didn't the untouched nursery demonstrate that? He hadn't changed a thing in that beautiful room. Last night, he had shown her with his lips and hands and body how much he'd missed her.

Juliette walked out of the bedroom to head downstairs, where she could hear Joe moving about in the kitchen. But as she was passing the door to the master bedroom she had previously shared with him, she stopped and reached for the door knob. Why did he no longer sleep there? What had motivated him to occupy one of the spare bedrooms instead? She opened the door and, leaving the door open behind her, walked further into the room.

Memories floated towards her, stirring her emotions into a way she hadn't expected. She walked past the king-sized bed where she had spent so many nights wrapped in his arms, when he'd come home from his work trips. She opened the door of the walk-in wardrobe and found her clothes still hanging there as if she had never left. She could even pick up a faint trace of her signature perfume. She came out of the wardrobe and entered the en suite bathroom. Some of the cosmetics and toiletries she hadn't bothered to take with her were on the marble counter and in the cupboards under the twin basins.

Surely he could have got one of his housekeepers to remove her belongings? Why hadn't he? Or had Joe been *expecting* her to return?

Juliette frowned and came out of the bathroom to find Joe standing in the open doorway of the bedroom, carrying a tray with tea and toast and preserves. His expression was hard to read. On the surface he looked relaxed and open but she could sense an inner tension.

'I was just bringing you breakfast in bed.'

'Why didn't you get rid of my things?'

He came further into the room and placed the tray

on the bedside table. He straightened to face her. 'I figured if you wanted them you would've taken them with you when you left or asked me to send them to you.'

Juliette searched his unreadable gaze. 'Were you always expecting me to come back?'

Something flickered at the back of his eyes and his mouth took on a rueful twist. 'No. I had given up on that score.' His tone contained a flat note of bleakness.

She sat on the edge of the bed and looked up at him. 'Joe...why don't you use this room any more?'

He ran a hand around his shirt collar as if the fabric was prickling him. 'I told you last night—I sleep better in the other room.'

'But why?'

Joe released a harsh-sounding breath. 'For God's sake, do I need to spell it out?'

Juliette kept her gaze trained on his. 'Yes, I'm afraid you do.'

He drew in another breath but this time released it less forcefully. He sat down beside her and took one of her hands in his. His fingers wrapping around hers in a protective cloak. 'Every time I came in here was another reminder of how I'd let you down. I couldn't be in here without thinking about you. It was easier not to come in here at all.'

Juliette lifted her hand to his cleanly shaven jaw. 'Is that why you left the nursery as I left it?'

A flash of pain went through his gaze. 'I can't even bear to say her name, much less go in there and be reminded of her.' His voice was raw with suppressed emotion, his jaw tightening against the cup of her palm.

Tears sprouted in her eyes. 'Oh, Joe, I can't say her name either. Some days, I can't even think it without falling to bits.'

Joe brought his hand to her face, blotting her tears with the pad of his thumb. His eyes were dry but pained. 'My whole career has been based on fixing things that are broken. Finding why things that shouldn't have failed, failed. But I couldn't fix any of this for us.'

Juliette put her arms around him and laid her head on his chest. 'I'm glad we're able to be so honest with each other now. It helps me to know I'm not the only one who feels so undone by what's happened.'

His hand stroked the back of her head in gently soothing strokes that made the last of the armour around her heart melt away. 'I wish I'd been there to support you better. There's so much I would like to have done differently.' His deep voice rumbled against her cheek—full of low, deep chords of regret and self-recrimination.

'It might have been different if we had known each other better at the time,' Juliette said, glancing up at him. 'I mean, if we'd had a normal period of dating before we married. I feel like I'm only getting to know you now.' When it was too late. Or was it?

He glanced at the tea tray with a wry expression. 'I'm trying to decide whether to feed you breakfast or give you a kiss first.'

Juliette linked her arms around his neck and smiled. 'Just one kiss?'

His eyes smouldered and he gathered her closer. 'Why stop at one?'

And he didn't.

A couple of days before the Paris trip, Joe came in to the morning room where Juliette was sketching. He had been on a lengthy Skype call in his study. 'Sorry that took so long,' he said, leaning down to press a kiss to the top of her head. 'Hey, it's great to see you sketching again.' He picked up one of her earlier sketches—one of him sleeping—and frowned. 'I look so relaxed.' He put the sketch back down.

Juliette swivelled on her chair to look up at him. Something in his expression sent off a distracted vibe. A subtle distance in his gaze. A slight disturbance in his tone.

'Is everything okay? Has something come up with work?'

'I've been thinking about this Paris thing.'

Juliette straightened in her seat, unsure what to make of his expression. 'You still want me to go... don't you?'

'I shouldn't have pressured you into going. I can go alone if you don't feel up to being social.'

Juliette rose from her chair and wrapped her arms around her middle, uncertain of what to make of his seeming reluctance to have her accompany him. Was he wary of being out in public with her in case people read more into their relationship than was true? After all, they weren't officially reconciled. They were having a break-up fling. Did he want to keep their involvement with each other out of the press? Or was there some other reason?

She turned her back to him and stared at the view of the ocean below the steep slopes, with their collection of old and luxury villas and the vivid splashes of colour and greenery. 'Are you worried I might say or do something I shouldn't? That I might disgrace you in some way?'

Joe came over to her and placed his hands on the top of her tense shoulders. He turned her around to face him, his expression etched in lines of concern. 'No. I'm worried people will make you feel uncomfortable. You know how it works at these gatherings. You get stuck next to someone who wants to know every detail about your life or tell you every detail of theirs.' He made a husky, clearing his throat sound and added, 'I know it's a fundraiser for stillbirth research and counselling services but people can still ask intrusive questions. I don't want you to be hurt by someone asking you about things you'd rather not talk about.'

Juliette's heart gave a funny little flutter-spasm.

He was concerned about her. He wanted to protect her.

She had done her usual jumping to conclusions by thinking he was somehow ashamed of her, worried she might drink too much and humiliate him. But it was nothing to do with any of that.

He genuinely cared about her.

She put her hands on his chest, her lower body flush against his. 'I've avoided a lot of social events for exactly that reason. What if someone asks me if I have any children? Or plan to try again? What am I supposed to say? Am I even allowed to call myself a mother when I didn't give birth to a live baby?'

Joe framed her face in his hands, his gaze tender as it meshed with hers. 'You will always be Emilia's mother. No one can take that away from you. No one.'

Tears stung her eyes and a lump formed in her throat. 'Y-you said her name…'

Joe stroked his thumbs across each of her cheeks in a slow soothing motion. 'Maybe some time in the future it won't hurt so much to say it. To think of her.'

'Maybe…' Juliette sighed and leaned her cheek against his chest. 'They say time is a great healer, but how *much* time?'

'As long as it takes, I guess.'

There was a small silence, broken only by the sound of his hand stroking the back of her head and their quiet breathing.

It was an enormous comfort to her that he felt the same sense of loss. She had unfairly assumed he was less affected because he hadn't been the one to carry the baby, to physically give birth, and that he hadn't been there to witness the birth. But she realised now his expression of grief was different from hers.

Not wrong, but different.

Juliette lifted her head off his chest and looked up at him. 'I can't avoid social events for ever. I want to go with you. It's important to support such valuable fundraising.'

A small smile flicked up the corners of his mouth and illuminated his gaze. 'We could make a long weekend of it. How does that sound?'

She linked her arms around his neck and smiled. 'It sounds wonderful. I haven't been to Paris for years.'

He pressed a kiss to her upturned mouth. 'How remiss of me not to have taken you before now.'

Juliette played with the ends of his hair that brushed his collar. But she was conscious of a small grey cloud of unease creeping closer. Paris. The city of love. Had he taken anyone else in the past? She wasn't aware she was frowning until Joe inched up her chin and smoothed the crease away from her forehead with a gentle finger.

'What's wrong, *mio piccolo?*'

Juliette forced a smile but it fell a little short of the mark. 'I guess you've been to Paris heaps and heaps of times with lots of other…people…' She couldn't bring herself to say the word *lovers*—the pang of jealousy was too intense.

His eyes softened and he drew her closer with one hand resting in the dip of her spine, the other gliding to the sensitive nape of her neck. 'You have no need to feel jealous, *cara.*'

Juliette slipped out of his hold and pretended an interest in straightening her sketches on the table. 'I'm not jealous. I know you've been to lots of places with lots of different people.'

'But none of them have been my wife.'

My wife. The words sounded so…so permanent. But they hadn't decided anything permanent about their relationship. They had discussed a lot of issues, yes. And grown closer in so many new ways. But Juliette knew there would be other issues to discuss. Difficult, painful issues—whether or not to have another child, for instance. That was one of the questions she most dreaded. For months and months since the loss of her baby, she couldn't bear the thought of trying again. Going through another pregnancy with fear and dread on board as well as a baby. A baby there was no guarantee she would deliver alive.

Juliette held onto the back of one of the chairs and glanced down at her ring finger. The vacant space seemed to mock her. He referred to her as his wife but there had been no renewed promises. No official reconciliation. No renewed commitment. No declaration of love.

She brought her gaze back to his. 'Have you told anyone we're…?' She left the sentence hanging, not sure how to describe their relationship. A fling sounded so tawdry. An affair even worse.

'No. Have you?'

She pressed her lips together and released her grip on the chair, using one hand to sweep her hair back over one shoulder. 'I didn't think it was necessary… under the circumstances.'

'Precisely.' Something about the delivery of the word was jarring. Discordant. Like the wrong note played during a musical performance.

Juliette ran the tip of her tongue over her lower lip.

'It would be silly to get people's hopes up. Lucy and Damon, for instance.' *Not to mention her own hopes.*

'But what if the fundraiser draws a lot of press attention? Aren't people going to assume we're back together permanently?'

The ensuing silence was too long. Why wasn't he asking her to come back to him for ever? Why wasn't he dismissing her concerns with a declaration of love?

'There isn't a law about divorcing couples attending a social function together.' Joe's voice sounded tight. Constricted. 'If anything, it will demonstrate how civilised we're being about the whole damn thing.'

She studied his tense features for a moment, wondering if he was having second thoughts about their divorce. But, if so, why hadn't he said anything? 'Joe...?'

He scraped a hand through his hair and released a rough sigh. 'The press will probably make a big thing of it, but that's to be expected. I'll try and shield you as much as possible.'

Juliette approached him, touching him on the forearm. 'I want to be with you.' She couldn't think of anything she wanted more. Not just the Paris trip but with him all the time. For ever. Was she a fool for hoping he would agree to a reconciliation? Maybe the Paris trip would cement their relationship—take it to a new level that would make him realise they had a chance to make it.

The tension in his face relaxed slightly and he cupped her face in his hands. His eyes searched hers as if he was looking for something he'd lost and hoped desperately to find again. 'The dinner is only for a couple of hours. We can spend the rest of the time doing our own thing.'

She linked her arms around his neck and pressed closer. 'I can't wait.'

CHAPTER TEN

THEY ARRIVED IN Paris on Friday afternoon and once they had settled into their luxury hotel Joe suggested they go shopping.

'Shopping?' Juliette looked at him in wary surprise. 'But I don't need anything.'

'How about a new outfit for tomorrow night?' He wanted to spoil her. To make this weekend as special for her as he could. To make this weekend last for as long as he could.

'I brought one with me. You don't have to waste money buying me expensive—'

'I insist, *cara.*'

Something flickered across her features. A tightening. A guardedness. 'Are you concerned I won't dress appropriately?'

Joe mentally kicked himself. He should know by now how proud and sensitive she was. He took her by the hands and brought her close to his body. 'You always look amazing in whatever you wear. Indulge me, *tesoro.* Let me spoil you this weekend.'

Her gaze slipped to the open collar of his shirt, her

teeth sinking into her lower lip. 'I feel guilty about all the money you're spending. This hotel, first class airfares, designer clothes.'

He tipped up her face to meet her gaze. 'Don't you think you're worth it?'

Her eyes swam with doubt. 'It's not about that...'

'Then what is it about?'

Her teeth did another nibble of her lip and she slipped out of his hold. 'We're not exactly acting like a soon-to-be-divorced couple, are we?'

'I wasn't aware there was a strict protocol we had to follow.' Joe couldn't remove the note of bitterness from his tone. The divorce word was becoming worse to him than the birthday and funeral words. Every time he heard it, his heart stopped and his gut clenched like a fist.

Juliette turned to pick up her silk scarf from where she had left it on the bed. She looped it around her neck and turned back to face him. 'It feels wrong, taking gifts off you when we're not—'

'Does it feel wrong sleeping with me?'

Her expression faltered for a moment. 'No.' Her cheeks pooled with a tinge of pink and her gaze drifted to his mouth. 'It doesn't feel wrong at all.' Her voice was a few decibels shy of a whisper. 'But I can't help feeling it should.' A frown pulled at her forehead as if she was trying to solve a deeply puzzling mystery.

Joe placed his hands on her hips, his body responding to her closeness with a hot rush of blood to his groin. 'It would only be wrong if one of us didn't want to. Or if one of us was involved with someone else. But, for now, we're involved with each other.'

Her mouth flickered with a vestige of a smile. 'Right.' She took a serrated breath and released it. 'For now.' She said the two words as if she was underlining them.

'If you're not okay with that, then you need to tell me.'

Her grey-blue eyes were clear and still as a lake but he sensed a disturbance just below the surface. 'I'm okay with it.' Her tone was confident, assured. Her smile a little too bright to be believed.

Joe reached for one of her hands and brought it up to his mouth. He pressed his lips to her bent knuckles, holding her gaze with his. 'Then let's make the most of it.'

A couple of hours later, Juliette felt as if she had stepped into Cinderella's shoes. Joe took her to various designer stores, where he proceeded to buy her not one, but several gorgeous outfits. She tried not to think about the money he was spending or why he was spending it on her. It was wonderful to be spoilt like a princess and wonderful to be in his company, walking hand in hand along the streets as if they were just like any other couple.

'Time for a coffee?' Joe said when they came across a street café.

'Lovely.' Juliette sat opposite him and took in the surroundings while they waited for the waiter to arrive. The leafy trees along the footpath created a canopy of dappled shade. The afternoon was mild with a light breeze that every now and again set the leaves above them into a shivery dance that sounded like thousands of pieces of tinsel. In the distance she could see the ancient cathedral of Notre Dame in various stages of repair after the devastating fire that had threatened the entire structure. It reminded her of her relationship with Joe—the savage fire of loss had ripped through their lives and left them both scarred shells of themselves. But maybe this time together would rebuild the framework of their marriage, making it stronger and more resistant to damage.

The waiter took their order and within a short time an espresso was placed in front of Joe and tea and a buttery croissant set in front of Juliette. She was conscious of Joe's gaze resting on her as she broke off pieces of the croissant. She glanced at him and held up a portion. 'Want some?'

He shook his head, his smile indulgent, and he patted his rock-hard abdomen. 'No, thanks. I have to think of my figure.'

Juliette laughed and put the piece of croissant back on her plate. 'Now you're making me feel guilty.'

There was a small silence.

'I've missed hearing your laugh.' He brought his cup up to his mouth, taking a sip without his gaze leaving her face.

Juliette could feel a light blush heating her cheeks. 'I can't remember the last time I laughed.' She sighed and added, 'It seems like a lifetime ago.'

He put his cup back on its saucer and reached for

her hand across the table. His fingers gently squeezed hers, his expression sombre as he looked down at their joined hands. 'I think I was probably five or six years old when I first heard my father laugh. A proper laugh, I mean.' His thumb stroked the empty space on her ring finger. 'I asked him about it once. He said he felt guilty about being happy.' His eyes met hers. 'Like he was betraying my mother's memory.'

Juliette placed her other hand on top of his. 'It must have been so hard growing up without your mother. Mine drives me crazy at times but I can't imagine not having her in my life.'

His mouth flickered with a smile touched by sadness. 'I could mostly put it out of my mind but now and again something would remind me I wasn't like the other kids at school. Lots of them were in single parent families but mostly it was from divorce or separation, not the death of a parent. Parent-teacher interviews were difficult, and on Mother's Day, when the teacher got us to make cards, I made one for my *nonna* instead.'

'Were you close to your *nonna*?'

'I adored her. She was a widow herself so she understood what my father was going through but she died when I was nine.' His mouth twisted. 'I never met my mother's parents. They refused to have anything to do with my father. They weren't keen on him as a son-in-law in the first place, so you can imagine how they felt once she died. They blamed him for her death. I'm sure it didn't help his grieving process.'

Juliette's heart ached for what he had been through.

So much sadness. So much loss. So much grief. Somehow it made what she had been through a little easier to bear. Just a little. 'I don't know how you coped with all that sadness. Did things improve at all once your dad remarried?'

'Yes and no.' Joe released her hand and picked up his coffee cup, cradling it baseball mitt style in one hand. 'My father was certainly happier. And my stepmother was nice enough but it was hard for her bringing up someone else's kid. A kid she had no history with, who she suddenly had to mother when she married my father. When they had two kids together, I felt even more of an outsider.' He lifted his cup to his lips and drained the contents, placing it back down on the saucer. 'And when my father died my stepmother no longer had to pretend to play happy blended families any more.'

If only he had told her this in the past. If only she had understood the trauma and sadness that had shaped his personality—the grief that had robbed him of a normal childhood and made him so cautious about relationships.

Juliette pushed her plate to one side and touched his hand where it was resting on the table. 'I wish I'd known more about your background when we first met.'

His eyes met hers, his fingers wrapping around hers in a gentle hold. 'I can't remember the last time I told anyone about any of this. It's not something I like talking about. Plenty of people have it much worse than I did.'

'Yes, but we were married and I should've understood you better.' She frowned and looked down at their joined hands. His wedding ring was a reminder that she was the one to leave their marriage, not him. Would he remove it once their divorce was finalised? Her stomach pitched at the thought of him being with someone else. She swallowed a tight lump and continued, 'I should've made more of an effort.'

Joe leaned forward and stroked a lazy finger down the curve of her cheek. 'None of this is your fault. You had your own stuff going on with your ex.'

Juliette sat back in her chair with a little thump and folded her arms and frowned. 'I wish you'd stop mentioning my ex. I don't even think I was truly in love with Harvey. I think I only continued with the relationship as long as I did as it seemed to please my parents.'

He studied her for a long moment. 'Were they pleased when we broke up?'

Juliette unfolded her arms and slumped her shoulders on a sigh. 'No. If anything, they thought I was being impulsive and letting my emotions overshadow everything. But I shut them down pretty quickly and they've said nothing since.'

'One could hardly blame you for being emotional, given the circumstances.' His tone was a disarming blend of gruffness and tenderness.

Juliette lowered her gaze, leaned forward and pushed a piece of croissant around her plate with her finger. 'I don't see much of them these days. They're always so busy with work. I know their careers are important to them but it always makes me feel I'm way down on their list of priorities.' She sighed and added, 'I wonder if it will change when they retire. *If* they retire, that is.'

There was a long silence.

Juliette chanced a glance at him but he was looking into the distance as if his thoughts had been pulled elsewhere. It gave her a moment to study his features—the frown of concentration, the sharply intelligent gaze, the chiselled jaw with its peppered regrowth, the sculptured contours of his mouth. Her belly flip-flopped when she thought about his mouth on hers, the silken thrust of his tongue, the heat and fire of his kiss.

He stirred his coffee even though she knew he didn't take sugar, his gaze focused on the tiny whirlpool he created in his cup. 'Some people live to work—others work to live.'

Juliette shifted uncomfortably in her chair. 'I suppose you think that makes me sound like a spoilt brat, insisting on being the centre of my parents' world.'

His gaze met hers. 'I don't think that at all. It can be difficult when our caregivers don't meet our expectations. Sometimes it's down to circumstances, other times to personality.'

Another silence ticked past.

Juliette shifted her gaze to the left of his. 'I was a change of life baby. An accident. A mistake.'

His expression clouded. 'Surely they didn't say they didn't want you?'

Juliette chewed the side of her lip. 'No. Never—it's

just a feeling I've had over the years. Having a child at their stage of life must have been an inconvenience. My brothers were eighteen and twenty. I spent a lot of time with nannies and babysitters and, of course, boarding school, which I hated. I think that's why I never did that well at school. I disengaged out of emotional distress.'

He touched her hand where it was resting on the table. 'Don't be fooled into thinking a bunch of letters after your name makes you smart. You are an intelligent and hugely talented artist.'

Juliette hoped her creative drive would come back stronger than before but it had taken such a blow with the death of her baby. Her motivation had been totally crushed and was only now flickering into life. 'Thanks.'

He smiled and waved a hand at her teacup. 'Would you like a refill?'

'No. I'm done.' She pushed back her chair while he gathered the array of shopping bags around his chair.

He paid the bill and within a short time they were on their way back to the hotel. Once they arrived, Joe handed the porter the bags and accompanied Juliette to the private lift to the penthouse.

'Why don't you have a bit of a rest before dinner?' he said as the lift arrived at their suite. 'I have a couple of things to see to.'

Juliette tried to ignore the little stab of disappointment that jabbed her. 'Will you be long?'

He leaned down to press a light kiss to her lips. 'Not long at all.'

* * *

Joe walked the streets of Paris, ruminating on how he had approached life's challenges. Juliette's comment about her parents always working had struck a chord with him. Ever since he was a young child, he had thrown himself into tasks, study, work, to escape the shadows of his childhood. The loss that had defined him since he'd taken his first breath. Being successful, wealthy and hard-working had given him a framework for his life that had never let him down until he'd met Juliette.

But now he could feel the foundations of his personality undergoing a change, like a fine crack running through concrete. A gradual destabilisation of his identity as a man who needed no one.

Who kept himself emotionally separate, distant. Safe.

But the more time he spent with Juliette, the wider the cracks grew, allowing him to envisage the sort of man he could be if he was able to let go of the past. A man who could love and be loved in return. A man who would no longer need to keep his emotions locked down. A man who could embrace his vulnerabilities and face whatever life threw at him with emotional courage instead of cowardice.

His feelings for Juliette were something he had tried so hard to ignore. And he'd been damn good at it so far. So good he'd convinced himself not to beg her to come back to him when she'd left. So good he'd not revealed things to her he should have revealed while they were together. Things that might well have made a difference if he hadn't been so determined to hold himself apart, as he had done with every other relationship, both intimate and otherwise.

But now his feelings were tiptoeing out of their hiding place, their tentative footsteps leaving soft little impressions on his heart that felt almost painful.

He looked down at the wedding ring on his finger, the symbol of his commitment. A commitment he wasn't entirely sure Juliette wanted from him any more. She had made no commitment other than to spend the next few days with him before she went back to London.

Could he dare to hope to change her mind?

Juliette had showered and dressed and was putting the finishing touches to her make-up in preparation for the dinner when Joe returned to their hotel. She met his eyes in the mirror of the dressing table. 'You're cutting it fine. Isn't the dinner at seven-thirty?'

He gave a crooked smile. 'It won't take me long to get ready.' He came up behind her and, slipping one hand inside his jacket pocket, retrieved a rectangular jewellery box. 'I found something for you when I was out walking.'

Juliette turned on the stool and raised her brows. 'Found? Like on the footpath?' She gave him a mock frown and waggled a reproving finger at him. 'You've been spending money on me again.'

He handed her the box. 'And why shouldn't I spoil you?' He leaned down to press a light kiss to the top of her head. 'Mmm... You smell beautiful.'

Juliette lifted her face to meet his gaze. 'It's the same perfume I've always worn.'

His fingers brushed beneath her chin in an idle movement, his eyes dark and lustrous. 'I know. I smelt it everywhere in the house after you left.' His mouth turned down at the corners as if the mention of that time caused him pain. He glanced at the jewellery box in her hands. 'Go on. Open it.'

Juliette looked down at the box and ran her fingertip over the gold embossed designer label on the black velvet lid. She prised open the lid and gasped when she saw a glittering diamond on a gold chain as fine as a thread and two matching diamond droplet earrings.

'Oh, Joe, they're gorgeous.' She could only imagine how much they'd cost. It was the sort of jewellery designer where one didn't shop if one needed to see a price tag before considering purchasing anything.

'Here. Let me put the necklace on you.' His voice had a gruff edge, his expression hard to read.

She handed him the box and turned so she was facing the mirror again, watching him carefully remove the diamond from its plush white velvet bed. She shivered when his hands brushed the sensitive skin of her neck as he fastened the diamond in place. He handed her the earrings one at a time for her to insert into her earlobes. Then he rested his hands on her shoulders and met her eyes in the mirror.

'You look stunning.'

Juliette touched the diamond with her fingers, the

earrings glinting like stars when she turned her head from side to side. 'I hope I don't lose one of them.'

He gave a grim smile that wasn't really a smile. 'There are worse things to lose, *cara*.' His deep tone echoed with a sadness that was almost palpable.

She placed one of her hands over one of his, pressing down on it in an I-know-what-you-mean gesture. Her throat thickened, her chest tightened, her eyes glistened. 'You'd better get dressed. It's almost time to leave.'

He looked as if he was about to say something— his brows moved closer together and his mouth opened as if in preparation to speak—but then seemed to change his mind. He gave her shoulders one last squeeze and turned away to get ready for the dinner.

The fundraising dinner was held in the ballroom of a private mansion within walking distance of their hotel. By the time Juliette and Joe arrived, the guests were making their way to their allotted tables after having drinks and finger food in the foyer. The room was decorated with simple and elegant arrangements of flowers and pastel-coloured paper rosettes and ribbons rather than less environment-friendly balloons.

Joe seemed to know many of the guests and introduced her to several people on the way to their place at the huge table but she found it hard to remember all their names. She smiled and shook hands with everyone, quietly wondering if any of them knew the circumstances about her and Joe's marriage.

Juliette was seated next to Joe, with a woman on

her left in her mid to late forties called Marisa, who was on the board of directors for the charity.

'I'm so pleased to finally meet you,' Marisa said with a warm smile. She glanced covertly towards Joe but he was talking to the man next to him and added in a lower tone, 'We so appreciate what you and Joe have done for our charity. It's really lovely too that you could make it here with him.'

'Oh, well, it was really Joe who did all the fund-raising. I'm afraid I had little to do with that at all.'

Marisa placed a gentle hand on Juliette's arm, her expression full of compassion. 'You don't have to explain. What you two went through is enough to tear apart any young couple. I should know. I had a still-birth in between my first and third child. It was horrendous. I think of him every single day. We called him Alexandre.'

Juliette looked into the other woman's now shimmering hazel gaze and for the first time in months felt less alone and isolated. 'I'm so sorry.'

Marisa's mouth twisted. 'He would have been ten years old last month. You never really get over it. You carry it with you. I was lucky I already had a child. I'm not sure I would have been game enough to try again if I hadn't. But I'm so glad I did. My two girls are my biggest joy.'

Juliette swallowed a tight lump in her throat. 'How soon did you...try again?' Her voice was as tentative as her thoughts on the subject of having another baby. It was something she had been thinking about ever since she'd walked into the nursery. The thoughts were mostly at the back of her mind, but lately they were creeping closer and closer. Close enough for her to imagine cradling a beautiful baby in her arms.

A live baby.

Joe's baby.

'Months and months,' Marisa said. 'I could barely look at my husband without bursting into floods of tears. But I'd always wanted a family and Henri did too. We decided it would probably help us heal if we tried again. And it worked. It doesn't mean I don't still grieve. I do, and badly at times, and so does Henri. But the thing that helped Henri and me was setting up this foundation a couple of years after we lost Alexandre. Joe's contribution has been invaluable. It's meant we can do further important research as well as adding to our counselling services. It was so very kind and generous of him, when he was going through such a difficult time himself.'

Guilt rained down on Juliette anew. Joe might not have visited their daughter's grave but he had done what he could to stop such a tragedy from happening to others. Instead of trying to understand things from his point of view, she had pushed him away, rejected him, marched out of his life instead of sharing the burden of grief with him—without allowing him time to process his feelings, which were just as valid as hers.

'He's…a very kind and generous person,' she said, her heart so full of love for Joe she found it hard to take her next breath. Love that had grown from the moment she'd met him. The first kiss, the first night together—the night where she had given herself to him so wholeheartedly. The night that had bound them together with a subsequent tragedy. Could they move past it?

Marisa gently squeezed Juliette's hand where it was resting on her lap. 'You'll know when it's the right time to try again. You'll probably always feel worried during any subsequent pregnancy—that's entirely natural and unfortunately unavoidable. But the sheer joy of holding your baby at the end is worth it. There's really nothing like it.'

Juliette squeezed the other woman's hand in return. 'Thank you for sharing your experience with me. I've found it so hard to talk to anyone about it. Some people in my life think I should have moved on by now.'

'Not Joe, though?' Marisa frowned.

'No, not Joe.' Juliette sighed and continued. 'I've been so hard on him. I was so caught up in how I was feeling that I didn't realise he was feeling the same, only expressing it a different way.'

Marisa nodded in empathy. 'Tell me about it. I often was so angry at Henri for the most ridiculous things until I realised it was misplaced grief masquerading as anger. I could handle feeling angry. What I couldn't handle was feeling profound gut-wrenching, inescapable grief. But eventually we worked through it and are stronger and closer for it.'

Stronger and closer for it.

Juliette mulled over that phrase as the more formal part of the dinner commenced. The award was finally announced and Joe led Juliette up to the podium. Press cameras went off and later a journalist requested an interview. Joe spoke briefly about the foundation and skilfully steered the journalist away from their personal situation. It made Juliette all the more uncertain of what he ultimately wanted from her. A fling before they divorced—or did he want her to stay with him for ever?

Stronger and closer.

Would those words one day define her and Joe? The desire to heal was so strong in her now. Stronger than her anger, which seemed to have dissipated like fog under the hopeful beam of sunshine. And she realised now a part of that healing included fulfilling her dream of having a family. Of being part of a loving partnership with her husband, raising children in a house where love and acceptance and nurture were at the forefront at all times.

Time was reputed to be a great healer, but wasn't love the best healer of all?

CHAPTER ELEVEN

THEY WALKED BACK to their hotel in silence. Juliette had so many questions to ask, so many doubts to address, so many hopes to allow the freedom to grow. When they were back in their room she turned to look at him.

'Joe? I wish I'd known about your work with the foundation. It means so much to me that you've tried to help so many others like us. I'm sorry I blocked contact with you.'

He slipped off his jacket and hung it loosely over the back of a chair. His mouth was pressed flat for a moment and his eyes looked pained. 'I was almost glad you blocked me. I was worried about upsetting you. Every time we talk about the baby...' his throat rose and fell and his voice grew raspy '... I see what it does to you. It hurts you.'

Tears sprouted in her eyes and she went to him, wrapping her arms around his waist. 'But it hurts me more *not* to talk about her. Losing Emilia will always upset me. It's normal and unavoidable. We suffered a terrible loss. But I want to move on as best I can and that includes talking about how we're feeling and when we're feeling it.'

Joe cupped one side of her face, his other hand going to rest on her hip. His gaze held hers in a tender lock that made her heart contract. 'I felt so powerless and frustrated our baby died. Giving to the foundation was the only thing I could think to do to remove some of that powerlessness. I figured by donating and raising large sums of money for research it would stop it happening to someone else. It helped me process my grief by actually doing something positive. I didn't want to be like my father, who was so prostrated by grief it took years for him to come out of it.'

Juliette stroked his jaw, leaning into his strong frame, her body responding to his closeness with its usual leap of excitement. 'I think you're amazing to have done that. It shows the wonderful man you are. Generous and kind and compassionate.'

He brought his head down so his mouth was just above hers. 'Don't make me out to be too much of a hero, *tesoro*. I have many failings.'

Juliette linked her arms around his neck. 'Kiss me, Joe. Make love to me.'

He drew her closer, his arms a strong band around her body, his mouth coming down on hers in a kiss that was soft and yet deeply passionate. Sensations swept through her body—hot, urgent sensations that made her weak at the knees. He lifted her in his arms, carrying her as if she weighed little more than a child, and took her through to the bedroom. He lowered her feet to the floor in front of him, his hands already setting to work on her clothes. Juliette got to work on his and within moments they were both naked and lying, limbs entwined, on the bed.

Joe's mouth came down on hers, firmer this time, his tongue entering her mouth to tease hers into erotic play. Molten heat pooled in her core, need pulsating deep in her feminine flesh. His mouth moved from her lips to explore the soft skin below her ear, his tongue flickering against her sensitive flesh until she writhed with pleasure. He went lower to her décolletage, tracing the fine structure of her collarbone and down to the gentle swell of her breasts. The action of his mouth and tongue evoked tingles and prickles and needles of pleasure through her breasts. Her nipples tightened, her spine melted, her need escalated.

His hand went to her hip, gliding to her bottom to tilt her towards him. '*Dio mio*, I want you so much.' His voice was a low, deep, agonised groan. He kissed her again, his tongue tangoing with hers until she was mindless with desire. He lifted his mouth off hers and rolled away to get a condom.

Juliette thought of telling him not to bother, that perhaps they should try for another baby instead of using protection. But she decided to keep that conversation for another time. A time when she had a better understanding of how he felt about her. He had never said he loved her. But she knew deep in her bones he cared about her. Cared more than he was probably willing to admit. And wasn't she a bit the same? She hadn't declared her love for him. Not yet.

Joe applied a condom and came back to gather her

close. His eyes were so dark with desire they looked densely black. 'I'm glad you came with me to Paris.'

Juliette pressed a soft kiss to his mouth. 'I'm glad I came too. And, speaking of coming…' She hooked one leg over his and gave him a come-hither look.

'Leave it with me.' He smiled a sexy smile and brought his mouth back down to hers. 'I'll see what I can do.'

During the night Joe reached again for Juliette, his arms gathering her close to his body. She made a soft murmuring sound and nestled closer, her head resting on his chest right where his heart beat a steady rhythm—but not for much longer. He could feel the quick uptake of his pulse as his body responded to her silky skin, her smooth limbs, the soft waft of her warm breath. The scent of her filled his nostrils, the glide of one of her hands against his thigh making his breath catch. His groin swelled, heated, burned at the thought of her touching him. Desire rolling through him in ever-increasing waves.

The moonlight coming in through the window cast her body in silvery light, making her look like an angel that had flown from heaven and lain down beside him. *Heaven* just about summed up what it felt like to hold her. To make love to her. To feel her body enclose his, to feel her respond to him hadn't lessened his desire but rather fed it, nurtured it, expanded it.

Her hand crept ever closer until she was encircling him with her fingers. 'Are you awake?' Her voice was a whisper that made his flesh tingle all over.

He smothered a groan as his body throbbed under her touch. 'I am now.'

She glanced up at him with shining eyes, a cheeky smile curving her lips. 'Do you want me to stop touching you?'

Joe felt like he would *die* if she stopped touching him. He rolled her over to her back and leaned over her with his weight propped on his elbows. 'How about I touch you to even this up a bit?'

He cupped one of her breasts, rolling his thumb over her nipple, watching her response play out on her features, in the catch of her breath, the parting of her lips, her gaze flicking to his mouth. His hand went down from her breast to the tiny cave of her belly button and then beyond.

'Oh...' Juliette gave a breathless gasp, her legs folding outwards to welcome his touch. *'Oh...'*

Joe moved down her body, using his lips and tongue to bring forth her earth-shattering response— a response that never failed to thrill him. Making love with her was on another scale from anything he had experienced before. A scale he had never reached with anyone else. Her response to him touched him at the centre of his being. Making him *feel* every movement of her body, every stroke and glide of her fingers, every soft press of her mouth, as if his body's nerves had been tuned to another setting. A higher, richer, more pleasurable setting.

Juliette flopped back down against the pillows, her face flushed, her eyes bright as gemstones. 'I'm not letting you get away with that without a payback.'

'Is that a promise?'

She smiled and scrambled to a sitting position, pushing him down so he was on his back. 'What do you think?' She straddled him and slid down his body until her mouth was close to his erection.

He sucked in a rasping breath. 'I can't think right now.'

'Then don't. Just feel.' And when she closed her mouth over him that was all he could do. He was reduced to sensations so powerful, so all-consuming, he thought he would lose consciousness. The teasing suction of her mouth, the sexy glide and the kittenish licks of her tongue made him fly into a vortex of mind-blowing, senses-spinning ecstasy.

He came back to earth with a deep sigh of contentment and brought her down so she was lying on top of him, her legs entangled with his. He stroked the length of her spine in slow movements, enjoying the press of her breasts against his chest, the beat of her heart against his, her hair tickling him where it cascaded over him like a mermaid's.

He listened to the gradual slowing of her breathing, felt her body gradually melt into full relaxation as she drifted off to sleep.

A long time later he too closed his eyes but it was a long time before he went to sleep...

On Monday morning Joe woke a little later than was normal for him. He turned to reach for Juliette but the space beside him in the bed was vacant. For a brief moment panic gripped him in the chest like a claw—a sudden, savage claw that reminded him of all the mornings he had woken without her beside him. But then the sound of her moving about in the bathroom relaxed his tense muscles like the injection of a prophylactic drug. Relief swept through him in deep calming waves.

After spending the weekend wandering around the city of Paris hand in hand, they were flying back to Italy this afternoon. He could not remember a time when he had felt such a deep sense of hope. Hope that their relationship had a chance to be restored, regenerated, renewed. But while Juliette had initially agreed to stay a couple of weeks, she hadn't said anything about staying longer. He *wanted* her to stay longer. He wanted to resume their marriage. To start afresh. To build on the new understanding they had now after spending time together.

Juliette came out of the bathroom already showered and dressed. 'Good morning, sleepyhead.' Her smile was as bright as the sunshine pouring through the window and his breath caught in the middle of his chest.

'Yes, well, you did wear me out a little last night.' Joe smiled and tossed off the bedcovers and slipped on a bathrobe in case he was tempted to take her back to bed and cause them to miss their flight.

She gave an answering smile but something about a look in her eyes gave him pause. 'Joe?'

He came over to her and ran his hands down from her upper arms to her wrists, gently encircling them with his fingers. 'What's on your mind, *cara*?'

She drew most of her lower lip into her mouth, holding it there for a beat before releasing it. 'You know how I said we should be honest about our feelings? Well, I don't want to go ahead with the divorce.'

Joe pulled her to him in a tight hug, his relief so immense it flooded his being. 'I don't want that either. I want you to stay with me.' His voice was hoarse with suppressed emotion, his heart thudding with joy. 'We'll start afresh. Go on a proper honeymoon this time. We can even renew our vows if that's what you'd like.'

She leaned back to look up at him, her grey-blue eyes clear. 'Why, though? Why do you want our marriage to continue?'

Joe could feel a ripple of unease slithering down his spinal column. 'You know why. We're good together. We understand each other better now.'

Her eyes drifted to his mouth. 'Joe, a marriage is not just about good sex.' Her gaze came back up to his. Direct. Determined. 'I love you.'

Joe knew he should fill the silence with the answer of those overused words but his mouth dried, his chest tightened. He had never said those words to anyone. Not even his father or Nonna. He had showed it in other ways, but saying those words out loud would trigger something primal in him. Born out of some kind of primitive desire to keep himself free of deep emotional entanglements.

'*Cara*, you know I care about you.' Somehow he spoke past the stricture in his throat.

Her expression faltered, hurt flickering through

her gaze, her mouth sagging at the corners. 'I don't want you just to care. I want you to love me. And I want us to try for another baby. I'm ready now. Please say you're ready too?'

Something in his chest gave way as if his heart had suddenly been dislodged, like an industrial crane losing its heavy load. He couldn't take a new breath. He became lightheaded, disoriented. Panic beat in his chest as if fists were punching inside his heart to escape.

Another baby... Another pregnancy... Another nine months of worry. Of dread. Of anguish.

Joe let his hands drop from around her wrists and stepped back, fighting for air. For composure. For safety. 'Whoa there. That's not something I can even think about. Not right now.'

She frowned, her mouth opening and closing as if she couldn't think of what to say. Then she took a steadying breath. 'Joe.' Her tone was level, calm, rational. 'I know you're worried about what might happen to me or the baby or both. I suspect most husbands would feel that way if they were asked, especially after going through what we went through. But we'll have the best of medical care and we can only hope this time the baby will be okay.'

Joe shoved a hand through his hair, his brain reeling so much it felt as if his skull would fracture. 'I'm not ready to discuss this.'

'But, if we're to stay together, we have to discuss difficult things as they come up. Isn't that what we did wrong in the past? We pushed it under the carpet instead of airing it up front.'

He moved to the other side of the room, unable to get his thoughts out of their frenetic maelstrom. It was like a tornado of terror inside his head. 'I'm not willing to discuss it. No way.'

Her eyes widened, her cheeks losing colour. 'No way...*ever?*'

He scrubbed a hand down his face, his chest still so tight he could barely inflate his lungs. His gut prickled with anxiety, his head pounded, his brain log-jammed. He wanted a reconciliation. It was all he wanted—to have Juliette back in his life. But to go through the stress of another pregnancy, knowing it could end like the last one, would be a step too far. A dangerous, frightening step that made everything in him freeze in panic.

'Look, I'm happy to resume our marriage—really happy—but having another baby is out of the question. I just can't face it. I'm sorry.'

Her brow was furrowed with confusion. 'But I thought you cared about me? I even thought maybe you...loved me, even though you seem unwilling to say the words.'

Love was something Joe had never expected to feel with any intensity. Whenever he felt the stirring of emotions he couldn't handle he blocked them. Deadened them. Denied them. He let out a long breath. 'I told you—I care about you.'

She moved further away, crossing her arms over her body. 'But you're not in love with me.' Her tone was flat, resigned, dull.

Joe swallowed against another tight knot in his

throat. 'I've never felt like this with anyone else, but as to whether it's the love you want, well, I can't guarantee it is.'

She met his gaze with a steady focus that was unnerving. Unnerving because he felt a horrible sense of history about to repeat itself. 'I spent so much of my childhood wondering if I was loved like my brothers were loved. Never quite feeling I made the grade. I didn't seem to tick the boxes my parents wanted ticked. I always seemed to disappoint them. It made me feel like an outsider in my own family. I don't want to live like that in our marriage. I want to be on an equal footing with you. A true partnership where we share everything openly and honestly.'

What could he say that he hadn't already said? He *was* being honest with her. Brutally so.

'I'm sorry you feel that way about your family. It's tough feeling like you don't belong. I get that. But a marriage like ours could be successful without the idealised, overly romanticised version of love you're talking about.'

Juliette ran her tongue over her lips and continued, her voice becoming husky. 'I could probably cope with you not being in love with me. I knew when you married me you didn't love me that way. But I want another baby at some point. It doesn't have to be right now. But how can we have a future together if you won't even discuss it?'

'Of course we have a future together,' Joe said, struggling to contain his poise. 'Hasn't the last week proved that? We're in a much better place than we ever were before. We know each other so much better and—'

'I know all that but it's not enough.' Her slim shoulders went back as if she was drawing on some inner strength to get her point across. 'I want a family, Joe. I want to be a mother so badly. I can't guarantee it will happen, especially given what happened last time, but I still want to try.'

The punching panic in his chest was at a manic stage, like a boxer going for the knockout blow. Desperate to get out of the ring no matter what.

'Look, children obviously are an important part of many people's lives. But we've been down this road and it nearly destroyed us. Why not quit while we're ahead? We can have a great life. Travel to anywhere at any time and never want for anything.'

Her eyes dulled, her expression faded, her throat tightened over a swallow. 'You never wanted her, did you? You never wanted a baby in the first place. That's why you don't want another one now. It's not part of your life plan. It never has been.'

'That's not true. I wanted our child as much as you did—'

'Tell me honestly. Do you *ever* want another child?'

The silence clawed at his guts, tore at his heart like talons.

'I'm not sure I can answer that.' He finally found his voice.

Her grey-blue eyes became glacial ponds, her expression hardening like a hoar frost. 'I think I get it now. Sorry for being so slow on the uptake.' Her tone chilled the temperature in the room to an arctic level. 'The problem as I see it is you don't want to have a baby with *me*. I'm the problem.' She batted her hand against her chest for emphasis. 'It's *me*.'

'That's not true,' Joe said, scrambling for a way out of this wretched conversation. He was in quick-sand and sinking. He could feel it dragging him down, down, down. He had seen whole buildings crumple and disappear into sinkholes. Could there be a bigger, blacker pit of despair for him to fall in? To lose her again? Not once, but twice?

But…another baby?

No. No. No. He couldn't go through it again.

Her spine straightened, her gaze determined. 'If you don't want to be the father of my child, then it's time for us to say goodbye.'

No! The word was a silent scream inside his head. A siren of blind panic. A high-pitched screech of fear that made his blood run cold. But, rather than voice it out loud, Joe curled his lip instead, determined not to show how undone he really was. He would climb out of that damn sinkhole and take control. He *had* to. He'd done it before. He would do it again.

'Blackmail doesn't suit you, Juliette. And you should know by now, I'm not the sort of man to respond to it.'

Her small neat chin came up and her eyes glittered with defiance. 'Then we are at an impasse.'

'Don't be ridiculous,' he began.

'I'm not being ridiculous—I'm being realistic,'

Juliette said. 'What would be the point in continuing our marriage if one of us isn't getting what we want? Who never gets what they want? I'd end up resenting you. Hating you for denying me the family I want so much.'

Joe strode over to her but refrained from touching her. If he touched her, he would agree to anything. He couldn't risk it. He needed time to process what she was demanding. It was too much for him to handle when they had only been back together a matter of days.

'There's always compromise in relationships,' he said, shocked at how calm and collected he sounded when on the inside he was collapsing like a badly constructed office tower. The very foundation of his being was under threat. He was teetering over an abyss of uncertainty, dread, uncontrollable danger.

Juliette met his gaze with a level stare. 'I know all about compromise. I'm the one who made all the adjustments, fitting into your life when we first got married. But I'm not prepared to compromise on this. It's not fair to ask me to. If you loved me, you would understand how important this is for me.'

'Then maybe I don't love you.'

One side of Joe's brain was shouting, *What are you saying?* The other was saying, *You're safe, for now.*

She flinched as if he had slapped her and, right at that moment, he had never hated himself more. But wasn't it better this way? He had always known on a cellular level he would not be enough for her. He wasn't good for her. He had all but destroyed her life by getting involved with her in the first place.

The blame for so much suffering was at his door.

'Then I think that's all that needs to be said.' Her voice was almost as calm and indifferent as his but he could see how much he had disappointed her. It was in every nuance of her face—the tight lips, the creased brow, the dullness of her grey-blue gaze as if a light had been turned off inside her. 'I won't be returning to Italy with you this afternoon. I'll fly straight home to London.'

Home to London.

The words were vicious hammer blows to his heart. But he had no way of defending himself without bringing more pain and uncertainty into both of their lives.

Juliette turned away and began packing her things into her weekend bag.

Stop her. Stop her. Stop her. Tell her the truth. Tell her how you feel about her. Don't let her leave like this.

But Joe did the opposite. He walked calmly, silently into the bathroom, and when he returned a few minutes later she was gone.

Later, Juliette could barely recall how she got to the airport and on a plane to London without displaying the devastation she felt. It was as if she had split herself into two people—one was calm and logical and rational, able to call a taxi, pay the driver and board a plane without a qualm. The other was a broken, shattered shell, limping through the steps to get her to somewhere safe where she could address her terrible wounds.

Joe didn't want another child.

Joe didn't love her.

He had never loved her.

She had fooled herself into believing otherwise. She had constructed a dream landscape where the pain of the past would fade into the background, not quite going away but no longer causing the distress it once had. A landscape where the birth of another baby would bind her and Joe in the joys of parenthood, their marriage thriving instead of dying. How could she have been so naïve? How could she have allowed herself to think they had a future when he was unable—*unwilling*—to love her?

Was there something wrong with her that she was destined to crave a love she couldn't have?

Juliette had always doubted her parents' love for her, seeing it as conditional rather than unconditional. She had thought Harvey, her ex, had loved her and had foolishly believed it when he'd said the words so often and so volubly. But that had also been a lie.

She huddled into her seat on the plane and looked listlessly out of the window at the clouds drifting by. Her heart ached as if an invisible corkscrew were driving through it on the way to her backbone.

So, it was finally over.

Her marriage to Joe Allegranza was dead.

Unsalvageable.

Could there be anything crueller than to dangle

hope in front of her and then snatch it away? Every kiss, every touch, every time they made love, she felt that he loved her. How could she have been so misguided? So fanciful? So deluded?

It was time now to move on and forge a new path for herself. A new future.

Juliette's heart gave another painful spasm.

Without Joe...

Joe spent the first week after Juliette left throwing himself into work, largely helped by a bridge collapse in northern Spain. Fixing other people's problems was the only way to distract himself from his own unfixable ones. But, as much as he found his work rewarding and challenging in equal measure, he began to realise it no longer filled the gaping chasm Juliette had left behind. His work was like temporary scaffolding holding up a compromised building.

He was the compromised building, constructed from materials that were now seriously out of date.

Stoicism, self-reliance, a fierce desire for control, emotional lockdown, an isolationist mind-set were no longer materials in a man's life that worked, if indeed they ever had. They were destroying him like termites in the foundations, quietly, secretly, stealthily destabilising and destroying the man he had the potential to be.

But where to start to fix such deep-seated faults?

He knew exactly where—at the beginning.

Joe's mother's grave was sadly neglected and a deep sense of shame washed over him as he knelt down beside it and pulled out the weeds from around her plot. He placed the flowers he'd brought with him in the stone vase and sat back on his heels to read the words engraved on the marble headstone.

Giovanna Giulia Allegranza
A loving wife and mother
Missed for ever

He had no knowledge, no physical memory of his mother, and yet he sensed how much she must have loved him. He was touched that his father had insisted the word 'mother' was included on her headstone even though she hadn't regained consciousness to hold Joe in her arms. Why hadn't he noticed that before now? All those times his father had dragged him to the graveyard, Joe had stood sullenly to one side as his father tended the grave with tears pouring down his face. It had repulsed Joe, made him feel his father was weak and unable to control his emotions, that he had loved his wife *too* much.

Why had he adopted such toxic notions about manhood? Why had he denied himself for all these years the full breadth and depth of his humanity? The ability to feel and express deep emotion, the ability to willingly relinquish control over things that couldn't be controlled in any case, to acknowledge his grief over the loss of his baby daughter.

And the deep and abiding love he felt for Juliette.

Why else was he struggling to make sense of his future without her? The emptiness she'd left behind could not be filled with work. No amount of work could ever do that. He loved her with a love so strong it seeped into every cell of his body like the pouring of concrete on a building site. His love was the solid, dependable, unshakable platform on which they could plan a future.

Joe stood from his mother's grave and glanced at some of the other headstones nearby. There were numerous stories of love inscribed there. Old love, young love and everything in between. Life had no guarantees. You could be lucky to live to ninety. Some, like tiny Emilia, didn't survive the nine months of pregnancy. Some didn't survive childhood or middle age, and yet others lived long lives and still they were grieved. Grief had no age limit. It was a human response to loving someone. It didn't matter how old they were—they were missed when they were gone.

Like he missed his baby daughter...

Pain gripped him in the chest and he blinked against the moisture at the back of his eyes. Could he do it? Could he visit that tiny grave and confront the raw grief that threatened to overwhelm him?

CHAPTER TWELVE

JULIETTE WAS IDLY sketching at her flat in London, her mind preoccupied with missing Joe. She hadn't heard anything from him since she'd left him in Paris. Not that she'd expected to—they had both said all that needed to be said. But when the doorbell rang her heart leapt and her deadened hopes took a gasp of air.

She opened the door and her shoulders slumped on a sigh. 'Oh…hi, Mum…' Her tone was jaded and unwelcoming even though she was craving company. Any company to distract herself from her misery.

'Have I come at a bad time?' her mother, Claudia, asked.

Juliette forced a weak smile. 'Of course not. I was just doing some drawing…' She led the way into the kitchen, where she had set up her art materials.

Claudia glanced at the sketches. 'So, you're working again?'

'Sort of.' Juliette shuffled the papers into a neat pile. 'I'm thinking about doing a children's book on loss. I thought it might help when kids lose a parent or someone close to them. Or even a pet.'

'That's a wonderful idea,' Claudia said, pulling out a chair to sit. She waited a beat before adding, 'Did you get the divorce papers signed?'

Juliette hadn't told her mother about the few days in Italy with Joe or the weekend in Paris, and re- alised now how awkward it was going to be to fill in the gaps.

She slid into the seat opposite. 'Mum…for a time I was considering going back to him. We caught up at Lucy and Damon's wedding and then I went to see him in Positano. I stayed for over a week and I re- ally thought we had a chance to make things work. I found out his mother died having him. How tragic is that? I realised while I was there that I love him. I know this might sound a bit fanciful to someone as rational and logical as you, but I think I fell in love with him the moment I met him. And I want to have another baby but he's adamantly against even discuss- ing it. I can't compromise on that. I know there's no guarantee I won't have another stillbirth but I want to try for another child.'

Claudia reached for Juliette's hand and gave it a motherly squeeze. 'Sweetie, falling in love like that doesn't sound fanciful at all.' She sighed and contin- ued. 'I might appear rational and logical to you, but I'm not always like that on the inside. I fell in love with your father in much the same way. It was so sudden and I always felt as if I had to prove myself to his parents—your grandparents—to justify him marrying me.'

'Really? But I thought Nanna and Pop adored you.'

Claudia's smile was rueful. 'They did, eventually, but mostly because I did everything I could to please and impress them. My Masters and PhD? That was my way of showing them I was as intelligent and capable as their son. Worthy of him.' Her expression faltered. 'When I got pregnant with you, I had just enrolled in my PhD. I couldn't bear the thought of dropping out and yet I was so torn about you. There were times when I hated leaving you with the nanny and other times when I couldn't wait to get away so I could concentrate on my work. I couldn't seem to win, no matter what I did. And, being an older mother, well, I just didn't have the energy and drive I had with your brothers.'

'Oh, Mum...' Juliette stood and came around to give her mother a hug around the shoulders. 'I think most mothers feel like they can't win.'

Claudia turned in her chair and grasped Juliette's hands. 'I wish I could make you happy, sweetie. The last few months have been so tough on you. But, given what you told me just now about Joe, it's been terribly tough on him too. He must have been beside himself the whole pregnancy. No wonder he doesn't want to go through that again. He wouldn't want to risk losing you.'

Juliette slipped her hands out of her mother's hold. 'He doesn't love me, Mum. He told me he cares about me. That's not enough. I want him to love me.'

Claudia frowned. 'Sweetie, are you sure he doesn't love you? One thing my long career in science has taught me is to look closely at the evidence. Examine every bit of data, check and double check and keep a rational perspective. Men aren't always good at expressing their emotions. Sometimes they don't even recognise what they're feeling. Years of being taught to suppress how they feel makes it hard for them to open up when they need to.'

Could her mother be right? But why had Joe let her leave both times without asking her to stay? Why hadn't he called or texted?

He'd left her stranded in a vacuum.

'I don't know...' Juliette sighed. 'I sometimes thought he loved me. He's so generous and kind. But he hasn't contacted me since I left him in Paris. Not even a text or phone call. If he cared about me, wouldn't he want to contact me?'

'We always expect people to respond to a situation the way *we* would respond, but each of us has their own way of doing things, their own framework or lens to view things through,' Claudia said. 'Joe strikes me as someone who takes his time to think about things before he acts. He's just taking longer than you would like.'

'But what if you're wrong?'

Claudia gave a soft smile. 'Look at the evidence, sweetie. It's all you can go on for now.'

After her mother left, Juliette bought flowers from her local florist and drove to the graveyard where Emilia was interned in a small village outside London. It never got any easier and it was particularly difficult on cold wet days when the miserable sky above felt as if it was pressing down on Juliette with the sole intent to crush her. But the sun was out today and birds were twittering in the shrubs and gardens that fringed the cemetery. The roses were in full bloom and the rich clove and slightly peppery scent wafted on the gentle breeze.

Juliette walked towards her daughter's grave but, as she got closer, something caught her eye. There was a new teddy bear with a pink tulle tutu sitting propped up next to the marble headstone. She bent down and read the card that was attached to the teddy bear.

To my darling Emilia
Love you for ever, mio piccolo
Rest in peace
Papà

It was Joe's distinctive handwriting. The combination of English and Italian a touching tribute to their baby girl's heritage. He'd been here. Recently. He had visited Emilia's grave for the first time since her funeral.

He was here in England.

Juliette turned and scanned the graveyard for any sign of him but, apart from an older couple standing next to a grave several metres away, there was no one else here. Her shoulders slumped and she turned back to Emilia's grave and set about placing the flowers in the vase. Just because he was in England didn't mean he would seek her out.

What else could he say other than what he'd already said?

Then maybe I don't love you.

How those words had tortured her, bruised her, destroyed her hopes like noxious poison sprayed on a delicate bloom.

Juliette drove back to her flat in London with a heavy heart. It was all very well for her scientifically trained mother to insist she look at the evidence, but how could she survive another rejection?

She turned the corner into her street and saw a tall figure standing at her front door. Her heart gave a leap, her pulse thudded, her hopes rose. She tried to play it cool by parking her car with casual ease, even though she felt like banging and crashing into the cars before and aft in her haste to get to Joe.

She walked towards him with her expression as blank as she could muster but she could do nothing about the way her heart was thumping. 'Hello.' How stiff and formal she sounded. As if she was addressing a cold caller or doorstep salesperson.

'Can we talk inside?' Joe's tone was gruff, his expression guarded.

'Okay.' She unlocked her door and went in, conscious of his tall frame coming in behind her. The scent of his aftershave teasing her senses, her body reacting automatically. Wanting to touch him. Be held by him. Loved by him.

The door closed behind him and silence descended. A weighted silence.

'I saw the teddy bear,' Juliette said.

'Yes, I went there this morning.' He swallowed and continued in a fractured tone. '*Cara*, can you ever forgive me for how I've handled everything? I'm ashamed of how blind I've been to how I feel about you.'

Juliette took a steadying breath, not quite ready to let her hopes run free. 'How do you feel about me?'

He smiled and took her hands in his. 'My darling, I love you. I think I've loved you since the first night we met but I've been denying it, suppressing it or disguising it as something else. It was cruel of me to say I didn't love you back in Paris. I can never forgive myself for that. But I was so threatened by your desire to have another child. It made me shut down in a blind sort of panic.'

Could she believe him? Could she risk further heartbreak if she was wrong about his motives for being here?

'How do I know you mean it? You might be just saying it to get me to come back to you.'

His grip on her hands tightened as if he was worried she was going to pull away. 'I deserve your scepticism. The way I blocked any discussion about having another child was a knee-jerk reaction, sure, but it was unspeakably cruel to send you away as if I cared nothing. I love you with every beat of my heart. I can't imagine life without you by my side. It is no life without you. I'm a robot, a zombie like my father was when he lost my mother.'

'You're not just saying this because you want me back?'

'I'm saying it because it's true. I can't be who I'm meant to be without you. I never thought there was such a thing as a soulmate but I've realised you don't find a soulmate, you *become* one.' He squeezed her hands. 'I've become the man I want to be because of you. I didn't know I was capable of such depth of feeling.'

'Oh, Joe...' She blinked back tears. 'I'm so frightened I'm going to get hurt again. It was so hard losing both you and the baby.'

He brought one of her hands up to his mouth, his eyes holding hers in a tender lock. 'You're not going to lose me, *cara*. I will always be here for you, no matter what. I can't guarantee we won't lose another baby. No one can guarantee that, but what you can count on is this—I will be with you every step of whatever journey our lives take us on.'

Hope blossomed in her chest. 'So, are you saying you'd consider having another baby?'

He brought her closer, his eyes dark and tender, so full of love it made her heart turn over. 'I'll probably be a nervous wreck throughout your pregnancy, but it will be worth it if we are so lucky as to be blessed with a child. The thought of losing you like my father lost my mother haunts me. It haunted me from the start but when I visited my mother's grave the other day—'

'You visited her grave as well?'

Joe gave a rueful smile. 'It was long overdue but, yes, I did. It was strange. I didn't see it in the same way as I had as a teenager. I saw all those other graves—lives well lived, others cut tragically short—and I realised no one can guarantee you won't experience grief at some stage. Having another child will test me in ways I don't want to be tested. But it's part of being human to experience grief sooner or later. And being human, fully human, means being able to give and receive and openly express love.'

He stroked her face and looked deeply into her eyes.

'I love you so much. I can't bear the thought of spending however much time I have left on this planet without you by my side. I have already wasted too much of it without you. Come back to me, *tesoro mio*. Please?'

Juliette blinked back tears and flung her arms around his neck. 'I never want to be apart from you again. I love you. I've been so sad without you. So miserable and empty and lonely. But we can take our time having another baby. We don't have to rush into it.'

'We will try for another baby after we renew our wedding vows.'

Juliette blinked. 'You really want to do that?'

He grinned. 'Of course. We can even get Damon's cousin Celeste to organise it. It will be a celebration like no other. I'll give her carte blanche.'

Juliette gave a soft laugh. 'You don't have to do that. The simplest ceremony will do me. All I need to hear is you say the words and mean them.'

'I will love and honour and protect you until I take my last breath.' He brought his mouth down to hers in a lingering kiss that contained hope and love and healing. He drew back to gaze down at her once more. 'You have made me happier than I ever thought I could possibly be. I will always feel sad about our baby girl. Always—but that doesn't mean we can't build a wonderful life together. We will support each other during the bad times and celebrate the good ones.'

Juliette hugged him tightly, so full of love and joy it was hard to get her voice to work. 'I can't believe you actually love me. I still think I'm dreaming. That I will wake up and you won't be holding me like this—that I'll be alone again.'

Joe leaned down to kiss the tip of her nose. 'You're not dreaming, *cara mio*. I didn't know it was possible to love someone the way I love you. But if you need any more evidence...' He brought his mouth down to hers, his sexy smile sending a tickly sensation down her spine.

Juliette smiled and stood on tiptoe to meet his lips. 'I'm a big fan of evidence.'

EPILOGUE

April the fifth, the following year...

JOE CRADLED HIS newborn son in his arms and looked down at his beautiful but somewhat exhausted wife. After a mostly trouble-free pregnancy, Juliette had gone into labour the night before his birthday, and at ten minutes past midnight Alessandro Guiseppe Allegranza had been born.

'Isn't he gorgeous?' Juliette said, a dreamy expression on her face.

Joe rocked the little bundle in his arms, his heart feeling as if it was going to explode with love. 'He's amazing, like his mother.'

He stroked a careful finger over the minuscule face—the tiny button nose, the twin wisps of dark eyebrows, the soft downy black hair. It was a miracle to hold new life in his arms. A new life that repaired some of the pain of his own birth that had taken his mother from him. A new life that would help them move on from the loss of their first baby, Emilia. Not as a replacement—no child could ever be that—but as a new chance to experience all the joys and challenges of parenthood.

'Happy birthday, darling,' Juliette said, beaming.

Joe smiled so widely he thought his face would crack. 'I couldn't have asked for a better birthday present.' He looked down into his baby son's face. 'And you, little guy, couldn't have asked for a better mother.'

* * * * *

REVELATIONS
OF A SECRET
PRINCESS

ANNIE WEST

This story is dedicated to Agnès Caubert,
Fabiola Chenet and all the other special women
who make up Les Romantiques.

Thank you for your friendship!

Thank you too for your work in hosting the
wonderful Festival du Roman Féminin and for
always making this visiting Australian feel welcome.

CHAPTER ONE

CARO EMERGED FROM the café, huddling into her coat as the wind swirled around her ankles and bit her face. Funny that her skin could feel numb with cold while inside she was all churning heat. Nothing could extinguish that fire inside.

Except the possibility she might fail.

She faltered to a stop, grasping a lamp post with one gloved hand, fighting nausea.

Her head told her success was unlikely.

Her heart urged her on. Not with logic, but with desperate hope.

She'd never been courageous or adventurous. From infancy she'd been trained to do as she was told, never make waves or put herself forward. Her one attempt to break free and make her own decisions had been disastrous.

But that was years ago. She'd changed, reinventing herself in the aftermath of tragedy and pain. Caro might not be naturally intrepid but she was determined. She breathed deep, swallowing sharp, sustaining Alpine air. She'd do whatever it took now to succeed.

Caro looked up the street of the famous Swiss ski resort, ultra-exclusive with its astronomically high prices. Tourists gaped at the elegant shop windows, but they'd be gone by evening, driven away by the chic resort's unaffordability.

Up a nearby valley was one of the world's most iconic mountains. In the other direction lay her destination. Setting her jaw, she crunched over a dusting of late snow and got into her small rental car.

Twenty minutes later Caro nosed the car around a bend and emerged in a cleared space that hung partway up a mountain. The view was spectacular but she barely noticed.

She'd assumed she was driving to a ski lodge or an architect-designed home positioned for a multimillion-dollar vista. Instead she looked up at a wall of pale stone, a fairy-tale profusion of towers with steep, angular roofs. There was even a portcullis, raised to reveal a cobbled courtyard.

Caro stared at the centuries-old castle. This was no romantic ruin. It looked solid and meticulously maintained.

She'd known Jake Maynard was rich but he must have money to burn to live here. Her research told her he hadn't inherited it. His permanent home was in Australia.

She set her jaw. Caro had seen behind the scenes of the rich and famous and knew human frailties lurked there as they did everywhere. Wealth and overt luxury didn't awe her.

That was the one tiny advantage she had. Caro clung to it, feeling the nervous lurch of her stomach, tasting desperation on her tongue. Slowly she drove under the portcullis with its security camera, feeling each bump of the old cobblestones. Then she parked in the corner of the courtyard, next to a sleek, black vehicle.

It was only when she switched off the ignition and heard the silence thicken around her that she realised her hands shook.

Firming her lips, she reached for her purse, flicked a look in the mirror and pushed the door open.

She could do this.

She *would* do it.

Two lives depended on it.

'Ms Rivage is here.'

At the sound of his secretary's voice, Jake reluctantly looked up from behind his desk. Neil stood in the doorway, his expression bland.

Logic had urged Jake to excise this woman from the shortlist. She didn't have the experience of the front-running applicants. Yet one small detail in her application had caught Neil's eye, and Jake's. Small but vitally important. He raked a hand through his hair and told himself he'd give her fifteen minutes.

Neil stood aside and she walked in.

Jake felt his eyebrows channel down in a frown, his senses humming like the rigging on a yacht when a sudden wind rose. The nape of his neck prickled and his nostrils flared as if sensing…something.

She looked like a nanny straight from central casting. Yet at the same time not. He surveyed her plain skirt suit, scraped-back hair and apparent lack of make-up.

What was it about her that didn't fit? He'd learned to rely on his instincts and right now they sensed…something.

He got to his feet and walked around the desk, hand outstretched.

'Ms Rivage.'

His hand engulfed slim, soft fingers, yet her grip was firm as she returned his gesture. Most of the other applicants had non-existent handshakes. Either they'd simpered up at him, or were content to let him take the lead. This one looked him square in the eye.

But only for a moment. Then her brown gaze slewed from his and he knew she stifled anxiety.

Of course she's anxious. She's applying for a job. She must know her qualifications aren't impressive.

Yet his sixth sense tickled, telling him this was more than interview nerves.

'Please, Ms Rivage, take a seat.'

She nodded. 'Thank you, Mr Maynard.'

Her voice was deeper than he'd expected, with a husky resonance that teased an altogether earthier part of his consciousness. Perhaps it was the hint of an accent colouring her perfect English. But Jake had never been swayed by a sexy accent. Not unless it was accompanied by an equally sexy body.

Caro Rivage's body was hard to define behind the boxy jacket and skirt. She was tall in those heels, just half a head shorter than he, and her long legs were slender. She subsided into the chair with a grace that seemed at odds with the sombre suit. Brown clothes, brown eyes, dark, dull brown hair. She should look forgettable yet Jake found it hard to drag his gaze away.

Maybe it was the neat way she angled her ankles beneath her, accentuating an innate femininity that plain suit belied. Or the creamy skin that contrasted so startlingly with the dark suit.

Not completely pale. His gaze traversed her small, lush mouth and high cheekbones, both tinted the palest pink. Not, he'd swear, from make-up. This looked like the genuine article, a peaches and cream complexion, unblemished by the years of sun exposure he was used to seeing in his fellow Australians.

She shifted, her eyes lifting almost to his, then away, making Jake aware he was staring. The knowledge disturbed him. He wasn't interested in Ms Rivage's skin. Even if it looked as soft as a petal.

He pulled out his chair and sank into it, sprawling comfortably. Again that swift almost-stare from his guest before she looked down and smoothed her skirt.

Was she afraid of men?

But then she lifted her chin and their gazes collided. He felt the impact as a wave of heat.

Jake stared back, intrigued. What was this sensation? Attraction? Surely not for such a sparrow, even if she did have nice legs and an intriguing face. Suspicion?

Something about her made him cautious.

'Tell me about yourself, Ms Rivage.' He leaned back, elbows on the chair arms, and steepled his fingers under his chin.

* * *

Jake Maynard's voice was a delicious rumble that she felt like a burr of pleasure in her veins. Caro blinked, ordering herself not to be fanciful. She was immune to male charm—once bitten, twice shy. Yet even as the thought surfaced, she knew this man wasn't trying to charm. Despite the gesture of welcome and the barest hint of a welcoming smile, she sensed an intensity of purpose that made her pulse quicken.

Or maybe it was the laser-sharp keenness of his grey eyes beneath coal-black eyebrows. It made his eyes seem diamond bright and knowing, as if he saw beyond her carefully constructed appearance to those secrets she hoarded close.

It took everything she had not to shift in her seat or betray any other sign of weakness. Or break away from that glittering stare.

She drew a deep breath, conscious of the unfamiliar new suit, the pantyhose and heeled shoes that felt so different from the comfortable jeans, skirts and flat shoes she'd worn for the past few years.

The very act of putting on these clothes made her simultaneously grateful for the camouflage and unsettled by the reminder of her other life.

One black eyebrow climbed his broad forehead towards thick, ebony hair, reminding her he was waiting. With that hard but handsome face, powerful physique and enormous fortune Jake Maynard probably wasn't used to women making him wait.

The thought dampened the worst of Caro's nerves, helping her focus. She'd been distracted by the aura of strength emanating from him, courtesy of broad shoulders. By even features and that slash of a dimple in one cheek when he offered his half-smile. By his air of strength and dependability.

As if any man could be relied on!

She folded her hands and began. 'My application speaks for itself. I love working with children and I'm very good at it. As you'll see from my references.'

Her chin lifted as if anticipating an argument. Even now her father's habit of squashing her self-confidence had its effect. She expected Jake Maynard to disagree with her claim, though it was true.

For too long those cool eyes held hers, then his gaze fell to the papers before him. Caro's breath rushed out in relief. She'd have to do better than this if she were to convince him and win the job.

The possibility of being rejected was unthinkable. She bit her lip as he looked up, brows contracting as he read her features.

'You don't have formal qualifications.'

'A degree in early childhood education?' She shook her head. 'My experience is all hands on. But you'll see I've done a number of short courses on specific early learning issues.'

He didn't bother to check her application again, letting it fall to the desk. Caro's heart plunged with it. Surely that wasn't it? He wouldn't write her off so easily, not when he'd decided to interview her!

'I have to tell you the other short-listed applicants have both practical experience, years of it, plus excellent formal qualifications.'

There it was, the brush-off she'd feared. Nausea churned at the idea of being given her marching orders.

'Have you read my references? I believe you'll find them persuasive.'

He sat back further in his chair, as if getting comfortable while he watched her squirm. He didn't bother glancing at her application.

Maybe the contrast between his bronzed skin and the

dark jacket he wore teased her imagination, or perhaps it was his almost insulting air of indolence, but for a second Caro fancied something demonic in the knowing slant of those dark brows. Something fierce and compelling and totally at odds with this comfortable room full of old, leather-bound books.

'I'm supposed to be awed because one of your referees is a countess?' Had he memorised her application? Caro was surprised he recalled that level of detail. 'Unfortunately for you, Ms Rivage, I'm not swayed by an aristocratic title.'

His sneer rankled. Stephanie was a dear friend as well as a client. She'd given her reference in good faith. Caro sat taller, fixing her slouching interviewer with a stare.

'The key part of the reference is the description of my work, Mr Maynard, not my employer's title.'

Those straight eyebrows rose as if he was surprised at her response. Did he expect her to sit silently while he picked her application and her friends apart?

'Her son faced a range of difficulties when I began working with him. Together we made considerable progress.'

'You claim all his improvement was because of you?'

'No. It was a team effort that included some specialised programmes. But I was there with him every day, a major part of that.'

That might not sound as good as *I did it all myself*, but it was the truth.

No sign of approval on those stark features. Maybe that was how Jake Maynard looked while processing information—gaze sharp, brow frowning and mouth pursed. The expression emphasised the heavy planes of his jaw and the slant of his high cheekbones. He reminded Caro of a picture that had fascinated her as a child, of a medieval knight frowning in concentration as he pinioned a flailing dragon the size of small Shetland pony with his lance.

Her sympathies had always been with the little dragon.

'You think four or five years working as a nanny and preschool assistant make you the best person to look after my niece?'

She'd been wrong. The steely glint in his eyes was more condescending than the medieval knight who hung in a dark corner of the upstairs corridor. It reminded her of her father's chilly stare. The one that through her childhood had reduced her to apologetic silence.

That, as much as her desperation, stiffened Caro's spine.

Slowly she shifted position, sitting back in her seat and lifting one leg, crossing it over her other knee, feeling the slide of silky pantyhose. A flicker in that grey-eyed stare told her Jake Maynard noted the movement.

For some reason her chest constricted, as if the air turned thick and hard to breathe. She refused to let it show, instead adopting what she hoped was a relaxed pose.

'I can't speak about the other applicants, but if I'm given the opportunity I'll devote myself to your niece totally. You won't have any complaints.'

'That's a big claim.'

'But true. I know my capabilities, and my dedication.' In that at least she was absolutely the best person for the job.

Her stomach plunged. He didn't look impressed. Why should he? No doubt he had hordes of ultra-qualified specialists at his beck and call. The very real possibility of being ejected without a chance to prove herself seemed more likely by the moment. Then where would she be? What other opportunity would she have?

Caro re-crossed her legs. 'Clearly you were interested enough in my application to interview me.'

Her pulse thundered in her ears as she stifled fear at the prospect of failing. She'd known her chances were slim yet she'd obstinately clung to hope. This was her one opportunity to make things right. If Jake Maynard had any inkling of why she was really here she'd be out of the door before her feet touched the ground.

The thought flushed heat through her, eddying deep inside and burning her cheeks. Was his niece somewhere close even now?

'Perhaps I was interested in meeting a woman so confident despite her lack of solid credentials.'

Caro stiffened. His tone hadn't changed, hadn't even sharpened, but his words were like harpoons piercing soft flesh.

Fortunately it took more than words or dismissive stares to discomfit her these days.

'I'm sure, Mr Maynard, you wouldn't drag applicants out into the wilds of the Alps on a mere whim.'

At least she hoped so. Surely this interview meant she had a chance?

'Wilds?' He shook his head. 'You object to the location? The advertisement made it clear this is a live-in position.'

If he was looking for an excuse to reject her it wouldn't be that.

'No, I'm quite content to live in the country. In fact it's what I'm used to.'

Silvery eyes bored into hers and Caro looked back calmly. Her heart might be hammering an out-of-kilter tempo and her palms might be damp with nerves, but she wouldn't show it. Better to take the initiative.

'I understand your niece is from St Ancilla—'

'Who told you that?' He leaned forward abruptly, hands planted on the desk, as if ready to vault across the polished wood. Now she registered what his chilly expression had concealed. Protectiveness.

Maybe it was the innate caution of a wealthy, good-looking bachelor, a target for the paparazzi. Yet Caro sensed his protectiveness was for his niece. Caro warmed to him a little. She was glad the little girl had someone to stand up for her and keep her safe.

Out of nowhere emotion swept in, blindsiding Caro. It rose, a choking ball of heat in her throat, making her swallow convulsively. It roiled in her belly and prickled the backs of her eyes. If only she'd been stronger—

'Are you going to answer me?'

Caro blinked and met that searing stare, hating that moment of weakness. 'I did my research before applying for the position.'

For the first time since she'd walked into this room, Jake Maynard didn't look completely in control, despite his perfectly tailored clothes, his big desk and air of authority. 'That's not common knowledge.'

Fear rippled through her. Had she slipped up already? Her mind raced, thinking through what she'd said.

'It may not be common knowledge here, but in St Ancilla it's no secret.' She paused. 'The accident that killed her parents was reported by the local press.' When still he didn't say anything Caro continued. 'I'm very sorry for your loss. It must be a difficult time for you and your niece.'

Caro's heart squeezed. If her information was right, and she knew it was, little Ariane had been orphaned twice. Once as a newborn and then again a month ago when her adoptive parents died in a severe storm. The poor mite had had a rough start to life.

Caro was determined that the child's future would be brighter. In so many ways.

'And you somehow linked that small news item to my advertisement? I don't recall the St Ancillan press mentioning me.'

He sounded sceptical and she couldn't blame him. In fact he sounded downright suspicious.

That was the last thing Caro needed.

Jake Maynard was a self-made multibillionaire. You

didn't become a world-class financier without being clever and insightful, or by taking people at face value. Why had she ever thought this might be straightforward?

The answer was simple. Because she needed it to be.

She smoothed her hands over her skirt, buying time to conquer her emotions.

'A friend lives in that part of St Ancilla and happened to mention that you were now Ariane's guardian.' Caro paused, hearing the slight wobble in her voice as she said the little girl's name. Stupid to let emotion affect her now. She couldn't afford any sign of weakness. This man would pounce on it mercilessly. She looked straight at Jake Maynard and spread her hands in an open gesture. 'Later, when I saw your advertisement I put two and two together.'

'I see.' He leaned back again and she tried not to let her gaze drift to those imposing shoulders or that strong jaw. 'You do get around, don't you? First in St Ancilla, now in Switzerland.'

Why couldn't Jake Maynard be easy-going and friendly? Eager to employ a nanny from Ariane's island homeland in the Mediterranean?

Caro met his gaze with the polite smile she'd perfected as a child. The one her father had approved when she needed to look happy for the press.

She had no intention of admitting she only knew of Jake Maynard's search for a nanny because she'd been seeking a chance to meet Ariane. Let him think she was in Switzerland for some other reason.

'Fortunately both air travel and the Internet are available to many of us now, Mr Maynard.'

A hint of a smile turned up the corner of his mouth and for a second Caro saw a glimmer of appreciation in that hard gaze, making it look almost warm. The effect was startling.

She sucked in a slow breath, to her consternation feel-

ing her bra scratch flesh that suddenly felt oversensitive.
Deep inside flared a kernel of heat that had nothing to do
with nerves. It felt like feminine awareness.

Caro told herself she was imagining things. She was
immune to men.

'You think I should give you the job because you come
from the same country as my niece?'

She brushed her sleeve, giving herself a moment's re-
spite from that searching gaze.

'I think it's useful that I speak the language and understand the culture. Such things are comforting, especially
at a time of loss.' She paused. 'Even if she's not going to
live there, there's a strong argument for her keeping her
native language.'

Slowly he inclined his head, as if reluctant to agree.
'Frankly that's the only reason you're here, Ms Rivage.
Because Ariane needs someone who can speak Ancillan
as well as English. She's lost her parents but I don't want
her to lose her heritage too.'

His voice hit a gravel note and something shifted inside
her. For the first time since Caro entered this imposing li-
brary she felt real sympathy for the man before her. His
expression hadn't altered yet that tiny crack in his voice
hinted at deep-buried grief.

He might remind her of a sexy fallen angel with that
blatantly raw masculinity and a simmering impatience that
bordered on arrogance, but he'd recently lost his sister and
brother-in-law. Plus inherited responsibility for his niece.

He probably wasn't at his best.

'I have some experience of dealing with loss, Mr Maynard. If you give me the chance I'll do everything I can to
support your niece and help her thrive.'

His eyes held hers and for the first time she sensed he
wasn't quite so negative. Was it wishful thinking?

She didn't have a chance to find out for there was a tap on the door and it swung open.

'Sorry to interrupt, Jake, Ms Rivage.' It was the secretary, Neil Tompkins, who'd escorted her upstairs. 'There's a call I really think you need to take. The Geneva consortium.'

Jake Maynard pushed his chair back. 'My apologies, Ms Rivage. This is bad timing but it's crucial I take this.'

Even so, Caro gave him credit, he didn't simply march out, but waited for her response.

'Of course, Mr Maynard.'

'I won't keep you long.' Then the pair disappeared, the studded oak door closing behind them.

Caro shot to her feet as if from a catapult. Sitting under that icy scrutiny had taken its toll. Leaving her bag beside her chair, she paced the room, drawn to the incredible vista of snowy mountains, so different from her Mediterranean home.

Her mind raced through what he'd said and how she'd responded. What she could have said better. What she could say to sway him on his return.

If the other applicants were so much more experienced it was unlikely he'd entrust his precious niece to her. On the other hand, Ancillan wasn't a common language. Its origins were ancient, with roots in classical Greek and even, the linguists thought, Phoenician, but influenced over the centuries by trade and conquest so it had traces of Italian, Arabic and even Viking borrowings. If she was the only applicant who could speak it she had a chance.

The door banged open and Caro swung around. But it wasn't Jake Maynard who entered, nor was it the door to his secretary's office that stood open. It was a door on the other side of the room.

In front of it, poised as if in mid-flight, was a small, dishevelled figure. Her frilly dress was rumpled and her plaits were half undone so her head was surrounded by a bright bronze nimbus of curls.

Caro's heart stopped.

She breathed. She must have, for she didn't black out. But she couldn't move.

Memory swamped her as the little girl turned a tear-stained face and drowned violet eyes met hers.

Caro felt a trembling begin in the soles of her feet and work its way up her legs to her hands and belly. She swallowed then swallowed again, unable to moisten her suddenly arid mouth.

She'd struggled, hoped and prayed for this moment. But nothing had prepared her for the raw shock of reality.

Those eyes. That hair.

She was thrown back in time to her own childhood. To the only person in the world who'd ever loved her. To gentle hands, tender words and a thick mass of curls of the same distinctive burnished bronze.

'Where's Uncle Jake?'

The little girl's words dragged Caro back to the present. She tried to smile but her mouth trembled too much. Her knees gave way and she sank onto the padded window seat, her hand pressed to her middle as if to still the tumult inside.

'He'll be back in a minute.' Her voice was barely audible, rough with emotion.

The girl's eyes widened. 'You speak like me!'

Caro hadn't realised she'd spoken Ancillan.

Then the girl she'd come all this way to find, the girl she hadn't known about till a few weeks ago, slowly crossed the room towards her.

Caro went hot then cold as relief, disbelief and wonder hit. She was torn between the urge to grin and the need to sob.

Or to gather Ariane close and never let her go.

CHAPTER TWO

OBLIVIOUS TO HER distress, Ariane stopped before her and held up a teddy bear that looked worn and well loved.

'Maxim's arm came off.' Her bottom lip trembled as she held up the separated limb. 'Can you fix him?'

It took Caro a moment to follow her words. She was so busy taking in the heart-shaped face, wide eyes and smattering of tiny freckles across that little nose.

Despite all the evidence Caro had told herself it was possible there'd been a mistake. Things like this—long-lost relatives and scandalous secrets—didn't happen in the real world.

But face to face with Ariane, doubt disintegrated. Those eyes, that hair, even the shy, questioning tilt of the head, were unmistakeable. Was it possible for a child to inherit a gesture, a way of holding themselves, if they'd never spent time with their birth family?

The impossible was real. Real and here before her.

Searing emotion smacked Caro in the chest. She gulped a noisy breath, unable to fill straining lungs. Her eyes filled—her first tears in years.

Instantly the little girl backed away.

That was possibly the only thing that could have helped Caro get a grip, the sight of Ariane retreating.

From somewhere Caro conjured a wobbly smile.

'I'm sorry. I didn't mean to scare you.' She lifted a hand to her eye, blinking back the unshed tears. 'I think I had something in my eye. Now, tell me about your bear. He's called Maxim?'

Ariane nodded but kept her distance.

'That's a fine name.' Caro resisted the urge to move

closer. She'd already upset the poor kid with her tears. It would do no good to rush this, though instinct urged her to wrap her arms around the child and hold her tight. 'Did you know there was once a king called Maxim? He was very brave. He fought off the pirates who tried to invade St Ancilla.'

Ariane took a step nearer. 'That's where I come from.' She tilted her head. 'Are you from there too?'

'I am.' Caro let her smile widen. She'd never allowed herself to imagine having this conversation, as if it might tempt fate into obliterating all her hopes.

This was a bittersweet moment. Sweet because after all the grief and years of emptiness, Caro had found the girl she hadn't known about. Bitter because of those wasted years.

But there was no time for dwelling on past wrongs. Suddenly Caro had never felt more alive, more brimming with excitement.

'What happened to Maxim? Was he in a battle with pirates too?'

Ariane smiled and Caro felt it like a dart of sunshine piercing her heart. 'No, silly. There aren't really pirates.'

'Aren't there?' Caro stared at the bright face with the dimpling cheeks and felt her insides melt.

Ariane shook her head. 'No. Uncle Jake said so.'

'Ah, I see.'

'So don't be scared if you dream about them. They're not real.'

'That's good to know. Thank you.'

Did that mean Ariane often had nightmares? Again Caro resisted the impulse to gather her close.

Ariane tilted her head, clearly curious. 'Who are you? You look…' her forehead scrunched in concentration '… like someone I know.'

Caro's heart thudded high in her throat. 'Do I? Who do I look like?'

She shook her head. 'I don't know.'

Caro drew in a slow breath, reminding herself Ariane was a little girl. She imagined Caro was familiar, possibly because they were from the same place. Maybe speaking Ancillan made her seem familiar. There was no more to it. Anything else was impossible, even if Caro felt the connection between them as a tangible bond.

'What happened to Maxim if he wasn't fighting pirates?'

Ariane pouted. 'I don't know. I woke up and he was like this.'

Caro eyed the bear, with its fur rubbed off on one side where he'd clearly been cuddled a lot. She'd guess Ariane usually held him by that arm and the stitching had given way after much use.

'That's easily fixed.'

'It is?'

'Of course. All we need is a needle and thread to sew him back together.'

Ariane stepped closer and held out the brown bear and his separated arm. 'Can you fix him now? Please?'

Those huge eyes in that grave little face would make any heart melt. As for Caro, it took everything she had to keep things light.

'I don't have any thread with me but we can patch him up till we get some.'

'Patch him?'

'Yes. If you get my bag from near the desk I'll see what I can do.' Because even now her knees felt too wobbly to take her weight.

She watched the girl dart across the room. Obviously Maxim was a much-loved bear. Who'd given it to her? Her parents? Her Uncle Jake?

Caro thought of the self-contained man who'd interrogated her across the desk and tried to imagine him with this

precious little girl. She couldn't conjure the image, but that
didn't mean he didn't care. He was protective of Ariane.

'Here.' She held out Caro's capacious bag.

'Thank you.' Caro barely stopped herself calling the
child by her name. 'My name is Caro. Can you say that?'

'Caro. That's easy.'

'And what's your name?'

'Ariane.'

'What a pretty name.'

'My daddy said he and Mummy picked it because I was
so pretty.' Those big eyes filled with tears and Ariane's
chin wobbled.

Caro's excitement shattered, her insides curdling. Ariane had lost her parents. She was grieving.

'I can see that,' Caro said slowly as she reached for her
bag and began to rummage in it. 'I know some girls in St
Ancilla who are called Ariane. They're named for a famous
lady. She was very pretty, but more importantly she was
kind and brave too.'

'She was?' Ariane blinked up at her, diverted.

'Oh, yes. She lived a long time ago before there were
good hospitals and medicines. When all the people were
very sick from a bad illness the lords and ladies shut themselves away because they were afraid they would get sick
too. But Ariane came out of her castle and visited the poor
people. She made sure they had food and clean water and
helped them get better.'

'I want to be like her. I want to help.'

'Well,' Caro said slowly, withdrawing a scarf from her
bag, 'you can get some practice now, helping Maxim. Here.
Can you hold his arm like this?'

Ariane nodded and stood by Caro's knee, head bent as
she concentrated on holding the bear and his arm in just
the right way. Caro felt the brush of her soft little hand. A
flutter of sensation rippled up Caro's arm, arrowing to her

heart. She tugged in a tremulous breath and focused on fashioning the scarf into a sling.

There'd be time for emotion later, when she was alone. She couldn't give in to it now. That would be self-indulgent, besides scaring a child who knew her only as a stranger.

But as Caro knotted the scarf, her attention wasn't on the bear but on Ariane, whose world had been ripped apart. Who needed stability, kindness and above all love.

Caro vowed that, whatever it took, she would be the one to provide that.

Jake stood in the doorway, watching the pair with their heads bent over the teddy bear.

There was nothing especially arresting about the sight. Yet there was something about the woman and the girl together that hit him like a fist to the ribs.

Because it should have been his sister Connie here with Ariane?

Jake released a slow breath from searing lungs.

That went without saying. He'd give everything he had to see Connie here, alive and well. But this skitter of preternatural awareness didn't spring from loss. Or not loss alone.

What was it about this pair that stopped him in his tracks?

They spoke Ancillan so he didn't understand their conversation. Yet he'd understood Ariane's sadness and the way Caro Rivage had directed the conversation, allaying the tears he'd seen brim in his niece's eyes.

His confidence in this woman as a potential nanny soared. Anyone who could make Ariane smile these days was good in his book. He liked Ms Rivage's sensitivity, the deft way she'd handled what looked like a fraught moment.

Not that he was ready to give her the job. Her qualifications were laughably light compared with some of the experts who'd worked in the field for decades.

Jake frowned, watching her wind something around the teddy's arm, murmuring to Ariane.

There was something there he couldn't put his finger on. Some...similarity between them. His nape prickled as instinct stirred.

It wasn't their colouring. Ariane's was vibrant whereas Caro Rivage had dull brown hair and dark brown eyes. Ariane's face was heart-shaped and Caro Rivage's was oval. Yet the slanting set of their eyes looked similar and maybe something around the shape of the nose.

He shook his head as his brain cleared. There *was* no link. It was merely the way they worked together, both intent, both speaking Ancillan. He imagined things.

For some reason his sixth sense had worked overtime ever since Caro Rivage arrived. So much that after the phone call he'd checked her application again at Neil's desk, looking for anomalies. But there was nothing that didn't fit. The references and qualifications of all the shortlisted applicants, including Ms Rivage, had already been checked.

His first assessment had been right. She was ordinary, not outstanding.

Jake always chose outstanding. He didn't have time for ordinary. That was how he'd built his business and his personal fortune, through excellence. Yet he couldn't stifle the idea that perhaps it wasn't outstanding Ariane needed but someone ordinary. Someone to help her grope her way back to normalcy after her trauma.

He frowned. That was crazy. He wanted the best for Ariane.

Jake ploughed his fingers through his hair. Maybe he was oversensitive when it came to choosing Ariane's nanny. This wasn't like his usual decisions. Then there was nothing at risk but money, albeit lots of it.

Where his niece was concerned, Jake refused to take risks. She'd been through enough. He thought of his sister and brother-in-law's car, crushed almost to nothing by a massive tree brought down in a storm. It was a miracle Ariane had survived when her parents died.

He owed it to her and Connie to keep her safe.

He stepped into the room. Instantly the woman in brown jerked her head up, those impenetrable eyes locking on his.

What was it about her that made his hackles rise?

Clearly, despite her apparent absorption in the child, she was attuned to his presence. Jake didn't know whether that was good or suspicious.

Or maybe, the idea surfaced again as their eyes held and his chest expanded on a deep breath, it wasn't suspicion tugging at him. Could it be attraction?

Jake dismissed the idea. Caro Rivage might have fine features and a certain understated elegance, and poise... definitely poise. But Jake preferred more in his women. Eye-catching beauty and scintillating personalities for starters. Jake didn't date dull sparrows.

Nor did he mix work and pleasure. No dating the staff.

He stopped before them, jaw firming. She wasn't staff. Not yet. Probably never.

'What happened to Maxim? Is he okay?'

Ariane looked up and he caught a fleeting smile. His niece was pleased to see him, even if not pleased enough to hug him. He stifled a pang of regret.

He couldn't blame her. He was still almost a stranger. His trips to St Ancilla hadn't been frequent and though he'd stayed with Connie and her family, he'd usually worked during the day when Ariane was awake.

'His arm came off. But Caro can fix him. We need...' She turned to the woman.

'Thread. Wool to sew his arm on.'

Ariane nodded. 'Wool. Do you have wool, Uncle Jake? Please? Then we can make him better.' Pleading eyes turned to him and Jake felt that familiar stab of discomfort.

It was crazy that he should be responsible for this needy child. What she required was someone who knew how to care for her. Someone who could fill the gaps he, with his lack of experience, couldn't.

'I'm sure we can rustle some up.' He hunkered near his niece, enjoying the way she smiled back, clearly delighted with his news.

What he hadn't counted on was discovering the surprisingly rich scent of the woman holding Ariane's teddy bear. Jake's nostrils flared as a hint of her warm, spicy fragrance reached him. It was the perfume of a sensual woman, not heavy but far more intriguing than the predictable floral scent he'd have expected of a prim sparrow. He inhaled deeply then wished he hadn't as his sense receptors shuddered into awareness.

Jake shot a look at her under lowered brows but she avoided his gaze.

Because she felt that jag of awareness too?

Grimly he yanked his brain back to order. There *was* no awareness.

'I'll call Lotte and we'll see if she has any wool, shall we?' The ever-efficient housekeeper would have some, or be able to acquire it.

'And a needle please, preferably a large one.'

Up close Caro Rivage's husky voice sounded surprisingly sensual. Was she trying to entice him into giving her the job? She was in for a rude awakening if she thought he'd be swayed by a sexy voice.

Yet once more when he looked she was all but ignoring him. Instead she smiled at Ariane as she put the teddy into the little girl's arms.

Jake stared, amazed at how that smile turned this passably pleasant-looking woman into someone almost…stunning. The joy in her expression could be bottled and sold as a tonic.

As if sensing his stare, she darted a glance at him then away, fussing over the sling she'd arranged.

'Please, Uncle Jake. Can you ask now?'

'Of course.' He got up and called Lotte on the house phone. The interview had been derailed by Ariane and her damaged bear. But perhaps that was a good thing. Despite requiring the best qualified person, he also had to find someone caring. Someone Ariane could relate to.

As he watched the two females together it seemed as if he'd found just that. Or, he amended, someone who could put on a good initial show but who might not have the depth of experience Ariane needed. The thought loosened the ribbon of tension tightening around his gut.

He didn't *want* to give Caro Rivage the job.

Yet there was no denying Ariane liked her. He owed it to his niece to give the woman a chance, despite his doubts. Without a solid reason to reject her she deserved that much.

Ariane spoke again.

'Can you speak English, Ariane?' that throaty voice asked. 'I don't think your uncle understands Ancillan and it's not nice to exclude him.'

Spoken like a true governess. As if he cared. He was just glad to hear Ariane sound so animated after weeks of being withdrawn and teary.

'Exclude?'

'It means to shut someone out so they feel all alone. It's not a friendly thing to do. You don't want to hurt your uncle's feelings, do you?'

Ariane shook her head yet she looked unhappy. 'But I like talking with you. It's like being home, talking with my...' Her mouth clamped shut and her little chin wobbled and Jake wanted to tell her he didn't give a damn what language she spoke. He hated it when she withdrew into that grief-stricken bubble where he had trouble reaching her.

He opened his mouth but Caro Rivage spoke first. 'Of course you want to speak Ancillan. I'm sure you'll soon be able to do that a lot.'

'With you?'

Jake's heart cramped as he looked into that woebegone little face.

'We'll have to see, won't we?' Full marks to Ms Rivage for not playing on Ariane's desperation to make promises she couldn't keep. She turned to the opening door. 'Now, is this Lotte?'

Jake crossed his arms and leaned against the desk to watch proceedings. As expected, Lotte had wool in several colours, plus needles and scissors. The housekeeper reached for Maxim, offering to sew him better, but she was forestalled by Ariane, who insisted Caro do it.

He saw the women's gazes meet, assessing and something more. Caro asked permission to use Lotte's supplies, then sought a second opinion on the choice of colour and needle size. By the time the two had discussed possible stitches and the need to reinforce Maxim's other arm, the women were firm allies.

Silently Jake applauded Caro Rivage. She knew she trod on the housekeeper's territory and had adroitly co-opted her as an ally rather than a rival. Lotte fretted over Ariane like a broody hen with a single chick yet now she smiled and nodded, praising the newcomer's stitching and telling Ariane that Maxim would be as good as new.

Caro Rivage was a smooth operator, able to read people's sensitivities.

Was that what she tried to do with him? Were those downcast eyes a ploy to make her seem the ideal nanny?

But she'd met his gaze steadily when she had to. He sensed she really was nervous, despite her show of calm. Clearly she wanted this job badly.

Was she broke? Her clothes looked new if unremarkable.

Maybe she wanted the kudos of working for him. A stint in his employ would open any door to her.

The idea eased his tension. Why shouldn't she want the job? This vague sense of something askew dissipated. The woman checked out. She had no criminal record and her references were good.

'Maxim looks as good as new,' he murmured when she cut the thread and handed the bear to a grinning Ariane.

'Thank you, Caro!'

Jake thought Ariane might even hug the newcomer, but instead she cuddled the toy while Lotte looked on, beaming from ear to ear.

Jake cleared his throat. 'Perhaps, Lotte, you could take Ariane for a snack while Ms Rivage and I conclude our business?'

It took some doing as Ariane didn't want to leave but finally they were alone. He watched Caro get to her feet. Her hands twisted together before she seemed to collect herself and let them fall to her sides. Her eyes met his and once more he felt the curious blankness of that dark-eyed stare. It struck him that when she was in control of herself she gave little away.

Jake was torn between annoyance and admiration.

'Shall I sit by the desk again?' She gestured to where she'd faced him across the expanse of glossy wood.

'No, Ms Rivage.' That deep voice rippled across her skin. 'The interview is over.'

Just like that dismay slammed into her. Her belly knotted with nausea. Caro flexed her fingers then linked them behind her back rather than press them to her roiling abdomen.

He couldn't dismiss her so quickly! They'd barely begun to talk when they'd been interrupted.

'I believe you should reconsider, Mr Maynard.' There.

Her voice was even, though a little hoarse. Amazing what desperation could do.

'Reconsider? You haven't heard what I have in mind.'

Amusement sparked in his cool, grey eyes as if delighting in her discomfort.

Outrage filled her. She'd been the butt of her family's amusement so often as a child that it grated. Because she was shy. Because she looked different. Because she didn't fit with the rest of them.

Okay, it was mainly her stepmother rather than her half-brothers who'd made her feel an outsider, but the wounds carved deep. Especially as her father had merely raised his eyebrows and told her not to be sensitive.

Caro planted her feet more firmly and met Jake Maynard's sparkling gaze with one of her own. 'Perhaps you'd like to inform me what you *do* have in mind?'

Her tone would have done her father proud. Cool, composed and superior. She saw Jake Maynard's eyes widen then narrow suspiciously but she refused to back down. This was too important. This meant everything.

'I had in mind to invite you to stay overnight. To give you a trial period with my niece.'

Caro felt the air whoosh from her lungs, leaving her gasping for breath. Only years of training at projecting the right image kept her on her feet, for her knees trembled like leaves in a gale. Her heart jammed up in her throat and there was a roaring in her ears, blocking out the rest of his words. She saw him speak, tried to focus and heard something about this not being a promise of employment.

'Well, Ms Rivage? You haven't said anything. Does that mean you're not prepared to stay?'

Caro shook her head, buying time while she found her voice. 'No, Mr Maynard, it doesn't mean that at all. I'll happily stay tonight and get to know Ariane.'

'Good.' He nodded but didn't smile. In fact he didn't look happy at all, though he was getting his own way.

Perhaps he was so used to everyone jumping to do his bidding he didn't consider how inconvenient it might be for a job applicant to make an unscheduled overnight stay. Fortunately Caro had the suitcase she'd brought to Switzerland in the car downstairs.

'Very well. I'll have my secretary draw up a simple agreement to cover us both in the event of any accident or liability during your stay.'

He really was a businessman through and through. Caro wouldn't have thought of that. But then she was in such a whirl she was barely capable of digesting what he'd said.

She watched him walk out of the door, heard the murmur of male voices in the outer room and reached out a hand to anchor herself. Her fingers clutched fabric and she blinked. She was grabbing the thick curtain as if it were all that kept her upright.

Caro sank onto the window seat, reeling. She felt hot and cold, anxious yet ecstatic.

She had a chance.

A chance to be with Ariane.

Her long-lost daughter.

CHAPTER THREE

'No, NO, EVERYTHING's under control, Mr Maynard. The young lady is excellent with her. It's good to see your niece smiling.' Jake heard the relief in Lotte's voice over the house phone.

Because, with a temporary nanny here, she had time to get on with her own work uninterrupted? No, that wasn't fair. Lotte had a soft spot for Ariane. He knew she was pleased to see the little girl happy.

As he was. Even if he wished Ariane responded as enthusiastically to him as she did to this stranger she'd only known a few hours.

Catching his thoughts, Jake scowled. He wasn't jealous. The idea was preposterous. He thanked Lotte and hung up.

'Dramas?' Neil looked up from his laptop.

'Apparently not.'

His secretary nodded. 'I thought so. I had a hunch about her—'

'So you said. But you'll forgive me if I refuse to rely on hunches where Ariane's concerned.'

Jake wanted solid evidence that the woman would be good for his niece. A couple of hours keeping her content wasn't enough to tip the scales in her favour. Not against the other applicants.

'You don't like her?'

Put that bluntly, Jake felt almost ashamed to realise he *wanted* Caro Rivage to fail. Because of some inexplicable hunch of his own.

He shook his head. He trusted his instinct. It had saved his life in his long-ago army days. Listening to it had proved invaluable since moving into finance too, where sometimes the truth behind a too attractive investment could have sunk him if he hadn't raised questions.

'I'm reserving judgement.'

He told himself it was true. He summed up people quickly, not having time to waste. But with this woman he found himself still guessing. Perhaps his inability to read her made him suspicious?

Usually women were easily read. They liked his money, his power, his body, or perhaps all three.

Jake's mouth twisted. How had he ever thought Fiona, his last lover, different? Because she'd lasted longer? It wasn't much of a recommendation. He didn't miss her and felt a judder of distaste when he thought of her. Her attitude to Ariane had sealed her fate. Now she was back in England with her privileged friends or perhaps cruising the Riviera, searching for his replacement.

Amazing that he'd considered even for a second being with her long term. Her double-barrelled surname and cut-glass accent, her knack of knowing anyone who was anyone at society events, should have pressed every hot button. He despised trust fund hangers on, expecting life to give them what they wanted. But she'd seemed so natural, down to earth and appealing. He'd been blinded by her quick mind, sense of humour and great sex.

Maybe his sister had been right and he'd begun to hanker after more than casual affairs. Fiona had been on the same page with that. She'd had the nerve to talk about Ariane being an unnecessary encumbrance when he, they, started a family.

The Honourable Fiona Petrie-Mathieson was a snob. Instead of helping when he found himself responsible for a grieving child, his lover had focused on the fact Ariane was adopted. She'd called her an anonymous baby, saying she could have been anyone's. The Honourable Fiona didn't want to pollute herself with ties to a child who didn't come from class or money. She'd suggested Ariane would be better with others of *her sort*, at an orphanage school Fiona *happened* to hear about.

As if Ariane weren't his sister's child and his only living family.

'No need to look so fierce, boss.' Neil raised his hands in mock surrender.

'Have I been giving you a tough time?' Jake leaned back and raised one eyebrow.

His secretary grinned. 'On a scale of ten? Let me think…'

Jake grunted out a laugh. They'd worked together for years. Neil could take anything he dished out and was no pushover. He also had a quick, analytical brain.

'Do *you* like her?'

'I told you she'd be good for the job.'

'Not what I asked. Do you *like* her? Trust her?'

Neil's amusement faded. 'You really *are* concerned!' He paused. 'I've barely spoken to her. She seemed…nice. Trying not to show she was nervous while she waited for the interview. But I felt she was genuine, not ignoring me because I'm a lackey nor buttering me up for information about you. And she has a sweet smile.'

Jake shook his head. 'A sweet smile? Good thing I'm hiring the nanny, not you.'

Neil shrugged. 'You asked. I like her better than the one with two Masters Degrees. That one might know the theories of child development but I'm not sure she'd cope with a carsick kid.'

Jake thought of that eye-opening car trip through the Alps when he discovered Ariane didn't travel well.

'You have a point.' He shoved his chair back. 'I'll leave you to finish up. I'm going to check on this would-be nanny.'

Jake was at the door when Neil spoke. 'There was one

other thing I noticed about Ms Rivage.' He turned and
caught the gleam in his secretary's eyes. 'She has spectacular legs.'

Those legs were on display when Jake reached Ariane's
playroom. Rugs lined the floor and padded window seats
held bright cushions and dolls. But it wasn't Ariane or her
room that snared his attention. It was Caro Rivage standing
on a small stool, arms raised above her head as she reached
for something on a high shelf.

Neil was right. She had spectacular legs. Fabulous legs.

She'd taken off her shoes and stood on tiptoe, the stance
accentuating the fine curve of her calf. She'd removed her
jacket. Jake saw it draped over the back of a nearby chair.
Her white blouse strained over her breasts.

Something dug into his belly, grabbing tight. His nostrils
flared on a quick inhale. His gaze tracked down to her toes
and up over the loosely fitted skirt to a lithe torso revealed
by that taut blouse. Then up the long, feminine arch of her
tilted neck to her bundled-up hair.

Jake's breath expelled in a rush that left him almost
light-headed.

Stripped of her conservative shoes and unflattering
jacket, Caro Rivage was slim, svelte, feminine and intriguing. A different sort of intriguing from the way he'd
viewed her earlier.

Except Jake knew that was a lie. Despite her prim pose
and drab clothes, he'd been aware from the first of this
woman's magnetism. It was a sly thing. Not overt like Fiona's blonde beauty and overtly sexy curves.

Even as he'd catalogued and dismissed Caro Rivage's
expertise, at another level, that of primitive male, he'd been
aware of the attractive woman behind the pursed lips and
downcast eyes.

Heat drilled down from his temples to his gut, boring straight to his groin.

Did this explain his resistance? Was it why he didn't want to employ her? Because he responded to her as a man to a woman, not a boss to a governess?

He sucked air into tight lungs. Business and pleasure didn't mix. He had no intention of beginning anything personal with a staff member.

After Fiona he'd found it easy to avoid the charms of the opposite sex. Except, to his horrified fascination, he realised sex was the operative word here.

Caro Rivage bit her lip, shifted her hips in a way that shouldn't be in the least provocative yet turned up his inner thermostat from hot to scorching. The tug of desire dragging at his groin told its own story. It wasn't one he wanted to hear.

But Jake prided himself on facing facts.

She wasn't gorgeous like the women he dated. She wasn't his type. He hadn't decided if he could trust her, yet he was attracted.

Urgently attracted.

Worse, he felt compelled to give her a chance despite his better judgement because his niece showed every sign of bonding with her. That rankled. Jake made a point of being the one to dictate terms. He didn't take kindly to being forced into decisions. But little Ariane had held herself aloof from everyone except her teddy since the accident that killed her parents. Seeing her shy excitement with Caro Rivage was a profound relief. It was the first time she'd smiled properly in a month.

What option did he have but to give this nanny a chance?

She expelled an exasperated breath that puffed up the strands of brown hair drifting free of her brutally neat bun. She looked ruffled and pink-cheeked and Jake knew a growing curiosity to see her flushed and rumpled for other reasons.

'Can I help with that, Ms Rivage?' His voice hit a resonant baritone note that betrayed the trend of his thoughts. He could only hope she wasn't as adept at reading men as she was little kids.

His deep voice came out of nowhere, lassoing her around the middle and drawing her off balance. Caro teetered on her toes, arms windmilling, then warmth enveloped her. Hard warmth that wound around her and held her steady.

She registered a broad palm and long fingers splayed across her hip bone. A solid body, all heat against hers, and near her breasts a head of tousled dark hair.

She hauled in a shocked breath and wished she hadn't. This close she could smell Jake Maynard's skin, warm and scented with bergamot and citrus. Her eyes sneaked shut for a self-indulgent moment, enjoying that fresh, masculine tang.

He was Ariane's uncle. A potential employer. An obstacle to be overcome. She couldn't think of him as a desirable man.

She hadn't considered any man in that way for years. Not since she'd been blindsided by Mike's smiling attentiveness, then gutted by his betrayal.

Reluctantly she looked down to Jake Maynard standing with his head a whisper away from her breasts. Dark brows contracted over brilliant grey eyes that no longer looked icy. Instead they reminded her of the heat haze she'd seen rising over boiling geothermal pools in Iceland. Heat drenched her skin and sank into her bones.

Still she shivered.

'You can let go. I'm not going to fall.'

She wondered if he heard her, though his gaze was anchored to her face.

'Even so. I'll get whatever you need. I'd rather you didn't take a tumble.'

His voice was brisk, his movements quick as he lifted her off the stool. Yet when he'd swung her to the floor he took his time releasing her. Caro was inordinately conscious of the weight and size of those hands. Of his tall frame, close enough to lean into. Of the tendril of beckoning male scent in her nostrils.

She stepped back smartly and he dropped his hold.

Belatedly she looked at Ariane, who'd turned back to the puzzle on the floor. Was it just Caro who felt the air thicken and clog when Jake Maynard was around? It must only have been seconds since he strode into the room yet it felt as if time had spun out far longer.

Panic whispered through her but she conquered it. She was stronger than this. No man would derail her plans.

'Thank you, Mr Maynard.' She pointed to the top shelf. 'There's a puzzle we wanted to try. If you could reach that one I'd be grateful.'

Of course he grabbed it easily, as she would have if he hadn't taken her by surprise.

'You like puzzles, Ariane?' Instead of handing it to Caro he crouched next to his niece. Caro registered the tautness in his folded frame as he waited for Ariane's response, and the ease of tension when she nodded and whispered that yes, she liked puzzles.

That was when Caro guessed some of his diamond-bright hardness might be down to something other than a demanding nature and a short temper.

Was he worried about Ariane? His movements as he settled himself beside the little girl were ostensibly easy, yet Caro saw how carefully he moved, as if not wanting to spook her. And though Ariane didn't move away, nor did she lean against his big frame. She didn't burrow close for reassurance as would be natural if she relished the comfort of a beloved uncle.

What was Jake Maynard's relationship with his niece?

As Caro put away the footstool and tidied a few toys, she observed them. Both were wary, treating each other with the politeness of strangers.

Caro huffed out a relieved breath. At least Ariane wasn't afraid of her uncle. If she had been... Well, she didn't know what she'd have done but she wouldn't have been able to watch without taking action.

The urge to declare herself and her relationship with Ariane was almost overwhelming.

Caro imagined announcing the truth, at which point little Ariane would fling herself into her waiting arms and it would be as if they'd never been apart.

Then what? Jake Maynard would simply relinquish his niece to her care?

She didn't even have to look at the obstinate angle of his jaw to know that wouldn't happen.

It was a nice fantasy but it would never be that easy. Announcing the truth would be complicated, especially since she had no intention of letting Ariane be taken from her again.

If she declared herself now she'd upset Ariane, who wouldn't understand why a strange woman claimed to be her mum. Plus she'd infuriate Jake Maynard who'd chuck her out of his castle before she could draw a second breath.

He'd think her mad.

Even if he didn't, if by some miracle she managed to convince him, he wouldn't let her stay. She'd seen his distrust and his protectiveness of his niece. If he had an inkling of the truth, she doubted she'd see Ariane again till they'd been through the mill of lawyers and courts. That could take years.

Caro pinched the bridge of her nose, tasting the rust tang of blood where she'd bitten her cheek.

She should have made a plan before coming here. A sensible plan with actions ready for every contingency. Instead, when she got this opportunity she'd sped here, needing to see Ariane.

Though it went against every instinct, Caro had to be patient. To wait, gain Ariane's trust and her uncle's. To work out how best to approach this.

Even if Jake Maynard didn't have a close relationship with Ariane, he cared for her. Caro guessed she was only here now because she and Ariane had connected. Not, she sternly told herself, because of their blood ties, but because they shared a common language.

It was ridiculous to think Ariane sensed their link though to Caro it was so blatant, so strong, she almost expected a fanfare and bright lights, as if a contestant on a TV show had won a fortune.

Abruptly the enormity of the situation hit her in slicing blows to her knees and stomach. She pressed her palm to her belly. There was a searing sensation inside, as if her baby had been ripped from her womb.

Caro's knees folded but she caught at a chair and collapsed on its cushioned seat. Ariane half lifted her head, looking for her, then, satisfied she was nearby, turned to Jake Maynard, pointing out something on the puzzle spread across the floor. Fortunately he was turned away from her. She hated to think of that intense scrutiny on her now.

Caro breathed through the pain, telling herself it wasn't real. There could be no physical pain now. It was well over four years since she'd gone through labour and an excruciatingly difficult childbirth.

But though her rampaging pulse slowed, the pain persisted.

It was the ache of loss, familiar because she'd endured

it so long. Strange to feel it now when for the first time she had hope for the future.

She breathed deep, absorbing the fact that she'd found her daughter.

It was a miracle.

Caro had never let herself believe it possible. The idea that her baby was alive somewhere without her had been the fraught stuff of nightmares, taunting her till she awoke tearful and distressed, to the real world where such things couldn't happen.

Except it had.

Her jaw clenched and pain spiked from her grinding molars. She knew who was to blame.

Her hands curled into fists that trembled with the force of her emotion. Slowly, each joint aching with effort, she smoothed her hands on her thighs, feeling the bunch of stressed muscles beneath the fabric.

One day there'd be time to think of confronting the person responsible. Not today.

Her gaze slewed to the bright head bent over the puzzle and her heart lurched.

All that mattered was that she'd found her baby. That she was with her. She'd do whatever it took to stay at her side. And she wouldn't let anything, including Jake Maynard, stand in her way.

Jake forked his fingers through his hair, leaning back in his chair and rolling his shoulders. He'd had enough for tonight.

Trying to make progress with this new scheme was like wading through treacle in cement boots. He'd thought it easier to do business in Switzerland where he could access the principals in person, and he'd been right, to some extent.

He swivelled his chair, surveying the tapestries on the thick castle walls. His lips twisted. A medieval castle was a far cry from his usual surroundings.

The exclusive location meant he'd been able to entice some of the key players to this ultra-private retreat after the international summit in the next valley. That had provided impetus to his plans, but not as much as he'd like. There was a lot of work to do.

He wanted to stay in Europe to see how Ariane went. He'd thought of taking her back to St Ancilla for a visit. He was torn between thinking it could ease her pain and fearing it might send her back into the blank state of shock she'd been in at the hospital.

She needed time and he needed expert advice. Meanwhile, they'd stay here. This castle, rented from an acquaintance, was as good a place as any to keep Ariane from the media limelight. If any more intruding journalists turned up he'd simply drop the portcullis.

Jake turned and noticed a scrap of wool on the floor. It must have fallen when Ariane's bear was mended.

His thoughts zipped from his niece to the woman he'd invited to stay overnight.

He couldn't quite believe he'd done that when he hadn't offered the better qualified applicants such a chance.

He got to his feet, shoving his hands into his pockets.

Caro Rivage had no criminal record and her references checked out. She was what she seemed, a woman who liked kids and had some experience with them. A woman well-regarded by her employers.

Yet something about Ms Rivage gave him pause. If only he could put his finger on it.

But how could he send her away after seeing Ariane's smile? The way she chattered with the woman, eager to be with her.

Jake stretched and looked at his watch. Almost midnight. He switched off the child monitor, knowing from the silence that Ariane was sound asleep. But he always checked on her before turning in.

Minutes later he reached Ariane's room. In the dim illumination from a nightlight he saw her curled up, thumb in mouth and her other hand hooked around her teddy. Jake's heart tugged.

She might not have been born Connie's daughter but Ariane was as much his niece as if his sister had carried her for nine months. Seeing the love in his sister's eyes for the tiny red-headed bundle, Jake had loved her from the first too.

He vowed he'd do better for her from now on. The first four and a half years of her life he'd been so focused on his projects that he hadn't spent enough time with his family, stopping by for quick visits and relying on long-distance calls to keep up to date.

Because he hadn't realised Connie would be ripped away.

That familiar pang filled Jake's chest as he thought of his older sister, moving across the world to be with the man she loved. After her early years of struggle it had been a relief to see her settled with a nice bloke.

Jake turned, ready for his own bed, and his gaze caught a figure sitting in the corner. A figure he hadn't noticed because it was as still as the massive, carved wardrobe behind it.

The hairs at his nape sprang to attention. His scalp prickled and even the hairs on his arms lifted.

Caro Rivage could have been a statue. Her absolute stillness was uncanny. As was the way her gaze fixed so intently on Ariane.

It wasn't surprising to see a nanny in a child's room but surely not like this? Suspicion stirred.

'What are you doing here?'

She jumped, her hand flying to her chest as if to hold in her heart. Her face swung wide-eyed towards him.

Instantly his urgent protectiveness of Ariane faded.

He'd never seen someone look so vulnerable. Her dark

eyes were…haunted. Her mouth gaped and her chest heaved as if she'd had the shock of her life.

This wasn't the expression of someone up to no good, but of someone utterly defenceless. Jake saw a terrible starkness in her face. Then her expression smoothed. She rose and crossed the room.

Did he imagine a pulsing charge of energy as she stopped before him? He frowned, thrown by the flight of fancy. Nevertheless, once more his senses stirred into overdrive in her presence. It was unlooked for and disturbing.

'I was checking Ariane.'

Jake darted a glance at his niece, still sleeping, then jerked his head towards the door. When they were in the hall he scrutinised the woman before him. The light was better here but it was impossible to interpret her expression. She looked self-contained, as if presenting an unreadable front came naturally.

Again his sixth sense twitched a warning.

'A glance would have told you she was settled. You looked as if you'd been there for some time. Why?'

Something stirred, a fleeting expression, and Jake realised how pale she was, how tightly she held her mouth. His gaze lowered, past a fast-flickering pulse at her throat to the enveloping jacket and skirt. She hadn't even been to bed?

She swallowed and something jerked in his belly as he watched her slender throat work, feeling the tension vibrate off her in waves.

Now, instead of suspicion, Jake felt concern. He was familiar with pain and he recognised its shadow in this woman's unnaturally still features.

'What is it, Caro? What's wrong?'

'Nothing's wrong.' Her lips curved in an unconvincing smile. 'I wanted to check Ariane before I went to bed. She's going through a difficult time and something she said made me think she was prone to nightmares.' She spread her hands in a wide, helpless gesture that told him more about her state of mind than her face did. 'Truly, I just wanted to make sure she was safe.'

Her words rang convincingly and for once instinct told him it was true. She *was* here out of concern for Ariane.

True but not simple. That awful vulnerability he'd glimpsed in her momentarily unguarded face, that wealth of emotion had bordered on anguish. It couldn't be about Ariane, whom she'd only known a few hours. So it had to be about another child. A child she'd cared for and lost? Cot death? Illness? Accident? The possibilities were endless.

Pity rose, a rush of sympathy that made him want to comfort her. He moved closer then stopped himself.

'Get some sleep. My room's next to Ariane's so I'll hear if she wakes.' Maybe if he gave her this job she'd sleep near Ariane too, but he hadn't yet made that decision.

She nodded. 'Goodnight, Mr Maynard.'

'Goodnight, Ms Rivage.'

When she'd disappeared from view he exhaled slowly, thrown by what had happened. He'd wanted to haul Caro Rivage into his arms and hold her close. To ease the grim shadows that rode her.

His nostrils flared and he stepped back into Ariane's doorway, glancing at the curled-up child.

Tonight had revealed several things.

Caro Rivage was serious about caring for his niece.

She carried some distressingly heavy burden.

And he, with no real knowledge of the woman, without even wanting her here, had been on the verge of easing her pain with his arms around her and his lips on that inviting pink mouth. He wanted to hear her sigh with delight instead of anguish. He wanted her to smile at him with the warmth she bestowed on his niece. He wanted…

No. She was *not* his type. He wasn't interested.

Yet he'd stood mesmerised by the gentle sway of her hips till she disappeared from view.

He'd been right. Caro Rivage spelled trouble. Yet for Ariane's sake he wouldn't turn her away.

Ariane's sake?

With a snort of self-disgust Jake turned and stalked into his bedroom.

CHAPTER FOUR

'I'M SORRY I don't have better news, Caro, but this situation is a minefield.' Despite the early hour, Zoe's voice was crisp. No doubt, as one of the finest lawyers in St Ancilla, she was used to cutting to the heart of complex issues. 'This is likely to become a protracted court battle unless the two parties come to agreement.'

Her words fell like sharpened blades, slicing the sinews at Caro's knees. She grabbed the carved post of her four-poster bed, letting it take her sagging weight.

She'd been excited when she saw who the caller was, hoping Zoe had rung because she'd found a simple way through what promised to be a legal nightmare.

Her lips twisted. Since when had anything in her life gone as she'd hoped?

Wishing for something wouldn't make it happen. A happy family, a man who'd love her for herself, a future with her precious child—she'd dreamed of them all but not one had become real. No matter how hard she'd tried.

Caro set her jaw. This time it *would* be real. No matter what it took.

Beyond the window was a magical vista of soaring mountains and sparkling, fresh snow. So clear and pristine. So different from the mess she found herself in.

'But surely the adoption wasn't legal? How could it have been when I didn't consent?'

She closed her eyes, her mind swimming with memories that had haunted her for years. The exhaustion, the blur of pain and fear, punctuated by moments of startling clarity when she realised something had gone badly wrong with the delivery. Her growing distress, and then...nothing, just blankness as the drugs took effect.

'That's something I'm trying to investigate. It's proving difficult.'

Caro dragged in a deep breath. She understood what Zoe wasn't saying. The impenetrable wall of denial and obfuscation that would meet her attempts to discover more.

Caro's father had pulled strings to arrange the adoption. He was a man adept at getting his way and as far as she knew no one had ever had the wealth, the will or the power to hold him to account.

Till now. In this he'd gone too far.

Sometimes, in her more desperate moments, she considered confronting him and calling him to account. Except she knew it would be like a gnat biting a bull. He'd swat her aside and immediately turn all his considerable power to making the problem go away. Then she'd be up against two powerful men, not one. Better to bide her time, for now.

'Difficult or not, there must be a way forward.' She bit her lip. 'I want to avoid a long court battle, for Ariane's sake especially.'

'It appears both sides can argue a legitimate claim to the child.'

She's not 'the child'. She's my daughter!

Caro clenched her teeth against the instinctive protest. Zoe was only doing her job, telling her the legal reality.

'My advice is to talk to her guardian. Negotiate. See if you can find common ground.'

Negotiate with Jake Maynard? The man was a world-class financier, regularly working with some of the largest and most successful corporations in the world. It was rumoured he was here for secret meetings with officials of unnamed governments. Caro couldn't imagine him negotiating with her. He'd be more likely to throw her out before she could do more than explain why she was here.

Then where would she be? Caro would fight with everything she had to win her daughter, but she wasn't fool enough to compare her power or negotiation skills with Jake Maynard's.

She couldn't quite stifle a choked sound of dismay.

'I don't mean straight away,' Zoe said quickly. 'Not till I've got to the bottom of the adoption process and checked some more precedents. Especially as Ariane's not in St Ancilla now. Different legal jurisdictions can complicate things.'

'As if they weren't already complicated.' Caro pushed her hair behind her ear, frowning.

'We knew that from the start,' Zoe's matter-of-fact voice cut through her troubled thoughts. She let a pause lengthen. 'Unless you don't want to proceed?'

'No!' Caro shook her head, her hair swirling again across her cheeks. She stalked to the window, pressing her palm to the cool glass. Along the horizon formidable peaks rose stark and seemingly unconquerable. Yet she knew that against the odds mountaineers had reached those impossible summits. 'I do want to proceed.' She drew a measured breath then said more evenly, 'I can't give up, Zoe. I can't.'

'Of course you can't.' Gone was the sharp voice of legal opinion, replaced by warm understanding. 'Who could, in your place?' The other woman sighed. 'Try to be patient. Time enough to talk to Ariane's guardian when I've done some more checking and we know exactly where we stand.'

As she ended the call Caro was torn between frustration and relief. Stupid to have thought there'd be any easy way through this, but after finding Ariane and spending time with her, it had felt as if anything was possible.

She'd gone to bed last night overcome by emotion at finally seeing her little girl. Being free to talk with her, watch over her as she slept. She'd assured herself it was a good sign that Jake Maynard had invited her to stay. He wouldn't do that unless she had a chance at the job.

Yet she didn't want to be a nanny. She was Ariane's *mother*.

No wonder she hadn't slept. She'd tossed all night, imagining one scenario after another where Ariane's uncle stopped her claiming her daughter.

Zoe was right. He was her uncle despite being no blood relation. Before Caro met him she'd wondered if he might be relieved to be rid of responsibility for his orphaned niece. That hope had died as she'd seen his protectiveness for Ariane.

Thinking about Jake Maynard disturbed her. He made her…unsettled.

Caro told herself it was because he had a claim to her daughter. His sharp eyes had softened when he watched Ariane. Clearly he was determined to do his best for her.

He'd never tamely give her up, even to her rightful mother.

That explained Caro's edginess. Because they were destined to be rivals, if not enemies.

It had nothing to do with the fact that he made her feel, for the first time in ages, aware of her femininity.

She couldn't be so self-destructive as to be attracted to the man who stood squarely between her and her daughter.

Caro stepped into the office, masking her nervously roiling stomach with a façade of calm. She was grateful for her father's insistence that she learn to conceal her feelings behind a show of well-bred calm. Being in the same building as her child for the first time in four and a half years tested her to the limit.

'Take a seat, Ms Rivage.'

Instead she stopped beside the desk. How could she sit while Jake Maynard paced the room?

He was even more intimidating than he'd been yesterday in his tailored business clothes. Those black jeans revealed muscled thighs and, when he moved away, a taut, rounded backside that turned her throat to sandpaper. His fine-knit pullover was a shade darker than his eyes and clung to broad shoulders and a flat belly. Even the way he'd pushed the sleeves up to reveal strong forearms dusted with dark hair did strange things to her insides.

He was potently masculine and far too disturbing.

And last night he'd called her Caro.

The knowledge beat in her bloodstream, slowing her pulse, making it ponderous with unexpected need.

For one crazy second she'd thought he might reach out to her as she grappled with yesterday's emotional onslaught. She'd been disappointed when he didn't.

When she'd thought of finding her daughter, she'd imagined Ariane's uncle as kind and ordinary. Not sucking up all the oxygen in the room. His presence shouldn't be electric, demanding, stifling the breath in her lungs.

How woefully underprepared she'd been.

He turned and surveyed her over his desk. No sympathy in his eyes now.

Not that it was sympathy she wanted.

She hurried into speech. 'I'd prefer to stand, thanks.'

One slashing eyebrow rose. 'You look like you're facing a firing squad.'

She inhaled roughly, her teeth digging into her bottom lip. How did he read her so easily?

He was right. After the way he'd quizzed her in Ariane's room last night, she knew he was suspicious of her. All through breakfast she'd been conscious of his piercing stare trained on her.

Did he hope to discomfit her? On the thought she pushed her shoulders back. He might be tough and used to taking charge but as an adversary he had nothing on her father.

Jake Maynard was a hard man but he seemed to play by honest rules, unlike her devious, despised dad.

'I'm expecting to hear your decision. And after sitting for the last hour with Ariane I'm comfortable standing.'

'As you wish.' He surveyed her in a leisurely way that made her skin itch. He might have all the time in the world but she needed an answer.

He must know she was on tenterhooks. Was this some extra test to pass? Despite her joy at being in the same building as Ariane, Caro felt as if she'd been scraped too thin by the emotional overload. She hadn't slept and her mind spun relentlessly like a mouse on a wheel, trying to work out the best way to deal with this fraught, complicated situation. She didn't have answers, just the certainty that whatever she did Jake Maynard wouldn't be happy.

'You still want to work for me?'

Caro's heartbeat accelerated, hope leaping. 'You're offering me the job?' She grabbed the back of the chair.

He raised his hand. 'Not quite.' Her heart plummeted. 'To be frank I still have reservations, but,' he forestalled her when she opened her mouth to respond, 'I've noticed Ariane has taken to you and how attuned you are to her.'

That was good, surely?

'But?' She leaned forward, willing him to put her out of her misery.

His eyebrows lifted as if he wasn't used to staff demanding answers.

'But my niece's well-being comes before everything else. I want to be sure I'm making the right decision, especially as on paper you're far from the best applicant.'

Caro choked back the impulse to say Ariane could have no better carer than her birth mother. But that would be disastrous. She couldn't reveal all too early and risk messing everything up. She had to choose her moment carefully, wait for news from Zoe. She guessed he'd resist her claim and he had far more resources at his disposal.

'So I'm offering you a job but with a six-month probationary period.' His crystalline gaze pinned her to the spot. 'If I'm satisfied with your work then we'll make it permanent.'

Permanent. That was precisely what Caro wanted.

But not permanent in the way he meant—with her as a paid carer.

Caro wanted her child. The right to love Ariane openly, to be acknowledged as her mother. Not because Jake Maynard employed her.

And, one day if she tried hard enough, maybe Ariane would love her back.

Caro's throat closed convulsively.

The situation was convoluted, with so much potential for failure. Caro met that questioning gaze. 'You accept?' One dark eyebrow slashed his brow as if he was surprised she hadn't eagerly accepted his proposal.

Caro hesitated on the brink of declaring herself. She abhorred lies yet she was deceiving this man, even if it was a lie of omission. Then she thought of Zoe's advice. And the very real possibility Jake Maynard would eject her when she revealed her identity.

So she curved her lips in the gracious smile she'd perfected almost before she could walk. 'That sounds ideal. I accept.'

'Good.'

He didn't smile. In fact, there was a crease between his eyebrows as if something bothered him. Caro silently vowed to do whatever it took to allay his doubts.

'Ariane already calls you Caro.' He paused, her name lingering in the silence. 'I'll do the same. And you can call me Jake. There's no need for formality in front of Ariane.'

A little shimmer of pleasure exploded deep inside as

Caro imagined the taste of his name on her tongue. Her pulse quickened.

A second later devastating self-knowledge slammed into her. To be thrilled at the prospect of saying his name? At hearing him say hers?

She blinked and concentrated on keeping her expression bland while inside anxiety coiled. Jake Maynard was a remarkably attractive man and she'd deliberately avoided such men for five years. Maybe that explained why he got under her skin. Whatever the reason, it wouldn't do. She had to keep her distance.

'Of course you may call me Caro.' She nodded briskly. 'However, I'd feel more comfortable calling you Mr Maynard.'

She watched his eyebrows lift, as if he were surprised to find someone who didn't instantly agree with him.

For a full ten seconds he said nothing. Finally he nodded. 'If that makes you feel better, Caro.'

Surely she imagined the way his voice dropped on her name and his intense scrutiny.

Abruptly Caro felt that, instead of blending into the background, she'd thrust herself into the limelight.

Exactly where she didn't want to be.

CHAPTER FIVE

A WEEK LATER Jake stood at his office window watching two figures track through a layer of white that was forecast to be the last, late snow of the season. They pulled a small toboggan.

When Caro had asked permission to take Ariane out he'd been sceptical. Since she'd left hospital in St Ancilla his niece hadn't shown interest in anything except staying inside with her teddy bear and toys.

He guessed her reluctance to go out stemmed from memories of the storm that left her parents dead and her trapped in their car, crushed beneath a massive tree.

Jake's belly clenched. At least Connie and Peter had died instantly.

He knew nothing about being a father, and not as much as he should about being a hands-on uncle, but he'd get there. He'd give Ariane the love and stability she needed.

Jake's mouth twisted. He wouldn't let her face what he and his sister had, a gaping hole where parental love should have been. It had been his determined older sister who'd given him the love, discipline and constancy their feckless mother hadn't.

He owed Connie everything and he was determined to give her daughter what his sister had given him. Once this deal was through he'd ease back, spending more time with Ariane. Which meant finding a permanent home. In Australia? St Ancilla? Renting a castle in Europe was useful for his current scheme but it was hardly the home his niece needed. Nor were his high-rise apartments in Sydney, New York and London. He'd get somewhere with a garden and plenty of sunshine.

He planted his hand on the glass, watching the pair skirt the castle. Ariane wasn't smiling but nor did she look nervous, as she had previously when he'd suggested an outing.

Caro had succeeded where he'd failed.

Jake stifled what felt suspiciously like jealousy. It didn't matter *who* helped Ariane come out of her shell of grief and shock. He should be pleased.

Plus, it reinforced the fact he'd made a wise choice offering Caro the position on probation.

Yet he reserved judgement on Caro Rivage.

Because he was drawn to her?

Jake forced the notion away.

Because of her patent wariness around him?

At first he'd assumed she suffered from interview nerves but it was more than that. He felt she watched each word, each nuance, always on guard. Did she have a problem with men in general or him in particular?

Yet she wasn't scared of him. She was...cautious. And he couldn't shake the idea that she wasn't all she seemed.

Jake frowned. Should he delve deeper? Get a comprehensive investigative report?

Or was he overreacting because she kept her distance despite the way she looked at him sometimes? As if she were fascinated, as inexplicably drawn to him as he was to her. Yet she avoided him when she could. It wasn't a response he was used to in women.

He huffed out a laugh. Was his ego so big he imagined a mystery because a woman didn't try to snare him? He should be glad. He didn't need that complication in his home.

He'd been cooped up inside too long, working on this deal. *That* was what made him stir crazy, not Caro Rivage. Maybe Ariane wasn't the only one needing fresh air.

Fifteen minutes later he approached a little valley on the far side of the castle. The air was so sharp he tasted it with every inhalation. Above was the wide blue bowl of sky and before him a cleared slope surrounded by trees.

It felt good to be outside. Especially when he heard childish giggles.

Jake's chest tightened. How long since he'd heard Ariane happy?

It unlocked memories of the last time he'd visited his sister on St Ancilla. They'd eaten outdoors under a vine-draped pergola. Connie and her husband had been the same as ever, the most content couple he knew, and little Ariane had been in high spirits, laughing at some nonsense game her father had invented with her. It had been idyllic and Jake had been glad to see Connie enjoying such happiness. She deserved it after those tough early years devoting herself to her difficult kid brother.

The sound of a husky voice interrupted his thoughts. It tickled its way through his belly then up his spine, drawing his shoulders tight.

Caro. Even if he didn't know the voice he recognised his response. The eddy of heat down low and the teasing prickle of awareness across his nape.

How was it a woman so prim and buttoned up had such a seductive voice? Last night he'd woken in a tangle of sweaty sheets, the echo of that throaty voice in his head. It had murmured an explicit invitation that made him feel as if it had been six months, not six weeks since he'd kicked Fiona out of his bed.

Scowling, he strode towards the sound.

To his surprise Ariane was on the lightweight toboggan alone, sliding down a gentle slope to where Caro waited on a broad flat area, arms wide in welcome.

It should have been his niece who captured his attention. Instead it was her nanny's amazing smile. Even from this distance it delivered a punch straight to his belly.

The sunlight on her hair picked out warm auburn highlights he hadn't noticed before. Suddenly she looked less staid and more vivacious.

She wasn't beautiful but still she was stunning. Jake frowned. It wasn't merely her hair and the colour whipped into her cheeks by the cold, but her look of sheer joy. Her smile was infectious. His mouth curled up at the corners.

Heat beat at his throat, his chest and lower. He wanted to see her smile at *him* that way instead of pretending his collar or the view past his ear was more fascinating. He wanted to see her flushed with pleasure and exertion, beaming up at *him*.

The realisation corkscrewed through him, jagging his libido and setting off alarms.

She was his *employee*. He still had reservations about her, nothing he could put his finger on but still…

'Well done,' he called out, heading towards them. 'You didn't tell me you were so good on the snow, Ariane.'

'Uncle Jake! Did you see? I slided all by myself.'

Her grin was the one he remembered from St Ancilla, from before the accident. It made his breath catch in his lungs. She'd always been a sunny child and he'd told himself she would be again. Yet seeing proof that with time and care she could recover from the recent trauma perversely reminded him again of how much they'd both lost, and how precious she was.

Nothing, he vowed, would upset her world again if he could help it.

'I saw. I'm very impressed. Was that your first time by yourself?'

She nodded so vigorously a bright coppery curl that had escaped her woolly hat danced around her face.

'Want to see me do it again?'

He nodded. 'I sure do. Then you could teach me.'

For answer she looked at Caro as if seeking permission. The nanny nodded. 'Remember, not too high, Ariane.'

Jake watched his niece climb off and head back up the slope, dragging the lightweight toboggan behind her. He was tempted to intervene and carry her burden, or offer to accompany her but he held back, seeing the determined thrust of her small chin.

He turned to find Caro watching him, an unreadable expression in her eyes. Instantly he felt that clenching awareness low in his belly, that hot swirl in his blood. Her arms were wrapped defensively around her middle. Did she too feel the tug between them, or was she just cold?

'I'll go and help her.' She made to turn and follow Ariane up the slight slope.

'No!' At his command she stopped, brows raised at his urgent tone. 'Let her do it herself.' Jake told himself he wasn't prompted by the need to keep the woman near him.

Caro looked over her shoulder at Ariane then nodded. 'You're right.' She slanted a look at him then away.

'What?'

She shrugged then met his stare. 'I might be wrong but I think, as well as the sheer fun of the slide, it's that sense of being in charge that she's enjoying.'

'Because everything in her life has upended?'

Caro nodded. 'All the things she could depend on have gone or changed. And though you've done what you can to establish a home and a routine, she probably feels the world is a scary place.'

The air Jake drew into his chest seemed thick and rough. She was right. Ariane had been through so much. She must feel powerless and adrift. Which was why it was important she have stability.

'You like working with her?' He hadn't consciously formed the question but suddenly he had to know. Providing the right carer for Ariane wasn't just a matter of him approving someone, but of that someone wanting to stay.

Given how Ariane responded to Caro Rivage it appeared that someone was standing before him.

Caro's eyes widened. 'Of course! Why? Aren't you satisfied with—?'

Jake raised a placating hand. 'I'm satisfied. So far,' he amended. 'I wanted to hear your perspective.'

Relief drifted across her face, making her expression unusually easy to read. It was another reminder of how rarely she let down her guard with him. So she really was invested in this job. 'I love caring for Ariane. I—'

She swung her head around at the sound of the toboggan approaching, then froze. A second later she was sprinting away from him across the flat little plateau towards the steeper slope at the edge of the clearing.

Jake looked up the hill, his gut curdling.

While they'd been talking Ariane had taken the toboggan high up the slope. Far higher than the track of her previous run. Now, with the added momentum, she was skidding downhill dangerously fast and at an angle that took her in a collision course with a stand of trees.

Jake's legs were already pumping, driving him through the snow towards the far side of the clearing, even though his brain told him he'd be too late. He was too far away.

His heart sank. So was Caro. She was stumbling, trying to make headway in the snow, but, as in a nightmare, seemed to be moving in slow motion.

His ears rang when Ariane's squeal of delight turned into a cry of fear as she torpedoed towards danger. He pushed himself faster, lungs burning, but knew it was impossible he'd make it in time.

The toboggan flew towards the trees and unspeakable visions filled his head. As a one-time soldier and peacekeeper he'd witnessed terrible injuries. But this was Ariane...

At the last moment, as impact with a tree seemed inevitable, there was a blur of blue as Caro threw herself at the toboggan. Snow sprayed as it spun, there was a resounding thump and a fall of white from the branches, obscuring his vision.

As he covered the last couple of metres Jake found himself praying.

Caro lay winded, her arms wrapped tight around the small, still body.

'Ariane! Talk to me.' The deep voice was raw with fear. A fear that matched her own. For the life of her she couldn't open her eyes and face what awaited her. Had she lost her daughter again? Permanently this time?

Anguish tore at her soul.

She thought she'd known fear before but it was nothing to the terrible yawning blackness that threatened to engulf her.

All she could do was hold on, *willing* her little girl to be all right. A tightness in her chest reminded her to breathe. She drew a ragged breath that sounded like a sob. Caro should never have taken her eyes off her, not for a second.

'Ariane!' The deep voice sliced the frigid air.

Large hands covered Caro's, pried them loose. She tried to resist, opened her mouth to cry out, when a little voice said, 'Uncle Jake?'

Caro's eyes snapped wide. Above her Jake Maynard filled her vision, surrounded by cerulean sky, like an angel in a painting. Except this dark angel's face was distorted with fear and, as she watched it transform, relief. Caro felt the same emotions unfurl within, so strong nausea punched her.

Her embrace weakened as her arms turned to water. Ariane moved out of her hold.

'Are you okay, Ariane? Where does it hurt?' That resonant voice was stark with emotion.

'I don't hurt anywhere.'

Caro could swear her heart dipped and lifted on the words. Ariane was okay, she was all right.

Her own eyelids flickered shut as emotion rose like a tide, filling her chest, closing her throat, forcing her to bite her lip against the sudden, appalling urge to cry.

'Caro?' That large hand was back again, this time lingering on the pulse at her throat then skimming up to her cheek and forehead. It was hard and surprisingly callused but incredibly gentle. Who'd have thought a man with such cold eyes could have such a tender touch?

'Is she...dead, Uncle Jake?'

The fear in Ariane's voice snapped Caro out of her reverie. After what had happened to Ariane's adoptive parents her fear of death wasn't surprising.

'I'm very much alive, sweetheart.' Even if Caro's voice didn't sound like her own, far too raspy and uneven.

When she opened her eyes this time two faces peered down at her. Dazed, she took in her daughter's hopeful expression and smiled. Her skin felt stiff, as if drawn too tight, but seeing Ariane smile tentatively back was worth the effort. Her heart thudded a double beat.

Then her gaze shifted to the broad-shouldered figure beside her daughter. Had she really thought Jake Maynard's eyes cold? They flared with a heat she felt all the way to her bones. For one suspended instant everything inside her stilled then burst into flame.

'Are you injured? Can you move?' His eyes belied his terse tone.

'Give me a minute.' She drew another quick breath, pressing the heel of her hand to her sternum, trying to force her lungs into action. 'I'm just winded.' Or too euphoric to feel pain. 'You're sure you're okay, Ariane? You didn't hit your head?'

Her daughter shook her head as tears filled her bright eyes. 'I'm sorry, Caro. I didn't mean to hit you.'

As if that wasn't exactly what Caro had aimed for. Better her than a tree.

'Why did you disobey Caro and climb right up the hill?' Jake's voice was low but steely and Ariane flinched. Caro told herself it was the voice of a man reacting to fear. They were lucky Ariane had escaped serious injury.

Seeing Ariane's tears spill, Caro found the energy to sit up, curling her legs under her and pulling Ariane to her. Her daughter burrowed close, her arms creeping around Caro's neck. Caro had never experienced anything like the burst of glorious happiness that exploded inside her.

This. This was what she'd missed all these years.

For so long Caro had been tempted to fantasise that her child hadn't been stillborn. But the fantasy was too dangerous and she'd forced herself to put it aside and face reality. Then, discovering Ariane *was* alive, Caro had been so focused on tracking her down that she hadn't allowed herself to imagine this moment. It had seemed like tempting fate into stealing away her daughter again.

She rocked Ariane, breathing in the scent of snow, pine trees and little girl. It was a perfume she'd remember for the rest of her days.

'Shh…it's okay, sweetie. No one's hurt.'

'Are you sure?' Jake Maynard frowned down at her, apparently still concerned about her. But Caro couldn't feel anything but the precious bundle in her arms.

'I'm fine.'

Ariane lifted her head. 'I won't do it again, Caro, I promise. I just wanted…' Her gaze flicked towards her uncle.

Suddenly Caro understood. 'You wanted to show Uncle Jake how well you could slide?'

Her ribs squeezed her heart. She'd seen Ariane's shy regard for the big man who was so concerned about her.

Ariane nodded. 'But I hurt you.'

'You must never do that again, Ariane,' Jake interjected, his voice gravelly. 'It's dangerous to go so high.'

Her little girl's head drooped lower and Caro rushed into speech.

'Ariane's promised never to do it again, haven't you, sweetie?' She watched her daughter's silent nod. 'And we're both okay.' Though Caro was beginning to feel an ache slide around her ribs and her shoulder throbbed. 'So why don't you show Uncle Jake how good you are at tobogganing? You could go together.'

Jake looked at her as if she'd sprouted another head and she hurried on. 'They say that if you come off a horse you should get on again straight away.' She met his stare, willing him to understand. There were enough scary things in Ariane's world without adding to them. 'I can vouch that it works.'

Caro had taken a toss off a pony as a kid and her father had insisted she get back on. It had stopped her developing a fear of horses, though they discovered later she'd fractured her wrist in the fall. She'd been more afraid of disappointing her disapproving father than of the pain.

But watching Ariane jump to her feet when Jake finally agreed there was time for *one* slide, Caro knew she was okay.

He pressed Caro again about injuries, but finally he was satisfied and she had time to gather herself, watching Jake and Ariane share the toboggan.

One slide turned into three, though at the end of each Jake strode across to check on her, his concern warming a part of her that had been frozen for a long time. Caro couldn't recall the last time any man had been genuinely concerned for her well-being. Not her father or brothers. Definitely not her ex-boyfriend who'd sold her out for personal gain.

By the time Jake announced it was time to go back, that he didn't want Caro waiting in the chill air any longer, Ariane was gleeful and her uncle's eyes had lost that stormy light.

Caro hoped that within a few days Ariane might forget how close to disaster they'd come. But her own spirits, after that initial burst of euphoria, plummeted.

It was clear Jake Maynard didn't merely feel obligated to look after his niece. He *cared* for her. And little Ariane beamed with pride and delight in his company.

What would happen when Caro claimed her daughter?

She had every right to do so. She'd been denied so much it hurt to think about the years of Ariane's life she'd missed. Even her name wasn't one Caro had chosen!

Once more she was tempted to come clean about her identity. Except Ariane was fragile and bewildered after losing her adoptive parents and Caro didn't want to add to her stress. She'd wait at least till she and Ariane had a good, strong relationship.

Plus there was another reason to delay. Jake Maynard was wealthy and powerful. If she went in assuming that because she had right on her side everything would be okay, things could go horribly wrong. Caro had been victim to the machinations of manipulative men. First Mike then her father. She'd be a fool to think Jake was any less dangerous.

He'd move heaven and earth to stop her claiming her daughter. Caro had little money of her own and her father would never support her in a court case. He'd do everything in his power to avoid scandal.

But that wasn't all. She drew a shuddering breath as she watched Jake, powerfully built and agile, utterly, fascinatingly masculine as he climbed the slope hand in hand with her daughter.

No, the worst of it was that Jake Maynard awoke something within her, a longing, that she'd never expected to experience again after years of numbness.

Desire. Not some vague sweet yearning but a piercing stab of need for his touch, his powerful body.

She sank her head in her hands. Was there any way out of this tangle?

CHAPTER SIX

JAKE COULDN'T STOP thinking about Caro Rivage. She was in his head every time he tried to read the report before him.

It wasn't figures he saw. It was Ariane's nanny, earlier today, throwing herself across the snow at risk of life and limb. Then later, limp and pale, making him curse himself for taking her word that she was uninjured.

He'd leaned down, about to lift her into his arms and carry her. For an instant he'd seen hunger in her expression. An answering beat of need had pulsed through his blood, but a second later her expression had morphed into something like fear.

Before he could prevent her she'd clambered to her feet, insisting on walking. But Jake wasn't fooled, he'd seen her stiff movements and insisted on a doctor.

Fortunately the doctor, checking out both nanny and child, had declared no harm done. Caro would suffer only bruising.

Yet Jake couldn't put her from his mind.

At least he knew he could trust her with Ariane. Caro might have been severely injured or killed with that desperate dive.

Jake's heart had been in his mouth. He wasn't used to being on the sidelines, watching others act. Guilt gouged him. He should have been the one to save Ariane but he hadn't been within reach.

The experience had changed him. Like varnish stripping away layers, there was nowhere now to hide the attraction he should *not* feel for his niece's nanny.

He tried telling himself it was because she was so good with Ariane. Even when his niece drew into herself or, very occasionally, acted up over something that to him seemed insignificant. There were times when he thought Caro too strict and others when her refusal to respond to a display of childish temper made him want to intervene. But he knew so little about child-rearing that he held back and each time he'd been glad, as Ariane became more like the engaging child he knew.

Frankly, those small displays of temper were a relief. When he'd first seen Ariane after the accident she'd been a shadow, withdrawn and wan.

Time, and Caro Rivage, were helping.

Yet hiring her hadn't been his best decision. Because no matter how he tried to distance himself, he couldn't ignore her. Or the awareness thickening his blood when she was near.

He didn't date staff.

He didn't pursue mousy women.

Yet, despite her penchant for wearing browns and dull navy, Caro Rivage wasn't mousy. The quiet manner couldn't conceal the lambent fire that blazed when she smiled at Ariane. Or when she forgot to be meek and treated him to a glimpse of that proud—and, he was sure, passionate— woman behind the mask.

That hidden woman made Jake's blood sizzle. He'd bet every million he'd made that hers sizzled too. Today her expression had made him want to forget every reason she was off limits. To break through the tension that hummed between them like electricity through a high-voltage cable.

He'd wanted to discover if she melted at his touch.

Even the way she dragged her hair into that tight bun, like a nanny a century ago, was perversely alluring. Instead of making her look frumpy, the style drew attention to the purity of her neck and jawline, and that small but exquisite mouth. Molten heat pooled in his groin at the memory of that mouth, as pink and delicate as a rosebud.

Rosebud? Delicate?

His last lover had been confident, sophisticated and gifted with a wide, mobile mouth that she used with sinful persuasiveness. *That* was the sort of woman he dated, clever, amusing and blatantly erotic.

Why did Caro Rivage tie him in knots? The other day he'd found himself pondering her neat collarbone, glimpsed beneath the V of another primly buttoned blouse, wondering if her skin was as soft as he imagined! He'd leaned in, drawn by the hint of sweet spice in the air as she moved, till he realised what he was doing.

Jake set his jaw, shoved his chair back and shut his laptop. It was midnight but he'd never settle to sleep. He'd work off this excess energy in the gym till he was too fatigued to think of rosebud mouths, creamy skin and that husky, feminine voice.

It was a good plan. The only trouble was, when he pushed the door open to the cellar fitness complex, there was Caro standing between the pool and the hot tub, head bent as she undid the belt of her robe.

Her hair, instead of being yanked back in a bun, fell in waves past her shoulders, making her look soft and young. The guarded, self-contained nanny was gone.

Jake's throat dried as she shrugged the robe off.

She was tall, slender but with a sweet, streamlined curve to her hips. She wore grey lace-edged knickers and matching singlet top. The outfit had none of the conscious seductiveness of a scanty bikini but she radiated an innocent eroticism that dragged his libido into raging life.

Every muscle tightened as blood hurtled to his groin. Every masculine response he'd fought to control roared into life.

Attraction.

Desire.

Downright hunger.

She must have heard the door or his sharp intake of breath because she turned and he saw her eyes widen before the swell of high, perfect breasts pressed against taut fabric caught his attention. She was braless and the little jiggle of her breasts as she sucked in air drove an arrow of carnal heat straight to his groin.

Through the thickening silence came a soft sound as the robe pooled around her bare feet.

Jake's brain told him not to move even as he covered the small distance and bent to pick it up. At the same time she did.

His fingers brushed hers and he stilled. The robe fell again and he drew in a breath scented with woman and warm spice. The perfume went to his head like a draught of fine cognac downed too fast.

She straightened and he grabbed the robe from the floor, discovering it still warm from her body. His fingers curled into the towelling, rather than reach for her.

She was Ariane's nanny. His employee.

Yet he couldn't move. His soles were cemented to the floor. He was so close he saw her shiver.

Watching the flush rise from her breasts to her throat and cheeks Jake knew she wasn't cold. He forced his gaze high and kept it there.

'You're having a swim?'

Congratulations, Maynard. Full points for observation.

His thought processes grew sluggish and it was the best he could do in lieu of marching back the way he'd come. That was what he should do but for the first time he could recall, his body refused to obey his brain.

She shuffled back a half step and he wondered in surprise if she found him intimidating. This last week she'd proved she was well able to stand up to him. He saw no fear in her face. Caro wore that guarded expression he'd come to hate, because his curiosity about her had grown insatiable.

He wanted to find out what went on behind that mask of calm as much as he wanted to taste her.

Neither, he told himself, was a good idea. He dropped the robe onto a lounger and managed his own half step away. The effort made him feel as if he'd run a half marathon.

'No. Not a swim.' The husky edge to her voice was pronounced, making it burr through his belly. 'I was going to try the hot tub, if that's okay.'

'Of course it's okay. Surely Neil made it clear you could use any of the facilities.' Jake wrestled with thoughts of Caro in the hot tub. Naked? The notion locked his knees so he hadn't a hope of walking away yet.

'I...thank you, he did.' She glanced down and away as if shy. Except that didn't ring true with the woman he'd got to know in the last week. Undaunted, courageous, fiercely determined, caring of Ariane and, when it came to herself, reserved to the point of blankness, that was Caro.

Besides, though he fought to keep his eyes on her face, he hadn't missed the way her nipples pebbled against her top. The area was well heated. He guessed it wasn't a reaction to cold, especially with that tell-tale blush.

Reaction to him?

The idea threatened his resolve.

He should go. He'd even managed to look past her to the door to the gym when she spoke in a rush as if needing to fill the throbbing silence.

'I thought the warm water might help.'

Jake's gaze wrenched back to her then down, skating over lithe curves to the expanse of pearly skin showing between her knickers and her top. A bruise marred her pale skin on one side, the sight reminding him of her bravery today and how he'd feared for her.

'Did the doctor give you something for pain?'

She tugged her top lower and she shook her head, hair

spilling around her shoulders. 'It's not that bad. I thought warm water might help me get to sleep. I feel…unsettled.'

Jake knew the feeling.

'I had a similar thought but I'm heading to the gym.'

Yet he didn't move.

Pale eyes blazed down at Caro. That silvery gaze was anything but cold. Wherever it touched her temperature soared.

Tonight, while she was suffering the after-effects of nearly losing her daughter on that snowy slope, the old, dark thoughts had circled again, waiting to swallow Caro whole. When she'd lost her baby the first time there'd been no one truly close to share her grief. Tonight she realised nothing had changed. Despite the friends she'd made in the intervening years, she was still essentially alone.

Except when she was with Jake Maynard.

The realisation slammed into her, fascinating and terrible.

With him she felt different. More alive. Less alone.

It had to be because they had a common purpose, caring for Ariane. Except as the atmosphere stretched taut around them she knew this wasn't about Ariane. It was about her as a woman and Jake as a man.

Did he feel this throb of awareness?

Caro couldn't afford to think so. Not with so much at stake. This masquerade. Ariane.

She *couldn't* risk her position here! She should run as far and fast as she could in the opposite direction.

But how could she leave when Jake looked at her that way? As if she were Venus herself, striking mortal men with yearning. A spark ignited deep inside that grew and grew as he ate her up with his eyes.

The old longing to be wanted rose again, her fatal weakness.

In childhood she'd hoped if she was good enough her

family would love her. When that never happened, she'd fallen for Mike, convinced too easily of his affection. Now here she was again, craving connection.

What would it be like to be truly wanted? And by Jake, the man who occupied too many of her thoughts both waking and sleeping.

Today she'd faced the stark reality of life and death. She'd almost lost her daughter. Was lucky to be alive herself. Recklessness rose. She wanted to live in the moment.

No. No. No! Think about Ariane. The reason you're here.

She set her jaw, summoning the will to move.

'Caro.' Jake's husky whisper carved a channel through her good intentions. His hands closed around her arms, gently enough that she could have broken his hold.

Caro told herself that was what she'd do. Soon.

His head swooped down, his lips brushing hers and she lost her train of thought.

That hard mouth wasn't hard at all. It was soft, tender, impossibly tempting. Long ribbons of fire unfurled within her and she saw showers of sparks behind eyelids she hadn't realised she'd closed.

Caro drew in a breath rich with citrus, bergamot and something she'd almost forgotten, that tangy, inviting scent of healthy male flesh.

The reality of Jake touching her, kissing her with infinite care sent need shuddering through her. She swayed and reached up to steady herself. Her fingers found soft cotton, taut over hot muscle. And more, his heart thundering as fast as hers. That undid her. The knowledge he was vulnerable too.

Caro splayed her fingers over his sculpted chest and felt him shiver.

She shivered too, the ripple starting at her nape and running down her arms, her spine and right through her middle.

One second. Just a second more, then I'll be sensible.

She'd firmed her hands on his chest, ready to push away when Jake let go of her arms. Dazed, Caro registered the grinding pain of rejection and told herself it was for the best.

Except it wasn't rejection.

Jake grasped her waist. Her top had ridden up and those hard fingers spanned bare flesh. Heat drenched her. She wanted those hands on her body. Everywhere. She no longer felt self-conscious that he'd found her in drab underwear since she didn't have a swimsuit here.

All that mattered was the intoxicating warmth of his touch. His deep hum of approval vibrated through her as her mouth opened to his and their tongues embarked on a dance of mutual seduction.

The taste of him. The tenderness. The languorous sensuality. There was heat, demand, a sense of bridled ferocity as he leaned in and she bowed backwards, losing her balance, reliant on Jake to keep her from falling.

Caro's hands slipped up over wide shoulders to the back of his head, fingertips slipping into thick hair that, like his mouth, was surprisingly soft.

Now there was no thought of leaving, of doing anything more than giving in to this compulsion.

Her breathing grew short and her pulse unsteady as the kiss became more than slow seduction. She needed Jake as surely as her oxygen-starved lungs needed air.

She gloried in it all. From the feel of his muscled thighs against hers to the possessive clasp of those powerful hands and the magic of his mouth moving with hers. She shuddered as Jake's tongue swept deep in a caress that detonated explosions right through her.

When he pulled back to nip at her lower lip, then press kisses to the corner of her mouth and down to her jawline,

Caro muffled a cry. He made her feel things she'd never felt before.

'Don't,' he murmured, nuzzling that sensitive spot at the base of her neck. 'I want to hear you.'

Her eyes snapped open. Eyes the colour of mercury, silvery bright, snagged hers.

'I want to know what you like.' His voice was different. Husky deep, like treacle over gravel, its rich abrasiveness turning everything inside her molten.

'Everything. I like everything.'

Caro didn't care that her voice betrayed her need. Not when he pressed close so his erection nudged her. She squirmed, planting her hands on his shoulders, trying to get closer.

'Everything?' One straight black eyebrow rose. His chest pushed her sensitised breasts as he drew a breath. Instantly her hard nipples ached and the ache drew down like an arrow, through her belly to the empty place between her legs.

She hesitated. A lifetime's practice in self-denial and caution closed her throat.

But not for long. Despite the alarm bells clanging in the back of her mind, and the hazy thought that for reasons she couldn't recall this was a bad idea, it felt so good. In Jake's arms Caro felt a wonder and a yearning that was totally new.

'Everything,' she gasped, cupping the back of his skull and tugging his mouth back to hers.

Now there was no languor, just fire and sizzling sensation. He looped an arm around her back while his other hand strayed over skin and fragile cotton, exploring, making her gasp. His fingers slid between her thighs, over her panties. She pushed up to meet his touch, eliciting a growl of approval from the mouth welded to hers.

The sound burred over her bare arms and slid like a liquid channel, down to the place where she burned for him.

Caro was aware of movement. The wide lounger behind her legs, then she was in Jake's arms, eyes popping open as he lowered her onto it and came down above her.

Fire was everywhere. Fire and longing. She plucked at his T shirt, drawing it up as she curled her ankles around his legs to stop him moving away. The press of his body set her alight.

'Wait.' It might have been an order except his voice was raw with a need that matched hers. Jake pulled back to straddle her hips, yanking his T shirt off.

Caro's mouth dried. She'd never seen a man with a body like his. Wide shoulders, a powerful, deep chest with a light fuzz of dark hair that accentuated the contours of muscles. Below that smoother skin, taut with more muscle that tapered to a narrow waist.

Caro reached for him but he caught her hands and shook his head. 'Soon.' He bent low, pushing up her old camisole top. Then he took her nipple in his mouth, drawing hard.

Caro didn't mean to cry out but the shocking delight was too exquisite. Need sang in her blood and she fought to free her wrists and reach for him.

'Patience, Caro.' He crooned her name, turning it into a caress as he moved to her other breast, using his free hand, his lips and tongue to work magic.

She felt almost overwrought at the sensations he evoked. After years of celibacy and emotional numbness, he brought her to life with a vengeance. Delight danced through her and the need for more, more, more.

When he moved lower, his tongue slicking her navel and beyond, Caro didn't know whether to weep or cheer. She loved what he was doing but she was teetering on an edge, where one nudge would make her fall off the precipice. She wanted to be with him when that happened.

Then his downward progress stopped. He traced a wide arc low across her belly. Then he looked up and the question in his eyes punctured the delirium of need.

'Caro?' For the first time since she'd known him, Jake looked hesitant. A line appeared between those dark eyebrows and his chest expanded as if on a sustaining breath. 'Are these what I think?'

Even then her bewitched brain couldn't make sense of his words. She levered herself up. He was looking at the pale striations across her abdomen.

Stretch marks.

Acquired during her eight and a quarter months of pregnancy.

Caro blinked, watching that tanned, capable hand stop on her belly. Jake's touch seemed more intimate than if he'd caressed her between the legs where she was wet for him. Sex was a finite thing, its pleasure fleeting. But carrying her child—that had changed her at the most fundamental level. It was the most precious thing yet also the source of an anguish that had haunted her for years.

She swallowed, her throat raspy and tight.

'You had a child?'

'Yes.' She didn't think of lying. She couldn't deny her daughter. Despite the masquerade she'd been forced to adopt to get close to Ariane, Caro would never do that.

It was madness to be upset now. The past was over. The future promised more than she'd dared hope for. Yet his question brought all today's emotions to the surface and pierced the armour she'd tried to build around her memories. Suddenly the past with all its terrible pain was upon her. Her guilt that she hadn't been able to keep her baby with her. She should have *known*, should have done something...

'Where is it now, Caro?'

'She.' The single word was automatic.

When the nuns had told her that her baby was dead they'd spoken of *it*, not *her*. There'd been no chance to see the child, no grave to visit, because her father had deemed it better.

Her father. He had so much to answer for. It had taken such effort even to prise out the information that she'd had a daughter.

Thinking of her lost baby as she, not it, had been a reminder that her child had been real, despite the determination of those around her to pretend she'd never existed.

Caro tried to swallow but her throat was completely clogged.

Maybe it was the gentle way Jake spoke, the concern in his eyes, now the colour of burnished pewter, dark with shadows. Maybe it was because she'd never had to answer that question before. Suddenly she felt as lost as she had years ago, both her body and her arms empty, her child taken from her.

She squeezed her eyes shut, willing the moment to pass. Trying to suppress the cold shivers.

'Where is she, Caro? Your daughter?'

It was his tenderness that undid her. She told herself it no longer mattered. She was over the grief, moving on to happier times. Yet it seemed that buried deep within was a residue of anguish that even recent events hadn't erased.

Frantically she gulped air and heard the terrible sawing sound of a woman on the edge. Past and present coalesced. Instead of seeing the little girl on the mountain who'd almost died today, it was the tiny, silent baby she'd barely glimpsed as they whipped it away. Adrenaline pulsed in Caro's bloodstream and her mouth crumpled.

'I lost her,' she whispered. 'I lost her.'

She gave up the battle and let the burning tears fall.

CHAPTER SEVEN

JAKE LAY BESIDE her and gathered Caro close, her head against his shoulder. Her tears tracking across him. His mouth set as she shook, her hiccupping breaths proof of her battle for control.

The contained, capable woman he'd begun to know disappeared. Wrapped against him she seemed fragile, slighter than when she stood up to him or when she'd kissed him. He tightened his hold.

'It's okay, Caro. Let it out.'

It didn't take an expert to know this pain had been eating away at her. Her tormented expression and the desolation in her eyes proved that. As did the fact she'd gone from the edge of rapture to blind grief in seconds. Her broken voice replayed in his ears and pity filled him.

How long had she carried this burden? Had today's drama dragged it to the surface?

Jake half rolled onto his back and pulled her across him while one hand went to the tumble of soft waves that had loosened as they kissed. He stroked her head, combing his fingers through her hair.

It was his fault she'd gone into meltdown. Why hadn't he smothered his curiosity?

But given Caro's age her baby would be young. He couldn't imagine her leaving her child in order to look after someone else's. It hadn't seemed to fit.

Now it did.

He swallowed regret, cursing his determination to uncover her secrets. Yet he was glad he knew.

Not because he was an expert in comforting distressed women. Though as a one-time peacekeeper in areas ravaged by natural disaster and violence he had some experience. But because his need to know about Caro was insatiable.

He was fascinated by her and not just because he'd doubted her suitability as Ariane's nanny.

His belly clenched as another shudder racked her. What would it be like to lose a child, one you'd carried in your body?

Jake remembered his sister Connie, her stiff upper lip as she'd told him via computer link about another miscarriage and their decision to adopt. He'd been on the other side of the world but he'd *felt* his sister's heartbreak. Jake had wanted to go to her but had been wary of interfering. The days of it being just the two of them against the world had gone. Connie had had her husband and Jake had feared intruding on their shared grief.

Who did Caro have?

There was no ring on her finger, no mention of a husband. Surely if she had a partner she wouldn't be so eager for a live-in position?

How long had she bottled up this pain?

Protectiveness engulfed him. Her abrupt transition from carnal excitement to anguish indicated she had a long way to go to come to terms with this.

Did you ever come to terms?

He hadn't given much thought to himself as a father, though over the last year he'd thought about creating a permanent base and finding a long-term partner. His experience of families and parents made him wary.

His father had abandoned them when Jake was born. As for his mother, she'd ignored her responsibilities, focusing on her own pleasure. With her stunning looks it hadn't been hard to find lovers who'd shower her with the trinkets, trips and the lifestyle she craved. That kept her away from home for weeks and months at a time till finally she found a rich aristocrat, holidaying in Australia, who wanted her long term. She'd abandoned her kids without a second thought.

Yet now he had Ariane, Jake discovered a strong streak of paternal protectiveness. It hadn't been simple, learning to accommodate a child in what had been a bachelor life. But he couldn't imagine life without her. Thinking of her rare smiles and growing trust made him glow.

If he were to lose her...

Jake rocked Caro in his arms, his lips moved against her hair as he murmured that it was all right. When, of course, it could never be all right.

Like a douche of iced water memory chilled him. The memory of Caro that first night, motionless and intent as she watched Ariane sleep. There'd been something so eerily focused about her that his sixth sense had prickled. He'd known something was wrong. Now he understood. Caro looked at Ariane but remembered her lost child.

Something plunged through his body, a weight descending to crash into his gut.

Caro's hiccups stopped and the shivers eased but she didn't move away. Instead it felt as if she was trying to burrow in his chest. Surprisingly Jake didn't mind one bit. She'd touched something inside. A chord of fellow feeling.

More. Something to do with Caro herself. He'd wondered what lay behind her façade of prim control. Now he knew at least one of her secrets. And she fascinated him more than ever.

Fascinated and attracted.

His mouth twisted. Whatever was between them, this wasn't simply sexual attraction. Sex was here—very much so, as his unsatisfied body reminded him—but so were compassion and something he didn't have a name for.

'Sorry.' Caro sniffed and rubbed her cheeks. 'I can't believe I melted down like that.' She moved her shoulders as if gathering herself to pull away. Jake's hold tightened.

'You needed to let it out.'

'Not like that. Not sobbing all over you like...' She paused and he felt the sear of her breath against his skin. It felt like a caress.

Despite everything, his body still equated Caro with sexual hunger. Jake shoved the knowledge aside, ashamed.

She lifted her head and red-rimmed eyes met his. 'I apologise. I don't know what came over me. I'm *never* emotional in public.'

Jake's eyebrows rose. 'It was hardly public.'

She shook her head and dark curls tickled him. 'It was weak and selfish to sob all over you.' She pulled back a little.

Normally the idea of a woman crying over him would make Jake avoid her. Even now he felt discomfited by the display of such visceral emotion. He'd learned to bury emotions deep. Yet when Caro voiced the same idea, as if her grief were shameful, he wanted to reassure her.

'It's been an eventful day. Emotionally charged. Seeing Ariane in danger triggered sad memories.'

Her gaze caught his and a zap like an electric current coursed through him. Then, in a flurry of movement, Caro scrambled off the lounger. By the time he stood she was shrugging into the towelling robe, wrapping it close as if for protection.

Jake's brow knotted. Surely she didn't think she needed protecting from *him*?

But seeing the hectic colour in her cheeks, he guessed she was embarrassed.

'Caro, I—'

'Please, Jake.' She paused, the picture of discomfort.

It was the first time she'd used his name. He wished it had been in the throes of passion instead of like this. His fingers curled hard and he shoved them into his pockets.

She opened her mouth to say something, something im-

portant by the look on her face, then she shook her head.
'I need to go.'

'Stay!' He made himself stand immobile rather than
reach for her. 'Have that spa. I'll leave you in privacy.' Stupid to feel rejected because she needed time alone.

Her mouth hitched at one side but it wasn't a smile. Sadness was there and a tension he supposed came from embarrassment. 'That's kind of you but I'll go to my room. I
need to think.'

She hurried away, leaving him staring.

Caro had plenty of time to think but it didn't help. Whenever she made up her mind to tell Jake the truth all the reasons it was a terrible idea crowded in.

Hair damp from the shower, wrapped in her fluffy robe,
she curled in the deep window seat of her turret room, her
back against tapestry cushions that softened the stone wall.
She hugged her knees and watched the sun rise with relief.

She'd spent sleepless hours staring at the massive peaks
glimmering pale against the starry night. The view had
been peaceful, at odds with the churning in her stomach.
She'd wrestled with her conscience. She couldn't let Jake
think her child had died. Or that she was simply a nanny.

He wasn't the cold-hearted man she'd thought. Jake was
caring, not just with Ariane but with her. He'd held her and
showed no impatience when her tears interrupted their passion. Her limited experience of men told her his forbear-
ance, putting her needs ahead of his, was rare.

The gentle way he'd embraced her, the way he'd rocked
her, no one had ever done that. Maybe her mother when
Caro was tiny, but no one since. When she hurt she was
expected to suck it up and get on with things. Even after
losing her baby—no, make that having her baby snatched—
she'd got little support. The nuns in the convent had seemed

kind but with a distant, impersonal charity. There'd been no hugs, no shoulder to cry on.

No one like Jake.

She'd known the man a week yet in his arms, with that deep voice murmuring reassurance, she'd felt such comfort. Such healing.

Caro drew a shuddery sigh. Her chest expanded with the first free breath she'd taken all night.

Watching dawn's rosy fingers spread across the mountains, turning indigo to peach, apricot and finally the dazzling white of snow, she made up her mind.

They all had to face the truth some time.

Today would be the day.

She'd do it one piece at a time. First the revelation that she was Ariane's mother. Then, after Jake had time to accept that, the rest. The full story would be a lot to absorb in one chunk.

Decision made, her tight shoulders dropped, the tension in her neck easing. Jake might react badly but the longer she delayed, the worse it would be.

Her relief lasted exactly fifty-five minutes. Till her phone rang while she was pinning up her hair, ready to find Jake. Few people had this number. Her lawyer, Zoe, and a couple of friends.

'Hello?'

'At last, she answers!' The terse voice splintered shards of ice down her spine. Caro froze, dropping the last hairpin. It seemed the only part of her still working was her heart, beating double quick.

'Father.'

'You remember who I am now, Carolina? That surprises me.' He thundered on. 'How dare you make me call you personally? I don't have time for this nonsense but my staff tell me you haven't answered their messages. You haven't said when you'll arrive for your brother's party. I'm forced to waste time doing the work of secretaries!'

His voice boomed so loud Caro lifted the phone from her ear. Remnants of old habits stirred. Habits of obedience and meekness. For years she'd let this man run her life and see where it had got her.

She wanted to scream that he'd stolen her child and let her spend years uselessly grieving. But she wouldn't scream, wouldn't respond to his bullying with emotion. Instead she'd be calm and in control, in contrast to his arrogant orders and malicious jibes.

When she *did* confront him it would be in person. She wanted to look him in those choleric blue eyes and let him see that he no longer had power over her. She wanted to see his reaction when the mouse of the family finally stood up to him.

'Are you there? Why aren't you answering?' Even at this distance that voice, like a thunderstorm crashing over mountains, made her skin twitch.

'I'm here, Father. And I did respond to the messages. I gave my apologies. I won't be able to attend—'

'Nonsense! Of course you'll be here.'

'Not this time.' Caro was proud of her even tone.

The silence that followed resonated with foreboding. No one, ever, said no to her father. Not her stepmother or half-brothers, not the prime minister, not anyone among St Ancilla's rich and powerful.

Caro almost wished she could see him, though the thought of being near him made her feel physically ill. Was there surprise as well as fury on that mottled face?

His voice when it came sent another polar freeze through her. 'Your brother's engagement is a major event. All the family will be there, you included.' He paused as if hearing her silent protest that she wasn't really part of the family. She hadn't been since he remarried and fathered the sons he'd so wanted.

'There'll be photos tomorrow evening before the first informal celebration. You'll be there and the rest of the week, doing your duty.'

Caro gathered her breath, storing it up in her lungs till she thought she'd burst. Her hands turned clammy and the butterflies in her stomach were the size of sea eagles.

'I'm afraid that's impossible. I—'

'I'll say this once, Carolina.' He said her name like an insult. 'It's vital we present a united front for this engagement. The wedding is important. Whatever you're doing in Switzerland you'll drop it immediately and come home.'

Shocked, her breath hissed in.

'Oh, yes, I know you're in Switzerland. My security staff keep me informed. I haven't asked them to dig deeper. I'm not interested. However...' he paused and the air turned heavy as if anticipating the next lightning strike '...if within the next hour my secretary doesn't receive details of your arrival time, I'll instruct security to find you and bring you home. By force if necessary. They're on standby. I'm told they can be with you within two hours.'

Caro opened her mouth to say kidnap was an offence when the line went dead.

The phone fell to her bed and she stared at it as if at a venomous snake.

Caro wrapped her arms around her ribcage where her heart thundered. She imagined the men in dark suits, driving vehicles with blacked-out windows. They gave her the creeps. They'd been the ones to spirit her back to St Ancilla when her father discovered her pregnancy, and to the isolated convent on the north of the island. They'd kept a discreet but not invisible watch on the convent and ensured she didn't run away before the baby was born.

She told herself they had no jurisdiction here. She could appeal to Jake for help. He'd protect her.

Then she imagined how that would play out. Swiss police, official reports, maybe press interest from those reporters who still kept an eye on this valley because of its connections to the rich and powerful.

Worse, she imagined Jake's reaction when he discovered not only that she was Ariane's mother, but who her family was, all in one terrible sweep. Fear pounded through her, drying her throat and churning her stomach.

She'd already decided she needed to handle this carefully. If he was bombarded with it all at once, especially with her father's henchmen battering at the door, he wouldn't take it well. He'd see her as the enemy, here to take Ariane from him any way she could. He was as likely to hand her to her father's goons as keep her from them.

Caro turned and paced, torn between distress and fury. There was something about all this she didn't understand. That final threat of her father's hadn't been simply because she'd annoyed him.

'It's vital we present a united front... The wedding is important.'

She knew enough about her father to understand he wasn't concerned about her brother's love life. It wasn't a love match but an arranged marriage. Why was her father so adamant they all be there, smiling and putting on a good show?

Caro shook her head. No time for that now. She had to figure out what to do. Unfortunately, she realised as she considered it from every angle, she didn't have a choice. Not if she wanted a chance to discuss Ariane's future calmly with Jake without her father interfering.

Jake strode the corridor towards his office. It was early but after a night of little sleep he might as well start work. The consortium he was trying to entice into this project was proving difficult to pin down. He needed to concentrate on that rather than Caro.

The woman perplexed him, intrigued and attracted him. He couldn't recall responding to any woman like this. Not even Fiona, his ex-lover, the woman he'd fleetingly considered as a possible spouse.

Every time he thought he had Caro pegged she surprised him. She awakened a host of unexpected feelings.

He turned a corner and slammed to a halt. There, silhouetted against the window, was Caro near the door to his office.

Jake recalled the feel of her slender body curving into his, the baffling intensity of the emotions she'd evoked and the less puzzling arousal. Then she'd worn next to nothing. Now she was in one of her drab skirt and jacket sets, in a colour that reminded him of mud. And still excitement throbbed in his blood.

She stared at a painting on the wall, the early sunlight limning her profile. Jake told himself she wasn't stunning the way some of his lovers had been, yet there was something about that pure profile, the angle of her chin, the neat curve of her ear and that long slender neck that drew his eye.

She moved and he caught a glint of russet in her brown hair. It reminded him of the fire that ignited in his belly last night. And of the volatile, passionate woman who'd turned to flame when he'd kissed and caressed her.

Heat punched low. All night he'd struggled against the need to go to her room.

To check if she was okay, he reasoned.

To take up where they'd left off, he knew.

Only the depth of her hurt had stopped him.

Caro swung around. Had she heard the sudden heft of his breath? Her eyes widened.

It was back, that pulsing heat. She bit her lip and he absorbed the fact she looked nervous, no, more than that. Scared. She swivelled back to the painting, fingers plaiting restlessly before her.

Her fear made him hesitate. She *couldn't* be scared of him.

'You like it?' Jake asked as he neared, forcing himself to look at the picture. He'd barely paid any attention to it. In the flood of morning light he discovered the face of a sombre man holding a globe and surrounded by maps and papers.

Caro shrugged and he noticed the movement was stiff, as if her shoulders were too tight.

Was she self-conscious after last night? He couldn't blame her, yet he wanted to make her turn and look at him.

'It's…interesting. At least four hundred years old.' She spoke quickly as if to fill the silence. As if nervous. 'I can't work out what it's doing here, in the direct sunlight. It should be in a protected position.'

'Maybe it's a copy.' Jake knew little about art and, though the castle's owner had provided an inventory, he hadn't looked at it. He was here to work, and build a relationship with Ariane, not stare at paintings.

Caro shook her head. 'Unlikely.' She bent closer. 'Highly unlikely.'

'You know old paintings?' If he'd been watching the portrait instead of her he would have missed her flinch.

'I studied art history.' She darted a sideways glance that didn't meet his eyes.

'I don't remember that on your résumé.'

She lifted one shoulder. 'I didn't finish and it didn't seem relevant.'

True, but Jake wanted to know more. Much more.

'It's my fault about the painting.' At his words she swung

to face him. Jake felt that familiar tug low in his belly when their eyes met. As if someone dragged a weight through his insides. 'It looked gloomy so I had it moved out of my study.'

'I see.' For a moment longer their eyes held, then her gaze slewed back to the painting and Jake found himself cursing her discomfort with him. He preferred her passionate and bold.

And eager for sex.

Heat spiralled like smoke up from his groin and he had to work at keeping his distance. Clearly she was nervous.

'I think you should move it.' Another darting glance. 'It shouldn't be here in the full sun.'

'I'll get Neil onto it.' He paused, watching the tic of her pulse at her throat and the way her hands refused to be still. 'Caro, we need to—'

'I have to—'

Both pulled up short. 'You first,' he invited.

Caro nodded but didn't look eager. 'In your office?'

'Sure.' He pushed open his study door and invited her to precede him. As she walked past he caught a hint of her warm, spicy scent and it went straight to his head. For a second he closed his eyes.

He'd be good. He wouldn't seduce the nanny in his office.

No matter how much he wanted to.

Caro's fingers twisted together, echoing the churning inside. This was more difficult than she'd thought.

She'd half hoped she could blame last night and the way she'd thrown herself at Jake on the high-octane mix of fear and elation resulting from Ariane's near accident. But it was still there, the desire for his touch, the yearning for his tenderness and passion.

Worse, she wanted to blurt out everything, ignoring the need to approach this carefully.

Hurriedly she looked down, veiling her eyes from that sharp scrutiny.

Her heart hammered and no matter how she tried she couldn't pull off the mask of composure she'd come to rely on. Because she wasn't just fighting her attraction to Ariane's uncle. Now her father had thrust his oar into these turbulent waters she felt in danger of being tugged under by forces too strong to withstand.

Now, instead of telling Jake the truth and trusting he was truly a decent man with Ariane's best interests at heart, she was forced to lie again. Because she couldn't afford to risk him withdrawing and taking her daughter away.

She felt sick.

'Caro?' A firm hand closed around her elbow. 'You look like you're going to keel over. Here.' He ushered her to a chair. 'Sit.'

She subsided thankfully, even as she castigated herself for weakness. This wasn't how she'd meant to face him. But when she'd seen him, all her hard-won resolve had disintegrated. She'd jabbered on about art instead of cutting to the point.

'Thank you. Sorry, I'm fine. I...' She shook her head. 'Something has come up. I need to go away for the rest of the week. I know it's not usual and I should give you notice but it's urgent.'

'Away?' His eyebrows tilted down. In curiosity or annoyance?

'To St Ancilla. I had a call from my...father this morning.' She couldn't suppress the shiver down her spine.

'Bad news?'

'A family matter. I'm needed there.' She paused and licked dry lips. 'Normally I'd never dream of asking for

time off so soon but I don't have a choice.' Her father had
seen to that. Caro straightened. 'I'd be back next week.'

Finally she looked him square in the face. What Jake saw
there made everything inside him still. Not just tension
but distress, and that fear he'd picked up on in the corridor.
He'd read it as embarrassment after last night's intimacy.
Clearly it was caused by something far deeper.

Not everything revolves around you, Maynard.

'Your family needs you.'

'I know it's inconvenient and I apologise but—'

He stopped her with a wave of his hand. Clearly this
was important. From her expression he guessed serious
illness or accident.

'Of course you can go.' What wouldn't he have given for
the chance to spend even a few extra minutes with Connie,
instead of being informed from the far side of the world
that his sister was dead? 'Take what time you need. Lotte
and I will manage.'

For a second her lip wobbled then she nodded briskly.
'I'll be back next week. You can count on me.'

CHAPTER EIGHT

'JAKE, DID YOU say it was St Ancilla Caro went to?'

Reluctantly Jake looked up from his emails. This project grew more complex by the hour and he wasn't devoting as much time to it as he should. He'd spent the morning with Ariane.

On the other hand, his niece's ease with him felt like victory. He owed her thawing, in part, to Caro, who'd done an amazing job in a short time. He'd been right to hire her.

Neil sank into the chair on the other side of his desk. His expression was unreadable, yet the fine hairs on the back of Jake's neck stood to attention.

'That's right. What's happened?'

Jake leaned back in his chair. A tough early life, a stint in the army then years devoted to wheeling and dealing in the turbulent field of international finance meant it took a lot to unnerve him.

'I tracked down another on our list of potential investors and discovered they were in St Ancilla for a big event.' Neil passed his tablet across the desk. It displayed a news article. If you could call it real news. Some royal event.

'So? Wait a few days then make contact.'

'Check out the photo. The second one.'

Jake looked again, scrolling past a photo of a young, formally dressed couple smiling at the camera with all the animation of marionettes. Prince Paul of St Ancilla and Princess Eva of Tarentia, just engaged.

Beneath was a group photo. An ornate balcony on an imposing building, crammed with elegant women and men in heavily decorated dress uniforms.

'And?' Jake had no interest in aristocracy. He did business with them but his personal experiences with them hadn't been happy. First had been the entitled foreigner who'd lured his mother away, on condition she abandon her kids. Then just months ago, his own girlfriend suggested he put Ariane in an orphanage rather than bother with her. Both had been uncaring of anyone else, expecting the world to revolve around them.

'Look closely. The one in blue.'

Jake frowned. Several of those uniforms were blue, plus a blonde in ice blue and…

He stared. It couldn't be.

Of course it couldn't. The woman in the deep blue dress was a vibrant redhead, not a brunette. Yet Jake felt adrenaline burst into his blood with a jolt.

He zoomed in on the woman, amazed at the likeness.

'Princess Carolina of St Ancilla. The King's eldest child.' Neil's voice was flat with suppressed excitement.

'*Princess* Carolina?' Carolina. Caro.

No. It was impossible. Mere coincidence.

Yet the buzz in Jake's bloodstream didn't abate.

'Yes, but she's not his heir. Her younger brother is. Carolina isn't in the limelight these days. She lives fairly quietly in the north of the island though she's very active in a number of charities, especially relating to children.'

Jake peered at the woman. She was a ringer for Caro, except for the clothes and hair. And the royal connections.

'Maybe our Caro is a distant relative.'

Our Caro? His choice of words made her sound—

'There's more.' Neil took the device and opened another page, handing it back. With his usual efficiency he'd collated a precis on the woman.

The Princess had a string of names, had been born almost twenty-five years ago and lost her mother early. Her father had remarried when she was two and she had three half-brothers. She'd studied in the US but didn't finish her degree. There'd been a scandal. He read headlines about wild parties and drug use. Jake wasn't surprised. Most of Fiona's privileged friends preferred parties to work. What did surprise him was that after returning to St Ancilla, Princess Carolina had all but dropped off the radar. She didn't live in the palace, merely appearing in the press at charity events or major royal celebrations like this, her half-brother's engagement.

He scrolled lower, studying the shots Neil had collected. Stiff and formal on the same balcony with her family when she was a little girl. Again in her teens, looking almost gawky despite her expensive clothes and with her flame-coloured hair now turning auburn, her head turned towards her father, her expression curiously closed. A shot of her with one of her brothers, both smiling for the camera but neither looking happy.

Jake began to feel almost sorry for her. Had the wild partying been rebellion after an unhappy childhood?

Then he scrolled lower and his breath caught.

This photo was different. Candid. He doubted she knew it had been taken. She wore casual clothes, her hair in a ponytail and she was in a crowd with other young people. At a party, by the look of it. She was half turned away, looking over her shoulder, but there was no mistaking the warmth in her expression as she smiled at someone beyond the camera. Her eyes, a remarkable deep violet, glowed. *She* glowed. Jake felt the impact of her joy judder through him.

He swallowed, mesmerised by those eyes. They were so like Ariane's that for a moment everything, his pulse and his breathing, seemed to stop. He'd always thought the colour rare. Maybe not so on St Ancilla.

He touched the screen, enlarged the photo and then his breath really did stop.

There, on the back of her shoulder next to the strap of her top, was a small birthmark shaped like a comma.

Jake had seen that mark three nights ago.

It had peeked out beneath the strap of a grey camisole when he'd held Caro in his arms.

By midnight the scowl on Jake's face threatened to take up permanent residence. His emotions veered between shock—he who'd believed nothing had the power to surprise him any more—fury and grim determination.

There was pain too, a sliver of hurt that he'd allowed her to play him as she had, but he buried that deep.

There was no time for such luxuries. With every hour came a new revelation. That was what happened when you could afford the best investigators.

No wonder the initial check of her application hadn't found any criminal record for Caro Rivage. She didn't exist, except technically, for Rivage was the family's name though royalty traditionally didn't use it.

Caro was royal. Daughter of a king. Her full name and titles took up four lines on the report filling his computer screen.

Jake stared at it and felt the blood jump in his arteries as if seeking a way out. His body was screwed so tight even an hour with a punching bag had done nothing to relieve it.

Once they knew which direction to pursue, the investigators hadn't taken long to prove Princess Carolina and Caro Rivage were the same person.

Some of what she'd said was even true. She had worked in a preschool. The references had checked out because she'd actually worked as a nanny for a couple of families. In between swanning off in couture clothes to charity events and royal parties. That in itself was curious. From socialite royal to nanny wasn't a normal progression. But she was definitely royal.

There was a photo of her taken six months ago at a ball, wearing a tiara and a complacent smile that made him grind his teeth. A tall guy with medals across his chest and a hungry expression was at her side, holding her as if he didn't want to let her out of his sight.

Jake swore and shoved his chair back, stalking the length of the room. He understood the feeling. The woman couldn't be trusted an inch.

Yet still he registered that hum of expectation deep inside. The expectation of what would happen when he held her in his arms again. Even her bald-faced deceit hadn't destroyed his desire for her.

He ploughed his fingers through his hair and spun on his heel, pacing again.

She'd lied from the first. Not only about her identity. About everything.

That scene by the spa? Had she waited for him, knowing he often worked out at night? She'd sucked him in with her passion and counterfeit distress. First reel him in by giving him a taste of what he wanted, a taste of mind-blowing sex, then play on his protective instincts to stop things going further. She'd teased and distracted him.

Ego told him she *had* been attracted to him. He'd seen the evidence almost from the first.

His brain said it was all a lie. Or if it wasn't, even if she had wanted him, she'd wanted something more, to lure him into feeling sorry for her. She'd wanted him in the palm of her soft little hands.

That sob story about needing to go to her family? The implication, unspoken but there in every throbbing silence, that some terrible tragedy had occurred? All lies.

She'd gone to a *party*!

Was the tall guy with the possessive look there with her? Or had she moved on to some other gullible bloke?

Jake frowned as pain radiated up his arm. He looked down and saw he'd pounded his fist against the stone wall beside the bookshelves. Gingerly he unfurled his fingers, feeling pain slice through his hand and seeing a graze of blood.

The woman had got under his skin in ways he could barely believe.

Even Fiona hadn't made him so furious. Because he'd begun to see her true colours despite her efforts to paper over the cracks of her innately selfish personality.

With Caro... Carolina, he'd been completely taken in. Except for that tingle of premonition that she wasn't what she'd seemed. He'd been distracted by his need to find a way to connect with his niece, and his attraction for a charlatan.

She hadn't just lied about her identity. If only that were the worst of it!

He shoved his hands in his pockets, peering out at moon-washed peaks, taking in the twinkle of lights further down the valley that made him feel, for the first time in years, as isolated as he'd been as a kid, shutting himself off in an attempt to lessen the pain of his mother's desertion.

He'd actually *felt* for Caro. Had wanted to care for her as much as he'd wanted her in his bed.

Whereas she didn't want him. She wanted Ariane.

Nausea swirled in his belly and he swallowed the rancid taste of disgust.

If the investigators were right, Ariane's birth mother was Princess Carolina of St Ancilla. Everything pointed to it. The way she'd been bundled home when news broke of her wild partying. Her seclusion at a convent on the northern end of the island for the better part of a year. The fact that Ariane's adoption took place in the same region and there appeared to be a link to the same convent.

As if that weren't enough, someone else had been investigating Ariane's adoption lately, requesting records and asking questions. A lawyer in St Ancilla. A lawyer related to the countess who'd supplied a reference for her friend, the masquerading Princess.

It was easy to see what was happening. A group of aristocratic friends colluding to help each other.

Why?

The answer made Jake's blood steam.

So the pampered Princess could get her hands on Ariane.

Jake shook his head, breathing deep and filling his lungs as far as they'd go. Even so it felt as if barbed wire wrapped around his chest, constricting his air, drawing tighter as his ire rose.

He didn't give a damn if some party-girl princess had a change of heart about the baby she'd abandoned. Ariane was better off without her. For what was to stop her changing her mind again?

What Ariane needed was love and stability. Family. That was where he came in. *He* was family.

Carolina of St Ancilla signed away her rights years ago. It was too late to change her mind. Ariane was his niece, his only link with his beloved sister.

He had no intention of giving her up to some spoiled, deceitful woman who used her body to get her own way.

A shudder stormed his frame as he thought of her giving herself to man after man, a commodity to get what she wanted. She was an expert cheat, given the way she'd fooled him. An expert at using sex and deception.

But she'd messed up this time.

He'd never release Ariane to such a woman.

He might have been born working class and only just avoided being made a ward of the state when his older sister stepped in to raise him. But he was a man to be reckoned with. Apart from his considerable wealth, he had powerful contacts.

More, forewarned was forearmed. He wouldn't wait till

the Princess tried to snatch Ariane, or filed a lawsuit to claim her.

Right now arrangements were being made to increase security on the castle and on Ariane in particular. No one would steal her away.

As for a lawsuit... His mouth curled disdainfully. He already had a team of the best legal experts onto it. Birth mother or not, Carolina wouldn't get custody. If he had his way she wouldn't get access to Ariane for years. By which time her whim to be a mother would no doubt have passed.

Jake's smile became a grin. He wanted to see her face when she discovered she'd been outmanoeuvred.

Caro's smile felt like a rictus and her fingers ached from shaking hands with the throng of people her father had invited to the ball. Yet a glance at the mirror on the other side of the palace foyer reassured her. Her smile appeared real and she looked as regal as jewels, haute couture and years of mind-numbing training in etiquette and deportment could make her.

Her father would have nothing to complain about tonight, at least as far as she was concerned. No doubt he'd find something else to take umbrage at. He was never happy unless unhappy with something.

What had possessed him to invite such a huge crowd? Not only royals and people from both St Ancilla and Tarentia, but a slew of others. There was an unusually high number of foreign bankers and financiers.

Surely the whisper she'd heard couldn't be true—that the royal finances were rocky.

Caro pushed the idea aside. Probably her father planned some new scheme and had decided to finance it with someone else's money.

She smiled at another guest, answering him in his native German, hiding a wince at his too hearty handshake.

Through the formal welcomes her mind kept straying to Ariane. Was she sleeping or was she beset by the nightmares?

Did she miss Caro?

Caro told herself it was too soon for that, though *she* missed her daughter with a permanent ache beneath her ribs. After years believing her child dead, the impatience to be with her grew stronger not less. She'd only just resisted calling again tonight to check on her. Lotte had been reassuring this morning when she phoned. That had to be enough.

Soon she'd be free to go back to the castle. To Ariane. And Jake.

Sinuous heat swirled through Caro's middle at the thought of Jake.

Feminine desire battled with trepidation whenever she thought of him. The man she'd almost given herself to. The man she wanted. She, who'd believed no man could ever again tempt her into intimacy, much less trust.

The man who'd been considerate and caring in a way unmatched by any other man in her life.

The man who stood between her and her daughter.

Except surely the person she'd seen behind the forbidding exterior and rapier-sharp mind needn't be an enemy? He wanted the best for Ariane. Surely, once he knew the truth he'd understand. Cooperate.

Caro clung to that thought through the last of the welcomes. In a couple of days she could return to Switzerland, see Ariane and explain to Jake.

He'd be surprised at first but he was no ogre. They'd find a way to negotiate this situation and—

'Princess Carolina.' The deep voice, like trailing velvet dipped in arsenic, wrapped around her.

Her thoughts shattered. Slowly, using every effort to

turn a neck suddenly stiff with tension, she looked to the next guest.

She felt herself sway, wondered distantly whether she might black out. But she didn't have the luxury of escape.

Jake Maynard stood there, superb in formal clothes tailored lovingly to his tall, broad-shouldered form. He'd looked daunting in business clothes, vital and handsome in a knitted pullover and jeans, raffishly sexy in gym gear. It shouldn't surprise her that in a bow tie and dinner jacket he was devastating.

Yet he stole her words as well as her breath. Caro stared up at the man watching her with the hooded silvery gaze of a predator. So handsome, with such a palpable aura of danger and power she instantly thought of a fallen angel. Or maybe that was because of the hot mercury stare pinning her to the spot.

'Or do you prefer to be called Caro?'

Nearby someone snatched a shocked breath at his effrontery but Caro was too busy standing tall when that poison-drenched voice wound tight around her, stopping the air in her lungs.

Without waiting for an answer he captured her hand. Instead of shaking it, he lifted it slowly, ostentatiously. He didn't bend his head, instead raising her arm high so she could see her pale hand in his as he pressed his lips to her fingers.

Involuntarily her fingers curled around his as energy jagged from her hand up her arm and down to her breasts and lower, to that empty space deep inside. The blood racketed around her body so fast she felt light-headed.

Caro heard a hissed breath, hers, then felt the convulsive shiver of her body's response. To him. To the anger sizzling in that half-lidded stare. And, heaven help her, to his bold challenge.

'Mr... Maynard.' Her hesitation made it sound as if she

was trying to remember his name, which was better than revealing how undone she was as he stood there, arrogantly stopping the queue of guests and holding her hand so close she felt the warmth of his breath on her fingers. The flesh across the back of her shoulders drew tight and her skin prickled. 'How good of you to attend.'

'You were expecting me?' His eyebrows rose as if in polite enquiry but Caro was busy reading the rest of his face. The grooves carved down his cheeks by the tight set of his jaw, the pronounced tic of a pulse at his temple and the flare of his nostrils as if assailed by some unpleasant smell.

Caro wavered on the verge of panic. She couldn't do this. Not here, not now. She needed quiet, a place to explain away from curious ears. She needed his understanding and compassion, not his enmity.

But finally Caro steadied herself. She had no option.

'I hadn't realised you were on the guest list but I hope you enjoy the ball.'

'I'm sure it will be most entertaining.' Still he didn't release her hand. She was conscious of the increasing number of stares trained on them.

'Please go on through.' She nodded towards the double doors flung wide to the gilded ballroom. Footmen stood on either side of the entry with trays of champagne. Beyond them guests milled, quaffing drinks, showing off their finery, chattering in anticipation.

Slowly he lowered her hand. But instead of releasing it, Jake curled his fingers around hers. His hold tightened into an implacable grip that matched the forbidding angle of his jaw. 'Perhaps you'd like to show me around, Your Highness?'

The suggestion defied royal protocol and good manners. She was here with her family to greet their guests.

'I'm sorry.' She made to pull her hand free but found it trapped. 'But I—'

'An excellent idea,' the familiar voice boomed from nearby.

Caro's face jerked around to find her father, resplendent in a scarlet uniform almost a perfect match for his colouring, beaming at them. Beaming! Her father!

Caro had a powerful moment of disbelief. So strong she wondered for a second if she'd strayed into a dream. Even her stepmother beside him wore a slight smile.

'You two young people go ahead. Enjoy yourselves. We're almost finished here.'

Inadvertently Caro caught the eye of a long-term diplomat in the queue, waiting to be greeted. In his eyes she saw a reflection of her own astonishment. Her father was a stickler for the rules, especially those promoting formality at court.

'Thank you, Your Majesty.' Jake inclined his head then, before Caro had time to catch her breath, he led her smoothly towards the ballroom.

As they stepped into the glittering room with its ornate ceiling paintings, crystal chandeliers and scores of massive mirrors, his breath whispered across her cheek.

'I'm sure tonight will be memorable.'

He spoke softly but the look in his eyes, and the feel of those long fingers manacling her wrist, sent a chill of deep foreboding straight to her marrow.

CHAPTER NINE

JAKE WAS KNOWN for his self-control. For an early responder in disaster zones it had been a quality almost as important as his skills at organisation and saving lives.

Yet tonight sorely tested him.

She tested him. Waltzing by on the arm of the man who'd held her possessively in that photo.

The simmering heat in Jake's gut rose in a seething flood of impatience. His plans to confront her in a quiet anteroom had been foiled by the press of people, all wanting to speak to her or him. Then there was the sheer formality of the proceedings. Her first dance had already been allocated and, short of hauling her away in front of a fascinated audience, he'd had no choice but to relinquish her.

He gritted his teeth, berating himself for the spurt of fury that had propelled him to the palace. He should have waited and chosen his venue better but his blood was up and for the first time in years he'd acted rashly. Goaded by the smiling redhead in the dark violet dress.

Simply watching her did excruciating things to his self-control. Jake told himself it was wrath but there was an edge to his anger that felt like more.

Like want.

Worse, like disappointment, because he'd felt something for her.

Except the person he'd begun to know was a mirage, constructed by the duplicitous woman now swanning around the dance floor. Her long skirt belled around her legs, calling attention to that tiny waist and acres of creamy skin bared by a dress that hung off both shoulders.

Jake's blood pounded in counterpoint to the beat of the

waltz. Colours blurred and faces flashed by but still he
had no difficulty keeping her in focus. Caro Rivage aka
Princess Carolina. She moved with a grace that despite his
anger evoked raw hunger in the pit of his belly. Or maybe
it was the smile she gave her partner, bending to murmur
in her ear.

They swept past and for a second violet eyes caught
Jake's. Wide, impossibly beautiful and, if he didn't know
better, scared.

No, this woman wasn't scared. Disconcerted perhaps
but she'd brazened it out, introducing him to guests as if
they really were simply acquaintances. Keeping up a flow
of small talk that made him want to muffle her mouth with
his till she was so breathless, speech was beyond her.

With difficulty Jake slowed his breathing, searching for
calm. They needed to talk. He needed confirmation of what
he'd learned. Needed her to admit it. Then he'd inform her
she had no hope of getting Ariane.

Sanity resurfaced. He told himself to wait till tomorrow
when he could see her alone.

Except that would give her time to regroup. He'd find
her surrounded by lawyers and royal officials who'd try to
deflect him. This was between the pair of them. He wasn't
in the mood to wait.

The music ended and her skirts spilled onto the gleaming floor as she curtseyed to her bowing partner. He was
Prince of Tarentia, Jake had learned. Brother to the woman
whose betrothal they were celebrating. How cosy. No doubt
the two royal families were close. Maybe there was a second wedding in the pipeline?

Jake grimaced as acid stirred in his gut. Caro inhabited
a privileged world where old family connections mattered
and worth was measured by inherited wealth and titles.

But her privileged past didn't give her the right to sail
into Ariane's life and disrupt it. To make the little girl be-

lieve her birth mother cared, only to be crushed when she
discovered the woman who'd borne her had no staying
power.

Jake knew how that felt.

He wouldn't let it happen to Ariane.

Stalking forward, he cut through the milling crowd to
Caro and her partner.

'My dance, I believe.'

He didn't wait for a response, ignored a protest from
the Prince and slipped his arm around Caro's waist. As he
claimed her he felt her jolt of response. Satisfaction stirred.
A second later the music started and Jake propelled her into
the centre of the dance floor.

He hadn't planned to dance, had decided merely to separate her from her partner, but this was the simplest way
to do it.

It had nothing to do with the greedy way his fingers
splayed over her narrow back. The surge of rampant triumph as he pulled her close. The way her eyes dilated and
that glossy cupid's bow mouth opened as if she couldn't
catch her breath. Or the sheer rightness of her slender form
in his embrace.

She matched his steps as if they'd danced together before. As their bodies had aligned perfectly when they'd
kissed and when he'd held her, sobbing in his arms.

Jake tasted disgust on his tongue. Those tears had been
faked. *She* was fake.

He glanced at the fine golden wires studded with purple
gems threading her auburn hair, the matching long earrings
that swung with her every move. Heard the swish of her
rich ball gown billowing around his legs. But the trappings
of royalty meant nothing to him. Glamour couldn't make
up for a good heart. The fact his body still responded to
her only made him more determined to wrest himself and
his niece free of her pernicious influence.

'So tell me, Princess Carolina. Since you're the eldest in the family, why aren't you married yet? No desire for a family and children of your own?'

Caro faltered and would have tripped but for Jake's iron-hard embrace. He didn't slow at her misstep, swinging her, if anything, faster into the next turn, so she had to clutch him to keep her balance. Hard muscle and warm fabric teased her palms.

The mention of children hit her like a blow to the solar plexus, the impact shooting through her body and turning her legs nerveless.

For a heartbeat, for two, she could do nothing but hang on and try to keep up.

She shouldn't be surprised he was such a superb dancer, he had the strength and agility of an athlete. Yet it was his words, not his moves that worried her.

How much did he know? Her double identity, certainly. Anger radiated from him in waves. But not, surely, the rest, about being Ariane's mother.

'No plans to settle down with your Prince Charming?' He didn't bother keeping his voice down and the glittering challenge in those icy eyes told her he relished the idea of her objecting and trying to quiet him. No doubt he'd say something more outrageous.

Was that why he was here? To embarrass her?

For several seconds her tongue stuck to the roof of her mouth. A lifetime's reserve, of doing as she was ordered and being the one to back down, urged her to murmur something placatory. She hated scenes.

The twisting distress in her belly urged her to flee.

Caro did neither. She looked him straight in the eye.

'No plans to marry, Jake.' She pronounced his name casually as if they were old friends. As if the taste of it on her tongue didn't evoke a clandestine thrill of self-destructive pleasure. 'And you? Are you looking for a wife? I could introduce you to some lovely women here.'

She let her gaze drift over the crowd as if searching for said women. As if she weren't avoiding his blistering contempt.

For years she'd caved at the first sign of her father's displeasure. Even now she was nervous about the prospect of facing the King when she finally got time alone with him. But for some reason, standing up to Jake, despite the knowledge he stood between her and Ariane, made her blood sing in her veins.

'I've no intention of marrying.' The words bit like glacial shards, grazing her skin. 'I have too much experience of lying, manipulative women to trust one that much.'

It was a direct body blow. Caro felt it smash through skin and bone, felt herself absorb it like soft flesh cushioning a knife thrust.

It didn't help that he was right. She *had* to lied to him. But how could she have done otherwise? She'd had her reasons, as he'd discover when she had a chance to explain.

'You need to be careful. You sound like a misogynist. You don't want to turn into a lonely old grouch.'

A flash of something that might have been astonishment lit his features then disappeared. His lips rucked up at one side in a derisory smile that perversely reminded her of how wonderful his mouth had felt on hers a few nights ago.

'No danger of that, Caro. There are always women chasing me. Some even smuggle themselves into my life undercover.' Her breath caught at the steely light in his eyes. 'But I can tell a woman on the make. They don't have a hope of getting what they want, no matter what inducements they offer.'

His gaze dropped slowly, insolently, to her mouth, then lower, to her throat, bare of jewels, then across her décolletage. Suddenly the beautiful dress she wore seemed totally inadequate to protect her from that scorching, lazy stare.

Indignation rose, fiery and glorious, eclipsing nerves and her innate dislike of scenes.

Abruptly, after months, no, years, of coping and carrying on despite the hurt, Caro reached breaking point.

She was tired of being wrong-footed. Of being assessed by men and found wanting. By her father, who'd ignored and belittled her because she wasn't a boy. By Mike, who'd read her gullibility then turned nasty when he discovered she wasn't the docile meal ticket he'd assumed. He'd taken cruel delight in telling her she was far below the standard of his usual lovers.

Now by Jake Maynard, who made her feel cheap. Because in a moment's madness she'd dared to act on the attraction shimmering between them.

It hurt. All her life those rejections had hurt.

She'd had enough.

With a strength that surprised her, Caro wrenched free of his hold and stepped back. She saw his eyes widen then she swung away through the swaying couples.

There'd be speculation and shocked looks but she didn't care. She marched on till she was out on the terrace, lit by flambeaux and still too full of people.

Behind her she heard something that might have been her name but it was drowned by the beat of blood in her ears. Turning, she headed inside again and down a corridor, the sound of her high heels clicking on inlaid marble matching the quick thud of her pulse.

Still she continued, past state rooms, dining rooms, libraries and offices, past startled footmen bringing supplies from the kitchens.

Her ball gown swung wide as she turned up a familiar staircase, skirts lifted for speed, her breath coming in raw gasps that betrayed her pain.

Along another corridor, right to the end of the palace furthest from the rest of the family's rooms. There, highlighted on a wall, was the victorious knight in armour, running a lance through a whimpering dragon. Caro didn't have to look to know the knight wore the same look of cold disdain Jake had as he'd stripped her soul bare.

Caro pressed a hand to her pounding heart and wrenched open the door to her rooms.

Sanctuary at last! At least for the ten minutes she'd give herself to regroup.

She swept in and turned to close the door but a dark figure loomed in the doorway. Before she could react Jake inserted himself into the closing gap, crossed the threshold then stood, looming over her.

'Perfect,' he purred in a deep rumble that danced along her bones. 'Just what we need, a quiet place to continue our discussion uninterrupted.'

Fingers welded to the doorknob, Caro struggled for breath. His effrontery left her speechless.

'No! I want you to leave.'

'Why? Are you scared to be alone with me? You'd rather have witnesses for this discussion?'

'It's not that.' Despite his anger she wasn't scared of Jake Maynard. More of her inability to deal with him until she had her emotions under control. With him she felt as if she walked a tightrope, one false move and she'd fall into…she wasn't sure what, but every sense screamed she couldn't go there. Especially with so much at stake.

Caro drew herself up, projecting the regal assurance the rest of her family did so well and for which she'd had to struggle.

'I didn't invite you here.' The sight of that big, brooding form in her private sanctuary sent a strange jolt through her. As if he trespassed on something more fundamental, more personal than a mere room.

'That's unfortunate, *Princess* Carolina.' He said her title as if it were tainted. 'We have so much to talk about.'

Caro hefted a breath that didn't fill her lungs and tried to get a grip. 'We do. But not here. Not now—'

Jake shook his head. '*Yes*, here and now. And as for you not inviting me, let me be absolutely clear.' He bent towards her, thrusting his starkly sculpted face into her space. 'I would never have invited you into my home if I'd known who you were. You owe me.'

Caro's eyes bulged at the venom in his voice. 'Look, I know my identity is a surprise and I regret not telling you in the beginning but I had excellent reasons—'

'To lie and cheat? Perhaps to steal too?' His eyebrows contracted in a mighty scowl and the atmosphere thickened as if a thunderstorm threatened.

'I don't cheat and I definitely don't steal!' Horror mixed with an anger she couldn't suppress, despite the voice inside telling her she needed to be calm and reasonable. That had always been her default position.

And look where it got you!

'So you say. But from where I stand you're a liar and a cheat.' He shook his head. 'To think I almost felt sorry for you with your sob story the other night.'

'I wasn't lying!' Her distress had been only too real.

'Except your baby didn't die, did it, Caro?' He stepped so close his breath wafted warm across her skin. 'Your child is alive and well.'

'You know?'

How did he know? It didn't seem possible. She'd never have believed it herself if she hadn't finally been told the truth by someone who'd been there. The knowledge staggered her. Her numb fingers slid from the doorknob and Jake shut the door with a solid thud, closing them together in the shadowy room.

'I know.' There was no satisfaction in his eyes, only a

burning emotion she felt like a brand on her skin. 'And I tell you now, you can't have her. You'll *never* have her. I'll do whatever is needed to make sure of it.'

'No!' She wasn't aware of launching herself at him but suddenly she was grabbing his lapels, leaning into him as if she could change his mind by the force of her desperation. 'Don't say that.'

His big body froze, all except for the rise of that wide chest and the quick flick of the pulse at his temple.

'Are you going to try using your body again to persuade me? It won't work this time.'

'I'd *never* do that!'

'No?' He looked so supercilious, staring down at her with hateful superiority. It dragged up memories of the many times she'd felt powerless, when others, principally her royal father, had twisted circumstances against her. 'You're saying you had no ulterior motives when you offered yourself to me? You weren't using your body to get what you want?'

Caro didn't want to think about what had happened that night by the spa, much less try to explain her actions. Not to this grim-faced stranger who bore only a superficial resemblance to the Jake Maynard she'd come to know.

That man was gone, if he'd ever existed outside her imagination.

Yet to Caro's dismay even his piercing disapproval didn't eradicate her profound response to him. Furious as she was, her body still registered the excitingly hard outline of his solid chest, the breadth of his shoulders that made her feel appallingly aware of her own feminine desires. A crazy part of her actually revelled in this flashpoint of physical intimacy though they were on opposing sides.

'Don't be insulting. I'd never do that.'

'No? Because you're a virtuous, responsible royal princess who never put a foot wrong?' Jake shook his head, his eyes not leaving hers, his tone censorious.

'Because you'd never make the headlines for drug use and drunkenness, would you? Or have an illegitimate child and abandon it and the father without a second glance?' Impossibly his expression hardened even more. 'Did you *once* think about where your child might end up? Leaving a vulnerable baby to the mercy of total strangers because you couldn't bother facing your responsibilities?'

Caro would have staggered back in horror except Jake wrapped a powerful arm around her waist, holding her against him.

'You don't deserve to be a mother.' His voice hit a low note that resonated through her bones. It reminded her of the terrible, insidious voice of despair that had hounded her darkest days after the loss of her baby. 'You might have been born with a silver spoon in your mouth but you're nothing but a selfish sl—'

The slap cut his words off, rocking his head to one side.

Pain burst across her palm and up her arm. Belatedly he captured her hand, pressing it against his shoulder. She saw his jaw work and the bloom of dull red across his cheek.

'You don't shut me up so easily, *Princess*. I'm not one of your lackeys, afraid to offend royalty. I tell it as I see it and as I see it you—'

Caro couldn't listen. Nerves stretched to breaking point, body shaking from the desperate surge of adrenaline filling her blood, she did the only thing she could think of to stem the flow of vitriol.

Rising on her toes, she smashed her mouth against his.

CHAPTER TEN

A THUNDERBOLT SHEARED through Jake, cementing his feet to the floor. His body rocked, hands clasping her tight.

As if he feared she'd step back?

Impossible.

She was a liar, a cheat. He couldn't trust a word that came out of that beautiful deceitful mouth.

Yet as Caro's lips sealed his and her soft breasts pushed against him something shuddered through him that wasn't abhorrence or repudiation.

Desire. Hunger.

Need.

A need so powerful it made a mockery of the diatribe that he'd spewed out. Even her resemblance to his faithless mother, abandoning her children because they didn't fit her chosen lifestyle, faded into the background.

In his arms he held fire and feminine passion. A desperation that matched his. She tunnelled her free hand through the hair at the back of his scalp, pulling his face down as she kissed him with an urgency that sent every sense throbbing into overload.

Already clinging to the borderline of control, Jake opened to her kiss, letting her tongue slip between his lips. He reciprocated, devouring her mouth with a thoroughness that spoke of this woman's seductive allure as much as his own recent celibacy.

Somehow this physical attraction survived disillusionment. Incredibly, it wasn't eclipsed by negative feelings. Fury and desire coalesced into something headier, stronger, hotter than he'd ever experienced.

He wanted to despise himself, wanted to wrench away

from her pliant body and the addictive sweetness of her mouth. Yet he couldn't.

She gave a mew of satisfaction that coiled through his vitals. He realised he'd bent her back over his arm, kissing her the way he'd like to take her body, with a single-minded carnality that already had him fully erect.

Jake tried to gather the ragged remains of his self-control. This was the second time she'd kissed him, each time trying to play him for a sucker.

Yet even that knowledge couldn't quell his need. It was bone-deep, undeniable and, it seemed, unquenchable.

The only way out was to make her pull back.

He covered her breast, warm and thrusting towards him. His grasp tightened and he heard again that encouraging purr in the back of her throat.

Jake told himself he was spurred by the need to make Caro retreat. He hooked his fingers into the top of the strapless dress and yanked. Impossibly soft flesh pillowed the backs of his fingers. He yanked again and the purple dress came down just enough to reveal a creamy, raspberry-tipped breast, not large but an exact fit for his hand.

Jake's erection throbbed as he covered her with his hand. Instantly an electric current zapped up his arm, lifting the hairs on his nape before shooting down, straight to his groin.

Caro watched him beneath drowsy eyelids. But there was nothing passive about that purple-blue stare. Jake felt the air freeze in his lungs as their gazes meshed.

Deliberately, driven by a compulsion he couldn't resist, he bent, kissing her nipple then drawing it into his mouth.

The assault on his senses was instantaneous. The delicious taste of her. The flood of rich, feminine scent, delicate yet sensuous in his nostrils. The incredible surge of arousal.

Far from repudiating him, Caro arched higher, lifting

her pelvis to bring her lower body flush against him, cushioning his erection against soft flesh.

Fumbling, Jake hauled down more material, exposing her other breast. He worked it with his hand, the other with his mouth, and the sound of Caro's faltering cry of pleasure drove him to more lavish caresses.

His groin was iron hard, forged and furnace hot.

For an instant, no more, he retained enough sense to hesitate, then caution shattered and he gave up the fight.

He wanted Caro so desperately his hands shook. The taste of her drove him wild. The sound of her panting, the hitch of her breath when he suckled harder, were pure encouragement.

So aroused it hurt to move, he straightened, pulling her upright and ignoring her pout of disappointment. With kiss-swollen lips and bare breasts pushed up towards him by the dislodged bodice, she looked like some raunchy male fantasy come to life. The contrast of all that exquisite bare flesh with the prim tiara still nestled in her bright hair made him feel as if he were debauching Cinderella.

Except those eyes, that mouth, held erotic awareness.

For this moment it didn't matter what she'd done or planned to do.

Who knew that fury and physical desire could be such potent bedfellows? That hate sex could be so powerful?

'Sorry?' He'd seen her lips move but his tumultuous pulse drowned the words.

'I said, don't you dare stop.'

Satisfaction crested like a curling wave thundering down onto a beach. Finally he had the real Caro. Stripped of lies and subterfuge. As vulnerable as he to the stark force of mutual attraction.

Ridiculously Jake's heart lifted. They both wanted this, both needed it. And when it was done the niggling ache he'd felt ever since Caro Rivage stepped into his world would be gone.

He couldn't wait.

Sliding his hands down warm silk to that slender waist, he lifted her off the ground, intending to find the bedroom. But the movement brought her exquisite, jiggling breasts high. His mouth dried, his ability to plan more than a few steps ahead disintegrated and instead he deposited her on a nearby piece of furniture. He didn't know what it was, only that its height meant she now sat almost level with his groin.

Without hesitation he stepped closer, hands in her voluminous skirts. Caro didn't try to stop him. Her knees fell open, inviting him closer, and her own hands were busy tugging his bow tie undone, ripping at his shirt.

Finally his questing hands met sheer nylon. He closed his eyes in frustration. He should have guessed a princess would wear pantyhose for a ball. He'd have to—

His fingers touched bare flesh. Stockings, not pantyhose. Elation rose. He touched lace between her legs, then, sliding his fingers beneath it, damp curls.

A shudder of lust racked Jake. He set his jaw, searching for the willpower to exhibit some control.

Soft hands palmed his chest, nudging his shirt and jacket wide. They slid down from chest to navel, to the top of his trousers. A second later nimble fingers undid his trousers.

His eyes snapped open as his clothes fell away and her hands curled around his length.

Arousal quaked through him. His skin pulled taut as heat shot hard and heavy to his groin.

Jake pulled her against him, his lips on hers, driving into her welcoming mouth.

There was no thought involved as he bent his knees to bring his erection to that sweet spot between her thighs. Or tugged her lacy underwear aside. Only the same instinct that made him plant one hand on her hip, tilting her towards him.

Something stirred in his brain. Some thought he couldn't catch. Something...

She shifted and suddenly he was there, the head of his shaft testing slick velvety heat. Her tongue swirled against his, her hand tightened on his length and the fragment of thought disintegrated.

Pulling her hand away, he planted it on his backside before drawing her legs over his hips and plunging into her beckoning depths.

Someone groaned. Was it him?

Caro's fingers wrapped possessively around his neck while she laid waste to his senses with that eager mouth. Her other hand clawed at his glute as if to hold him exactly where he was.

But Jake couldn't stay still. With a deliberate slowness that took him right to the edge of sensory overload, he withdrew then thrust again, deep and sure. Instantly she quivered. Tiny ripples of movement that coalesced into a powerful, clenching shudder that drew tight around him and hurled him over the edge with her. It was too soon, far too soon, but he was powerless to resist the force of this rocketing climax.

He was no stranger to sexual gratification but this pleasure was so sharp, so intense he lost himself utterly.

Instead of darkness there was light and colour. The deep blue-purple of the sky at twilight surrounded him, drugged him, lulled him through the force of that potent climax until, a lifetime later, it resolved into Caro's wide eyes, holding his in dazed wonder.

Jake shivered as aftershocks powered through him and he spilled again and again in hot, urgent pulses.

Even when it was over he couldn't process anything like a clear thought. Only the need to stay where he was, lodged within her, eaten up by those big violet eyes, with her long legs wrapped tight around his hips and his soul in paradise.

Finally, tentatively, he shifted his weight, only to feel her hands clutch tighter as if she couldn't bear the separation.

He understood the feeling. They hovered in a cushioned cloud of ecstasy.

Yet as the thought rose, so did others. Jake remembered the sheer perfection of losing himself in her intimate heat, pulsing hard and unfettered.

Because he hadn't used a condom.

The realisation cramped his gut and foreboding feathered his spine.

Jake closed his eyes, silently cursing his loss of control. It had never happened before and he'd believed it never would. How had it happened? Because Caro Rivage was a sexy siren who drove men out of their minds?

He breathed deep, inhaling the smell of sex and woman. To his amazement, despite the shock of his dangerous behaviour, Jake found it arousing.

Was this how she'd got pregnant with Ariane? Driving some poor sod crazy with desire so he forgot to take basic precautions?

No. Jake wasn't such a poor excuse for a man. He'd acted of his own volition. It had been his responsibility as much as Caro's to think about safe sex. He'd failed. For the first time in his life he'd let his libido conquer common sense. He despised himself for that.

Drawing a deep breath, he withdrew, clenching his teeth and shutting his eyes at the tormenting friction against sensitive skin.

If he wasn't careful he'd be ready to go another round with her and make exactly the same mistake. Even now he was tempted to forget everything but the need to bury himself in Caro's lush body and take them both to heaven again.

Which was why his movements were quick as he yanked

up his underwear and trousers. He didn't trust his control when they were skin on skin.

Control? He grimaced. He had none around this woman.

The sooner he put a distance between them, the better. Sex with the enemy was a mistake. One she'd hope to exploit in her favour. Best he set her straight immediately. Jake opened his eyes and his mouth at the same time but what he saw stopped the scathing words he was trying to form.

Instead he cursed under his breath.

For Princess Carolina hadn't moved. She sat, tiara at a tipsy angle in that dark red hair, cheeks hectic with a blush that spilled all the way down her throat and covered her trembling breasts. Her hands were clamped, white knuckled, to the edge of the carved wood where she perched and her shoulders bowed forward as if in defeat.

Despite the temptation of those perfect breasts, it was her expression that compelled his attention. Lines of pain gathered around her mouth and furrowed her forehead. Worse, glittering tear tracks spilled down both cheeks.

He'd hurt her.

She'd conned him and led him on. But he'd hurt her, and the sight of her pain made him feel wrong inside.

Caro closed her eyes, just for a second. *Then* she'd be strong. Then she'd pick herself up and face what had to be faced as she'd always done. Because there was no alternative. She was alone, always had been, with no champion but herself. She didn't have the luxury of weakness.

But when she'd seen Jake grimace…

There'd been no mistaking his disgust, the shudder of distaste as he pulled away. Disgust at what he'd done. Disgust at *her*. Because she'd lied and because he'd given in to the raging need for sexual completion that had sprung up between them like a clawing beast.

There'd been nothing civilised about their coupling. It

had been raw and intense, fulfilling a primitive need that was beyond her limited experience. Sex with her ex-boyfriend had been pleasant but not compulsive. Caro didn't understand the desperate woman who'd invited, gloried in being shoved onto an antique chest and taken without finesse or preamble.

It didn't matter. What mattered was that Caro had loved it. Had exulted in being ravished with such urgent thoroughness, eager for Jake in that visceral way as if she'd waited for him her entire life.

It had been glorious. *He'd* been glorious and made her feel special, strong, *wonderful*.

Until he realised what he'd done and hated himself. As he hated her. He'd stuffed himself back into his trousers so fast she guessed he feared she might touch him again. As if her touch tainted.

She recalled the ugly words he'd shot at her like bullets from a gun.

A great shudder built behind Caro's ribs in the vicinity of her heart. It curled round to her spine then up to her skull and down to her pelvis. Finally, mastering herself, she swallowed, put her shoulders back and forced her eyes open.

To find a grey gaze surveying her with what looked like concern. Something skimmed her cheek. She jumped then realised it was Jake's hand.

Caro leaned back. She should pull up her bodice, she realised as she registered her unfettered breasts and the discomfort of the boned bodice pushing them high. But her hands were too unsteady. Besides, he wasn't looking at her bare breasts but her face.

'You're crying.'

'Rubbish.' She turned her head away and began to wrestle with her dress when gentle fingers brushed her cheek again and she felt the smear of wetness there.

Caro stilled. Blinked.

Horror slammed into her. Bad enough to see his distaste, but to have him witness her distress was mortifying. This was the second time she'd cried in front of him. She, who'd spent years burying her emotions!

'I was rough. I hurt you.' Jake's voice sounded different, not the familiar mellow rumble that tickled her insides but taut and scratchy.

'You didn't hurt me.' Caro looked down, focusing on the bodice she couldn't tug up. Probably because she was sitting on the dress, holding it down. Desperately she shifted her weight, trying to drag the skirt higher so the bodice would move.

'Then why are you crying?'

'I'm not!' The tears must have escaped earlier.

Instead of moving away, Jake confounded her by capturing her chin in his broad palm and lifting it so she had to look him in the face.

'You looked like you were in pain.'

Of course she did. No woman wanted to be abhorred. But Caro couldn't bring herself to say that. The pain was still there but she masked it as she'd learned to mask so much.

'You're wrong. I'm fine.'

Except for the anguish deep inside. And the other, disturbing sensation that urged her to lean into his touch and ask for more, as if she had no pride.

Those pale eyes were intent. 'If you weren't in pain, why did you cry?'

Caro shrugged. 'It was an intense experience. It surprised me.'

She waited for him to say something offhand or derogatory. Instead she thought she saw a glimmer of understanding in his face. Until his next words.

'Not because we had unsafe sex?'

It was like being smacked in the face. Her head reared

back in disbelief. She gave up struggling with her dress and wrapped her arms protectively around her chest, as if to ward off his words. But, pressing her thighs together, feeling the wetness, she realised it was true.

How could she not have given it a thought? With Mike she'd been the one to insist on safe sex, despite his protests. It had been like fate laughing at her to discover she was pregnant, given the precautions they'd taken.

Her eyes locked with Jake's and she read her surprise reflected back. And more. Something that again, fleetingly, looked like understanding.

'I'm safe,' he said. 'You won't get any health problems from me.'

Except a possible pregnancy.

Caro bit her lips rather than blurt the words. Her first accidental pregnancy showed she was, or had been, very fertile. Her mind boggled at the idea of another baby. Jake's.

His forehead creased as watched her. 'This is where you're supposed to say you're clean too.'

'I'm clean too.'

'You don't sound very convincing.'

Probably because she was still stuck on the possibility of pregnancy. If it could happen once...

'How many lovers have you had lately?'

Caro frowned, his terse tone penetrating the fog of shock. 'None.' Then, when he lifted his eyebrows in disbelief, 'Well, one, but years ago. When I got pregnant.'

For long moments nothing moved except her blood pumping and the unsteady rise of her chest with a new breath. Jake looked as if he'd been turned into a statue. A frowning, disbelieving statue.

'You're telling me you've only had one lover?' At least his voice wasn't starkly accusing, but his disbelief tore at her self-respect.

She hiked her chin higher, profoundly glad that her crossed arms covered her bare breasts.

'Is that a crime? I don't ask how many you've had. I take your word that you're...clean.' She was lucky she was too, given what she'd discovered about Mike's lifestyle.

'What about the wild parties that made the headlines? The drugs and sex that made your father bring you home?'

Cold shivered through Caro. 'You know about that? You really are super-efficient, aren't you?'

Jake's shoulders lifted. 'I employ Neil for his efficiency.'

Nausea curdled her insides. She thought she might actually be ill. Bad enough that Jake, who despised her, thought the worst. Somehow the idea of Neil, the quiet, funny man who had treated her with such kindness, believing the press reports made her feel like vomiting.

'It wasn't true,' she said finally, her strangled voice not her own.

'Sorry?'

Anger rose and she was glad. Anything was better than feeling defeated and miserable. Caro stiffened her spine and met his gaze proudly. 'The stories weren't true. My boyfriend, Mike, was the one who partied to excess and took drugs, though I didn't know about the drugs till later.'

'How very convenient.' His mouth curled and suddenly Caro had had enough.

Ignoring the need to cover herself she put both hands to his chest and pushed. He was physically stronger but eventually he stepped back, leaving her free to slide off the high chest onto her feet. Caro gritted her teeth, her clammy hands slippery on the silk as she tried to right her dress. But the bodice refused to rise.

'Let me.' A big hand covered her shoulder, turning her. Before she knew it he'd lowered the zip of her dress.

'Stop that! I don't want—'

'Try again now that the dress is loose.'

He was right. She hadn't been thinking clearly. Of course it was easier without the bodice tight around her middle. This time the material rose easily and she sighed in relief.

A second later the zip rose and with it the touch of Jake's fingers on her back. Fire sizzled from there, loosening her spine and her resolve. Did she imagine his touch lingered then slid into a caress?

Setting her jaw, Caro stepped away, almost crying out at the loss of his touch. It made no sense. His distaste should have cured her of any attraction yet to her shame she still longed for Jake Maynard.

'It's time we talked.' To her surprise his tone had lost that harsh, hurtful edge.

She glanced at the time, realising in horror that they'd been away from the ball longer than she'd imagined.

'I should go back.'

Then she caught their reflection in the mirror on the far wall. Jake looked stern but attractive, the only sign of their carnal interlude his sexily rumpled hair and missing bow tie. Already he'd done up his shirt.

She, on the other hand, looked utterly…wanton. Her lips were swollen, her hair a mess and her designer dress suggestively crushed.

'If you show up looking like that you'll create a scandal.' He might have read her mind.

'If I go back wearing something else it will be just as bad.' She lifted a hand to the tiara listing to one side. She wanted to take it off but it was secured with scores of pins and her fingers shook.

Caro was damned no matter what she did.

'Father will be livid.'

To her surprise the thought, instead of making her feel worse, lifted her spirits. She hadn't set out to cause a scandal at her brother's party. From Paul's expression since she'd returned to St Ancilla he had too much on his mind to worry about gossip. His would be an arranged marriage but Caro suspected it wasn't a happy arrangement. However, the idea of annoying her father, childish as it was, pleased her. She still hadn't had the opportunity to confront him alone about stealing her baby.

Caro swung around to Jake Maynard. The man who'd once been so warm and kind. The man who'd been so cruel that remembering his words slashed at her soul. The man who was her enemy. And her lover.

The man she wished would sweep her up in his arms and take her back to that rapturous place she'd known for such a short time. At least now he wasn't sniping at her. He was ready to listen.

'You're right.' She felt the weight slide from her shoulders. 'It's time I told you everything.'

CHAPTER ELEVEN

She switched on a lamp and its mellow light turned her into a mediaeval illumination with her rich auburn hair, violet-blue eyes and deep purple gown.

Jake sat on an armchair opposite and reminded himself not to trust her. Just because she made his pulse hammer with longing, because her mix of defiance and melancholy twisted him inside out, didn't mean he could relax his guard.

Yet it was hard to reconcile the woman who'd clung to him as if he were her whole world with the scheming liar he knew her to be.

He ignored the treacherous urge to sit with her on the sofa. This time he'd think with his head, not another part of his body.

'How did you change your hair, your eyes?' It wasn't the most important question but he still wasn't accustomed to her flagrantly exquisite colouring.

She looked like a painting by an old master brought to life. Except the memory of her toned, surprisingly strong body was vivid. This woman was no delicate work of art. She was bold and so alive his skin tingled being close to her.

Because you still want her. Despite everything.

Their eyes locked. Jake's pulse thudded.

'Coloured contacts and a rinse. I visited a hairdresser in St Ancilla to get me back to my natural hair colour for this week. The rinse wouldn't have lasted anyway and that would have given me away. But I was impatient to see Ariane.' Her mouth crinkled in a moue of self-derision. 'When I finally discovered where she was I couldn't wait. I acted rashly, but I had to see her as soon as possible.'

She shrugged and Jake was surprised at how the simple movement of bare shoulders could so entice. He jerked his gaze back to her face but Caro wasn't looking at him. Her eyes were fixed in the distance.

'What was the plan? To snatch her?'

Now Caro looked at him, her face full of astonishment. An act?

'I'd never do anything like that. Apart from anything else, Ariane just lost the only parents she knew.' Did he imagine her voice wobbled on the word 'parents'? 'She's struggling to cope with the changes in her life. Kidnapping her…' Caro shook her head, staring as if *he* were the one at fault. 'She needs stability, not more trauma.'

Caro drew a deep breath. He watched as she sat straighter, chin up, hands loose in her lap. With the movement she became more regal, more untouchable. He fought the urge to go over there and reduce her to the desperate lover she'd been minutes ago. Sexual awareness still thickened the atmosphere and his body was taut and eager.

'I acted on impulse applying for the job. My lawyer advised me to wait before confronting you. And I thought if I told you the truth you wouldn't let me see her.'

Jake's hackles rose. There, she finally admitted it.

'You plan to claim Ariane.' Bitterness filled his mouth.

'She's my daughter.'

Caro spoke quietly but with a pride Jake couldn't mistake. Nor did he miss the sparkle in her eyes.

Just as well he'd taken the precaution of increasing his niece's security. He hadn't brought her to St Ancilla. He didn't trust this woman's royal relations not to twist the law in their own country and rip Ariane from him.

He shook his head. 'You gave up your rights to her when you abandoned her.'

Despite her wounded look he didn't hide his disdain. He abhorred mothers who deserted their children.

'Let's get one thing straight.' Jake leaned forward, his hands fisted on his knees. 'You're not Ariane's mother. My sister was. She and her husband were the ones who sat up with her through the night as a baby. Who suffered the sleepless nights. Who played with her and loved her and taught her everything she knows. *Not* you. It never *will* be you. Not while I've got breath in my body.'

Jake's words were arrows, piercing her heart. Reminders of all she'd missed. All she hadn't been able to give her daughter.

Would Ariane ever forgive her for that?

Caro swallowed convulsively, ignoring the blistering pain as the acid of his hatred penetrated. How could she have given herself to a man who despised her?

Yet even on opposing sides, Caro felt that trembling awareness that was always present around Jake. Shame engulfed her. Even now she couldn't conquer her yearning.

'It wasn't like that. I didn't abandon her.' Caro drew a shuddering breath. 'She was taken from me.'

Jake lifted his eyebrows in disbelief.

Finally he spoke. 'They still believe in fairy tales here? You'll have to do better than that, Princess Carolina.' She hated the sneering way he said her name. 'No one could take your child unless you wanted it gone. You were an adult, a mother. You had responsibilities. So did your lover. Yet you both gave her up.'

His words echoed the guilt that dogged her in the darkest hours. The shame, the belief that somehow she should have intuited the truth and stopped them taking her baby.

Caro blinked, feeling the hot glaze at the backs of her eyes but refusing to shed more tears.

'Ariane's father died before she was born.'

Jake stilled, a frown descending. Then he shook his head. 'You're after sympathy?'

'No!' She looked down at her hands, twisting in her lap. 'All I want is for you to hear me out.' She'd hoped to skate over some details but Jake already knew so much and had put the worst interpretation on those. She had to make him understand. 'Can you do that?'

For answer he crossed his ankles and leaned back in his seat, his silvery gaze fixed on her like a steely skewer.

For all his sprawling arrogance Caro had the crazy urge to get up and kiss him full on the lips till he lost that haughty attitude and scooped her close. Because, bizarre to admit it, she'd found not just carnal satisfaction with him but something more. Something that had, for a fleeting time, felt strong and real and good.

How many times could she fool herself into believing what she wanted to believe? Surely Mike had cured her of that.

Shifting her gaze to the small landscape painting on the wall beyond Jake, Caro cleared her throat. 'After school I was allowed to study in the USA. It was the first time I'd lived outside the palace.'

'And you kicked over the traces, of course.'

Her gaze slewed back to his. 'There's no of course about it. I was nervous but excited. To have the freedom to make my own friends, not the ones approved by my father...' Looking at Jake's stony face, she gave up trying to explain.

'I spent a lot of my time studying. Art history mainly. I'd hoped eventually to work in a gallery or museum.' That dream was long gone. She frowned, dragging herself back to the point. 'When I was there I met Mike, another student. He was everything I wasn't. Confident, outgoing, charming—'

'You do yourself a disservice.' Jake's drawl interrupted her. 'You were all those things at the ball tonight.'

Her eyes darted to his then away. 'Learned skills. In Mike it was innate. He was...' She shrugged. 'Actually, he wasn't the man I thought he was. But I fell for him. We became lovers and I was as happy as I'd ever been.' The change had been amazing after her dour family situation with her perpetually disapproving father and a stepmother who saw her as an encumbrance.

'We did go to parties and some of them got out of hand, but I usually left early. I wasn't into drugs.' Which was why she hadn't realised the signs that Mike was. She'd truly been naïve. 'Then I found out I was pregnant. I suspect Mike tampered with the condoms.'

'Another bit of embroidery, Caro? Young guys aren't generally eager for parenthood.'

'Mike wasn't like most guys. I discovered later that he saw me as a ticket to wealth and privilege. Getting me pregnant was his insurance policy.' She met Jake's narrowed eyes and hurried on. 'At first it was so romantic. He proposed and I accepted. I thought we were in love and we'd have a wonderful future. Until I came home early one day to find him in bed with another woman.'

Jake leaned closer, his disbelief replaced by anger. He muttered something savage that, though it couldn't change the past, made Caro feel better.

'I was devastated.' Looking back now, she'd had a lucky escape. Cold iced her bones as she imagined not discovering Mike's true colours till after the wedding. She rubbed her hands up her arms.

'I dumped him and when I refused to take him back he turned nasty. He wouldn't give up. His moods became erratic, possibly because of the drugs he was taking.' Caro shivered, remembering how he'd frightened her.

'He threatened you?' Jake's gaze darkened.

'It doesn't matter now. What matters is that he contacted the palace. He told my father I was pregnant, hoping my father would force me into marriage. He's very strict and wouldn't abide me bringing up an illegitimate child.' Caro grimaced, remembering.

'But you didn't marry.'

'No. My father paid him for his silence.'

So much for the undying love Mike had professed. Even after all this time that had the power to wound. All her life she'd longed for love. She had only the vaguest recollection of her mother's warmth. 'With Mike's help the press got hold of stories of me partying wildly. My father used that to explain my return to St Ancilla.'

'And your lover?'

Caro tilted her head, surveying Jake. Why the curiosity when he knew Mike was dead?

'He used the money to indulge himself. He died of an overdose months after I left.'

'I see.' Jake scowled and Caro wondered what it was he saw. 'So you came back here, to your family.'

Her mouth twisted in a smile that held no humour. 'Not to the palace. Nor to my *family*.' She drew a sustaining breath, remembering how frightening it had been, hustled from the airport by a team of anonymous men who wouldn't even speak to her, much less tell her where she was going. 'I was taken from a private airport to a convent on the other end of the island. I was kept on the estate there till after the birth. My only contact with my family was a note from my father saying he'd see me after my little problem was resolved.'

'And you agreed.' Was Jake's anger directed at her or her father? Suddenly tired, Caro didn't care.

'Of course not. I walked out several times. When that didn't work I tried to sneak away. I didn't get far. His security team had the place under surveillance and they were very…efficient.' Even now the sight of her father's minders made her feel sick in the stomach. 'I had no phone or computer and my friends didn't know where I was. My father said nothing but I discovered later that *"sources close to the royal family"* hinted I was recuperating from an unspecified health condition.'

Caro saw the flash of confirmation in Jake's expression and knew he'd read those rumours that she'd been in rehab or recovering from a breakdown.

Sitting, recounting those days was too much. She got to her feet and paced to the window, clutching the curtain as she looked across the royal gardens, lit with thousands of lights for tonight's party. Her father would be furious at the scandal she'd caused. Already gossip would be in full swing.

But now the prospect of his temper didn't make her cringe. She wouldn't give in to his bullying any longer now she had something to fight for. Ariane.

'I gave birth there.' It was easier speaking about it with her back to Jake. Despite her father's wishes, Caro had resolved to raise her baby, even if it meant leaving St Ancilla with nothing. But she'd underestimated her father and her weakness after the birth.

'It was long and difficult.' She'd lost a lot of blood and drifted in and out of consciousness. 'I never heard the baby cry. I didn't see her, just the midwife's back, taking her away. They told me she was stillborn.'

Caro swallowed and unlocked her stiff fingers from their death grip on the curtain. She pressed her hands to her stomach, remembering the terrible anguish of that night, fighting the urge to bow her shoulders and curl in on herself.

She focused on the garden illumination and the strains of music in the distance.

'It took a while to recover. Afterwards I refused to return here, except for official events. I made my home at the far end of the island, working with children.' Caro cleared her throat, striving for a lighter tone. No need to explain that after losing her baby, she'd been driven to connect with other children.

'Recently I was contacted by the younger of the two midwives who'd been at the birth. She'd just had her first child and…' Caro faltered then made herself continue. 'She said she'd always felt guilty about what happened that night. But it was only when her daughter was born that she knew she had to tell me the truth. She said my baby was alive. That it was taken away, she assumed for adoption.'

Caro forced down the tangle of distress choking her throat.

She'd have to do better than this when she confronted her father. The knowledge gave her the energy to turn and look at Jake.

To her surprise he was no longer sitting, but stood mere paces away, on the other side of the window. His expression was unreadable yet he radiated tension. It hummed from him, making the hairs on her arms stand up.

'You know the rest.'

His hooded gaze raked her. 'I have the resources to check your story.'

Because even now he didn't believe her? The knowledge sent adrenaline buzzing through her, as if she'd taken a shot of spirits. A laugh emerged from her dry mouth. 'Is that a warning? Go ahead. The more corroborating evidence, the stronger my claim to Ariane.'

It was the wrong thing to say. That half-lidded stare turned laser bright and, despite her resolve, trepidation scuttered down her backbone.

But Caro was done with giving in to bossy men. She wanted her daughter and no one was going to stop her. She met Jake's narrowed eyes with determination.

Jake gritted his teeth, refusing to argue. Time, and the best investigators and lawyers, would give him the ammunition he needed. No matter what had happened in the past, Ariane was his niece and she needed him. He'd protect her with his life.

Yet Caro Rivage muddied the waters with her story. He'd felt anger and sympathy stir. Dangerous undercurrents when this woman was his rival for Ariane.

She was challenging, dangerous. Around her his emotions became stronger, more unwieldy.

Through her story he'd felt horror, sympathy and outrage but even now he didn't know whether she'd manipulated him. Her story was far-fetched and he wanted to dismiss it as fantasy. Except no one was that good an actor. He'd not only seen but felt her distress and pain.

There was a chance her story was true.

When she'd talked of her lying scum boyfriend her expression had revealed bitter betrayal and Jake had felt the urge to smash the guy's face. His skin crawled at the idea of her father keeping her captive, cut off from friends.

As for stealing her baby... Surely no father would do that!

Yet Jake knew that simply having children didn't make someone a caring parent. His mother was a case in point.

Had Caro given him a sob story to win him over while she found a way to get Ariane? Watching that challenging stare, he was torn between doubt and the desire to believe.

And desire of a different kind, for carnal pleasure. Their quick coupling hadn't eradicated it. Instead it was as if one taste of her no-holds-barred passion left him addicted.

It was appallingly difficult to focus on the past.

Had she abandoned Ariane or had her daughter been stolen? That was the crux of the matter. If she was lying she was the best liar he'd ever met. His gut told him she spoke the truth. Yet he needed evidence.

'I'll reserve judgement till I have proof you didn't give her away.'

Instead of her being downcast at his words, her expression lightened. 'I'll arrange a meeting with the midwife.'

She looked almost excited. The contrast with her earlier vulnerability was almost painful to observe. Surely that meant he could trust her.

Except people could be bought, stories altered.

'You do that.'

Jake wouldn't easily be convinced. He clenched his jaw against the wild see-saw of emotions. He was used to assessing situations quickly, trusting his instinct and taking decisive action. This uncertainty, the conflict between his desire to believe and the knowledge he couldn't, yet, was maddening.

'Well…' for the first time since she'd stormed out of the gala she looked uncertain '… I suppose it's time you returned to the ball. Do you need me to show you the way?'

Jake frowned. 'I'm not interested in the ball. I only came here to see you.'

The words echoed with a profound resonance. It was truer than he'd thought. Even now, when he knew he'd get no further proof tonight, he was magnetised by her. He didn't want to leave.

Whether it was the sexily mussed look of her ripe lips, untidy hair and crumpled dress, or the deeper thread of sympathy stirred by her story, Jake didn't know. But he felt…connected, drawn to her. Though he couldn't allow himself to trust her.

His voice must have revealed his doubt. He saw her react, her pupils dilate and her body sway infinitesimally nearer, till she jerked back.

'It's late. There's no proof I can give you tonight.'

'You want me to go?'

Caro felt her eyes widen as Jake's low voice rumbled through her.

She opened her mouth to say of course she wanted him to leave. He'd been brutally insulting. He'd made her feel like dirt.

Right before he'd made her feel as if she'd found heaven.

A squiggle of arousal stirred deep inside and she rubbed her damp palms down her skirt. Jake's eyes tracked the movement. To her dismay her nipples budded against her silk bodice while between her legs that slow circling ache of want started up anew.

Caro swallowed. She tried to summon a convenient lie. *Yes, I want you to go.* But her tongue didn't cooperate.

'Caro?' That gravel-wrapped-in-velvet voice reminded her of the night she'd kissed him and he'd held her while she cried. It was rough yet tender and strangely reassuring. It shouldn't be. They were on opposing sides.

'I—'

'Because I don't want to leave.' His features took on a grim cast, the planes of his face stark and sheer.

'What *do* you want?' The words came this time, breathless and quick.

'You.' He didn't move closer but it felt as if he did. As if he'd reached out and trailed his hand over her flesh, awakening dangerous longing. 'Us. Together. Again.'

'You despise me.' She summoned her pride as a last defence against his appalling power to tempt her. He'd flayed her with his insults. She wouldn't forget that soon.

He shook his head. 'I did, before you told me what happened.'

'You're saying you believe me?' It couldn't be so easy.

She was right. 'I told you, I'll reserve judgement till I have proof.'

He drew a slow breath and for the first time she realised he was as tense as she. His big chest rose in a shudder and the muscles in his jaw worked as if he held himself back with difficulty. 'But I still want you. More than ever.'

The words, delivered not in challenge but with devastating honesty, loosened her knees. Caro snatched in air to her overworked lungs but couldn't fill them.

'I've wanted you from the moment you sashayed into my office looking ridiculously sexy in that brown outfit. You made me feel like some Victorian reprobate, lusting after the staff.'

Caro stepped back in shock, straight into the window embrasure.

'You were attracted then?'

The voice of self-preservation told her it didn't matter. Nothing mattered but Ariane. Yet it wasn't true. This—whatever it was between her and Jake—was so powerful she felt it at a visceral level. In his arms Caro felt renewed, happy, vibrantly alive.

It made her weak when she needed to be strong. But oh, what weakness!

Even angry, desperate sex with this man had felt profound.

Surely it was a catastrophic mistake to give in to it, yet it felt anything but wrong.

'You couldn't tell?' He stepped close and she felt hot all over from that silvery stare. 'I thought it was obvious.' Another deep breath. This time that broad chest came within a hair's breadth of her breasts and she had to fight not to lean into him.

Caro shook her head. 'Sex would complicate things between us.'

Jake's mouth rucked up at one side in a disarming smile that turned her insides molten. 'A bit late to worry about, don't you think?' He paused. 'Whatever the rights and wrongs, we find ourselves in a...fraught situation. Why not indulge in a little recreational pleasure to relieve the tension?'

He made it sound not only logical but laudable. This man was incredibly dangerous!

And yet... She wanted badly to put aside her hurt, even for a short time.

'And afterwards? We part as enemies?'

He lifted his hand, feathering one finger down her cheek, then across to her mouth where her lips promptly opened for him. Heat drilled deep inside and she shuddered as she inhaled the citrus and male scent of his skin.

'How about we call a truce?' he purred. 'Till the negotiations begin.'

It was absurd. Reckless and irresponsible.

Utterly tempting.

Caro shuddered, her senses on overdrive. She told herself to be sensible. She opened her mouth to spurn him and heard herself say, 'Perhaps just once.'

The words were barely out when he scooped her into his arms. He carried her as easily as if he did it every day, leaving her hyper-aware of his strength and a sense of well-being. It was crazy but nevertheless real.

Then they were in the bedroom and he put her on her feet, reaching to flick on a bedside lamp. Caro waited for the frenzy of need, the urgent hands, hard on her body, that had so excited her before.

Instead, to her surprise, Jake lifted his hands to her hair. Gently, with deft patience, he drew out the pins that secured her tiara and kept her hair up. He wore a lazy half-smile as his fingers moved in her hair in a series of caresses that made her shiver all over.

Finally he removed the delicate tiara but instead of stopping, those hard hands massaged her scalp, turning her boneless. The exquisite sensations, the unhurried intent in those glittering eyes and the stroke of his breath on her skin turned it into the most amazing foreplay.

Caro's head fell back, her hair cascading in waves

around her shoulders. She clutched his upper arms as he kissed her jaw, her throat and down, down, down to the low-sitting line of her bodice.

That was only the beginning. Caro had expected fast and hard. What she got was endless patience and a sure sensuality that made her realise how limited her experience was. Mike had never seduced her with such infinite patience, or with such devastating knowledge of how to excite her.

By the time they were on the bed, he in boxers and she in nothing at all, she was quivering with anticipation, her breath coming in broken snatches. Finally, unable to wait, she reached for him, hand closing around his fabric-covered erection.

'Wait.' Hard fingers encircled hers and she saw Jake grimace as he throbbed against her touch. 'We need a condom.' His ragged voice made her realise that in this passion they were equals.

She almost smiled till his words sank in.

'I don't have any.'

He frowned, head turning to the bedside table.

'Not there. Not anywhere.' She pulled her hand away, feeling almost embarrassed. As if it were a crime to be celibate! 'I don't have sex.'

Jake stared as if he'd never seen her before. Because he hadn't believed her when she'd said there'd been no one but Mike? But before she had time to take offence, his mouth curled up in a sexy grin that made her heart leap against her ribs and her throat jam.

'You do now, Princess.' He kissed her quickly but with a naked intent that had her writhing beneath him.

Then suddenly she was bereft as he rose and reached for his trousers. Moments later he was naked, rolling a condom onto his impressive erection.

Caro swallowed hard, overwhelmed by her need for this magnificent man. She told herself her emotions were more profound because of the intense circumstances, the roller coaster of hope and fear since she'd heard Ariane was alive. But as Jake met her eyes and that ponderous pulse of connection pounded between them, Caro feared it was more.

He came to her, held her, kissed her, then, despite his arousal, slowly explored her with his mouth and hands. By the time he reached her sex, his breath a caress, she couldn't take any more.

'No!' He lifted his head and Caro stared, overwhelmed, at the sight of him there between her legs. One more touch and... 'I want *you*.'

'I haven't finished—'

Raising herself on her elbow, she reached for him, her hand sliding through the dark silk of his hair. 'Please.'

The teasing light in his eyes faded, replaced by something that felt heavy in her chest. Something warm and almost reassuring. Jake prowled up her body and carnal excitement stifled everything else.

This time when they came together it was slow and sure and almost familiar as he held her gaze and she held him. This time the fizz of sparks didn't explode as fast but the way their bodies rocked together, the searing strands of fire threading through her at every movement, every breath, every touch, made the climax more compelling.

Caro's orgasm bore down upon her, first in tiny ripples that made Jake's eyes glint with approval. Then in great undulating waves that made her cling and bite her lip against the urge to cry out.

She hung suspended, held from oblivion only by that grey gaze. Then his wide shoulders quaked, he flung his head back and powered deep inside and ecstasy took her.

CHAPTER TWELVE

JAKE WOKE ALONE in her bed.

Daylight streamed in yet he couldn't bring himself to move. Caro's 'perhaps just once' had turned into a long, vigorous night. Good thing he'd had condoms in his wallet. The more he had her, the more he wanted, and Caro had been equally needy.

Now he was content to wait for her to emerge from the bathroom.

Last night's madness could have been a major error. The last thing he needed, if it did come to a court case, was a sexual relationship with Princess Carolina muddying the waters.

Yet he couldn't regret that amazing night.

His belly warmed at the memory of her coming apart in his arms, her generous passion and his exultation. Caro had been everything he desired, though more than once he'd observed surprise at some of his caresses, and his ability to bring her multiple climaxes. Ego suggested the quality of his lovemaking surprised her but he suspected she really had been pretty inexperienced.

Which put an intriguing slant on what she'd told him. Some of it was true, possibly most of it. But he couldn't accept it all without proof, despite what felt like the best sex of his life.

It was tempting to believe they'd shared something extraordinary. His sated body and the smile tugging his lips confirmed it. But Jake was cautious. He preferred to ascribe this feeling to a particularly compatible woman and recent celibacy.

Jake surveyed his surroundings, curious at the difference between this room and the rest of the palace. Despite its high ceilings, ornate plasterwork and spacious dimensions, it wasn't as opulent. The furnishings looked comfortable, the fabric on the armchair in a shaft of sunlight actually looked frayed.

Probably because Caro only stayed here occasionally. But the bookcase on one wall, stuffed full, proved it was more than a convenient bolthole. Intrigued, he investigated.

Children's books jostled with classics and tomes on art. On one shelf was a stack of sketch books. He plucked one, leafing through and discovering drawings of formal gardens, a servant in livery and a bird on a branch.

He turned, looking for information about the woman he'd spent the night with. Nearby was a single framed photo. The resemblance was so intense Jake's pulse jumped.

Picking it up, he saw a woman of about thirty with Caro's slim build. Her hair was red but not Caro's dark auburn. This woman's was lighter, matching Ariane's, and her eyes, deep violet with that familiar slanting angle that made them look mysterious and happy at the same time, looked like Ariane's eyes, and Caro's.

This must be Caro's mother. Ariane's grandmother. She held a baby with a fuzz of reddish hair, one tiny hand reaching towards her mother.

Abruptly Jake put the photo down, recalling Neil's report on Princess Carolina. She'd lost her mother when she was tiny. Her father remarried almost immediately. This photo seemed to indicate a bond with a mother she could barely have known, rather than with the woman who'd raised her.

He thought about Ariane losing her adoptive parents. And Caro's story of having Ariane stolen from her.

What if it were true?

What if the passionate woman he'd bedded wasn't a spoiled princess who hadn't wanted her child? What if she'd genuinely believed her child dead, the maternal bond broken, as with her own mother?

Something lodged in Jake's belly. A weight that, against the laws of physics, rose within him, crushing his lungs and stopping his breath.

He swung around, needing to find her. She'd been in the bathroom a long time. Too long.

Jake walked past a wooden-faced footman on the ground floor. Either the servants were used to guests ending the night in a royal bed, or too well trained to bat an eye. He didn't care. What he cared about was locating Caro.

His need to find her had grown from a niggle to a presentiment of trouble. No matter how unaccustomed she was to nights of passion, it was unlike the woman he knew not to face him this morning. His nape tightened.

Finally, when he was almost at the ballroom, he heard a loud voice. Pushing open a not quite closed door, he found himself in an empty sitting room. On the far side French windows stood open to the garden. Following the sound of voices, Jake stepped outside then realised the conversation was taking place in the next room. He moved to another set of French windows and looked inside. It was a study with gilded antiques and floor-to-ceiling books that looked, unlike the ones in Caro's room, as if they'd never been opened. The occupants didn't notice him on the threshold.

King Hugo of St Ancilla sat behind an oversized desk. Caro stood before him in a tailored skirt and jacket, spine straight and chin up. Jake silently applauded her, for the monarch wasn't holding back his tirade in mixed English and Ancillan. Jake's stomach curdled at his blistering vitriol.

He was about to make himself known when Caro spoke.

'I did what you insisted, came back and attended every

event this week. As for leaving early last night...' She shrugged. 'I'm not here to discuss that.'

'How *dare* you speak to me like that?' The King's face darkened.

'Oh, I *dare*, Father.' Amazingly Caro's defiant tone made the King stop, eyes widening. 'I only came here because you threatened to send your goons to haul me back, and, in the process, wreck my plans.'

'Plans? You don't have plans. You spend your time playing at being a preschool teacher. It's time you toed the line and came home.' He sat back, an ugly smile on his face. 'I've a mind to organise your wedding next. There's a banker in the US I'm cultivating.' His tone turned sneering. 'I know your weakness for Americans.'

Any thought Jake had of revealing his presence died as Caro turned parchment-pale. She wouldn't thank him for witnessing this.

Besides, it could be his chance to discover whether she'd told him the truth.

'Or perhaps the Australian you spent the night with. We could turn your scandalous behaviour to advantage, put pressure on him to come up to scratch. His fortune is huge.'

Jake was absorbing that when Caro stepped up to the desk. She slapped her hands down and leaned forward.

'Make your plans for my brothers, not me. I wash my hands of you.' She drew a deep breath and Jake, seeing the light glinting on her bright hair, realised she was shaking. 'I know what you did. The lies you told, the laws you broke.'

For a moment the King said nothing. When he spoke his voice was venomous. 'Careful, Carolina. I've let you go your own way for years but I can bring you to heel like that.' He snapped his fingers.

Slowly she shook her head. 'Not this time. Not any more.' She straightened, her hands clenched. 'You stole my child. You had her illegally adopted without my consent.'

Jake's hand closed so hard on the door frame that pain shot from his palm up his arm.

It was true. Unbelievably it was true.

His mind boggled and his stomach dropped.

He'd got her so wrong.

The things he'd said last night!

Jake rocked back as guilt and horror filled him.

'There was never any question of you keeping it.'

'Her. I had a girl.'

'A bastard.' Her father shrugged. 'As if I'd allow that blot on the family name. I did what I did for the family. You should be grateful—'

'Grateful? Hardly. I know where she is and I'm going to get her. We're going to live together. I'm going to raise my daughter the way a child *should* be raised and—'

'You'll do no such thing. Put the idea from your head right now. Unless you'd like another year living under guard till you see sense?'

Jake couldn't take any more. He rapped on the window frame, feigning a smile as they whipped round towards him.

'Good morning, Your Majesty... Carolina. I hope I'm not interrupting.' He paused, looking from one to the other, willing Caro to follow his lead. She looked pale, her features drawn.

He'd heard enough to suspect that, with only a little more provocation, her father would have her clapped in a dungeon or a tower, guarded by sentries. Jake recalled her bleak expression when she'd spoken of being held against her will by the King's security men. Until he could get her out of St Ancilla, she wouldn't be safe.

Jake didn't question his determination to get her away. She'd told the truth. He owed her more than an apology for last night's scathing words.

'Not at all.' The King recovered first, stretching his mouth into a smile like a hungry shark's.

'I'm so glad.' Jake stepped into the room, standing beside Caro and planting his palm reassuringly at her back. She shivered and he had to bite back the words he longed to fling at her father. Instead he made himself smile. 'Carolina promised to show me something of the countryside today, didn't you, darling?'

She blinked, her brow furrowing at his words. Before she could speak Jake ploughed on.

'I must thank you, Your Highness, for the invitation to last night's event. It was spectacular. I'm honoured to have been invited.' He smiled as if his one aim in life were to hang out with pampered aristocrats, then added the bait. 'Especially as I understand there are some interesting investment opportunities in your country.'

Ignoring Caro's scowl, he watched the King and saw his ruse had worked. Perhaps Neil was right and the royal coffers weren't as plump as they used to be. He'd noticed a number of high-profile financiers attending last night, including a few involved in his latest project. It wouldn't hurt if the King thought he planned to stay and look at business options.

'It was our pleasure to have you here.' No sign of a scowl now on that crimson face. 'You must accept our hospitality for the rest of your visit.'

'You're most kind, Your Highness.' Jake slipped his hand from Caro's back to capture her hand. He squeezed it reassuringly. 'I'd hoped to make an early start on our sightseeing. Unless...'

He let his words trail off as he gave Caro a melting smile. Best if her father thought he was unaware of the dark undercurrents in the room.

'Of course. Carolina, see you take Mr Maynard to the business park on the way out of the city.'

Caro opened her mouth and Jake spoke first. 'That

sounds perfect. But maybe on the way back. There are other sights Carolina promised to show me first.'

'I'm sure there are.' The King's suggestive chuckle curdled Jake's belly but he kept his expression light.

Finally, to his relief, Caro spoke up. 'That's right. We'd better leave now if we're to fit everything in.'

'Come and see me when you return, Carolina.' It wasn't a suggestion but an order.

Jake wore a calm face as they traversed the palace. He was determined the servants wouldn't see anything amiss, though restraining his seething emotions took concentration. Caro's hand was cold in his and she moved stiffly, shoulders high and face blank.

He was torn between slashing guilt over the way he'd treated her, disbelief at the enormity of what he'd witnessed and the desire to do serious damage to the man they'd just left.

Jake had thought his own mother appalling. She had nothing on Caro's father.

They remained silent till they reached Caro's rooms. As the door shut, Jake wrapped his arms around her, breath expelling in a rush when she didn't push him away. He didn't deserve her trust.

His scorn last night proved he had no filter and precious little control where Caro was concerned. He'd told himself he was furious on Ariane's behalf but this was more, much more.

Caro leaned close, fracturing his thoughts and filling him with relief. He inhaled spice and woman, her hair tickling his cheek, her body warm and trembling.

His arms tightened. 'I'm getting you out of here. Now.'

Caro let Jake lead her from the helipad along the path to the castle. She'd been away less than a week yet spring had arrived in the Alps. The air was warm and the snow had begun melting. Further down the slope she saw the first traces of wildflowers. The air felt fresh with promise and the fragrance of growing things teased her nostrils.

While she felt chilled.

Everything had happened quickly. Maybe she was in shock. The confrontation with her father, then Jake spiriting her off St Ancilla in a private jet, followed by this short hop in a helicopter. She wasn't used to anyone, especially a man, coming to her rescue. That added to the air of unreality.

If ever she'd doubted Jake's ability to make things happen, today would have disabused her. He'd made one call while she gathered her most precious possessions in a large shoulder bag. Her mother's photo, her mother's jewellery that she'd worn last night and some illustrated books she'd had when she was young and had always wanted to give her own child. Then they were heading to the garages and from there to an airfield.

All the time fear tingled down her spine as she imagined her father's reaction when he found her gone.

She had no illusions that his threat to hold her by force was bluster. He was ruthless. While she was in St Ancilla he had all the power, despite what the law said.

'I have to thank you. Getting me off the island.' She stopped and turned to Jake as the helicopter lifted off and its throbbing thunder retreated.

He looked the same, dark-featured, broad-shouldered and with the air of calm competence that reassured.

Alarms tripped in her brain, warning that she couldn't relax her guard, couldn't rely on anyone but herself. Yet it was too late. She'd gone so far with him, in so many ways, she couldn't pretend none of it had happened.

It felt as if a lifetime had passed since they met.

'There's no need for thanks. I was glad to get away too.' There was so much to discuss but neither was eager to start. They'd barely spoken on the trip. Caro because she grappled with a barrage of emotions and Jake because he was busy working on his phone. Because his business couldn't wait or because he realised she needed some quiet time?

Pewter-grey eyes surveyed her. 'You're feeling better now you're off St Ancilla?'

Caro breathed deep and nodded, looking away to the magnificent vista of fields, forests and soaring mountains. On the other side of the valley towering waterfalls, fed by melting snow, plunged to the valley floor.

'I wouldn't have got away so easily without your help.' She faced the horrible truth today had revealed. 'I love my country but I can't stay there. Not with my father's threats hanging over me. If he sends his men after me...'

She shivered and hunched her shoulders despite the warm sunlight on her back. To be virtually exiled from her homeland was bad enough. To fear returning because it could only be on the King's terms was even worse.

'Don't worry. I've got people working on it.' Caro raised her eyebrows but before she could question Jake continued. 'Let's talk about it later. For now just know you're safe.' He gestured to the castle, golden in the sunlight, its machicolated towers charming yet sturdy, its massive walls solid. 'I'll make sure no one, not even the King of St Ancilla, can harm you or Ariane here.'

'Thank you. That's...good of you.'

It meant everything to have breathing space to decide what to do next. To know her daughter, and she, were safe for now.

Caro felt stiff facial muscles twinge as she smiled. 'You're sure you're the same man who stalked into the palace last night with vengeance in his eyes?'

He'd looked like an avenging angel.

There was no answering humour in Jake's features. If anything he looked even grimmer.

Warmth enveloped her hand and she looked down to see he'd captured it in both of his. Heat radiated from his touch and the tension stringing her muscles began to ease.

'I owe you an apology.' Jake winced. 'I jumped to conclusions about you that were unfounded and hurtful. Can you forgive me? I cringe when I think of what I said. The way I treated you, in private and in front of others. You didn't deserve that. I lost control and I'm ashamed.'

Caro read his remorse. His words, his contempt, had hurt. Badly. With a lancing pain that drove right to her heart. But he hadn't known the truth.

'I can't blame you for doubting my word. I came here in disguise, lying to you.' She paused. 'I apologise for that. My only excuse is I was desperate, scared I'd lose the chance to see my daughter.' Caro tried to summon a smile but it felt like a grimace. 'I was afraid if I told you who I was you'd stop me seeing her when I'd just learned she was alive.'

'Caro, you don't—'

'I do have to explain. I hated lying. I knew soon enough that you loved her and wanted to protect her, but I knew you'd see me as an enemy, particularly when I told my story. It was so far-fetched. You were right, it does sound like something from an old story.' The sort that had evil stepmothers and awful curses.

Caro's stepmother wasn't evil. Just wrapped up in her own family with no warmth to share for another woman's child. As for her father, he was larger than life with his selfish, manipulative ways and towering temper.

Not for the first time she wondered what life would have been like if her mother had lived. Everyone said she was gentle yet fun-loving. Caro had a horrible feeling life with her royal husband would have been hellish.

'Nevertheless, I should have waited to be sure of the facts.' Jake's stern voice sliced her thoughts. 'Abandoning children is a hot button for me. I saw red and acted before thinking. Believe it or not, that's not my usual way.'

He looked down to where his thumb described a half circle again and again on the back of her hand. He seemed so abstracted she guessed he had no idea of the powerful, delicious sensations his caress evoked.

Here she was, fleeing her country, her father and her King, with her life in chaos. Yet she found it impossible to concentrate on her problems because of Jake Maynard and the feelings he evoked.

She tugged her hand free, ignoring that twitch of dark eyebrows.

She cradled her fingers, warm from his touch, in her other hand. 'Don't worry. I'm tougher than I look.' She'd had to be. 'I'm not about to collapse in tears or have a breakdown.'

Caro was acutely aware of the fact Jake had seen her at her lowest ebb, unable to stop the grief she'd carried for so long. She'd wept in his arms, finding a solace she'd never known before. But she wouldn't do that again. The humiliation of having him witness that scene with her father still cramped her insides. Even though it had convinced Jake she told the truth, she hated him thinking she was a helpless victim.

His smile when it came was crooked but totally disarming. It set light to her last defences like flame to paper. She could almost hear the whoosh of conflagration as her resistance crumbled to ashes.

'It seems those stories about your breakdown years ago were exaggerated.' His smile died and Caro read concern in his smoky gaze. 'You don't have to convince me you're strong, Caro. To get through what you did, to keep going, and deal with *him*...' He shook his head. 'That takes guts.'

Caro's heart swelled. It was the first time she'd received such a compliment. 'I've never held my own against him before. I let him—'

'Don't!' Jake raised a palm to stop her. 'Don't blame yourself. He was your father and your King and he held all the power.'

Jake's stare pinioned hers. Instead of her feeling cornered, her confidence rose, a warm glow that felt like happiness.

They stood, gazes locked. Caro didn't want to move. The quality of Jake's regard, how he made her feel about herself, were new and precious.

'I've got one question.' His voice made her blink.

'Yes?' Absurdly, now the worst was over, she was breathless.

'Do I have to call you Carolina now?'

She smiled and took a half step back, suddenly aware she'd canted towards him. 'I've come to loathe my full name. My father insists on it but as he's usually in a bad mood he makes it sound ugly. My friends call me Caro.'

Jake bent forward in a formal bow as if he were a master of court etiquette. 'May I call you Caro?'

Did that mean he saw her as his friend?

Caro wasn't sure whether to be pleased. She should be. It meant he trusted her. Yet given her deep-seated, confusing feelings for him, 'friend' was such a lukewarm word.

'Of course.' Looking into his eyes, she felt a zap of energy that warned she was vulnerable to this man. Hurriedly she gathered her wits. 'And now? What happens next?'

Caro would call her friends in St Ancilla and her lawyer, to warn them the King would be on a rampage when he discovered she'd left. She didn't think he'd take out his wrath on them but he could be unstable when crossed.

'Next?' Jake's smile was easy. 'We'll work it out one step at a time. There's no rush. For now concentrate on the fact you and Ariane are safe.'

Caro swallowed. He didn't want her thanks yet he gave her so much, refuge when she needed it most. They still had to work out Ariane's future. Ostensibly they were on opposing sides, yet Jake treated her as someone to be protected.

The knowledge stirred the most poignant feelings. Here was a man she could respect as well as...

'And us? Is there an us?' Instinctively she lifted her chin, ready to pretend it didn't matter if he said last night's passion had been a mistake.

Jake's face turned unreadable.

She'd give anything to know what he thought. Did he regret having sex? Was it gauche and embarrassing to mention it now they'd moved on from those moments of heightened emotion?

She wished she knew one-night-stand etiquette.

'Do you want there to be?'

Caro had imagined this morning that confronting her hectoring father would take all her courage. Yet, looking into that piercing gaze that gave nothing away, her heart thudding against her ribs, she discovered her courage could still be tested.

She craved more of what she'd experienced with Jake, that soul-searing passion that went beyond anything she'd known. Yet with everything so uncertain—

'It's okay. You don't need to answer now, Caro. Shall we take that one step at a time too?'

She slicked her dry lips, searching for the right words when a shout made her turn.

Rounding the corner of the castle were Jake's secretary Neil and Ariane, hopping beside him.

Abruptly it hit her, the fact that she was here, safe for

now from her father's machinations and with her daughter. Her incredible, lovely daughter. Caro's breath shuddered through her as relief and joy filled her.

'Come on, Caro.' She felt Jake's hand warm at the small of her back. 'It's time to see your little girl.'

CHAPTER THIRTEEN

JAKE SURVEYED THE pair sitting across from him and fought to hide his response to the picture they made.

Ariane had begun the trip down the mountain's steep cog railway on the seat beside Caro. But as Caro pointed through the carriage window, his niece had climbed onto her lap. Now Caro's arm rested around Ariane's middle as they chattered about the view and the quaint Alpine farm-houses.

His ribs tightened at their glow of happiness. His niece and her mother. Not that Ariane knew Caro was her mother. They'd agreed to keep that quiet till Ariane was better able to understand.

But she was still his niece and always would be.

His lawyers said there were legal arguments on both sides, for him as Ariane's permanent guardian, and for Caro as birth mother. Though they thought, despite the wrong done years ago, they could successfully argue that the continuity of living with him would be best for Ariane.

Jake felt no triumph at the news.

He didn't *want* a legal wrangle with Caro.

He watched their faces, alight with pleasure as Caro spotted hikers with a frolicking dog. Two shades of red hair, one coppery and the other a deep, ruby auburn, touched as they craned to look. Two sets of violet eyes and two smiles, each capable of twisting his heart.

He wanted Ariane with him. And he wanted Caro.

The twist of heat moved from his chest to his groin. He *had* Caro. She'd been his lover ever since St Ancilla.

That first night back he'd been surprised by the rap on his door. When he'd found Caro there, huddled in a robe with her hair in waves around her shoulders, he'd pulled her inside, expecting to hear her appalling father had managed, despite Jake's precautions, to contact her with threats.

It had taken all Jake's once considerable restraint to hold back from her, invite her to sit, turn his brain to tactics to stymie the King's machinations.

But instead of talking about her father or Ariane, Caro had surprised him. Gone was the wan woman who'd left St Ancilla beside him. Instead he'd been visited by the ardent siren who'd given herself so generously the night before.

Had he held back? Worried about taking advantage when he knew she'd been rocked by recent experiences?

Jake counted himself a decent guy, if hard-nosed in business. But he wasn't into self-abnegation. He'd hauled Caro into his bed. For the last ten days he'd made sure she was satisfied, more than satisfied, there.

He truly was selfish. He had Caro each night and still he wanted more. He had no name for this craving. To possess her physically. But more too. To bask in her smiles. Enjoy her in ways that had little to do with sex.

'Uncle Jake…?'

He found two pairs of eyes on him.

'Sorry?' He yanked his thoughts to the present. Their trip up the mountain. His sense of victory when he'd finally persuaded Caro it was safe to take Ariane out. That her father's henchmen couldn't grab them. Even then she hadn't relaxed till his own security staff boarded the next carriage, keeping a discreet distance.

Jake hated the need for such a precaution but the deeper the experts dug, the less he trusted the King to behave reasonably. He'd do whatever it took to keep Ariane and Caro from the monarch's reach.

'What are you thinking, Uncle Jake? You look funny.'

'Do I?' He met Ariane's bright eyes, so like her mother's, and felt his fluency desert him. His brain went com-

pletely blank. Because he'd been thinking about sex with
Caro and how his need for her kept growing, not dimin-
ishing with familiarity.

'This sort of funny?' he asked as he crossed his eyes.

Ariane giggled and the tight sensation in his chest eased.
He loved hearing her happy.

'Or this?' He stuck his tongue in his cheek and scrunched
his eyebrows down.

His gaze caught Caro's. She was smiling, the shadows
he sometimes saw in her eyes banished.

Elation hit. By rights it should be because he was finally
on the verge of closing the deal he'd come to Switzerland
to accomplish. Or because he might have found a way to
protect Caro and Ariane from the King long term. Instead
this burst of happiness came from the sight of Caro's eyes,
dancing with approval as he made a fool of himself in front
of a bunch of tourists.

The realisation shook him. Her smile and her approval
had such power.

What did that mean?

And what did he intend to do about it?

Caro lay on her back, heart pounding, legs weak as over-
cooked pasta and a smile of well-being curving her lips.
How often had she felt like this in Jake's bed, basking in
the afterglow of his loving?

The man had a knack for diverting her worries about
the future and her conniving father. And the sight of Ariane growing more confident and loving proved that good
things *could* happen.

They hadn't discussed Ariane's future. It had been
enough to know she was safe from the King. Despite furious messages from her father Jake had somehow managed
to convince him to keep his distance. But they'd have to

face their problems. Caro wasn't naïve enough to believe this state of glorious limbo could continue.

Zoe had rung today, warning again that winning custody of Ariane wouldn't be simple. She favoured a negotiated arrangement with Jake. Which suited Caro. She couldn't imagine them on opposing sides in court. Yet nor could she envisage Ariane living part time with her and part with Jake, possibly on the other side of the world.

She should be relieved Jake hadn't forced the issue. Yet they couldn't go on like this despite his insistence that for now Ariane needed calm and stability. But Caro had never found the right time to shatter this peaceful interlude.

Caro rolled onto her side and watched the early light gild the mountains. She'd found peace here, such happiness, she didn't want it to end. Not only for Ariane but for *her*.

The bathroom door opened and there Jake was, naked but for a towel around his hips, his hair damp and the muscles in that glorious torso shifting as he moved. Despite her satiation Caro felt the tug of attraction deep inside.

Longing for him filled her yet she knew their peaceful bubble must shatter. Was today the day?

'You're awake?' He approached, smiling, and she smiled back, almost accustomed to the fillip of joy gathering behind her breastbone. No one, ever, had made her feel the way Jake did. The thought lodged and Caro stilled as its implications penetrated.

'Something wrong?' He watched her as she struggled to stifle a sudden, disquieting idea.

'No, nothing.' She made a production of turning to plump up pillows behind her and sit up, drawing the sheet under her arms. By the time she faced him again she had her calm face on, the one she'd learned in the palace, forged under the lash of her father's contempt and her stepmother's disapproval.

Yet her heart pounded wildly and perspiration prickled

her hairline. Her powers of concealment weren't as good as she'd hoped for Jake sat beside her, frowning. He took her hand and she experienced that familiar jolt of delight.

'Are you worried about a possible pregnancy? Because of that first night?'

Heat blossomed in her cheeks. 'It's unlikely, given the timing.' That was what she'd told herself again and again. 'Time enough to worry about that if it happens.'

'You wouldn't be alone, Caro.' His thumb stroked the back of her hand. 'I'd look after you. I don't abandon my responsibilities.'

And that, Caro realised as her heart landed somewhere near the floor, was part of the problem. She didn't want to be a responsibility to Jake. Nor did she want to be a rival for Ariane. She wanted to be someone he—

'I was going to wait till later but now's as good a time as any. We need to talk, Caro.'

His gentle tone, the way he watched her, assessing her reaction, made her heart skip. Tension crawled along her shoulders to the back of her neck. Was he going to say he'd decided he couldn't give Ariane up?

It was stupid to jump to conclusions but a lifetime of disappointment, of things going against her, had conditioned Caro to expect the worst. She tugged her hand free and folded her arms over her chest.

'I agree. We can't continue this way indefinitely.'

Keen eyes surveyed her. What did he see? She had the unnerving notion he saw far more than she'd like.

'My time in Switzerland is almost over. The project I've been working on is complete.'

Caro's eyes widened. Despite telling herself this wasn't permanent, she hadn't thought about Jake leaving. Distress coated her tongue.

'It's not long term?'

He had investments globally. From the snippets she'd

heard between him and Neil she'd imagined his current work continuing.

He shrugged. 'It is, but now everything's in place I don't need to be here. My role was to cajole the other investors into participating.'

Caro frowned. 'Is that normal? Moving from place to place with each new investment?'

Jake shrugged. 'This wasn't business in the usual sense. It's a pet project. I had to chivvy reluctant investors.'

'Surely if you can prove they'll make a good return they'd agree.'

'You're assuming the investors would reap the financial rewards.'

Now Caro really was intrigued, despite the low-grade frisson of nerves, reminding her they had more personal things to discuss. Was that why she was eager to talk business? To put off the evil moment?

'You make it sound like a great mystery.'

He laughed. 'No, at least not now we've got agreement. I developed a self-perpetuating investment scheme. But instead of profits returning to investors they'll be channelled into programmes for child victims of war and natural disaster. I came here to lobby some powerful corporations and governments. Especially corporations that need to rehabilitate their reputations as global citizens.'

'Companies that could do with positive press?' Caro could name a few. 'You tapped into the high-level talks here to establish a charity?'

The region regularly hosted talks between governments and attracted lobbyists from some of the world's most powerful corporations.

'There's nothing like face to face meetings to drive a project, especially when you're asking for substantial sums they'll never see again.'

Caro sat back, taking in the satisfaction on Jake's face.

He glowed like a man who'd sealed a deal to make his fortune. Instead the deal was for others.

'Why children? Why in war zones?'

'Not just war. In areas hit by tsunamis, hurricanes, any large-scale disorder.' His eyes held hers. 'You don't think it a good cause?'

'I think it's wonderful. I'm just curious.'

She'd thought she knew Jake. Living with him and Ariane, seeing him with his staff, she'd discovered many sides to his character. This was something new. He loved Ariane but she'd thought that was because he was her uncle. Maybe there was more to his motivation.

His gaze slid to the window. 'I spent a few years in the army. We were deployed in the Asia Pacific region mopping up after natural disasters, and once after a civil war. Some of the children…'

He stopped and Caro realised he wasn't seeing the glorious Swiss scenery. Her heart squeezed as his features tightened.

'Children are the most vulnerable, especially if separated from family. It can take years to reunite kids with remaining family, if there *is* any. Most disaster support is for food and shelter. Only a few agencies address the longer term process of finding secure, loving homes for lost children.'

Caro heard emotion beneath his words. She recalled images of disaster-ravaged zones worldwide and shuddered, imagining Ariane alone and lost.

Jake must have seen her shiver. His hand covered hers. This time she didn't object.

'What you're doing is important. Clever too, to target the big companies to contribute.'

'It will be good PR for them.'

Caro guessed Jake wouldn't claim any of those kudos. She wanted to say she was proud of him but stopped herself. She had no right to sound proprietorial, even if she felt it.

After her earlier revelation she needed to be careful.

'I didn't know you'd been in the army,' she said, trying to distract herself.

'It wasn't a long career. I didn't have the temperament for being ordered about.' At her questioning look he said, 'I got into trouble as a kid and my sister convinced me it was a ticket out of the place we lived.'

No mistaking his bitterness. 'You weren't happy at home?'

Reading the tension in those broad shoulders, she wondered if he'd answer. But eventually his lips curved in a rueful smile. 'It probably wasn't too bad but I was trouble. A misfit. My sister told me if I didn't sort myself out I'd end up in gaol. I was starting to act out.'

'Your sister, not your parents?'

Gunmetal-grey eyes met hers. 'I never knew my father and my mother abandoned us on a regular basis. She only came home when her latest boyfriend dumped her. The last time she left I was barely fourteen but Connie looked after me, stopped me from going into foster care.'

The air whooshed from Caro's lungs. No wonder he had a thing about lost children. And women abandoning their kids. She remembered his lacerating words when he thought she'd abandoned Ariane. No wonder he'd been so savage.

'Yes.' He nodded, as if reading her thoughts. 'I've got baggage. Usually I keep it under wraps. But with you…' He shook his head. 'It was like a red rag to a bull. I'm sorry I—'

'Don't.' Caro put her hand up. 'It's in the past. So you went into the army. That's a far cry from finance.'

Jake spread his hands. 'The army taught me discipline and that there was a big world out there. It gave me the drive to work hard and improve. Then my sister and I had a windfall. There were plans for a giant shopping complex in our suburb but the planners forgot to acquire a small parcel of land.' He smiled reminiscently. 'Ours. We lived in our grandparents' tiny house in a rundown neighbour-hood but suddenly it was worth a fortune. Connie used her share to travel. I invested mine and got a job in the city, learning finance.'

'And never looked back.'

Caro marvelled. From troubled teen to billionaire took a lot of doing.

'Oh, I had setbacks. But I found mentors and learned from my mistakes.'

Jake made it sound something anyone could do. Caro thought of herself, all those years giving in to her father, not even able to look after her own baby—

'Hey.' He cupped her chin. 'What is it?'

Her heart turned over at his gentle touch.

'Nothing. Except that I'm incredibly impressed.' She tugged in a sharp breath. She'd avoided the inevitable for too long. Time to confront it. 'What did you want to talk about? You said it was time to leave.' Caro was proud of her even tone. 'Where will you go?'

'Somewhere to make a home for Ariane. I'd thought of St Ancilla, till your father...' He lifted those bare shoul-ders and Caro followed the movement, remembering how she'd clung to that broad expanse when they made love. 'Maybe Australia or—'

'Australia!' Caro's voice hit a shrill note. 'If you take Ariane I'll never see her.'

He dropped his hand. Caro's heart dropped too.

'Unless you come with us.'

'Sorry? You want me to move to Australia?'

'Or somewhere else. I'm open to suggestions. Some-where we can make a home for Ariane.'

We. Her heart thundered. He'd said *we*.

'What, exactly, are you suggesting, Jake?'

He hesitated and to her surprise, Caro saw uncertainty on his face. It couldn't be. This was the man who'd stalked through a royal ball like an avenging angel intent on retribution, uncaring of scandal. Who'd spirited her away from her father and kept her safe from his machinations. Jake didn't do uncertain.

'We could bring Ariane up together.'

She couldn't think of anything she'd like more. Her pulse tripped and she had to stifle a surge of elation. It didn't seem possible.

'Together, not taking turns looking after her?'

'I want her to have stability and a loving family.' He paused, his long fingers squeezing hers. 'We could be that family.'

Caro tried to speak but the words stopped in her chest. She told herself to breathe, think this through, not jump to conclusions. Yet her heart leapt.

Less than twenty minutes ago she'd had a revelation, discovering the reason Jake affected her so profoundly.

Because she loved him. She'd fallen completely, devastatingly in love with Jake Maynard.

Her feelings for Mike hadn't been love, more excitement at escaping her restrictive life, the thrill of being wanted. He'd been her first crush. And he'd cured her of crushes for life.

Till Jake. Honourable, protective, tender, funny. He was everything she hadn't dared hope for. And now he talked about them making a family.

Because he'd fallen in love too? Excitement scudded through her.

Jake leaned in, warmth in his eyes. 'We could make it work, Caro. A marriage of convenience for Ariane's sake. What do you say?'

CHAPTER FOURTEEN

JAKE SAW THE fire in Caro's bright eyes die. It didn't flicker or fade. It was snuffed out in an instant.

In the same instant cold engulfed him.

Her lips thinned as she pressed them together. Within his grasp her hands jerked then stilled. She blinked once, twice, the dark pupils widening, making her look wounded, as if he'd hurt her.

Yet it was Jake who felt the punch to his gut, like a hunting knife jabbing flesh, piercing a vital organ.

He forced himself to breathe slowly. She was surprised. She wasn't rejecting him.

'It's a perfect solution, don't you see?' He sounded more confident than he felt. Like a desperate salesman giving a final pitch. That made him pause. He didn't do desperate. There was no reason for the anxiety gripping his belly.

'I realise it's an unusual solution to our situation.' Actually it was perfect. 'But think about it. Ariane needs stability and a family to love her. We're that stability. We give her that love. Even after such a short time I see the difference since you came into her life. We can be all she needs. And we're good together, you know we are.'

Jake made himself stop. He wasn't a snake oil salesman, pushing her into a purchase she'd regret. He knew she'd enjoyed this time together since leaving St Ancilla. It wasn't only her relief at leaving her father's kingdom, or even, he suspected, being with her daughter. Caro revelled in his company and his lovemaking. She'd been gratifyingly eager for both.

Yet Caro looked anything but eager as she slipped her

hands from his and hitched the sheet high. She trembled so much Jake could see it.

The blade at his belly twisted, gouging deep.

Jake had never laid himself open to rejection by a woman. Not after being rejected time and again by his mother. He'd kept his relationships with women to simple sexual transactions. This was the first time he'd put himself on the line.

It was impossible she'd shun him.

Yet his pulse juddered as he looked for a sign of understanding and agreement.

'But...marriage?' She frowned as if marriage to him was some distasteful medicine.

'Why not?' He shrugged his bare shoulders, chilling now despite the warmth of the room, and wished he'd waited instead of rushing into this. Instead of getting the easy agreement he'd anticipated, he had the unnerving sensation her response wouldn't be an enthusiastic 'yes'.

Would he have done better dressed for business in his office, with Caro sitting on the other side of the desk? The idea was preposterous. Yet—

'Isn't it a bit extreme? Couldn't we share custody, six months with you and six with me?'

Something heavy shoved down through Jake's middle. Disappointment or something stronger? Because she didn't leap at his suggestion. He told himself they discussed a pragmatic arrangement, that she wasn't rejecting *him*.

'You said it yourself. If we live on opposite sides of the world one of us would miss seeing her when she's with the other. This way she gets both of us.'

And we get each other.

'Besides, if you're pregnant, wouldn't it be the best outcome?'

Any thought that argument would clinch the deal died as

Caro's face leached of colour. It was like watching flesh and blood turn to parchment and it curdled the hope within him.

'You're covering all bases, aren't you?' Instead of admiring his foresight, it sounded oddly as if Caro resented his pragmatism.

'We have to be practical.' He waited for her to agree. When she said nothing he went on. 'Neither of us want to fight for Ariane in court.'

Finally, to his relief, she nodded. At least there was one thing on which they agreed.

'We need a solution for Ariane that will work for us both. Why not stay together? Build on what we already have? I can see it working.'

He could see it so clearly he had to bite his tongue from insisting she must too. It was the best, the only solution.

'Can you?' Her gaze held his. It wasn't the look of a happy woman. A woman offered security and caring, plus wealth beyond most people's imaginings. Offered *him*.

Suddenly, instead of a billionaire with the world at his feet, Jake felt like someone else. Someone unwanted, never good enough even to hold his parents' attention.

The sensation lasted only a second but it rocked Jake to the core.

So when Caro thanked him politely and said she needed to think about it he merely nodded and stood, forcing himself to rise and walk away on stiff legs.

The sun was warm on Caro's face as she drank in the peaceful scene. White-topped mountains that now seemed like friendly guardians rather than sombre presences. The alpine meadow dotted with the season's first flowers was tranquil, the only sound her daughter's voice.

Caro inhaled the scent of meadow grass, listened to Ariane's chatter as she played with Maxim, and willed herself to feel happy.

She had so much to be thankful for. They were safe, they were together and they were far from her father's influence. He still sent irate messages but it seemed he had more on his mind than pursuing his errant daughter. Money troubles, said Jake, who'd made it his business to find out. Significant money troubles, which explained why her father hadn't done more than bluster about her absence.

Caro and Ariane were building a real bond, which grew stronger daily. It was more than she'd once dared hope for.

She owed Jake so much. He made this possible. He could have prevented her seeing Ariane till the legalities were sorted out but he wasn't that sort of man.

Unlike her domineering father, Jake didn't play with people and their emotions for his own ends. He was decent, honest, reliable, and he cared for Ariane so much it was impossible not to love him for that alone.

As if Caro didn't love him anyway.

Her chest tightened painfully. It shouldn't be possible after so short a time but her feelings were clear. She loved him as surely as she loved her daughter.

How much longer would he wait for her answer?

How much longer could she pretend she didn't know how to reply?

Last week he'd offered her a convenient marriage as a solution to their tangled situation. Ariane would acquire a family. Caro and Jake would get to be with her permanently.

It was simple and workable.

Except Caro wanted more. She wanted someone to love *her* for herself.

She reminded herself she'd have Ariane's love. But she'd grown greedy. Having spent this time with Jake, she wanted it all. The physical intimacy and more besides. She wanted Jake to care for her, not as a co-parent but because she was unique, someone he didn't want to live without.

Not because she might carry his child.

Caro looked at the tiny daisies in her hands, the flower chain she was making crushed.

When she'd asked for time to think Jake's expression had turned wooden. She'd seen the shutters come down before he strolled away to dress. Since then there'd been a barrier between them. Even in bed, at the height of passion, when Caro was on the verge of blurting out her feelings as he drove her to peak after peak of pleasure, she was aware of something different in Jake. As if he held something of himself back.

Jake gave her everything except love.

She'd lived without love all her life. She could live without it now, especially as she had Ariane. Her daughter would grow to love her, Caro felt it in her bones.

In time, if she wanted, there'd be more children, and she'd love them too. She should take what she was offered and be content.

'What's wrong, Caro? You look sad.'

She turned to find Ariane regarding her solemnly. Though her daughter was brighter and more relaxed now, she was sensitive to negativity, still easily worried.

'Nothing at all.' Caro smiled. 'I was thinking how peaceful it is here.'

'Maxim likes it. He's not sure he wants to live somewhere else.'

'Somewhere else?'

The solemn little face nodded. 'I heard Uncle Jake and Neil. We're moving.' The little girl swallowed. 'Will you come too, Caro?'

And that, of course, put her personal woes into perspective. What was more important than Ariane?

Caro leaned in and cuddled her daughter. 'That's the plan, sweetie.'

So it was decided.

All Caro had to do now was tell Jake she'd accept his marriage of convenience.

She'd marry the man she loved, yet it felt as if she gave up her soul. She'd have to spend her life pretending not to love him. Learning not to care when he wearied of their passion and sought pleasure with other women.

Caro set her jaw and pushed her personal feelings aside. They weren't as important as Ariane.

An hour later, as Caro headed to Jake's office to tell him her decision, her phone rang. She'd tired of her father's staff calling her old number to harangue her and had changed it last week. Was it Zoe? This would save Caro calling to tell her there was no need for legal action.

'Hello?' Caro tried to sound bright and happy. But the smile she forced felt like a grimace.

'At last.' Her father's voice struck like a blow. Caro stumbled to a halt, her stomach churning. Once more he'd managed to get her private number! Before she could gather her wits he went on, his voice serpentine with venom. 'Don't even think about hanging up, Carolina, or I'll make your lover pay.'

The sun was sinking when Caro forced herself up from the window seat where she'd slumped. Every joint felt stiff, as if she'd aged a lifetime in an hour. Not that her father had stayed on the phone that long. His call had been brief but it had changed everything.

Earlier this afternoon she'd felt sorry for herself, on the verge of marrying the man she loved to make a family with him and her daughter.

She hadn't known how lucky she was!

Now that choice was denied her. She had to give Jake up and Ariane too. Her father had made that clear. He was a man who didn't make empty threats.

It didn't matter that Jake had done nothing wrong, had

broken no law. If her father vowed to destroy him he would. Even if it took years, he'd manipulate the truth, plant evidence, bribe people, all that and more, to destroy Jake's reputation and his business. The King had the contacts and the lack of scruples to do it. He'd even threatened extradition to St Ancilla on trumped-up charges relating to the disbursement of Jake's sister's estate and alleged mismanagement of an investment scheme there. He'd ensure Jake didn't get a fair trial. Destroying his reputation would devastate his business.

Unless Caro gave up her daughter and returned, alone, to the palace.

He'd taken his time planning his revenge for the way she stood up to him. It was something he excelled in. How had she let herself forget that?

The threat had made her realise too that her father would continue to influence their lives, spreading poison that would eventually infect Ariane, unless she, Caro, gave her up. There'd be no escape and ultimately Ariane would suffer.

Caro's throat constricted but she refused to cry. Now, more than ever, she had to be strong.

She didn't know how she was going to walk away from Jake and Ariane but she had to believe her daughter would be fine without her, because she'd have Jake. It wasn't as if Ariane knew Caro was her mother. Now she never would. Caro would have to get Jake to promise that at least.

Yet, here in her room, the room she hadn't slept in since returning from St Ancilla, Caro wondered how she'd find the strength to do what she must.

But surely it was simply one step then another, like after Mike's betrayal. And when she'd believed her baby dead.

Drawing a deep breath, Caro took a step, then another, towards the wardrobe where her suitcase was stored.

* * *

Jake had waited long enough. The days had stretched out and still Caro hadn't given an answer. She drove him crazy.

She made love as ardently as before, yet their emotional connection had severed.

He'd given up being patient. It was time for answers.

Answers he got as he opened the bedroom door and saw Caro with her back to him, suitcase open on the bed.

For a second that seemed to last for ever his feet stuck to the floor. He couldn't move, could barely process what he saw. But only for a second. He crossed the room and she swung around.

There was a flash of something in her eyes. Relief? Pleasure? Something that made the bleakness inside ease and hope surge.

Then it disappeared. Those violet eyes turned dull and shadowed, dropping to his chin.

He knew why. She'd decided he wasn't good enough. Why marry a commoner when she had handsome aristocrats hanging off her every word? He'd seen them at the ball, panting after her.

The weight within his ribs crushed him. His lungs laboured. Jake had to force himself to stand still and not haul her to him and insist they could work this out.

'This is your answer?' Another time he'd have winced at the raw emotion in his voice. 'Were you going to tell me or just let me work it out when you vanished?'

She jumped at his lashing words and Jake was torn between wanting to soothe her and wanting to make her hurt as he did.

Had he ever felt such pulsing, writhing pain? He had a hazy recollection of something similar as a kid. The day he'd come home from school to discover his mother had cleared out again. Jake shoved the memory aside. He'd given up caring about his mother. But he cared about Caro. He'd thought…

She lifted her face slowly, as if reluctant to face him.

'I was going to tell you. I'm sorry, Jake. But I…' She shook her head and her glorious hair, loose around her shoulders, shifted like a living thing, attracting all the light in the room. It was burnished in shades of blood and rust, like the metallic tang of defeat filling his mouth. 'I've given your suggestion a lot of thought but it won't work.' She opened her mouth as if to say more then paused. 'It's time I left.'

She turned away and reached for a blouse, folding it methodically.

That was all the explanation he deserved?

His anger notched higher and so did his determination. He never quit. Never gave up on something worth fighting for.

Jake snagged a rough breath, then another. This wasn't the end. He refused to let her go like this.

'So you're going to fight me for custody of Ariane.'

Caro jumped and the blouse fell to the bed. For a long time she stood, utterly still, though tension emanated from her. He felt it like waves pummelling him.

'No… I've decided that won't work.' She picked up the blouse once more and began folding it with excruciatingly slow movements. 'Ariane is better off with you. You're her uncle. She knows you, loves you.' Caro's voice wobbled alarmingly and Jake felt its echo reverberate inside him as a shudder of astonishment.

He couldn't be hearing this. It was impossible. After all she'd been through Caro would *never* contemplate renouncing her child.

'You're giving up your *daughter*? The daughter you wanted so desperately? So desperately you came here under false pretences. So desperately you stood up to your father?' Jake stalked across to stand behind her shoulder. She hitched an uneven breath as the fabric in her hands became a mangled ball. Jake felt like mangling something himself. 'I don't believe it.'

What was going on? Did she find him so repulsive she'd give up Ariane rather than stay with him?

He couldn't believe it. He knew Caro. Even if things weren't as good between them now, she'd proved again and again that she was attracted to him. He'd cherished hopes it was something deeper than attraction.

Those narrow shoulders straightened. Her chin lifted and he caught a glimpse of Caro's proud profile.

'I've made my decision.' A pause, a long pause, so fraught Jake sensed she struggled. But if this was hard, why not accept his proposal? 'Ariane will be happy with you. I know you'll look after her. With me...' Her shoulders rose. 'It's better if she grows up without any connection to my family.'

Jake pounced on the mention of her family, a glimmer of hope easing the raw ache in his gut.

Because he couldn't believe she'd spurn him otherwise? Was he so desperate?

The answer was a resounding yes. For days he'd been on tenterhooks, giving Caro space to decide. In that time one thing had become abundantly clear.

That he had his own reasons for offering marriage and they weren't confined to Ariane.

Jake needed more from Caro. Not convenience. Not a mother for his orphaned niece.

He needed Caro for himself.

She spread the blouse on the bed a third time, smoothing then folding it. But her hands shook. Jake stood so close he felt the tremors, heard her uneven breathing.

This took more from her than she wanted to admit.

'What is it, Caro?' His voice was husky, rough with emotion he struggled to leash. 'What's wrong?'

'Nothing.' Her movements quickened, the fold lines on the shirt askew, but she didn't stop, almost throwing it into the suitcase and reaching for another.

Jake wanted to make her look at him but he didn't dare touch her. Not yet. He feared that if he did he wouldn't let her go.

'Why not marry me and give Ariane the life we both want for her?'

The life we both want for ourselves.

'I made a mistake. I'm not cut out for motherhood. I need to—'

'Caro.' Her name was a caress as he closed his arms around her, pulling her gently back against him, revelling in the feel of her there, where she belonged, even if she was rigid with tension. 'Tell me what's wrong. I know something is. You're a terrible liar.'

He felt the sob rack her though she stifled it. Still she didn't relax. Instead her movements grew quicker, her breathing too, as she leaned away from his restraining hold, grabbing fistfuls of clothes and tossing them into the suitcase.

'Please, don't make this more difficult, Jake. I don't want to marry you. We'd make each other unhappy and that wouldn't be good for Ariane.'

'And if you're pregnant?' He slid his palm to her abdomen. He'd told himself he'd support her if there was a baby. In fact he was thrilled Caro might carry his child. He'd begun to imagine what the baby would look like, how it would feel in his arms.

'I won't be. The odds are against it.'

She spoke so softly he had to crane to hear. Which brought him to the spice and warmth scent of her skin. Jake closed his eyes and inhaled. That undid him.

'Sweetheart, tell me what's wrong. I promise we'll find a way to deal with it.' Jake didn't care that his voice revealed his feelings. 'I want you with me. You and Ariane.'

If she'd been tense before it was nothing to her iron rigidity now. It felt as if she didn't even breathe.

'No! It's impossible. We can't.'

But Jake was listening now, really listening. He didn't hear rejection but desperation. A woman who didn't care for him or her child wouldn't sound as if she were being torn apart.

Her pain wrenched at his vitals. He'd do anything to take the hurt away.

He kissed the curve where her shoulder met her neck and felt her instant response as if her knees gave way. He gathered her closer. Caro's breath became a sigh and instead of fighting his hold she angled her head a fraction to allow unfettered access.

Triumph rose. Relief so profound it almost overwhelmed him.

Jake lifted one unsteady hand, pushing her hair aside, nuzzling that sensitive spot as she leant against him.

Even if she didn't feel the same way about him, he could work with that. He was determined, single-minded and patient when he needed to be. He'd *make* her love him if it took years.

'You want to be with me,' he murmured against her skin, feeling her shivers of response.

She tried to move away, but Jake was implacable. He needed to understand and it seemed the only way to learn the truth was when he weakened Caro's defences. Her words confirmed it.

'Let me go, Jake. Please. You're wrong, I don't want you.'

Her body told another story, as did her voice. She sounded desperate but not convincing. Scared rather than angry. Of what? Surely not of a future together?

'I don't believe you.'

She stilled.

'What happened, Caro? What are you frightened of?'

'I...' She shook her head as if she'd run out of lies to distract him.

Gently Jake turned her to face him. Her eyes were wide and her mouth a crooked line of pain but it wasn't rejection he saw in those purple-blue eyes. It was fear.

Surely not of him? Jake was processing the possibility when abruptly his mind clicked into action.

'It's your father, isn't it? He contacted you.'

The instant flare of her eyes told him he'd hit the truth.

Silently Jake cursed. He'd done everything he could to stymie the King's attempts to reach Caro and thought he'd succeeded. What he'd learned in that confrontation between father and daughter at the palace had horrified him. Now the man turned even more vicious and unstable. Not simply because Caro dared defy him but because the house of cards he'd built around himself was being swiftly and methodically exposed.

Jake hadn't hesitated to probe into the monarch's affairs. Between them, professional investigators and Jake's well-placed business associates had uncovered an unsavoury, not to mention illegal web of financial misappropriation and fraud. King Hugo regarded the public purse as his own, but the structures he'd used to hide his misdoings were crumbling under pressure.

'That doesn't matter.' Caro's face was drawn and tense. 'I can't live with you and Ariane—'

'I still don't believe you.' Her head jerked up and she looked him in the eye. 'You want to be with us but you're frightened.'

How he welcomed her spark of annoyance. Seeing her frightened made him desperate. 'Has anyone ever told you you're arrogant, Jake Maynard?'

As a diversion it might have worked, once, weeks ago before he'd got to know Caro. 'Yes. You have, and it's true. But I'm right. You can't lie to me, Caro, you're no good at it.'

It was true, despite her earlier masquerade. Deliberately, lifting his arms wide, he stepped back, giving her space, though it went against every instinct to release her rather than embrace her.

Jake needed her to trust him.

'Tell me what he said, Caro. Playing by his rules hurts all of us.'

Finally she nodded. 'He demanded I return. He wants me there, to marry someone he's chosen.'

'Or what?' Jake kept his voice even despite his building fury.

'Or he'll destroy you. He means it, too,' she said in a rush. 'He hates me for repudiating him and you for taking my side. He'll find a way to bring you down. He said he'd make it his mission, no matter how long it takes.' Caro reached for Jake, grabbing his hands as if to convince him by sheer force. 'He'll bring trumped-up charges against you, get someone to testify you broke the law in your financial dealings—'

'Is that all?' Jake threaded his fingers through Caro's, melding their hands.

'All? Don't you understand? He'll destroy your reputation and then your business! You don't know how devious he is, the lengths he'll go to.'

'Oh, I know.' He should have been prepared for this, but he'd thought there was no way the King could worry Caro here. 'What I don't know is whether you'd stay with me if it weren't for his threats.'

She shook her head, the picture of desperation. 'Jake, please, listen. He'll wreck everything you've worked for. I can't let him—'

'He won't, Caro. Because he's about to go under.' Jake willed her to focus on his words, not her father's threats. 'He's stolen funds and borrowed against assets that don't belong to him. He's dipped into the public purse on a huge scale.'

Finally she was taking it in. Her eyes grew huge.

'He got careless and some of us in the finance sector have been doing our own investigating.' Because he needed to protect Caro and Ariane. 'He's a spent force, Caro. Don't believe his bluster. This is a last-ditch effort to save himself through you. My guess is he thinks I'll call off the creditors if he has you in his clutches. Believe me, he can't touch you. I promise.'

His pulse thundered through the silence and he watched as, gradually, the fear eased from Caro's face. If Jake had had any doubts about her belief in him, the fact that she took his word now proved otherwise. It warmed him from the inside out in a way only Caro could.

'*You* did all that? But why?' She frowned. 'You didn't know he'd threatened you.'

Seeing her puzzlement, Jake realised how alone she must have felt all those years. Had there ever been anyone to stand beside her? He swallowed, his throat constricting painfully. Her stoicism and determination really were phenomenal.

'You don't know?' Jake's voice stretched. He'd hoped she'd understand. 'For the same reason I hope you really want to marry me.'

His breath grew shallow, his lungs working overtime. No longer was he a savvy investor, a world-class businessman, secure in his success. Jake hovered on a knife edge between hope and disaster.

'I fell in love with you, Caro. I want you, not for Ariane but for myself.' He lifted her hand to his lips and allowed himself a fleeting kiss to her hand, taking courage from the throbbing pulse at her wrist. 'I know it's been a short time but I've never been more certain of anything.'

Jake watched emotions chase across her face, so fast he hadn't a hope of deciphering them. Her fingers shook in his grip.

'Caro?' His confident words deserted him. It emerged as a croak.

'You love me?' She shook her head and he slipped his other hand up to cup her cheek, holding her steady so she could read the truth in his eyes. 'It's not possible.'

'It is. That's why I took it badly when you needed time to think about marriage.'

'You said it was a marriage of *convenience*!' Jake heard her outrage and hurt and understood how badly he'd blundered with that impulsive proposal. But he'd been so excited at the idea he'd been unable to wait.

Now he had to get it right.

'It's taken me a while to confront what I feel. I'm not used to loving.'

Or being loved. His heart rose in his chest as he waited for her response.

'Nor am I.' Suddenly Caro was laughing, though it sounded ragged. And beautiful. 'I can't believe it.'

'It's true, absolutely true.' He stroked his thumb across her velvety cheek, watching her pupils dilate. 'What I don't know is how you feel about me.'

Their eyes locked and he felt that slam of connection, as real as a fist to his heart.

'Even when I hated you that night of the ball, I was afraid I loved you too.' Her words were magic, her expression mesmerising. 'Since then...it's been so hard feeling the way I do about you and thinking you didn't reciprocate. I don't know how I came to love you, Jake, or when, but I do. Totally. You devastated me when you offered a convenient wedding. I thought you only cared about Ariane, not me.'

Jake was filled with mingled pain and ecstasy, torn between exultation and regret.

He was spellbound by her luminous joy that belied the hurt she described.

Caro loved him!

His face split with a grin and he felt like whooping. Or kissing her senseless, except he needed more of her beautiful, wonderful words.

He planted her hand on his chest where his heart danced to a rackety beat and looped his arm around her, drawing her close where she belonged.

'Caro, I'm sorry. I'm better with numbers than emotions.'

'You're wrong, Jake. I've seen you with Ariane. I know how deeply you feel about her.'

'Not just about Ariane.' He revelled in the feel of her right here against him. With her hand on his chest she could feel his heart thundering out the truth. 'Will you be mine, Caro, for ever? I need you.' To his surprise, Jake discovered the admission, far from weakening him, made him feel stronger than he'd ever been.

'But my father...'

'Trust me to deal with your father.' Jake would let nothing come between him and the woman he loved. 'He's going under, Caro. He won't be in a position to threaten any longer.'

'Of course I trust you.' Her free hand slid to his shoulder, her grip firm and possessive. He loved it.

'So you'll marry me,' he pressed. He wanted everything clear between them, despite the urgent need to taste and caress her.

Her smile turned from misty to mischievous and he loved that too. 'Do you always negotiate this hard?'

'Only when our happiness is at stake. I won't allow anyone to stand in the way of that, king or no king.' What Jake felt for Caro, and what he saw shining in her expression, were too precious to abandon.

Caro's smile died and she rose on tiptoe, cradling his face in her palms. 'I love you, Jake.' The words filled him with awe and gratitude. 'If you're really sure...the answer is yes, because I don't think I can live without you.'

Jake drew his first easy breath in days. Caro was his. She loved him and they had all their lives to be together.

With a groan of release he gave in and covered her lips with his. Caro was as eager as he, kissing him back with all the fervour, all the caring a man could want. Jake sank into her, losing himself and finding more, far more. Together they were magnificent, one entity forged of trust, respect and love. He'd never felt so strong, so blessed. Gratitude vied with desire.

When, finally, they pulled apart enough to haul air into starved lungs, Jake looked down into a face made even more beautiful because of the gift they shared.

'You make me the happiest man in the world, Caro.' Maybe other lovers said it too. All Jake knew was that no one meant it more than he. 'Let me make you just as happy.'

EPILOGUE

'THERE YOU ARE! I followed the giggles.'

Caro spun around in the shallow end of the infinity pool overlooking the blue Pacific Ocean. There he was. Jake. Her lover, her man, her husband. Just back from meetings in the city, he'd shed his jacket and tie and was rolling up his sleeves as he crossed the flagstones.

Their eyes met and, as ever, she felt that hard pump of blood as if their hearts realigned to beat in sync. He smiled the slow, sexy smile that undid her as easily as his deft hands undressed her each night.

'Uncle Jake!' Ariane squealed and splashed out of the pool to cling to his legs. 'We waited and waited for you.'

Jake lifted his niece onto his hip, regardless of her wetness. Ariane's heart gave a great thump as she saw them together, the big man and the adoring little girl, bonded by a love so strong sometimes Caro had trouble believing this was real. Their family was better than any fantasy.

'Sorry, sweetie. But I have to work sometimes.'

Jake had reduced his hours, but their home on Sydney's exclusive northern beaches allowed him to commute to the city occasionally. Very occasionally. Mainly he worked from home, or delegated.

'Did you have a good day?' He bent his head towards the little girl and Caro smiled as Ariane described her day in detail. The withdrawn child she'd met in Switzerland was gone. Now Ariane was confident, secure and adventurous, already making friends with other local children.

Caro got out of the pool and went to fetch a towel, but Jake got in the way.

'Haven't you forgotten something important, Caro?' Ebony eyebrows lifted over teasing eyes.

'Well, if you don't mind getting even more wet...' She leaned close, kissing him soundly. When she pulled back he was grinning. His eyes held a promise that sent anticipation sizzling all the way to her toes.

'You're not listening, Uncle Jake. We have a surprise.' Caro blinked at Ariane's words. When Jake looked at her that way...

'A surprise?'

Her daughter nodded importantly. 'A visitor.'

Jake's eyebrows rose and Caro clarified. 'A visitor tomorrow.'

Ariane nodded. 'But I want to look for a book to share with him. Can I go now? Please?'

Fifteen minutes later, leaving Ariane dry, dressed and sorting her picture books, Caro returned to the terrace with its ocean views. The view had never looked so good as now with Jake powering through the pool wearing only surf shorts.

'A visitor?' He waded to the edge of the pool and stood between her knees as she sat with her feet in the water. Jake pressed a luscious kiss to the base of her neck. Caro's nipples pebbled and her thoughts frayed.

'Mm hm.' She tilted her head so he could nip his way up her neck to that spot below her ear that drove her insane. 'Paul.'

'Paul?' His voice was a husky whisper.

Caro planted her hands on Jake's wet shoulders and leaned back. She couldn't kiss and think. 'King Paul of St Ancilla. We invited him, remember?'

The last couple of months had been dramatic with her father bowing to pressure and abdicating in favour of his eldest son. There'd been some scandal but the full depths of the old man's deceit and theft hadn't been made public.

The ex-King had quietly retired to a small estate on a distant island. The public didn't know he'd been banished. Meanwhile Jake helped Caro's brother work to restructure the royal debt with an ambitious plan of reinvestment and repayment. No one had the stomach for unseating a monarchy and destabilising a nation, so long as the man responsible was out of the equation.

'You're happy with that?' Jake's silvery eyes turned piercing.

'I said so before, didn't I? Paul could do with some time out, away from the court and the press.' And his mother and fiancée, though she didn't say that. Caro guessed neither of the women were particularly supportive but the way Paul had stepped up to his responsibilities, his honesty and genuine concern at their father's wrongdoing, had impressed her.

'The press will follow him here.'

Caro shrugged. 'I'll cope. I'm used to it, remember. Besides, if we accept his invitation and spend part of each year in St Ancilla we'll be in the spotlight even more.' She cupped Jake's harsh, handsome face in her palms. 'Are *you* sure you want to take that on? Associating with royals. Going to balls and such?'

'It's your home and your heritage, Caro, and Ariane's. I can cope if you can.' The glint in Jake's eyes grew wicked, turning her insides liquid. 'I enjoyed my first royal ball enormously.'

'It wasn't the ball but what came after.'

'I have a weakness for princesses.'

Caro huffed in mock dismay. 'Then you can't go to royal events. Who knows what princesses and duchesses there will be, even queens?'

Jake's expression made her pulse stutter. 'How could I notice them, Caro, when you've shown me what love is? You're Queen of my heart.'

That organ rolled over, beating frantically against her

ribs. 'Sometimes I think you're too good to be true, Jake Maynard.' Her words were husky with love.

'I *know* you are, Caro. Which is why I intend to do everything I can to make you happy. Now come here and kiss me.'

* * * * *

COMING SOON!

We really hope you enjoyed reading this book. If you're looking for more romance, be sure to head to the shops when new books are available on

Thursday 6th March

To see which titles are coming soon, please visit
millsandboon.co.uk/nextmonth

MILLS & BOON

Coming next month

A SCANDAL MADE IN LONDON
Lucy King

'Miss Cassidy?' said the concierge a moment later, his voice bouncing off the walls and making her jump. 'Mr Knox will see you now.'

Finally.

'The lift on the right will take you directly to the penthouse.'

'Thank you,' she said, mustering up a quick smile as she got to her feet and headed for said lift on legs that felt like jelly.

The doors closed behind her and she used the smooth ten-second ascent to try and calm her fluttering stomach and slow her heart-rate. It would be fine. She and Theo were both civilised adults. They might be chalk and cheese, but they could handle this. What was the worst that could happen? It wasn't as if she was expecting anything from him. She just had a message to deliver. It would be fine.

But when the lift doors opened and she stepped out, all thoughts of civility and messages shot from her head because all she could focus on was Theo.

He was standing at the far end of the wide hall, with his back to a huge floor to ceiling window, feet apart, arms crossed over his chest. The interminable rain of the morning had stopped and sunshine had broken through the thick cloud. It flooded in through the window, making a silhouette of him, emphasising his imposing height and the powerful breadth of the shoulders. Although clothed in jeans and a white shirt, he looked like some sort of god, in total control, master of all he surveyed, and she couldn't help thinking that if he'd been going for maximum impact, maximum intimidation, he'd nailed it.

Swallowing down the nerves tangling in her throat, Kate started walking towards him, her hand tightening on the strap of her cross-body bag that she wore like a shield. His gaze was on her as she approached, his expression unreadable. He didn't move a muscle. His jaw was set and he exuded chilly distance, which didn't bode well for what was to come, but then nor did the heat suddenly shooting along her veins and the desire surging through her body. That kind of head-scrambling reaction she could do without. She didn't need to remember how he'd made her feel when he'd held her, kissed her, been inside her. She needed to focus.

'Hi,' she said as she drew closer, his irresistible magnetism tugging her forwards even as she wanted to flee.

'What are you doing here?'

The ice cold tone of his voice stopped her in her tracks a couple of feet away, obliterating the heat, and she inwardly flinched. So that was the way this was going to go. No 'how are you, let me take your jacket, would you like a drink'. He wasn't pleased to see her. He wasn't pleased at all.

Okay.

'We need to talk,' she said, beginning to regret her decision to deliver this information in person. With hindsight, maybe an email would have sufficed.

'There's nothing to talk about.'

'I'm afraid there is.'

His dark brows snapped together. 'Your sister?'

'She's fine,' she said. 'Thank you for what you did for her.'

'You're welcome.'

'Did you get my note?' Shortly after he'd fixed her finances she'd sent him a letter of thanks. It had seemed the least she could do. She hadn't had a response.

He gave a brief nod. 'Yes.'

'She loves the flowers.'

'Good.'

'It was thoughtful.'

'It was nothing.'

Right. Beneath the force of his unwavering gaze and impenetrable demeanour Kate quailed for a moment and was summoning up the courage to continue when he spoke.

'Are you in trouble?' he asked sharply.

'That's one way of putting it.'

'What?'

'Sorry, bad joke,' she said with a weak laugh although there was nothing remotely funny about any of this.

'Get to the point, Kate,' he snapped. 'I'm busy.'

Right. Yes. Good plan. She pulled her shoulders back and lifted her chin. 'There's no easy way to say this, Theo,' she said, sounding far calmer than she felt, 'so here goes. There's been a...*consequence*... to our...afternoon together.'

A muscle ticked in his jaw. 'What kind of consequence?'

'The nine-month kind.'

There was a moment of thundering silence, during which Kate's heart hammered while Theo seemed to freeze and pale. 'What exactly are you saying?' he said, his voice tight and low and utterly devoid of expression.

'I'm pregnant.'

Continue reading
A SCANDAL MADE IN LONDON
Lucy King

Available next month
www.millsandboon.co.uk

JOIN US ON SOCIAL MEDIA!

Stay up to date with our latest releases, author
news and gossip, special offers and discounts, and
all the behind-the-scenes action
from Mills & Boon...

 millsandboon

 millsandboonuk

 millsandboon

It might just be true love...

MILLS & BOON

THE HEART OF ROMANCE

A ROMANCE FOR EVERY KIND OF READER

MODERN

Prepare to be swept off your feet by sophisticated, sexy and seductive heroes, in some of the world's most glamourous and romantic locations, where power and passion collide.
8 stories per month.

HISTORICAL

Escape with historical heroes from time gone by. Whether your passion is for wicked Regency Rakes, muscled Vikings or rugged Highlanders, awaken the romance of the past.
6 stories per month.

MEDICAL

Set your pulse racing with dedicated, delectable doctors in the high-pressure world of medicine, where emotions run high and passion, comfort and love are the best medicine.
6 stories per month.

True Love

Celebrate true love with tender stories of heartfelt romance, fro the rush of falling in love to the joy a new baby can bring, and a focus on the emotional heart of a relationship.
8 stories per month.

Desire

Indulge in secrets and scandal, intense drama and plenty of sizz hot action with powerful and passionate heroes who have it all: wealth, status, good looks…everything but the right woman.
6 stories per month.

HEROES

Experience all the excitement of a gripping thriller, with an inte romance at its heart. Resourceful, true-to-life women and strong fearless men face danger and desire - a killer combination!
8 stories per month.

DARE

Sensual love stories featuring smart, sassy heroines you'd want a best friend, and compelling intense heroes who are worthy of th
4 stories per month.

To see which titles are coming soon, please visit

millsandboon.co.uk/nextmonth

LET'S TALK
Romance

For exclusive extracts, competitions
and special offers, find us online:

facebook.com/millsandboon

@MillsandBoon

@MillsandBoonUK

Get in touch on 01413 063232

For all the latest titles coming soon, visit
millsandboon.co.uk/nextmonth